HER PERFECT LIE
A PSYCHOLOGICAL THRILLER

MARY STONE
CAROLINE CLARK

Copyright © 2025 by Mary Stone Publishing

All rights reserved.

No part of this book may be reproduced in any form or by any electronic or mechanical means, including information storage and retrieval systems, without written permission from the author, except for the use of brief quotations in a book review.

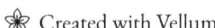 Created with Vellum

Mary Stone
To Krissy...
Thank you for loving my son as if he were your own and for giving life to the incredible woman who is now my daughter. We are family, and I'm so grateful for you.

Caroline Clark
To my parents, who gave me my love of thrillers and adventure. To the incredible MS team, thank you for putting your trust in me. But most of all to my wonderful readers, your support and sharing of my books has meant the world to me. Love you!

DESCRIPTION

**My marriage to Dr. Thad LaRue is perfect. Idyllic.
So why do I feel like he's hiding something...again?**

Two years ago, there was another woman. Younger. Prettier.
When she fell to her death on the cliffs, it was ruled a suicide.
But I've always wondered...

Now, there's a new woman—our beautiful, divorced neighbor.
She says her new boyfriend calls her "his lucky day."
The exact words Thad once said to me.

It's just a coincidence. I'm just paranoid. Or crazy.
The result of the oxy and wine that numbs the pain from my accident. From life.
Right?

To find out, I invite her to our annual holiday party.
The next morning, she's found stabbed to dead.

Two women. Two affairs. Two deaths.
Every woman Thad touches ends up dead. Except me.
Or is it because of me?

From bestselling authors Mary Stone and Caroline Clark, Her Perfect Lie is a twisty, unputdownable thriller perfect for fans of The Last Mrs. Parrish, The Couple Next Door, and The Perfect Marriage. Dive into a chilling journey where perfection hides deadly secrets—and no one is safe.

CHAPTER
ONE

I can do this. I can do anything for the man I love.

I've done worse, of course. I've downloaded the Flowery app to increase my vocabulary in a sad attempt to get the in-laws to accept me. I've purchased scratchy lingerie and even attempted a striptease once to keep Thad intrigued after baby number two. And I've done what every woman who's ever been married—broken into his phone in the bathroom in the middle of the night to spy on his messages.

But it's best to not think about that right now.

Right now, I need to gird my loins in preparation for the lions approaching my den. Okay, that might be a little dramatic, but not by much. But seriously, my in-laws are the most self-centered, pretentious, sons of—

"Coop." Thad steps around the kitchen island and places a hand on my shoulder with that confident grip that says he's always in control. "Cooper. Honey, are you with me?"

Leaning into him, I catch a whiff of his cologne, a blend of sandalwood and something that practically screams effortless luxury. "Sorry. I spaced out."

The low hum of the refrigerator paired with the soft clink of silver on fine china has me in some mental *Twilight Zone* as I plate our meal, transferring the bite-size masterpieces from the takeout cartons onto serving plates. It's a delicate maneuver, arranging every morsel as if the dinner somehow sprang from our oven, not from the kitchen of the island's fanciest restaurant.

On the counter, the Wedgwood Colonnade Gold plates, a gift from his parents, gleam with an almost judgmental air. Their conservative gold trim makes them look like they're hosting an aristocratic dinner party instead of covering my very practical attempt at saving face. If plates could sneer, these would.

Thad gallantly helps. At six feet, with a lean and muscled body he's a little too proud of, he looks out of place in the kitchen. He places roast potatoes onto the plates with about as much finesse as a clown juggling watermelons. "One potato, two potato, three potato, four," he sings as he plops them in place.

His goofy commentary warms the cold, expansive kitchen that's much too big for the four of us. He winks at me, a spark of mischief in his ice-blue eyes as he adjusts a roast turkey platter and spills a little on the counter. "Eh, I've had a good run." He nudges the dish slightly off-center and wipes up the mess.

The laugh we share grounds me. I reach up and brush aside wavy light-brown strands that have just started hinting at the need for a trim. His hair grows so fast. But the smile he gives me makes my knees weak. We're united. He's on my side completely. It's comforting against the backdrop of our elaborate deception. I love to cook, but my in-laws are never satisfied. They've always made me feel that I'm not good enough for their dear Thaddeus Grayson LaRue.

Tonight, Thad wanted to ease my stress and play a little

game, substituting a catered meal for a home-cooked one to fool his parents, especially his mother, Dot. A private joke between us.

"You know she's still going to moan." He waggles his eyebrows as he pats my butt. "I reckon the first barb will be within five minutes."

"Wouldn't bet against you." I doubt Dot'll make it that long without exploding.

"This'll be fun. Especially as this came from Château Meridian, her favorite eatery. She'd choke if we told her."

I swat his arm. "We can't ever tell her." Though the thought of Dot choking...

It's good to be this close. The absurd but fun deception will shield me from the criticism we're bound to face. Over the years, Dot's constant barbs have flattened my confidence and made the weekly meal with his parents less enjoyable than a root canal.

The table is complete.

Thad stands back and nods in approval. Though I don't have his confidence that our switcheroo will help with my in-law situation, I have to admit that the food looks amazing and smells delicious. At the very least, I'll enjoy a good meal, if not the company.

My stomach rumbles as I shove the empty takeout containers into the bulging recycling bin. It's overly full, and I grapple with the lid that refuses to close.

The last thing I want is for Dot to see my ruse. She'd interpret it as proof that I'm just as useless as she thinks. Finally, it slams shut, catching my finger in the process. "Shit."

A second after the swear word slips out, my daughter glides around the corner, her blond curls bouncing with each shuffle of her sock-clad feet. She's kicked off her shoes again. Where? I groan, knowing I'll be looking for them for hours.

At five years old, Grace has mastered sock-skating across

the kitchen tiles. Her eyes grow big before her eyebrows scrunch together in a reproachful frown. She claps her hands over her mouth, but a giggle escapes through her chubby fingers.

She skids to a stop next to me and tugs at my apron, looking up with her best attempt at a serious face. "Mommy, you said a bad word." Her voice is a mix of excitement and scolding. "That's a quarter for the swear jar."

Her brown eyes sparkle with mischief, clearly delighted to catch me in the act. Grace's enthusiasm for enforcing our house rules makes me smile. She steps back, her small hands planted on her hips as she mimics a stance she's seen me take a hundred times.

"Sorry, sweetie." With an exaggerated look of contrition, I cross to my purse and pull out my wallet. Grace watches every move with all seriousness.

Mouthing another apology, I drop a dollar into the crystal vase swear jar on the windowsill—I've mentally cursed at least three more times in just the past hour, so that's fair. Turning, I brush a lock of hair from her forehead. She's warm. Her cheeks are too pink, her eyes too bright. I press my hand against her forehead. Definitely a fever. "Let's keep an eye on that temperature, okay?" I murmur, more to myself than to her.

Thad dances into the kitchen, kissing my cheek before scooping our daughter into his arms. She lets out a shriek of joy. He pulls out his phone and swipes the screen. "Sweet Home Alabama" fills the house. Grace loves belting out the words to one of her favorite songs. He winks at me as he twirls her around the room.

I watch them for a moment, love filling my every cell.

The playful atmosphere can't fully ease the undercurrent of tension tugging at my nerves. Maybe it's the time of year, but something nags at me.

The doorbell rings, cutting through the last notes of the song. Thad kills the music as he sets Grace down. "Go tell your big brother it's dinnertime." He waggles his eyebrows once more. That gesture always fills me with warmth.

Grace takes off at a run, screaming Elias's name.

"Showtime." Thad winks over his shoulder as he strides to the door, a note of forced cheer in his voice. Does he dread these meals as much as I do?

As Thad opens the door, I smooth my apron. It's not merely a part of the dinner deception. It's armor against the night ahead, and I'm ready to face whatever comes through. As if Dorothy and Howard LaRue are two overdressed dragons, ready to sizzle me in their fire of judgment.

May my stuffing hold strong. Thad's with me. We've got this.

The dining room buzzes with the low hum of conversation, punctuated by the occasional laugh from Elias and Grace. They're distracted by the new coloring books I gave them, intently filling in vibrant hues that starkly contrast the snowy view outside.

"Is that really necessary at the table?" Dot's face shows her disapproval.

"Give the kids a break, Mother." Thad takes his seat while I serve. "Beats a Nintendo Switch."

"A Nin what?" Dot raises her eyebrows. She sports a summer-blond, impeccably styled bob, but neither the color nor the classy cut hides her age.

"My game console, Grandma. You ripped me a new one for playing with it last week."

"Elias, manners at the table, young man. You could talk

instead of..." She waves her hand, her head shaking in disappointment. She does not wear confused well.

Elias meets her gaze, his ice-blue eyes sparkling with a mix of seriousness and challenge, the kind only a seven-year-old with a penchant for perfection could muster. "I can teach you to play later." His light brown hair is a little long and falls over his forehead as he leans forward, his face intent. He's gonna look just like his dad. "It's easy and fun. I'm sure even you could learn."

Thad laughs and coughs to hide it.

Dot flashes him a bewildered look, which makes me bite back a smile.

The aroma of the roast turkey mingles with the subtle notes of oak and cherry as Thad pours a rich Château Pétrus into our goblets.

As I place Dot's plate down perfectly centered in front of her, her eyes narrow, and I bite back a laugh. *Say something nasty, I dare you.*

As if reading my mind, Thad waves a glass at me, one side of his mouth lifted in the slightest smirk. It's always a better bottle for the parents. This one is a merlot. I take comfort that Thad selected something he knew I'd like.

"There's been a lot of snow this early in the season." Howard raises his glass in a mock toast. "What does that say about global warming?"

We live on Cape Fleur Island in Maine. What does he expect?

Thad takes a long sip, not bothering to reply. Anything he or any of us says would only start an argument.

"To a load of nonsense." Howard takes a sip as Thad rolls his eyes at me. I refuse to join my father-in-law in his toast.

Dot seizes the moment to steer the conversation toward a topic close to her heart. "Did you hear about Roger Hemmings, Thaddeus? He's just accepted the chief of surgery job at Massachusetts General." She pauses like a singer waiting for applause. "Quite the achievement, isn't it?" Her gaze flicks toward me as I take my seat.

She doesn't outright say my name, but the insinuation that I'm holding Thad back is implicit. After all, it's not the first time.

Thad nods, acknowledging the news with a tight expression. "Roger was always driven. It's great to hear he's doing well. Did he ever get married?"

"Not yet, but a good match is in the offing." Dot picks at her food. "One that will no doubt benefit him."

I bury my annoyance with a sip of wine.

With a calculated casualness, Dot turns her attention to me. "It really is wonderful to see people like Roger taking such opportunities to excel. Makes you think about all the possibilities one could have. If one really pushes for it. If one isn't held back."

Tightening my jaw at her bluntness, I muster a diplomatic response. "Absolutely. Seizing the right opportunities can make all the difference. Like marrying young to have children and moving someplace safe to raise them."

Thad reaches over and squeezes my hand.

Howard chimes in like a trained dog. He's blissfully unaware of the tension. "Indeed, it's all about strategic choices. They pave the way for future success. Maybe you should leave this island and come back to the mainland. There's more opportunity. I'm sure we could find you a better position."

"I'm happy here." Thad takes a bite of the food and nods to me in approval. "Very nice."

"Thanks, my love."

Dot's gaze lingers on Thad. "We always imagined Thaddeus would end up in a prestigious hospital. At the top of his career. But, of course, everyone finds their own path."

"Sitting right here, Mother." Thad meets my glance with a half wink.

A giggle escapes, but I pass it off as choking and press my freshly ironed napkin to my mouth.

Dot takes another bite, chewing in confusion. She doesn't want to admit the food is good. Turning her attention to the children, her face softens. "And what about you two? What big dreams do you have? Will you follow in Daddy's footsteps, Elias, or maybe chart a bold new course?"

Grace goes first, bouncing in her seat. "I want to be like Mommy."

"Oh, how...nice." Dot's gaze flicks back to Elias, her nose turning up. She's clearly gritting her teeth. "And you?"

"I like the big boats in the harbor. I want to sail and catch fish like Liam's dad." The pride and excitement on his face are wonderful. At just seven, he's so sure of the future. A future that will no doubt change many times over the years.

He doesn't need her pressure. He needs to be a child, have fun, and explore possibilities. Tensing, I hope Dot won't shoot him down.

"What about your father's career, a doctor or a surgeon? That's very respectable, very lucrative."

"What's *lucrative* mean? You always use funny words, Grandma Dot." He screws up his face and waves his fork in a circle. A small blob of potato drops onto the table.

Dot *tsks*, and Thad chokes back another laugh.

But Elias doesn't notice such things. Not yet. That's my boy. He shovels in another forkful of food and chews like only a young boy can. The mouth is technically closed, but you still see a lot of food mashing around in there.

Well, so far, this isn't the trainwreck that last week's family dinner was. I may never have to cook for them again.

My back twinges as I shift in my seat, and I'm finding it hard to sit still. It's been bothering me more lately, the ache settling in like an uninvited guest that refuses to leave. I wish I'd taken another painkiller. Instead, I drain my wine glass. Thad reaches across and fills it up. We'll need another bottle soon.

As I start to relax, Dot grimaces. With her perfectly timed knack for pricking the bubble of any jovial moment, she leans over her plate, eyeing the turkey with calculated scrutiny.

And even though she doesn't have her husband's ice-blue eyes, she can still freeze you with one look. "Is there any gravy for this turkey?" Her voice slices through the children's chatter. "It's a little dry."

I nearly spit out my wine before passing across the gravy boat. Thad smirks. Dot just can't resist sticking in the knife.

No sooner have I settled back in my chair than Howard chimes in. "These carrots are on the rubbery side." His tone is as dry as his wife's turkey.

Across the table, Thad catches my eye as he deftly navigates the conversation, steering clear of any culinary confessions. He really does have a knack for maintaining appearances. I wonder just how long he'll keep up this charade tonight. Probably the whole night. He's always been so good at keeping things under wraps—a skill that serves him well in his profession.

Looking at our children, I watch Elias digging into his food without a care in the world. He catches me, his eyes ice blue like his father's and grandfather's, and his lips curl into a grin. I smile back and turn to Grace, my stomach knotting at the redness of her cheeks. The light film of sweat on her forehead. As if on cue, the color drops from her face.

Before I can react, she leans forward and vomits all over her dinner plate.

The chatter and clinking of cutlery come to an abrupt stop.

Dot recoils in her chair as she delicately places her napkin against her lips to shield herself from the offense to her sensibilities.

Bet Thaddeus James never dared to vomit.

Beside her, Howard's reaction is less about disgust and more about discomfort. He glances from Grace to Dot and back, his hands making a brief helpless gesture before settling into a clasp under the table.

Despite being a doctor, Thad's face is full of panic. *Men.*

I'm up in an instant, my chair scraping as I scoop Grace into my arms. Her small body trembles against me. Elias, ever the concerned big brother, follows closely behind.

Is it wrong that I'm relieved to escape?

It doesn't take long for Dot's sharp tones to pierce the air and chase me up the stairs.

"That's what happens when you allow your children to attend filthy, germ-infested public schools. Thaddeus, why are you so against sending them to a proper boarding school? One on the mainland? Are you trying to sentence them to a life of mediocrity?"

Grace whimpers into my shoulder, her small frame trembling. Holding her close, I know I should rush her to the bathroom, but I'm frozen to the spot.

Thad's response is quick. "Lay off, Mother. Cooper's doing her best. She's been working her ass off between the kids and her business. The last thing she needs is you criticizing her parenting."

"She's rubbing off on you. Language, young man."

"She's my wife. She's doing an amazing job. Leave it."

Hearing those words, I could run down the stairs and hug him or hit her. I can't decide which.

Born Cooper Anne Moynihan, a middle-class nobody, I know the superior Dorothy Lorinda LaRue will never believe I'm good enough for her boy.

I strain to hear more.

Elias squeezes my arm, a silent plea, and Grace murmurs something incoherent, her head burrowing deeper into my neck.

"Sorry, kids." The plush carpet muffles our footsteps as we rush down the wide hallway. We pass by walls adorned with pricey artwork and some cool family photos. Dot's approval doesn't matter right now. Nothing does. Not when I've got a sick kid in my arms. This is real parenting.

As the soft gush of water rushes from the faucet, filling the marble bathtub, I begin the quiet, familiar routine of cleaning up after a child's sickness. The splash of the water, a gentle reminder of the everyday tasks that ground me.

"Mommy, I don't feel well."

"You're okay, sweetie. We'll have you in bed soon." I kiss her forehead.

As I wash the remnants of the night's meal from Grace's face, shirt, and hair, the weight of Dot's words and Howard's expectations presses down on me. I glance up at the lighted mirror over the sink, and tired eyes stare back at me. I feel like I'm forty-four, not thirty-four. There are deep circles under those eyes and some gravy on my cheek. I can't help but wonder, not for the first time, if Thad ever doubts our life together. Am I good enough?

With Grace clean, I leave the children and run to her bedroom to grab her PJs. As I cross the landing, Dot's voice rockets up the stairs. "Well, Thaddeus, do you really need another decade to realize her best is not good enough?"

Those words sting. It's as though I don't matter, as if I'm not one of them. The urge to race down there and bitch-slap the woman is overwhelming. Better not. Violence and vomit, what an evening.

Does Thad regret choosing me over the life his parents mapped out for him?

Rushing back to the bathroom, I help Grace into her PJs.

Her movements are slowed by fever. Elias looks on, worry creasing his brow as he whispers reassurances. This is my world, my reality.

The love and the chaos, the messy, beautiful life we've built. It's mine, and no amount of condescending remarks can take that away from me, no matter how much they sting.

CHAPTER
TWO

That Sunday, Thad's home office, typically his private domain, is being used as our therapy room. Like a kid in the principal's office, I'm sitting stiffly on a sofa opposite Sydney Fram, our licensed marriage and family therapist.

The last time I was in the principal's office, it was for blowing raspberries at Ronnie "Rocket" Hargrove. This is more serious. This is our marriage.

Sydney sits across from us in a matching leather chair. Her short brown hair, cut into a chic, no-nonsense bob, frames her sharp features. She regards us with the serene expression she's worn since day one. Every session, as she measures us up, I wonder what she's really thinking. Does she believe the faces we both put on before meeting her, or can she see into our souls? Someday, maybe I'll find the courage to ask her.

I scrutinize Thad as he makes small talk with Sydney. She's nothing like his type, and boy, that was no accident. A neutral, understated suit with a splash of colorful earrings. No bombshell curves or flirtations nature. Nonthreatening, professional, with warm brown eyes that show a mix of empathy and piercing insight.

The antique grandfather clock announces the top of the hour with a deep, resonant chime. Satisfied that there continues to be nothing between them, I sit back and watch Sydney scribbling in an open notebook on her lap.

My throat is dry, my pulse pounding—the typical pre-therapy jitters I can never shake. There's also that touch of discomfort in my lower back, which makes me wonder if I should've taken a painkiller. These sessions are important. I need to concentrate, and right now, I'm finding it hard to sit still.

So here I am, all wiggly on the leather sofa, my legs crossing one way, then the other, the silk of my blouse pressed cold against my back. I'm all kinds of uncomfortable, like *about to get a colonoscopy* uncomfortable.

Meanwhile, Thad lounges beside me, his arm draped casually over the back cushion, his fingertips grazing my shoulder. He might as well have a cocktail with a mini umbrella in the other hand. I'm relieved Sydney agreed to come to the house, though.

Grace is still recovering from last night, and I couldn't bear to leave my sick kid with Allison, our sitter.

Grace and Elias are just outside in the den, watching cartoons on the big screen. The muffled laughter and music filter through the heavy oak door. It's a relief to hear her giggling. And we're so lucky Elias is so protective.

My perfect family. I smile and clasp my hands together on top of my knees. *Ready.*

"Cooper, Thad." Sydney's voice is soft and calming. "I'm so glad we could meet today, especially under the circumstances. How are you both doing?"

Thad clears his throat and sits up a bit straighter. "Great, Sydney. Honestly, Cooper...she's amazing. She's become such a bright light in this community. Everyone adores her.

Sometimes, I think she's even more well-known and well-liked than I am."

Sydney flashes him a smile that doesn't quite reach her eyes.

Thad chuckles, shaking his head in wonder. "Have you seen Marco's recently? The signage and the interior transformation. Coop's turned that place around. Marco is now her biggest fan. Well, her second biggest."

He waggles his eyebrows in that fun way. It feels good to hear him believing in me, even in a controlled environment with his therapy face on.

"I have." Sydney jots a note in her book.

If only I could read it. I would love to know what she writes about us.

"You turned that drab old pizzeria into a vibrant hub. You should be proud, Cooper. How is work overall?"

The praise dispels some of the morning's heaviness as I think about my work. "It's going really well." My voice is laced with genuine enthusiasm I don't have to force. "I love the creative aspect, giving new life to places like Marco's. Understanding the owner's vision and bringing it to life...seeing a local spot become a community favorite is incredibly rewarding."

I take a breath, and she seizes on the pause, asking me to reflect on the balance of my professional and personal life.

"It's busy, sure, and juggling it all can be challenging, but honestly, I wouldn't give it up for the world. There's something so fulfilling about using my skills to help others achieve their dreams. It's more than a job. It's a way to connect with the community and make a real impact."

Sydney nods, her expression soft and bland. "It sounds like you've found a true passion in your work. That's an important anchor, especially during turbulent times, which are inevitable in any marriage."

I shift on the couch, slightly away from Thad. What did that last comment mean? I jump back into talking about my work. Doing so reminds me of the parts of my life that are entirely my own, untouched by the chaos of personal uncertainties. It reinforces my resolve to maintain this piece of myself, no matter the struggles elsewhere in my life.

"And how are you coping with the Christmas season?"

That question is not so easy to answer. This time of year brings back memories of the loss of my mom. "I'm doing okay." Before I can elaborate, before Sydney can push for details, Thad jumps in.

"Cooper's doing so well." His hand finds mine and gives it a squeeze. "Honestly, I hit the jackpot with you, honey. Getting a do-over. I'm all in." He shrugs forward, letting go of my hand and opening his arms. "These sessions...they've worked. We're solid. I'll never let her down again." His hand rests back on my shoulder. Warm, protective.

I swallow hard against a sudden lump in my throat. Therapy has brought us here. It keeps us here. "Hey, I'm the lucky one." I think of his words the previous night. "You've got my back, always stepping in when your folks get to be too much. It means the world, really."

"You bet." He squeezes my hand again. "You and the kids are the world to me."

Then why do we need a therapist? a voice deep inside asks. I push it down. *I* need these sessions. The thought of quitting therapy fills me with dread.

Even so, his praise feels too much, and I want to pull away. But that would look wrong. We're happy. We've got our problems handled.

Though if that's true, if we've truly solved our problems, why do I sit alone at night? We don't hike the trails anymore. I miss the old, easygoing, fun-loving couple we used to be. We've lost our spontaneity. Everything is staged now.

"Do you think Thad's parents put undue strain on the relationship? I know how difficult this time is for you." Sydney's right eyebrow is raised.

"They're around a lot during the holidays." I hug myself. They make me feel inferior. I hate Dot's stupid pointy face framed by that stupid, perfect platinum bob. I want to punch her nose. But I would never say any of that. I look at Thad again, cock my head and smile adoringly. "You never hesitate to put me first. To put our family first. That means so much to me."

Sydney leans forward, shifting her gaze evenly between Thad and me like a good therapist. "So how do you both feel things are going in your marriage?"

Thad's so relaxed. "I think we're doing well. We have a beautiful home and healthy kids. My job is great, and Cooper's career is flourishing. We're really blessed."

I nod, feeling the weight of the unspoken truth his generic words mask. "Yes, we're grateful for so much." My voice is steady but cautious. "And these sessions with you, Sydney, they've been instrumental. They help keep everything in balance, don't you think, Thad?"

"Absolutely." Thad's face stiffens almost imperceptibly. "Though I wonder if we might be ready to start reducing our sessions. We've gained a lot of tools. Things are going great. I've been wondering…do we really need this anymore?"

Bastard. But I keep my mask on.

Sydney watches us closely, her pen poised above her notebook. "It's good to hear you feel equipped, Thad. But you didn't tell me how your marriage is. Neither of you did."

"I thought I did. It's great." Thad shrugs. I feel a tug of irritation at his nonchalance.

"Cooper, what about you? Do you feel the same way about your marriage? Is it 'great?'"

Great compared to what? I don't ask the question though.

All marriages have stresses and potholes and bumps in the road. I honestly don't know a single couple without problems.

"It is. We love each other and have so much. Thad's work is so engrossing. My job is great. The kids are great. Everything's great." *I just said great twice? Or was it three times? I can't think of anything but great.*

I want to mention the lonely nights. The fact that he seems so tired and often his interest in me is lacking. What if it's starting again? But instead, I just press my lips together.

"How do you feel about decreasing the frequency of our sessions?"

How do you feel about me pulling every strand of hair out of your head?

A quick throat-clear breaks the tension. "Our time here matters. It's like a safety net, making sure everything we've worked so hard for stays intact." My gaze shifts to Thad, a silent plea for understanding.

"We don't need it, honey. We're moving on. You have to take the training wheels off sometime."

I hunch my shoulders and picture him riding a bike over a cliff top. Training wheels, indeed.

Smile, Coop.

Sydney's eyes crinkle at the corners. She's trying to see past the masks.

Good luck with that.

We talk for twenty more minutes. She asks more questions, and we answer with the same perfect, cookie-cutter responses. I feel needy, though, wanting to hog her time and say something, but I don't know what.

Don't leave us, Sydney. Just...don't.

"The progress you've made over the past two years is commendable." Sydney looks up from her notebook. "In fact, I think Thad's right. We could probably start scaling back our sessions to once a month. You've built a solid foundation. The tools are there. I have every confidence in your ability to maintain this positive momentum. Why don't we look at our calendars and set a date for after the new year?"

My leg begins to shake. I grind the heel of my boot into the Persian rug. We can't scale back our sessions. The thought alone sends a spike of anxiety through my chest. A film of sweat breaks out across my back where my silk blouse meets the leather of the couch. These meetings with Sydney are our lifeline. They keep Thad focused on what matters most. Me. The kids. Our family.

Without that constant reminder, that accountability, I dread to think what could happen. I think of the time he hung up when I walked into the room last week. How he's locked his phone.

Thad and Sydney are checking dates.

"I can do any day." Is that pathetic?

Thad's nodding along, a satisfied grin on his lips.

We schedule something for mid-January.

Sydney closes her notebook with a soft snap and rises from her chair. "Keep up the fantastic work. My door is always open if you need anything before our next session. Have a great Christmas."

We walk her to the front door, Thad's arm resting on my shoulders as we thank her profusely.

As soon as she's gone, Thad turns to me, his eyes bright with excitement. "Can you believe it? We're in such a good place. We don't need Sydney anymore. She thinks we're doing so well. I mean, we are great, aren't we? Better than ever."

Thoughts of the nights he's been working late and the perfume on his shirt last week torture me.

I force a smile, trying to ignore the unease swirling in my gut. "We are." My voice sounds hollow to my own ears. "I'm so happy. Truly happy."

The perfume means nothing. He's a doctor. He has to get

close to his patients. I'm being paranoid. He had puke on his shirt the week before. I didn't get paranoid over that.

His strong arms envelope me. Over his shoulder, I glimpse our reflection in the entryway mirror. The perfect couple. But something about the image feels off, distorted. Like I'm looking at strangers wearing our skins.

But that close?

To transfer perfume?

I push the thought away. I don't feel like the blond, sun-kissed society wife. Instead, I feel like a middle-class girl who ended up with more than she ever imagined. A girl who fears the truth will catch her if she stops running. Sydney's the only thing holding me together. I can't drop to once a month.

Thad releases me, still grinning. "I'm going to go check on the kids. Maybe see if Elias wants to toss a football around."

I'm still reeling. *Once a month.* What will happen in between?

As Thad disappears down the hall, I drift into the den in a daze. Grace is curled up on the sofa, her little face peaceful in sleep. I sink down beside her, drawing her into my arms. Stirring slightly, she nuzzles into my shoulder with a contented sigh.

Closing my eyes, I breathe in the sweet smell of her hair. My daughter. My children. My reason for everything. Thad and Elias are laughing as they play. But the anxiety continues to churn within me, a rising tide of dread.

"We're moving on." Thad had seemed so confident. *"We're in such a good place. We don't need Sydney anymore."* The thought should comfort me, but a bone-deep terror fills me instead. Because in a dark corner of my heart, one I can barely acknowledge, a single searing question burns.

If we stop going to therapy, what if he does it again?

Letting go of Grace, I leave the room, heading to the kitchen to grab a much-needed glass of wine.

CHAPTER
THREE

Twinkling lights and homemade decorations create a warm, inviting atmosphere. Reds and greens paint the elementary school hall with holiday cheer. The gymnasium is packed to the rafters, benches stacked with parents, everyone focused on the makeshift stage where children fill the space with the joyous sound of singing. Their enthusiasm is infectious as they belt out "Jingle Bells."

One little boy with messy brown hair and bright-red cheeks is missing each note, his voice changing pitch on every third word. The girl beside him is screeching "jingle bells" and very little else with a broad, toothless grin as she bounces up and down on her heels. Her excitement is infectious.

In contrast, Elias is very serious, eyebrows knit together, his little hands clenched into fists. He's a perfectionist, just like his dad, which brings happy tears to my eyes.

In front of him, a little boy is picking his nose. His parents are near the stage. "Joshua," they call, "knock it off!" and a wave of laughter goes around the hall. He holds up his finger for them to inspect as the rest of the children sing with the tinkling piano.

Grace is looking right at me, grinning and trying not to giggle. I nod and give her a thumbs-up. She doesn't seem to know the words to freaking "Jingle Bells." Boy, am I going to hear about that from Miss Pointy Face. Dot's eyes will narrow. *"Really, what do they teach the children in that place?"*

Grace reaches out to hold the hand of the girl next to her. The two of them stop singing and start laughing. I squeeze Thad's hand, and we crack up too.

A teacher holds up both hands, motioning the children to stop. The performance cuts to a solo of "Frosty the Snowman." A young boy sings with the voice of an angel. Shuffling feet add to the performance. Joshua destroys the moment with a cackle. At least it wasn't another booger.

On the opposite end of the row, Thad's parents sit rigidly, their backs straight, chins held high, hands on their laps. They're probably afraid they'll catch cooties if they touch the armrests.

In the back, a baby starts screaming, and Dot shakes her head with a tut. The look she shares with Howard says it all. In contrast, if he were here, my dad would chuckle and turn to give the struggling parents a sympathetic look. Unlike the LaRues, who had a nanny to help raise Thad, he'd understand, as a single dad who raised a daughter all on his own.

Angelic little voices start singing "Winter Wonderland," and I'm toast.

A lump forms in my throat as tears burn my eyes, and that familiar ache blooms in my chest. I shouldn't be thinking about this. I should be watching the stage, but now I can't get past it.

Twenty-four years ago, I was singing that very song at my own school Christmas concert, and I was angry at my mom. She never showed up to watch my performance. It stung.

Worse still, my dad got up and walked out in the middle of my performance.

"Winter Wonderland." Such a joyous tune, but my worst song ever...

The recital was over. I grabbed my coat and ran outside. Dad was with a police officer and Ms. Cater, the art teacher. I ran to him to yell about how he ruined the concert, but he was crying. I'd never seen him cry. He scooped me into his arms. Ms. Cater was crying too.

"What's wrong? Where's Mom? Why's everyone crying?" And before I even knew what had happened, I was crying too. I'd never seen my dad so sad. It was terrifying, and the nightmare hadn't even begun.

"Rudolph the Red-Nosed Reindeer" brings me back to reality. As the song ends, the audience erupts into applause, and the concert is over.

My mom passed away on a day just like this, before a concert just like this. My dad worked so hard to make sure I had everything, but a child needs her mom. I was ten.

Did I have enough time to learn what a mother should be? Is that another of my shortcomings?

As Thad and I make our way to the stage, he glances at his Rolex, a frown creasing his brow. "I have to get back to the clinic. Sorry. Patients to see, and I'm already running behind schedule."

Even though it's his lunch break, I feel abandoned. I invited Dad to the kids' recital, but he begged off with claims he had to work. Is that true? He could be avoiding the reminder of how I ripped our family apart. Maybe Thad's avoiding me too.

Why must this time of year be so hard?

With a goodbye to his parents, Thad's gone. They piggyback on his excuse, wave to the kids, and follow him out.

Swallowing down my displaced anxiety, I watch as the kids

leave the stage and head off to their afternoon classes. Elias waves at me before he disappears through a side door, and my heart swells. Maybe I can face the next part of my day now.

Squaring my shoulders, I follow a stream of parents heading toward the PTA meeting scheduled for immediately after the recital. As elbows bump mine, my mom's absence is a physical ache—a tangled web of emotions and memories, a wound that refuses to heal no matter how much time passes.

When I enter the classroom designated for the meeting, disgruntled mumbles already echo around the room. No one wants to still be in the school. We have better things to do. Well, everyone except Felicia Muntz, the twenty-seven-year-old dictator with her straggly brown hair and peppy attitude.

It's the last PTA meeting of the year. Despite the holiday season's approach, the air is thick with the tired resignation that only a room full of overextended parents can muster. The joy from the earlier performance has evaporated, leaving behind stiff shoulders and tired faces.

The room is chilly. Everyone's wearing a coat.

Would it hurt to turn the heater up?

I cringe inside. That sounded just like Miss Pointy Face.

A cold chair of hard, molded plastic waits for me as I slip into the back row. Pulling my coat tighter around my shoulders, I note Felicia taking her place at the podium.

Her voice is sharp, and as she's slightly too close to the microphone, the initial squeal cuts through the murmur of side conversations. "Thank you, everyone, for joining us on such short notice." Her tone implies that the notice was anything but short.

The agenda is a drone of budget talks and event planning, none of which seem to warrant dragging us here when we should be preparing for the holidays. Several parents are discreetly checking their phones, their faces lit by the soft glow of the screens.

Felicia's voice rises and falls in a rhythm that's become painfully familiar over the years. I've never clicked with most of the other moms. They seem to mesh so well, while I'm the odd one out, benched on the sidelines when the players get called. Their easy vibes are just out of my reach. Or am I the one who guards her privacy like a fortress?

Beth Hopner, my bestie, chose the saner option and ditched today's meeting. Smart move on her part.

That brings a smile. I should follow her lead, emulate her confidence, but I don't. I do what the doctor's wife is supposed to do.

Beth says my problem is that my purse cost more than some of their cars. I can't help that.

A collective groan ripples through the crowded room as Felicia launches into a pitch about extracurricular participation quotas. She stands at the front, her eyes alight, oblivious to the growing discontent.

She's outlining her plan with eager gestures, insisting every student must engage in at least two extracurricular activities per semester to foster well-rounded development. Her voice rings with a passion that's more imposing than inspiring.

From the back, a man named Russell Barnes raises his voice over the murmur of dissatisfied parents. "We should table this discussion for next year." The strain in his voice suggests this is a battle he's tired of fighting.

Beside me, a woman named Linda—I can't remember her last name—juggles a fussy toddler on her hip. She shakes her head. "Our kids have enough on their plates. Let them join if they want to, not because they're forced to."

Felicia presses on, steamrollering over their concerns with a determined nod. "I appreciate your input, but this initiative is crucial for our students' growth. We'll be moving forward with implementing the program next term." The smug grin on her face sets off mumbles around the room. I know I'm not the only one who wants to slap it right off.

As the meeting finally wraps up, the parents stir, stretching and gathering their things with relieved sighs. The room's atmosphere shifts as casual conversation replaces the formal monotony. Some parents drift away, while others converge into familiar little circles.

Two moms from Grace's class wave me over, their smiles warm and inviting. They're mid-discussion about a bake sale and a group outing to see the holiday lights.

"Cooper, you should join us." Tammy Brooks's tone is warm and genuine.

"Thanks, but I've got so much going on right now. Another time maybe." The words are automatic. Even as I say them, I know they've heard this excuse from me before.

Next to her, Amiko Tanaka doesn't say anything at first. Instead, she tilts her head ever so slightly, her sleek black bob shifting just enough to catch the light. A delicate brow arches, and her lips press into the faintest of lines—a reaction so minute, it could almost be missed.

Almost.

"Of course," she finally says, her tone silk-wrapped steel. "Another time, perhaps."

Why do I always do this? Sabotage my chances to make new friends? With a nod and a "happy holidays," I walk away.

I wander through the cliques, feeling a little lost and overlooked. The crowd moves along, and I'm pulled with them down the hallway. I overhear snippets of holiday plans, the chatter providing a comforting, if mundane, distraction.

A voice cuts through the noise, sharper and more focused than the rest. It's Maggie Donovan, a woman who, like me, has never quite fit into the neatly packed boxes of island social life. However, with Maggie, the reason is crystal clear.

While most of us are bundled up in thick coats, she's

wearing a red dress, low cut and nightclub ready. I detect actual sequins on the trim. I hate being so judgmental as much as I hate the touch of envy winding through me as she stands with a group of mothers who normally snub me. They want to hear what she has to say.

Swallowed by the crowd, I catch glimpses of her animated gestures, painting her words in the air.

"He's just wonderful." Maggie flounces her hair, and her grin says it all. "You wouldn't believe some of the sweet things he texts me." She's holding up her phone but angling it so the screen is hidden.

I find myself inadvertently tuning in. Even *great* marriages can use a bit of excitement. Maybe I can pick up a pointer or two.

Maggie can certainly hold court. I'll give her that. This time, though, there's something different about her—a lightness I haven't seen before, making her even more captivating.

"Who is he?" Celia Garrison, that poor woman, always looks like she needs a nap and a trip to the salon.

"Sorry, ladies. My lips are sealed." Maggie's voice is filled with delight.

I clutch my purse and follow the crowd past her. The echo of Maggie's laughter rings off-key in my ears, and I slow my pace.

Something shifts beneath the surface of these mundane exchanges, tugging at the edges of my consciousness, whispering that all is not as it seems.

Maggie's voice pierces the din like a cold draft. "He says I'm his lucky day."

The words stop me dead in my tracks. That phrase, those words. Those exact words. Those aren't meant for her. Those are *my* words. Thad's special phrase just for me.

Or so I thought.

Thad whispered those exact words to me, his breath warm against my ear, during those first intoxicating days of our courtship.

Meeting me was his "lucky day."

Swallowing down a rush of bile, I want to go over there and rip her phone from her fingers. This can't be happening—again. I think of his words just yesterday.

"We're great."

The clatter of chairs and the hum of departing parents fade into a blur.

Maggie. Divorced Maggie. Attractive, divorced Maggie with her low-cut dress and swaying hips could not possibly be speaking about Thad. My Thad.

Could she?

The rational part of me scolds me for jumping to conclusions based on an overheard snippet of conversation. Six words cannot destroy our marriage.

Can they?

Push it away. It's impossible.

I think about the distance that has crept back into our marriage. The long nights I sit at home while Thad works late. The perfunctory kisses he gives me, the distance growing between us.

My stomach roils.

I should run up to Maggie and sniff her. Compare her perfume to what I smelled on Thad. Rip the bandage off.

Yes!

No.

It's time to confront Thad, demand the truth, but the memory of our past confrontations holds me back. Thad has a way of turning things around, brushing off my concerns, making me feel paranoid and petty. His words would be soothing and reassuring on the surface. Designed to quell my fears while hiding his betrayals.

No. This can't be true. He's fought too hard to rebuild a good marriage. He spends too much time at work, and he's often tired, but that's normal for doctors. It doesn't mean anything. He would never...not with a woman like her.

He likes them younger...

I push through the heavy doors, the bitter winter air slapping my cheeks. The parking lot is slick with a thin layer of ice, and the sky is gray and unyielding. I fumble for my keys, my fingers clumsy and stiff. My breath forms small puffs of fog in the air, each one proof of the chill that has settled deep in my bones.

As I sob back my frustration, Maggie Donovan's words play again and again, an unwelcome mantra.

"He says I'm his lucky day."

No. The words are hollow, unconvincing. It simply cannot be Thad. I love him too much to allow these seeds of doubt to take root. Too much to watch our lives disintegrate over idle, overheard gossip.

Unlocking the car, I slide into the driver's seat and stare at the row of barren trees lining the school driveway. Their branches are stark and fragile against the dull sky. Could Thad really betray me again?

With a deep, shaky breath, I pull away from the curb. My mind races, the specter of betrayal sitting heavy in the passenger seat beside me.

It's happening again.

CHAPTER
FOUR

"He says I'm his lucky day."

The thought of that scheming hussy in her red dress manipulating Thad has got me pacing the hallway outside the kids' rooms. I'm fidgety as the evening stretches on and counting down the minutes until lights out. I'll create a traffic lane in our newly installed plush carpeting if I keep this up.

No. He wouldn't do it. We've been through therapy. He's been amazing. I grapple with the lingering doubts from the PTA meeting and mentally kick myself for going. I should've ditched it like Beth did.

Thad's working late again.

Shut in his office below us, the door closed.

Keeping me out.

Talking to that redheaded bitch, a voice whispers.

Or slumped over his desk, working hard to get finished for the holidays, another one answers.

"Shut up, the both of you." I open the door to Grace's room.

Her nightlight casts gentle, dancing figures across the ceiling—unicorns, moons, stars. She's silhouetted against the glow, playing with her favorite bear, Beary Potter, still bubbling with the inexhaustible energy of a child who's just shrugged off illness.

"Bedtime."

"Not tired." The protest is accompanied by a spirited twinkle in her eye and her hands on her hips, once again mimicking the pose I strike when Thad pisses me off.

"Tired or not, you know the drill, young lady."

She's bouncing up and down, chasing the unicorns and giggling.

"Mommy, I'm not tired. I could stay up all night."

"No, you can't, my little one." I brush a stray lock of hair from her forehead. Her eyes are bright, but the telltale signs of fatigue are written in the faint circles beneath them. "Now." My voice is a little firmer.

She bounds over and jumps on the bed.

I pull back the quilt. She crawls inside and looks up at me. "Mommy, what's therapy?"

The question catches me off guard, her curiosity piercing the fog of my self-pity.

Dammit—she must've overheard us. I want to blame Thad, but it's both our fault. As I kneel beside her bed, the soft fabric rustles under my touch.

"It's just talking, sweetie."

"Talking? Why not say *talking*?"

"It's talking out your problems. You know, if you ever have any worries or problems, you can talk to me about them."

Her mouth opens.

I put a finger to her lips. "There's a time and a place for talking, and now is the time for sleep."

I kiss her forehead. The challenge stays in her eyes, replaced by a grin.

"We'll talk about it more when you're older, okay?" I press a remote, and the room dims to a cozy twilight where unicorns still dance across the ceiling. My baby can sleep and hopefully forget she ever heard the word *therapy*.

Leaving her room, I pause outside Elias's door.

"Just turning off, Mom."

I walk in and kiss his forehead. "Good night."

Padding along the hallway, down the stairs, and over to Thad's office, I listen for the faint sounds of his presence—the tap of a keyboard, the murmur of a late call.

A sense of loneliness washes over me. Why don't I walk in and ask if he wants a drink? Or tell him to call it a night? There were times when I slipped into that room in nothing but a robe, sitting on his knee and kissing him silly. That always stopped him working. I reach for the door.

There it is. His voice is low, indistinct. Who's he talking to?

"Don't even go there," I say before I can think of the redheaded temptress.

Turning away, I pull out my phone to call Beth, needing the anchor of her voice—however slurred it might be tonight.

"Hey." I keep my tone casual to mask the tightness in my chest. "You missed another thrilling PTA meeting."

Beth's laugh booms through the speaker as I make my way to the kitchen. "Let me guess. Felicia ruled with an iron fist, and everyone pretended to care while texting themselves a list of all the presents they still need to buy?"

"Pretty much." My spirits lift a bit. "She was ranting about extracurricular participation again."

"Bet that went down like warm vomit."

I bark a laugh. The familiarity of our banter provides a brief respite. "You got that right. Totally oblivious to the mood of the room. She just carried on and on and on."

"Like always. What does she think we do all day?" Beth sighs dramatically. "Seriously, with work, homework, and keeping them fed and in clean clothes and the boogers off their faces, who has the time for her latest scheme?"

"Amen."

The line fills with the soft clink of glass against glass, and I imagine Beth refilling her wine. "She doesn't have a clue." Another pause for a wine slurp. "So spill it. Did anything juicy happen, or was it just the usual drivel?"

I hesitate, the name on my tongue feeling like a betrayal. I want my own glass of wine. "Maggie Donovan was there... gushing about some new man."

Acid burns in my stomach. *It's not Thad.*

Beth snorts, the sound distorted by another sip. "Maggie? She's a hoot. Check out her Facebook if you want a laugh. It's a crash course in post-divorce crisis management."

The suggestion lingers in the air, a tantalizing and terrifying prospect. Curiosity wars with dread. What if Thad's name pops up somewhere on Maggie's timeline? What if there's a picture of them? That is some serious crazy talk happening.

"I might just do that." My voice is lighter than I feel. "I forgot I called to confirm the time for our coffee meet."

"Dang, I was gonna call you. Mia has a doctor's appointment. Can we rearrange for next week? Oh, I might be away. We'll figure something out."

"Sure. Is Mia all right?"

"It's just a checkup. I forgot to put it in my planner, but they pinged me to confirm."

We say our goodbyes, and I end the call. Dropping the phone, I uncork a merlot and pour a glass.

Seated at the kitchen table, the bottle at my side, I let the first few sips of wine warm and relax my insides. A hesitant tap unlocks my tablet.

Another sip...okay, a gulp of wine.

With a deep, steadying breath, I tap the icon and search for her name. There are lots of Maggie Donovans, but the right one is easy to spot.

Taking another swig of wine, I tap her picture.

Maggie's profile loads, and I'm immediately bombarded with images and posts that paint a vivid portrait of a woman reveling in newfound freedom. Each scroll reveals more of Maggie's wild escapades.

There's a photo from her "divorce party," where she's clad in nothing more than provocative lingerie, surrounded by friends raising champagne flutes. The contrast between her reckless joy and my mindful misery is like watching a puppy try to frolic when they're stuck on a four-foot leash.

She's fun and exciting like I used to be.

Stop it. Thad never wanted slutty. Not for a wife.

There's a picture of Maggie in tight leather pants, posing before a line of gleaming motorcycles. The caption, *Single and ready to ride*, is like a punch to the gut.

She's looking for a man, and I doubt she cares who he is. Or if he's married.

I set my wine glass down with a clink. But there are other implications she hasn't thought of. The page is public—exposed to anyone, everyone. My heart aches as I think of her children, especially her seven-year-old daughter, who's in Elias's class.

Maggie is undeniably beautiful, but she doesn't care about anyone but herself. She wouldn't care about stealing my husband. Not one little bit.

Attempting to see things from another perspective, I try to understand the appeal. Could the thrill of escape tempt someone like Thad?

Yuppers. And it's happened before. Do they know each other?

It's a small island. Of course he knows her.

"He says I'm his lucky day." Maggie's words echo, taunting

me. I replay them, trying to convince myself it's a coincidence, a common phrase. But the seed of doubt has already been planted.

The only person I've ever heard say that was Thad. How long ago was it that he spoke those words to me? Years. Before he proposed. Does he think I forgot? Maybe it's a reflex, something he says without thinking.

Anyone could've said those words to her. Why won't my damn mind let this go? There's no proof.

Just a paranoid wife.

CHAPTER
FIVE

The clink of breakfast dishes is deafening as I mechanically prepare toast, barely tasting the coffee I sip between tasks.

I subtly reach into the junk drawer, the perfect hiding place, and my fingers search the clutter until they brush against a bottle. No one goes in here. It's one of those *forgotten in plain sight* places that hide beneath the radar.

I glance over my shoulder. Thad's still in the shower. Quietly, I pop one of the pills. It'll ease the pain of the dull headache and the discomfort in my lower back. And take the edge off my paranoia. Bonus. Since that day on the trail, since injuring my back, the oxy has kept me going.

Breakfast is quiet. Coffee for me. The kids finish their eggs and toast before running to the den to watch TV.

"Thanks, Mom," I call after them, the sarcasm heavy.

Nothing.

Okay, kiddies, maybe Dot's right. It's time for some lessons in manners.

Thad walks in, staring at his phone. He looks exhausted. Maybe they're working him too hard at Cape Fleur Medical

Associates. That's why he's so tired. A thought surfaces, sharper, clearer—he's a partner. He can slow down if he wants to.

Though he's tired, he looks happy, almost eager. He wants to get to the office. Could it be?

No. Push that thought down.

He loves his work. The holiday period is always so busy. Everyone leaves things until the last minute. People mingle, catch more bugs. It makes sense that work is crazy. Like all of us, he's trying to put everything to bed in time for the break. The last thing he needs is a neurotic and suspicious wife stirring up trouble.

It's that time of year, I tell myself. I always get antsy around the anniversary of Mom's death. Everything hits me harder. I have this irrational fear that people will leave me. Now, like a psycho, I'm pushing Thad away.

He leaves with a perfunctory kiss on my cheek. I still have ten minutes before the kids need to catch the bus. Grabbing my coat, I take the back door and sneak to the detached garage. Ignoring the big doors, I head down the side to a pedestrian door, leaving it unlocked as I enter. Inside, tucked into the shadows, is my secret stash. A pack of Marlboro Lights hidden in an old coffee tin. Lighting one, I take a long drag, closing my eyes and leaning against the cold wall, letting the moment stretch a little longer.

Peace, for just a moment.

"Okay, kids, grab your bags." I head back inside and suck a mint, hoping they can't smell the smoke on my clothes.

"Ten more minutes." Grace is a champion whiner. "It's almost Christmas. We won't do anything in school anyway."

"Sorry, sweetie. Them's the rules."

Elias jumps up, and they grab their bags and coats and hustle to the door. I give them both a quick kiss as they put on their boots. With seconds to spare, I herd them outside just in time for the bus.

Relax.

My first meeting of the day isn't for a few hours. I do a quick tidying-up of the kitchen, all marble and shiny surfaces that flash my reflection back at me—haggard, exhausted. No match for Maggie Red Dress.

With that done, I perch on the edge of the counter to answer some emails until it's time to go. Not good for my back, but the pain pill is dulling my senses.

After a quick drive through the snow, I pull up to Marco's Pizzeria. The heaviness of sleep deprivation and unresolved worries weighs on me like a suffocating cloak, dragging at my shoulders and clouding my mind. It's all I can think about. I push it all away with an angry grunt.

Across the parking lot, Marco's vibrant sign, designed by me, sways gently in the breeze. He tells me his business has doubled since I started helping him. He already made terrific pizza. He just needed some signage and social media marketing to get the word out.

Inside the restaurant, the oven's warmth and the scent of baking dough provide a welcome comfort.

Marco greets me with his usual robust laughter, his voice booming through the space. "Cooper. Perfect timing." He waves me to a window booth cluttered with fabric swatches and color palettes. "I've got some big plans for the back section. You'll love this."

"Let's hear it." I try to match his energy.

Marco unfurls a large blueprint on the table and starts pointing animatedly. "Okay, picture this. We turn that dreary back room into a buzzing hub for the island's youth. I'm not sure what needs to be in there. What do kids want these days? Maybe whitewashed walls and pictures of Italy?" His hands carve the air as he outlines the space. "Board games?"

"Um." I wake up my tablet and swipe over to the artwork I've designed to advertise the new venture. "How about this? Neon lights, graffiti art, a couple of retro arcade games, the works."

His grin broadens even more. "*Magnifico*." His ideas spill out faster than I can capture them, more Italian smattered throughout his sentences. "We could have modular furniture, right? Something cool that's also...*funzionale*. Functional. You help me set this all up. Get it done."

"That's not really what I do."

"But you do such great work. I need help." He gives me a lost-little-boy look that he knows is going to work.

I relent. "Sure, we can look at it, work something out."

"*Bellissima*. I'll get more coffee."

Interior design is not really my forte. My job is to design the marketing and pull it together with the business's brand. To make that brand pop. But I can apply those skills to what he wants. The plans he's drawn are good.

"How do you like it?" He places the coffee and some little chocolates on the table.

"Great! This could work." My stylus moves rhythmically across the screen, translating Marco's vision into tangible designs. The colors pop—bold, bright, and full of life, just like Marco's description. I start with some graphics for an advertising campaign. Teenagers enjoying pizza in the new room.

"I love it, but I want more. What will bring them in besides the great pizza?" There's enthusiasm in his eyes, but a little worry too.

What do kids want? "How about a dedicated gaming area?"

Marco's eyes light up even more, if possible. "Say more."

"Depending on your budget, you could set up consoles for tournaments. It'll be a hit with the teens. I'm sure of it. You could even run some competitions. That would tie in well with the marketing."

"That's perfect. *Bellissima*. I see now why you're so *brillante* at this."

His passion is infectious, and his praise gives my wounded ego a much-needed boost. I imagine the space coming to life. "If you like it, we can start on the designs."

Marco claps his hands. "With your magical touch, it will be the best. Just the best!" He uses both hands to blow me a kiss.

"Thanks, Marco."

As I sip my coffee, a flash of red slices into the gray day outside. Maggie Donovan strides past the pizzeria's front windows, a showy flamingo parading her vivid colors and capturing the eye of every red-blooded male.

Long scarlet hair cascades from beneath a chic faux fur hat as she glides along. Her high-heeled boots make her hips sway provocatively. Does anyone really walk like that?

Her presence is a jolt of electricity, snapping me back to reality and pulling me out of the creative reverie I was lost in moments before.

Marco notices too. "Ms. Donovan's been prowling the neighborhood like a…a *cagna in calore* since her divorce. That woman is nothing but trouble." Despite the jocular delivery and the flush to his cheeks, there's no mistaking the undercurrent of censure in his voice.

If my Italian is correct, he called her a bitch in heat.

He shakes his head, but his gaze still tracks Maggie's progress down the street until she disappears.

What's the Italian phrase for "pick your tongue off the floor, man?" I force a laugh, trying to shake off my unease.

As Marco looks back at me, I can't help but wonder, *Would a man like him stray?*

The sickening possibility ties my stomach in knots. If kind, loyal Marco could fall prey to Maggie…a nauseating sense of déjà vu hits me. Just like the last time I suspected Thad of cheating.

CHAPTER
SIX

Marco pulls his gaze back to me. "What is our next—"

"I...I have to go. Something urgent came up." I push to my feet, barely gathering my materials in my haste.

He looks taken aback but nods, concern flickering across his features.

I rush out of the pizzeria, and the bell above the door jingles sharply as the cool air hits me with a harsh slap. My pulse races with a mix of fear and determination.

Stop, dammit. She walked past the window. This means nothing.

As I slide behind the steering wheel, my hands tremble against the supple leather, slick with a faint sheen of anxious sweat. I push start, and the engine rumbles to life.

A strange compulsion grips me, irrational but irresistible, hooking into some primal part of my psyche. Without fully understanding the reasons behind my actions, I idle in the parking lot, fixated on Maggie's sleek figure as she emerges from one store and disappears into the welcoming entrance of another vintage boutique.

Leave. Go. Push the stick into drive, and point the car toward home. Forget this momentary lapse of reason.

But I can't. Some invisible force keeps me tethered here, watching, waiting.

It's irrational. She's done nothing to warrant this behavior —nothing but look sinfully good in that dress and utter those six innocuous words.

I hate her. The way she dresses, the way she walks, everything. I'm envious, and I hate that feeling. And I hate her for making me feel that way.

The temptation to follow her inside is overwhelming, fueled by a tempestuous cocktail of trepidation, envy, and the troubling sense of my own inadequacy. In the face of Maggie's allure and effervescent charm, my self-worth withers. I'm insignificant, nothing, a nobody in her radiant presence.

Revulsion courses through me, a bitter self-loathing that propels my hand toward the phone. Sydney's number flashes in my mind—yes, I have my therapist's number memorized— a beacon of clarity amid the tempestuous sea of my thoughts. Her grounding presence, her incisive wisdom, would cut the Gordian knot of my obsessive suspicions.

Even as my fingers hover over the keypad, ready to tap those digits in the old-fashioned way, I hesitate, paralyzed by a fresh surge of warring emotions.

Dammit, I love Thad, so why don't I trust him? Surely he's done enough to earn back my trust.

He encouraged Sydney to come to the house, showing flexibility and understanding when Grace was sick. If he didn't care, he could've postponed that session.

He skipped lunch for his kids' Christmas concert.

He defended me to his parents on the Night of the Catered Meal. Our private joke. If he didn't love me, he wouldn't do those things.

This is why I fell in love with him. Marriages have

problems, but we got over ours, and I should stop looking for more.

Thad and I have worked hard to rebuild our relationship and forge a bond based on trust and mutual respect. We've come so far, overcome so much, that the idea of him risking everything for a fleeting dalliance seems absurd, especially with someone as high-profile and recognizable as Maggie.

"Be sensible, Cooper," I say aloud. "You're just torturing yourself, punishing yourself and Thad for what happened to Mom." The logical part of my brain knows I push people away at this time of year. Knows I fear they'll leave me.

He's done it before, whispers the voice in the darkest corner of my mind. *You heard what she said. "He says I'm his lucky day."*

The thought is a blade, sharp and cold, a cruel voice that seeks to undermine everything we've fought for and sacrificed to be together.

Maggie exits the vintage boutique, bag in hand. Another low-cut red dress, no doubt.

What am I doing? Sitting here like a stalker.

With a deep, shuddering breath, I put the car in gear and drive away, the boutique receding in my rearview. The tightness in my chest eases slightly, but the worries linger.

Way to go, Cooper. Behaving like a maniac.

I make a quick stop at the gas station. As I wander the aisles, my arms quickly fill with snacks—colorful bags of chips and sweet treats that will make Elias's and Grace's eyes light up in delight. I shuffle toward the checkout, the familiar crinkle of the bags a comforting sound. They're also for me.

In line, the customer ahead of me is wrapped in a bulky coat that swallows his frame. He wears fingerless gloves, his fingers red and chapped as he fumbles with a stack of scratch-off lottery tickets. My gaze inadvertently drifts to the tickets, each emblazoned with bright-green shamrocks and bold yellow lettering that spells *LUCKY*.

I can't catch a break.

On the way home, an idea forms. I need to get Thad in the same room with her. To know for certain if this is more than just jealousy.

The empty house greets me. I wish the kids were home, but they're not due for a couple of hours. My to-do list is a mile long, but all I can think about is Maggie, my thoughts are already racing ahead to my next move.

Dropping the goodies on the counter, I grab a bag of lime-flavored tortilla chips. Tearing them open, I hop on my computer and log into the PTA website. My fingers fly over the keys like a woman possessed. I locate Maggie's email from the parent list.

"Wait!"

Thad'll be furious if he finds out what I'm doing. But if it comes to nothing, he'll never know. Crafting a message about misplaced invitations to our annual Christmas party, I hit send. The click of the mouse is the exclamation point on my bad idea. But...it'll get Maggie and Thad in the same room and quell my suspicions.

Or light them up even more.

That done, I work on my laptop, attentive for any ping of a return message. I prepare a couple of quotes, send an invoice, and reply to a few questions. The afternoon flies by, and before I know it, the kids are home.

Grace is shaking snow out of her hair and giggling. Elias is stomping his feet.

"How was your day?"

Elias steps into the mudroom and neatly takes off his boots, lining them up with precision against the wall.

"Lots of snow." Grace tosses her coat at the mudroom

wall. It misses the hooks and lands on her boots in the middle of the floor. I give her a hug, but she pulls free and darts past me.

Elias hangs his coat carefully on one of the brass hooks as if he's a young officer in boot camp. Everything so precise, so neat.

"School was okay, I guess. We did math today. Fractions. Mrs. Whitman says I'm getting better at them, but they make my head hurt. Oh, next year, we're starting a science project to grow something from seed. I picked a sunflower 'cause it's the tallest, and I want to win the biggest plant contest. Oh, and recess was fun. I beat Tommy in tag."

Grace snags a bag of chips from the counter and races to the den. The TV comes on.

"Grace! Boots." No reply comes back, so I tidy them up, and Elias and I leave the mudroom.

Soon, they're both happy in front of the TV. I give them a bag of candy to go with the chips and wonder if I'm spoiling them too much.

Thad'll be home soon. I slide a meatloaf into the oven and put away some clothes. And now there's nothing to do but wait.

My phone buzzes. It's Thad.

Tied up at work, babe.

You've got to be kidding.

My thumbs stab the screen. *Hurry home. Love you.*

The evening stretches on interminably. I go through the motions of dinner, baths, and bedtime stories with robotic efficiency, my attention constantly drifting to the clock. Each tick is a reminder that Thad's still at work. Or possibly with her.

I'm just loading the dishwasher when my phone buzzes on the counter. The screen lights up with Beth's name.

I swipe to answer. "Hey. What's up?"

"Girl, I almost ran off the damn road today." Beth's voice is a mixture of panic and humor. "Snow's coming down like it's got something to prove, and the ice is no joke. Man, it was scary. Luckily, I bumped a little tree. Really slowly. It saved the day."

"Are you all right?"

"Yeah, nothing to worry about. My old jalopy bounces pretty well."

"Beth, you're a really crappy driver." I snort. "You could run off the road in perfect weather."

"That was only once." She laughs, and all my tension slips away.

"Just be careful. I don't want you rolling off a cliff or into the bay. Who would keep me sane?"

"I'm telling you, the ole girl's built like a tank. She can take it. Anyway, did you hear about Sheila, the mom with the pink obsession?"

"No. What's she done now?" I lean against the counter, settling in. Beth always knows the latest gossip.

"She's leaving her husband. Apparently, he's been fooling around with that new yoga instructor. The one who's way too flexible for her age."

That cuts a little close to home. I bite back the urge to spill my suspicions about Thad. "Seriously." I roll my head to stretch the muscles in my neck. "Wow. Are you sure? I didn't see any sign of that when I saw her this week."

"I've got my sources." She's hilariously smug. "Trust me. By tomorrow, the whole school will know. Betcha five bucks she starts posting inspirational quotes on Facebook."

"Five bucks? Please. She'll have a whole Pinterest board by morning."

"I figured you'd like a little island drama. How's everything over there? Kids good?"

"We're great." I barely manage to refrain from a Tony the

Tiger rendition. "It's a madhouse as usual, but we're hanging in there. You and yours?"

"Ah, I admit, I needed a break from the kids. I locked them upstairs so I could grab a glass of wine and have a chat."

Another snort escapes. Beth has three kids, two girls and a boy, ranging from four to ten. Somehow, she manages alone. I love how she's always happy, always full of energy. "Might join you in the wine."

"Do. Well, hang in there a little longer. The rabble are getting restless, and this snow's not letting up anytime soon."

"Yeah, yeah, tell that to your jalopy, and be careful."

It was good to chat, and I'm already looking forward to the next bit of scandal Beth will scoop. I just hope it's not about Thad and me. Does she already know?

After the call, I finish a few chores, but I can't stop myself from constructing vivid scenes of betrayal, each more torturous than the last.

He's smiling at the woman with the flowing red hair. The prettier woman, the bustier woman. The woman with no baggage who's just out for fun and "ready to ride." The woman who is not his wife.

Thad's handsome face, his eyes locked onto Maggie's, his laughter mingling with hers in a way he once reserved for me. The scene shifts, growing steamier, their hands brushing casually, the touch lingering, electric.

It shifts again to the privacy of a dimly lit corner at some upscale bar, their casual flirtation escalating to an intimate embrace, a stolen kiss. Still kissing, they leave the bar.

I shake my head.

Don't follow them into the hotel room.

I've refreshed my email compulsively going on three hours now, the screen a blank witness to my unraveling. She's bound to have read it.

What's she thinking? Is she laughing at me? Worried that I know the truth? Glad?

Just reply already. Waiting like this is a thousand needles stabbed straight into my eyes.

CHAPTER
SEVEN

When Wednesday rolls around, a ferry horn cuts through the air as it docks at Cape Fleur Island. My breath mists in the cold, my nerves tingling. The minutes stretch until I finally spot Dad disembarking.

Kerry Moynihan's broad shoulders, clad in a heavy wool coat, stand out among the other bundled passengers. Snowflakes dust his hair and settle on his eyelashes as he gets closer. He blinks them off and throws me a smile.

"Daddy."

"Hey, kiddo."

We embrace. I breathe in comforting sandalwood cologne with a touch of pine. He likes to whittle, and I think of the horse he once carved for me.

"I'm so glad you're here."

"Wouldn't miss it, Coop." His voice is rough with emotion. "You look a little pale, kiddo. Everything okay?" His brown eyes search mine.

I push away the anxiety that has become my companion, especially since he bailed on the kids' recital. I'm not going to burden him with my silly fears. This time of year is hard for both of us. The memories of our shared loss. Raising me as a single parent took so much from him. The last thing I want is to give him more worries, more reasons to fret when he already carries so much. Who knows if my problems will be the last straw that breaks our bond? I couldn't bear him deciding that I drag him down too much after all he's sacrificed for me already.

Even so, I'd love to fall into his embrace and sob my heart out.

Grow up, Coop. Stop being so darn selfish.

"It's just the usual holiday madness."

The drive home is filled with small talk, but his attention settles onto me often. My bravado is not fooling him as much as I'd hoped.

"Sorry I couldn't make it to the recital."

With the glow of the dashboard casting his face in shadow, I struggle to determine his expression. Whether his features hold true sorrow that he had to work or relief that he didn't have to relive such painful memories, I can't tell. "The kids missed you."

He grins, but maybe sadness does touch his eyes. Because I didn't say I missed him too? "Good thing I get to see them soon."

A few minutes after we get home, I'm making coffee when the kids run through the door and dive into his arms.

"Grandpa, Grandpa! Come see my drawings." Grace grabs her grandpa's hand, dragging him to the table. Her coat lands in a heap on the floor, but she's too excited to notice. I pick it up to tidy it away, ruffling Elias's hair as I pass him. I stop for a moment. Scattered over the table is a mass of vibrant colors. Grace's drawings are bold splashes of paint forests with smiling crayon animals and stick figure families. Everything in them is smiling.

I watch my dad swallow as she pulls out one picture. A

rainbow with glitter glued to each arch proudly reads *I love Grandpa* in wobbly pink letters. Seeing him so happy makes my day.

I turn away and head to the coffee machine.

Once the coffees are downed and drawings inspected, we start fetching boxes of decorations from the garage, from the same shelves that hold my coffee-tin cigarette stash. We pop on a Christmas playlist, and Mariah Carey fills the room with holiday cheer.

"What should we do first, Grandpa?" Grace's eyes are wide as she picks through a box of garland, sparkling lights, and ornaments as if they were precious treasures.

"What would you like to do, missy?"

"There's too many choices."

Reaching into a box, Dad pulls out a bundle of gold tinsel and hands it to her.

"Let's make the tree the prettiest ever." Grace unravels the tinsel and holds it up.

"Sounds like a plan." Dad turns to Elias.

"Can I hang the star?" Elias digs through a box labeled *Christmas tree* and plucks out the gold star.

Dad looks him up and down. "I think maybe you can reach."

"No, he can't." Grace giggles as she pulls out another garland. "He's too little."

Dad picks Elias up and pops him on his shoulder. "I don't know what you mean."

"Cheating." Grace points at him, giggling.

"Let's get the rest of the decorations done before we do the star." He sets Elias down, and Elias carefully places the star aside.

Wham! provide us with Christmas nostalgia as they sing about last Christmas while Elias and Grace dart back and forth, their laughter mixing with the music.

We watch the kids place baubles on the tree from across the room. Dad pauses from stringing lights along the mantelpieces and looks at me. "At the ferry, you seemed a bit off."

Elias tries to grab a Santa decoration before Grace can get to it. He slips and knocks a reindeer off the table. "Sorry."

"You lost." Grace grabs the Santa and runs from the room. Elias picks the reindeer up and looks at me.

"It's fine. Go on."

He runs out, and I turn my back, ignoring Dad's question.

"You don't escape that easily. You seem stretched thin." Dad flicks his gaze to the doorway. The children are out of earshot. "Is it just the holidays, sweetheart?"

Subtle, Dad. "I'm fine. You know this time of year is… hectic."

"No, you're hiding something. Is everything all right between you and Thad?"

The mention of my husband, the mere implication of trouble, tightens the knot in my stomach. "We're fine. Really." I avoid his probing gaze and focus on untangling a particularly stubborn knot in the lights. Grace runs in and clambers onto the sofa, draping shiny tinsel across the cushions.

I shuffle closer to Dad so Grace can't hear us over the Boss belting out another Christmas tune. "I'm tired. That's all. You know how it is with the craziness of the holidays."

He nods, but his furrowed brow tells another story. He's not buying it. Not fully. "You'd tell me if there was more to it, right? I know Thad's a good man, but if things are tough, if something's going on, you know you can always tell me anything. I'm here for you, no matter what."

His words are meant to reassure, I know, but they land with a weight that sticks in my chest. Of course he's here for me. Of course he wants what's best. But there's something in his tone, in that subtle insistence, that twists my gut. A flicker of hurt ignites—does he really think I wouldn't tell him? That I wouldn't trust him enough to lay it all out, no matter how ugly?

The truth is, he's not wrong. There are pieces I can't share, not yet, maybe not ever. But it still stings, the implication that he's waiting for me to falter, to prove him right about whatever suspicions are bubbling under that concerned dad expression.

I smile tightly and squeeze his arm. "I know. Thanks. But really, it's just the holidays. Nothing more than that." The words feel brittle as they leave my mouth, and his eyes linger on me like he's weighing whether to push further.

"I asked first," Elias shouts as he holds up the star for the Christmas tree.

"But I want to do it." Grace jumps up, trying to grab it from him.

This is normal family life. Silly squabbles over who does what. But something's missing.

"Coop, you can talk to me."

The worry in Dad's tone hits hard. I want to tell him everything—the late nights, the scent of perfume, the time Thad hung up when I came into the room.

Forget it. It sounds pathetic.

It's a burden I can't lay on his shoulders when my selfishness took the best of his life. My mom. The memory tugs at me, sharp and unrelenting. That day, I pressed and begged, desperate for her to come. Guilt has burrowed so deep, it feels like a second skin. Asking for anything now feels impossible, like tempting fate all over again.

Dammit, let that go.

Maybe I have to let this foolish fear about Thad go too. There's no proof, nothing tangible to justify my spiraling paranoia...nothing but those six haunting words.

"He says I'm his lucky day."

"We're good, Dad. Really, we are." My voice is a little firmer.

After studying me for a long moment, he finally nods, seemingly satisfied. However, I still see the lingering worry in the lines around his eyes. I hate that my troubles are clouding the holidays.

For the rest of the day, I put on my best performance. I laugh a little too much, throw myself into decorating the house and tree with forced enthusiasm, and reminisce with exaggerated fondness about previous Christmases. By the time I drop my dad at the ferry, he seems reassured, perhaps convinced by my Oscar-worthy display of holiday cheer. But the second he boards the ferry, I shed the mask.

I'm left utterly alone with only my thoughts for company.

Once I return home and get the kids in bed, my knees feel as if they can no longer support the weight of my worries. Hot tears sting my eyes and blur my vision. What should I do? The house is dripping in gold and sparkling like Santa's workshop.

My phone vibrates. It's Thad. A tingle of excitement precedes sinking dread. At this time of the day, there's only one thing he would call about.

"I'll be late tonight, honey. Another emergency."

"It's okay. I understand. Love you."

He's gone with a click.

Doctors work late. It's a mantra as worn as an old record. Thad loves me.

Yeah, right. As if "working late" isn't the oldest excuse in the cheater's handbook.

Merlot sloshes against the inside of my goblet as I stomp up to the Christmas tree and yank the cord from the wall, killing the twinkling lights. Standing in the darkened living room, I take a generous sip and another.

He didn't say "I love you" back.

Everything has to be fine, I tell myself, *because the alternative is unimaginable.*

CHAPTER

EIGHT

The next morning, I glance over at the George Nelson ball clock, with its wire spokes radiating outward and terminating in retro-colored spheres, on the dining room wall. Forty minutes until Allison arrives to babysit. Winter break has begun, so she's looking after the kids while I attend a meeting with a client. It's also one of those days when I feel like shit and want an oxy.

Thad left two hours ago, early and without even a coffee. I'm trying to forget the distant look in his eyes.

He's just busy.

For the rest of us, breakfast is Froot Loops. Grace is conducting a rendition of "Jingle Bells" using her spoon as an accompaniment.

Elias is on his console playing some game that emits a harsh, gritty sound, along with groans, hisses, and explosions. He's joining in with all of them, and my skull's about to explode.

Boom...hissssss.

"Jingle all the way." Grace adds a jubilant "Hey!"

punctuating the melody with a bang of her spoon and sending milk everywhere.

I knock over my coffee cup, and a lake of beige joins the milk. I bite down a hefty swear jar contribution and grab a cloth.

My phone buzzes on the table. A stack of Grace's drawings shake, and I pat them, finding the phone. I'm half expecting, half dreading it might be her—Maggie. But it's just a work email. My client wants to reschedule for after the holidays.

Thank you, Jesus.

"Hey, kids, looks like Mom's off for the day."

"Yay." Grace's shout could crack glass.

I cancel the sitter and flitter around the house, looking for something to do. Everything is already done for the annual Christmas party.

Relax. Dammit, relax.

"Let's make a centerpiece for the dining room table."

Grace lets out another *yay*.

While they grab their boots, I sneak an oxy. We head out into the snow to gather pine cones and greenery. Outside, Grace bites into an acorn she dug up and wails about its the bitterness. Elias laughs so hard, he topples into a snowbank, his giggles infectious enough to crack my mood just a little.

Once we get back inside, they arrange the decor, stabbing bits and ends into floral foam. Grace is shoving things in with abandon. Elias is all serious, taking his time in choosing the right piece. He tries three bits of ivy before settling on the right one. I recheck my email for the millionth time. Nothing.

"Mom, look." Grace holds up a scraggly centerpiece, beaming with such pride.

"It's perfect, sweetie." I give her a hug. "You've got a real talent."

A pine cone falls off. Elias laughs while adding some holly to his own display.

I want my marriage to work. I love Thad. The thought of life without him leaves a hollow feeling in my chest.

Elias has finished and holds up his own creation. It's a study in careful precision. Each pinecone set in a spiral around the evergreen. Pride lights up my smile.

"Well done."

"Will Dad like it?"

"I bet he will."

I refresh my email once more. Nothing.

Upon closing my eyes, an image of Thad and Maggie kissing projects onto my lids. Angry with my frazzled mind, I push it aside.

A cherished memory replaces it. A picnic on the clifftop. We lay on a blanket as the sun set and the stars came out during the Perseids meteor shower. I can still feel his breath on my ear, the touch of his lips.

I make a decision. "Let's surprise Daddy with a latte."

"We're going to surprise Daddy?" Elias's eyes light up.

"Daddy, Daddy, Daddy." Grace jumps up and down.

Kids in the car, we drive to the Bean Dock, a café I rebranded last year with a sleek new logo, advertising campaign, and menu design. The place is thriving. We grab some drinks and set off for the clinic.

"Can't wait to see Daddy." Elias clutches his hot chocolate.

"Me, me, me." Grace bounces in her seat as much as the safety belt will allow.

"Me too." I guess the late nights have bothered them. I forget they're often in bed by the time Thad comes home.

We walk into the clinic lobby. It takes me a moment to comprehend the scene on the other side of the glass atrium doors. When it does, my heart plummets.

There, standing next to Thad, unmistakable with her

bright-red hair, is Maggie Donovan. They have their backs to us.

I freeze.

It appears innocent. A patient talking to the receptionist. A doctor talking to a nurse. Neither is aware of the other. But to me, the proximity, standing inches from each other, screams intimacy.

I grip the coffee cups, my knuckles white as drops of hot liquid slosh over my hand. "Shit."

"Mommy!" Grace eyes me. "Bad word."

"Sorry. Mommy burned her hand." I can't move.

Maggie laughs. Thad does nothing, oblivious to her presence. Yet something feels staged, as if I'm watching actors in a play.

Elias's voice breaks through my thoughts. "Mom, what's wrong? Daddy's right there."

Keep your voice light.

I take a step back. "It looks like Daddy's too busy for surprise coffee."

Grace sighs, her head falling back on her shoulders. "Daddy's always busy."

I about-face, and the kids mimic the move, exaggerated and unhappy. We walk out.

The coffees hit the trash can. With the kids strapped in the car, I stare at the clinic. They're still there. Maggie and Thad, just small figures through the window, just so close. A plaintive "Mom" comes from the back.

"Sorry, kids." The image of Thad and Maggie, almost touching, haunts the drive home.

With the kids in front of *Peppa Pig*, I grab another oxy.

The day drags toward evening. I spend my time folding laundry, organizing the kids' toys, and watering the drooping houseplants. Perhaps they're feeling the tension too.

After a quick, distracted dinner, the kids chatter, and I

nod and mumble as I check my emails. Refresh. Nothing. Refresh. Still nothing. My inbox mocks me with its emptiness.

Springing to my feet, I tidy up a living room that's already spotless. I attack the sofa cushions, fluffing them aggressively and punching them more than they deserve.

The relentless ticking of the wall clock grates on my nerves as I slouch back onto the couch. Tick, tick, fucking tick. Could time move any slower?

Daylight fades into twilight—wine time—and we watch the Kratt brothers transform into jaguars. The kids soothe my nerves with their wide-eyed wonder, but as the show ends and I tuck them into bed, the peace ebbs away, leaving me alone with my churning thoughts.

A glass of wine in hand, I pace the living room. "Maybe I should sit him down, calmly and rationally, and ask what's with all these late nights."

Pausing by the window, I stare at my reflection. "I have to ask how well he knows Maggie. But I can't just throw accusations. That would make him defensive."

I turn away and pace again, a caged jaguar myself. "Sydney would want me to listen, to approach this with understanding, not confrontation."

Rehearsing the conversation, I practice being calm. This can be a composed exchange if I keep my cool.

"Breathe, Cooper. Don't just rush in. Think of what you want to achieve." Sydney's counsel echoes in my mind. I have to stay calm and rational.

Finally, Thad's car pulls into the driveway. The door opens. I rush into the hallway. Calm.

"You're late again."

Dammit.

"Sorry. It gets busy at this time of year with the holidays and all." Thad's tone is weary, and he looks everywhere but me. "You know this, honey."

"I invited Maggie Donovan to our Christmas party." I regret the words the instant they leave my mouth, but it's too late. I scan his face for any sign of guilt, any flicker of emotion.

He looks genuinely confused. "Okay?"

"Do you know Maggie?" My voice is tight, rising. *Control, Cooper. Control.*

He shrugs. "Sure. I've seen her at the clinic. She's Simon's patient. Why? Where's this coming from?" His gaze flicks to the glass in my hand. "How many have you had?"

The words sting. The accusation that I'm overreacting fuels my anger. "Just how well do you know her?"

Thad runs a hand through his hair. "I'm tired, Cooper. If you're coming unhinged…again…can you just let me know?"

My jaw clenches. "Don't do that. Don't dismiss me. Not after what you did. Not after Laurel."

He sighs heavily, a sound of resignation. "We're past that. You know you get emotional this time of year. I understand, honey, but I'm going to bed."

As he retreats upstairs, my mind races. Can anyone truly move past an affair? Especially one that ended so tragically.

The quiet amplifies every ugly doubt and suspicion, and the specter of Laurel Hackert that haunts my darkest, most buried thoughts rises to the surface like a long-lost ghost ship.

CHAPTER NINE

Friday morning unfolds like a carefully choreographed dance, both of us ignoring last night's unpleasantness. His overuse of "yes, honey" over the morning meal grates on my nerves, but I bite my tongue, not wanting to be a bitch.

As I tidy up breakfast, the kids, oblivious, chatter about Christmas as Thad pushes them out the door for a snowball fight. Alone, I slip my hand into the junk drawer. The orange prescription bottle feels heavy in my palm. I glance over my shoulder before quickly dry-swallowing an oxy.

Thad leaves for work as usual, with no kind word or kiss for me, but returns on time to prepare for the Christmas party. I marvel at his ability to float above all the crap.

We still say nothing.

As evening approaches, he emerges into the bedroom from our walk-in closet, resplendent in a midnight-blue Tom Ford suit that accentuates his broad shoulders. The silk pocket square, a swirl of ice blue, matches his eyes perfectly. He adjusts his cuff links—my anniversary gift—with practiced ease.

As I fasten the clasp of my diamond necklace at my vanity, Maggie swirls through my thoughts. Will she show up tonight? She never responded to my email. How will I know if he's cheating if I can't get them in the same room? Maybe I blew any chance of seeing his natural behavior with her when I confronted him last night anyway. Surely he'll be careful now.

But when I examine him for any hints of guilt, he's just Thad. Tired but normal Thad.

"Shall we, honey? You look absolutely stunning in that dress."

I glance at the bedroom around me. The Maria Theresa chandelier hangs above, its lead crystals catching the light, casting dancing sparkles across the room. It would look at home in some palace with its air of refined elegance, but the warmth it once brought feels long gone. Now, its beauty is cold and distant, like us. The opera-mauve walls feel heavy, crushing, but it's the Warhol on the wall that catches my eye.

The *Muhammad Ali* stares back at me, all bold fists and masculine bravado, completely out of place in a room that's supposed to be a romantic sanctuary. Thad's trophy. He had to have it. "A symbol of strength," he said, puffing out his chest like he'd just gone twelve rounds himself. "The background's purple. Perfect for the room."

Sure, but not a matching purple. And romantic? Not even close. It glares at me from its spot on the wall, a smug monument to every argument Thad just *had* to win, and every compromise I regret making.

Smoothing down the shimmering fabric of my emerald Chanel gown, I take Thad's arm, inhaling the woodsy sophistication of his cologne.

Thad leans in close as we descend the grand staircase, his breath warm against my ear. "We make quite the couple, don't we?"

"We do." I push aside my doubts, willing myself to trust him.

The party buzzes with festive energy. Glasses clink and champagne flows as guests flit from one glittering group to another, their faces flushed with merriment. Thad works the crowd, shaking hands and delivering jokes like a pro while I try to match his poise, though a slight tightness around my eyes betrays the strain I feel.

She's not coming. Put it behind you.

Thad is lost in the crowd, his charm working its magic on our guests. Handsome, rich, and well-dressed, he's undeniably appealing. I can't help thinking he's quite a catch, and I'm the one who caught him.

For a while.

Vivian Holloway waves me over, her blond updo as intricate as ever. She's the town treasurer.

"Cooper, darling!" She air-kisses both my cheeks. "This party is simply divine. Tell me, where did you get this exquisite buffet? I simply must have them for my New Year's soirée."

"Vivian, you're too kind. Château Meridian. I'll send you details. How's Charles?"

"Wonderful, now that he has more time."

I'm about to respond when the door opens. There, accompanied by a blast of wintry air, Maggie Donovan stands, her chin held high. Conversations pause as she saunters in with an air of unearned familiarity.

I can no longer hear a thing Vivian says as my entire being is pulled to Maggie. Her vibrant red hair cascades in glossy waves over bare shoulders. Her red dress is daringly plunging, hugging every curve. It should be too much, but it works.

Male eyes linger a fraction too long on her swaying hips and ample cleavage, and searing heat floods my face as I turn to search for Thad. He's still working the room. The consummate host, he doesn't seem to have noticed Maggie's arrival.

I toss back the rest of my merlot. The wine does little to soothe the tension. I excuse myself from my conversation with Vivian and step forward to greet Maggie, keen to root out any underlying intentions. "Good evening, Maggie, and welcome."

"It was so nice of you to invite me." Her tone is edged with something I can't quite place—smugness, perhaps? Her presence in our home feels like an intrusion. I'm troublingly aware that I might be sabotaging my own peace. Subconsciously testing my limits on how much heartache I can endure. Seeking punishment, a strange penance for unconfessed sins.

"I'm just so happy you could make it." The lie is like glass in my throat.

"Sorry for not replying sooner." Maggie's voice is like warm milk spiked with bourbon. "My calendar's exploded since my divorce." She fans herself. "It's been terrific, if you know what I mean." Her elbow bumps mine as if we're conspirators.

My expression purposefully neutral, I spot Thad with his parents. Dot's glacial stare as she examines Maggie's attire mirrors my feelings toward the woman.

Meanwhile, I'm dressed like I've come straight from the nunnery. My Chanel gown is designed to exude sophistication rather than allure. Despite its designer label and flawless fit, I'm a lanky, prepubescent teenage girl next to Miss Va-Va-Voom here. The only thing I've got on display is my earlobes.

Thanks, Chanel.

"Your home is simply exquisite." Maggie's attention roams greedily around the room.

I fight the urge to slap her. *Get a grip.*

"That's very kind of you." I step away. "Please, help

yourself to some wine." I've done my duty and want to put some distance between us. However, Maggie sticks to me like glue, her suffocating presence never more than a few inches away as she glides along in my wake, undeterred by my obvious discomfort.

I spot the Forbes couple, Jerry and Gavin, effortlessly stylish and always polished. I dive across the room to speak to them. Jerry's sharp suit and new beard complements Gavin's understated elegance. I don't know them well, but they are the kind of couple who are perfectly at ease in any social setting, and anything's better than small talk with Maggie. When I check the space at my elbow, I find it's worked. She's gone.

After we exchange greetings, I ask about their daughter. "How's Evie?"

"She's just come home for the holidays." Jerry is glowing with joy.

Out of the corner of my eye, I watch Thad. He navigates the crowded room, deftly steering clear of Maggie. It's either a response to our fight or a glaring red flag.

Next stop, the bar. I grab for another glass of merlot. Just as my fingers graze the stem, it's whisked away. Maggie's back.

"Thank you." Her eyes carry a hint of amusement as she raises the wine.

Tightening my jaw, I grab another glass for myself. With forced politeness, I clink hers and take a drink.

"My Samantha's smitten with Elias. She gushes about him after school almost every day. Wouldn't they make the most adorable couple?"

An image flashes unbidden—Elias and Samantha, hand in hand. My anger boils, but I hold my expression like stone. The thought of my son's brilliance dimmed by proximity to Maggie's offspring is unbearable.

When did I become this person? This...Dot?

The thought of my mother-in-law's smug satisfaction if

she knew I was mirroring her elitism makes my skin crawl. But here I am, mentally crafting a pedigree for my seven-year-old's future mate.

"Elias is friends with everyone. Excuse me." I retreat to the safety of the buffet, adjusting dishes to shake off the unease clinging to me like a second skin.

Around me, the party buzzes. Laughter rings out from a group that includes Thad's partner, Dr. Simon Hughford, and his wife, Angela, chatting near the fireplace. Across the room, our neighbors, the Carters and the McGills, are caught up in a lively debate about holiday traditions, their voices blending with the festive tunes playing softly in the background.

The wine is flowing, and as I close my eyes, the party swirls around me, a kaleidoscope of laughter and festive chatter. When I open them, there's Maggie. Seated away from Thad, not even glancing at him. Doubt flickers within me. There's nothing between them.

At the bar, I pour more merlot, downing it quickly. A bottle of wine a night. The pills for my back, originally a remedy, have become a crutch. They don't just dull physical pain. They mute the sharp edges of reality.

I set the bottle down, a sliver of control emerging amid the haze. Maybe Thad was right. Maybe there's no fire behind the smoke I'm sensing, nothing between him and Maggie.

Beth arrives at my side. I hug her tight, like a buoy in rough seas. "The kids were a nightmare," she explains with a roll of her eyes. "How are Grace and Elias?"

"They're with the sitter. Bribed with pizza, *Minecraft* for Elias, and *Frozen* for Grace. For the five hundredth time. If only life was so easy for us." I hand her a drink. "What are yours up to?"

"They're making Christmas cookies. They'll soon be in a sugar coma, and the house will be dusted with flour and blobs of dough."

Steering us to a cozy corner, I position myself where I can still keep my eye on most of the guests and one in particular. We sink into plush armchairs, and I take another gulp of wine.

"So how have things been, really?" Beth's voice is low.

"Oh, you know, the usual holiday madness. The kids are super excited about Christmas, and I'm just trying to keep up with everything. Work's been great, though," I add quickly, hoping to steer the conversation toward safer waters.

Why don't I tell her?

"That's good to hear." Beth's eyes remain thoughtful. "But you seem…I dunno, frazzled." She touches my arm lightly, a show of support.

Because telling her would make it real.

I hesitate before forcing a laugh. "No, nothing to worry about. Thad's just busy with the clinic. You know how it is this time of year. Everyone's catching something. Plus all the holiday events…it gets a bit overwhelming."

Beth would laugh if I told her. She'd tell me I was crazy.

But what if she didn't?

"Well, if you need to unload or just escape for a coffee, you know I'm here, right? We moms have to stick together."

"Absolutely, and thanks, Beth. It means a lot. How was the drive over?"

She covers her mouth and shakes her head. "I made it in one piece. God bless snowplows."

I want to sit in the corner with her for the rest of the night, but that would make me a bad host, and Dot would no doubt say something about it at our next dinner. We rise and mingle through the crowd, laughing over the outlandish holiday sweaters that some guests have chosen to wear.

"Can you believe we used to think these were so crass?" I tease, nodding toward a neon depiction of Rudolph.

Beth chuckles. "Now they're the height of fashion."

"And they wind Dot up," I whisper despite the music.

"Bonus."

We drift from one group to another, Beth introducing me to a new couple she met at her yoga class—Chloe and Lucas Jennings.

"I love how your house opens up. So much room for a party."

They're right. We have a game room next to the dining room. Thad had the original wall replaced with large pocket doors, and the whole thing opens up for nights like this.

As the evening wears on, Beth checks her watch and sighs. "I hate to be a party pooper, but my sitter can't stay late."

"No worries. Coffee soon."

"Absolutely." Beth gives me a quick hug. "I'm here if you need anything. Anything."

With that, Beth's gone. I try to enjoy the party and set aside my suspicions. Thad's by the pool table, looking relaxed. I shimmy my shoulders to shake the stress out.

Like a scene snapping into focus, Maggie struts toward the bathroom—which, inconveniently, or perhaps too conveniently, takes her right past Thad.

Though I tell myself it's nothing, my feet carry me in her wake. Peering through the crowds of partygoers, I watch as the space between them diminishes. Is it my imagination, or is the air around them charged, thick with unspoken tension?

Thad's gaze lifts from his conversation with Simon. His gaze appears to lock with Maggie's, and time seems to slow. There's an unmistakable flicker of recognition, a pause that lingers too long. A silent exchange crackles between them. A damning confirmation follows—a deep blush blooms across Thad's cheeks. He tries to mask it, lowering his head, but he's not quick enough.

Unspoken tension, my ass. I can smell the pheromones from here.

Spinning on my heel, I storm back to the kitchen, my

earlier composure crumbling to dust. I need another pill. I rummage in the depths of my purse, fingers searching for the small bottle hidden there. I finally grasp it, flipping out a pill with a stealthy flick of my thumb. I swallow one with a gulp of wine, trying to drown the tidal wave of betrayal.

All I can think about is Laurel Hackert and the dangerous road I'm slipping down once again.

CHAPTER
TEN

The final guest closes the door. Even after the hired wait staff is done cleaning up, the party's residue lingers—laughter fading into the soft clatter of dishes and the tangy scent of spilled wine. I stagger a little, wondering if we'll talk about it. Thad, still in his midnight-blue suit, moves plates on the island with clumsy, albeit well-meaning, gestures. The silk square in his breast pocket now hangs limp, like it's just as tired of keeping up appearances as I am.

The memory of that stolen look burns. "I saw your special little moment with Maggie Donovan." I blurt out. "You thought you were so careful, but you couldn't help it, could you?"

He whirls around, eyes icy and hard. "Coop, you're being crazy. I never saw the woman. There was no moment, special or otherwise."

His dismissal pierces through my drunken haze. "I—"

"The problem here isn't me. Our problem is you're drunk out of your mind, as per usual, and I saw you pop one of those pain pills. I know you don't need them."

"What? I—"

"Your back is fine." Thad shakes his head in a manner reserved for Elias when he won't eat his veggies.

Heat burns my cheeks, a flush of anger and embarrassment at being caught. I grip a glass, squeezing the stem to the breaking point. I want to throw it. "You're blaming me? That's rich."

"I've been watching you, honey." His tone is mocking. "Mixing oxy with alcohol." Once more with that head shake.

"You...you...asshole."

He tilts his head but doesn't acknowledge me. "We see it a lot. People get addicted."

"I'm not addicted."

He raises an eyebrow. I want to wipe the stupid, smug look off his face.

"Honey, I wanted you to come through it, give you time to get it together, but I think you need an intervention."

"Don't you dare gaslight me. I know what I saw."

"Pills and wine, honey. It's a horrid combo. One that messes with your mind. It's no wonder you don't know what you're talking about."

He's learned something from all that therapy I've been forcing on him. Just not the lesson I wanted.

"This is your fault. The pills, my injury, my drinking." I fire the words at him, but I'm too angry, too drunk to put the real reasons behind them. I'm just scatter-shooting accusations.

He throws me a look of sorrow, of pity.

Is he right?

The room sways. Or maybe I do. Shit, I am drunk.

"Honey, you're not thinking clearly."

"That hurts." My voice quavers, thick with the caustic mix of long-buried anger and unresolved anguish simmering dangerously close to the surface.

"And Maggie Donovan?" Thad's tone drips with

condescension. "Do you honestly believe I would take that woman seriously?"

I recall his family's lofty Ivy League expectations. "No, but you'd have no qualms about boning her." The words tumble out, and even I hear the slur.

If he ever took me seriously, he surely can't now.

Thad scoffs, the sound sharp and dismissive in the quiet of our post-party kitchen. His demeanor is suffused with the arrogance only ample alcohol can provide—he had his fair share too—treating me as though I'm a child lost in her fantasies, not a wife voicing her legitimate fears.

I try to lock gazes with him, but my vision swims. "There was a time," I make each word sharp and deliberate, "when I would've swallowed your lies whole. Treated them like gospel." I straighten my spine, willing the room to stop spinning. "That time is dead and buried, like your head in Laurel Hackert's tits."

"Cooper." He almost laughs the word. "If you'd just sober up, we could talk sensibly."

I cut him off with a bark of laughter. "Sober up? That's rich coming from you. Tell me, *Thaddeus*, how many drinks does it take to forget you have a wife?"

His face hardens, a muscle twitching in his jaw.

Good. Let him feel a fraction of the turmoil roiling inside me.

"I'm going to bed." I point a finger at him. "Don't follow."

Turning on my heel, leaving Thad and his protestations behind, I climb the stairs and wonder idly if this is how it feels to cut the strings off a puppet. Each step takes me further from the script we've been following, from the perfect couple we pretend to be.

In the bedroom, I slam the door. Let him sleep on the couch, surrounded by the wreckage of our marriage.

CHAPTER
ELEVEN

My skull threatening to split open the next morning pulls me out of sleep. My tongue's bloated, and my throat's as dry as a cactus in the Mojave. Fragments of last night won't let me rest.

Maggie's smug, ruby-lipped confidence as she sailed out of our party haunts me. *You invited her, dummy.*

That look between her and my husband. His blush.

Thad's disgusted expression.

My shrill voice.

The satisfying slam of a door.

What did I say?

Did I end my marriage?

I reach for Thad, but the bed beside me is cold and empty.

Despite my anger, despite the bitter words hurled like daggers and telling him not to follow me, a foolish part of me hoped that he'd come to bed, apologies spilling from his lips as he gathered me in his arms.

The clock reads 7:03. My phone flashes.

My fingers fumble, vision blurring as I swipe. Once. Twice. Third time's the charm.

Not Thad.

Beth's called three times.

She never calls this early.

My thumb hovers over the Call icon, trembling. Do I want to know? Can I afford not to?

I call her back, and she picks up on the first ring. "Cooper, have you heard the news?" Her tone is laced with urgency.

"News?" I echo.

"Maggie Donovan was found dead this morning." Beth's voice cracks.

"Dead?"

The word hits like a gut punch, and for a moment, the phone feels slippery in my hand. Beth keeps talking, her words a blur of details. My heart pounds, every beat echoing in my ears. Maggie. Dead.

The room squeezes as the words sink in, and I'm not on the couch anymore. I'm in the garage, standing in the side doorway, cigarette in hand, staring out at the snow. The cold bites at my cheeks, but it doesn't wake me from this half dream, half nightmare.

Smoke drifts from my lips, curling into the frosty air, and the memory—or vision, or hallucination—presses in like a suffocating blanket. It's overwhelming. I see the garage. Snow. Trees. Maggie's smug, overconfident smirk. Is this the pills? Fragments of memory swirl, refusing to coalesce into a coherent picture.

Not again!

"What?" I sit up and swing my legs over the bed. The room tilts around me. I clutch the nightstand.

"She was stabbed." Beth takes a breath. "Her body was found at the southwest entrance to the woodland trails."

"Are you sure?" That's just behind our house.

"The police are calling it homicide." Beth gives a mirthless laugh. "Sorry. Of course it's murder. Who could do that? I can't imagine it in our quiet little town."

I picture Maggie's bloody body in the snow. The image turns my stomach. "I...I don't know," I manage to choke out. I watched Maggie leave the party alone last night. Happy. Fine. Alive.

"Nothing like this has ever happened on the island," Beth continues, her fear weighing heavily on each word. "An actual murder. Can you believe it? It's like something out of a nightmare. How safe are our kids?"

I try to process the unthinkable. "No, I can't..." My words trail off as nausea overwhelms me, the shock and horror of Maggie's fate twisting my stomach into knots. I mumble that I have to go and drop the phone as my legs carry me to the bathroom just in time for the merlot from last night to make a violent reappearance.

Maggie's dead, her life cruelly snuffed out. My marriage—what's left of it—might be safe from her interference, but at what cost? Did I wish her dead?

Don't be ridiculous.

I lie on the cool bathroom tile for a minute, just in case there's a take two. It feels nice, oddly comforting, and my stomach settles. That's when a terrifying thought pops into my head.

Two years ago, I caught Thad with Laurel Hackert. He was furious I found out, worried about his reputation—that I'd leave him, that it would all come tumbling down. The LaRues' perfect marriage ended because little ole Thad couldn't keep it in his pants.

But Laurel died before it all came out. *Suicide*, my brain screams. That was a suicide. Nothing like this.

Laurel left a note and had a history of depression. Still, her death conveniently removed a complication from our lives. With Laurel gone, he couldn't cheat. His problem, our problem, died with her.

Maggie's death is too close to us. She was in our house just last night, laughing and mingling. Why did I invite her? This is my fault. And now she's gone. Murdered.

Who would do this?

The thought knocks around my brain like an unwelcome visitor, lurking, refusing to be ignored. Who could've done this? There must be suspects. Someone from her life, some shadow I don't know about. People don't just end up dead without some terrible backstory.

Laurel died. No, Laurel committed suicide. She had a whopper of a backstory. This gives me pause.

Stop it. It's just a coincidence.

Maybe someone followed Maggie from the party. Some stranger we hadn't noticed. An angry ex, a jealous friend, someone from her job, from her neighborhood who held a grudge.

She threatened our perfect life. No, Thad would never. It's ridiculous. Absurd. Just stress and paranoia. And the pills.

But Laurel died after I found out about her.

Stop this. I think of Maggie's Facebook page, *ready to ride.* That's much more likely to bring out a killer.

Judgmental much?

I have to find out the truth, no matter how devastating. When I drag myself up, my legs tremble like a newborn fawn.

As I stumble along the hallway, the family photos mock me with frozen smiles. Our wedding day, Thad's grin so broad. Grace as a Halloween pumpkin. Elias's first day at school. These are true moments. They build a family. A life.

Our marriage is perfect in these pictures. Idyllic.

Lies. It's all lies.

An urge to smash Thad's grinning face, to shatter the illusion, nearly overtakes me. Instead, I look closer. In our fourth anniversary picture…is that a flicker of impatience in his eyes?

How long has he been acting?

As I race to the kitchen, every nerve screams for a pill.

Thad's already there, grabbing a coffee. He doesn't even look at me but storms out of the room. "Heading to the shower."

Before I can even consider telling him about Maggie, he's gone. I glance at the George Nelson ball clock—a symbol of precision and perfection, of Thad's obsession with the image we project. It's barely seven thirty. So much for perfection.

I need answers. To know what happened to Maggie and if it has anything to do with us.

And if it has anything to do with what happened.

CHAPTER
TWELVE

Two years earlier...

Creeping around the bend, tires crunching, I followed Thad's car. The gentle snowfall worked in my favor, obscuring his vision. He wouldn't be able to see me, to recognize the vehicle trailing him on the deserted roads. I fell back, and his Mercedes disappeared. The tracks in the snow were all I needed to lead me forward.

My stomach churned. He'd been so aloof. Was that why I was doing this? Marriages ebbed and flowed. It was normal. Secretly following your husband wasn't.

As the tire tracks turned away from town, it dawned on me where this road led.

Our trail. He's going to our freaking trail.

The place of many happy memories, kisses, hikes, the kids laughing, picnics. The best views on the island...well, in our opinion. Now he was desecrating it with some floozy.

You don't know that.

Whispering to her like he whispered to me. The snake.

My rage grew as I drove on and on to our place. Nearly there.

My hands clammy on the steering wheel, I found Thad's car parked in the lot, a light dusting settling on its roof. Beside it, another vehicle lurked, anonymous, under a thicker blanket of white.

It could be a coincidence.

Grow up, Coop. You know.

Cutting the engine, I gritted my teeth. Two sets of footprints led from the cars, both pronounced. They walked away together.

Turn back now. Behave. Like a good wife should.

What was I doing here? This was the third time I'd followed him, driven by a gut feeling that something was profoundly wrong in our marriage. The easy laughter that once filled our home had dwindled to strained smiles. The effortless connection we'd shared seemed as distant now as the frosty horizon.

Thad's behavior had grown increasingly aloof. Why would he sneak off to the cliffs alone if there were nothing to hide?

Go home.

I was already reaching for the door handle, my body moving of its own accord.

With a deep, steadying breath, I stepped out of the car. The door slammed shut like a gunshot. I winced and cursed under my breath, hoping the sound hadn't carried.

The trail was rocky and steep, and I cursed myself for wearing pumps in the snow. In my defense, I wasn't expecting to hike through a damn blizzard. I wasn't dressed for the terrain. Or weather. Or any of this.

My babysitter probably questioned my sanity with how randomly I kept calling for her services. But I had to take the chances to follow Thad when I could get them. Sometimes that happened to be on my way home from working with a client.

I climbed the trail despite my heels sinking into the snow. Quietly. Carefully. My feet unsteady, my vision blurring in the crisp wind, my breath misting in the frigid December air.

The cold bit at my cheeks, the sharp air burning my lungs. When I had to stop to unstick a heel yet again, I froze with indecision. There was still time to turn back. To go home and pretend I never saw him. We could paper over the cracks, play happy family if I sucked it up and acted the ignorant wife.

But I couldn't. The Cooper who trusted was gone. I needed the truth. Good or bad, I needed to see what he was doing.

Snow dropped onto my neck from the overhead tree branches as I picked my way up the trail. Even as I shivered, cursing my lack of preparation, I admired the scenery. It was beautiful. Evergreens, dusted with white, led up to a cliff top that looked out over the beach and to the ocean. Romantic.

Each step on the snowy track seemed heavier than the last, and my feet were freezing, but I pushed on. Those footprints beckoned.

This trail was like an old friend. Thad and I once cherished this place as our secret retreat. Dread pooled in my stomach. Our spot was now his spot—his adultery alcove, his love nest, his sleaze den.

At last, I reached the top.

Edging forward, I peered through the pines and spotted them.

The wind carried a snippet of conversation, too faint to decipher. A woman's giggle—no, a girl's giggle. She was young.

Too young and slim. Like a teenager. His hand rested on her butt. Her face tilted up with an adoring look, she laughed at something he'd said. He kissed her, deeply and passionately.

Slapping my hand over my mouth, I stifled a cry. Our life, our love, crumbled to dust before my eyes. What was I supposed to do now? Confront him? Leave? Scream?

Vomit rose up my throat as I fumbled for my phone, fingers numb and clumsy with cold and shock. Tears blurred my vision before splattering onto the display. It wouldn't swipe. I tried again, smearing the screen dry on my arm. The camera app opened with a soft chime muffled, fortunately, by wind and waves.

Click, click, click.

CHAPTER
THIRTEEN

Present day...

The murmur of the local news filters down from the screen on the kitchen wall. It's situated in the alcove above the table. Normally, I don't turn it on. As more conjecture about Maggie's last moments fills the airwaves, I regret doing so this morning. It feels like a car crash. I can't turn away, and I can't not listen, but I hate what I hear.

It's a constant reminder of the crap that's descended on our quaint little town. On our home. Maggie, our guest—Thad's possible lover—is dead.

He's in the shower. Does he know about her fate?

Pouring batter onto a hot pan, I try to block out the commentary, but at the same time, I'm desperate to hear it. I catch enough to know they're spinning it into something sensational.

The blond anchor, Kathy Burnside, is in full dramatic mode. *"Maggie Donovan, a well-known member of the community, was last seen attending an exclusive society party at the home of a prominent local doctor."*

While the batter sizzles, I check the knife block. It's fully stocked.

Stop it.

I freeze, the spatula clutched in my hand, when the camera cuts to a still of Maggie laughing at some event. It's not here, at least.

I close my eyes, squeezing out the headache as Kathy's voice, more suited to feel-good stories about local bake sales and high school football, drips with barely concealed excitement as she discusses the "*shocking tragedy that has rocked our community to its core."*

When I toss the pancake, it lands on the edge of the pan. I shake it back, my attention still drawn to the screen.

"Authorities have yet to name a suspect, and the investigation is ongoing. Sources close to the case have revealed that several key figures at the party are being questioned."

When will they come here? Why are they not here already? Will I...will *they* find out Thad was sleeping with her?

I want to scream for it all to go away.

"We have a real whodunit in our little town."

I shuffle the pan. The pancake will soon be ready. While it's cooking, I look in the cutlery drawer. Wow, we own lots of knives. Are any missing? I don't have a clue. I slam the drawer shut.

The voice changes to a man's. I glance up. Kathy's co-anchor, Tom Harding, picks up the thread. His deep baritone rumbles from the speakers as he asks how such a heinous act could occur in "*our sleepy little slice of heaven."*

The scent of burning pulls my gaze back to the stove. "Shit!"

"Mom, swear jar." Grace eyes me with the moral authority of a five-year-old cop.

"Sorry, sweetie. As soon as breakfast is cooked, I'll pay my dues."

I rescue the pancake, more or less. The base is a little charred, but Elias won't notice if I add extra blueberries and syrup.

Tom Harding is still talking. *"Local residents are in shock, and police are urging anyone with information or security footage to come forward as the investigation intensifies. "For those just tuning in, we're following the tragic discovery of Maggie Donovan's body early this morning. Local dog walker Dolores Fairbanks made the shocking find, and authorities are continuing their investigation."*

I add more batter to the pan, but I'm thinking about Maggie Donovan. Society party. Our house. Thad.

Nudging the volume down, I wish I'd had the foresight to switch the channel to something—anything—else. Maybe I'm being too sensitive.

The kids are playing with their tablets. They're a little quieter than normal.

I peer out the front window. Our usually tranquil street is a circus. Police cruisers and news vans are parked haphazardly, their presence both comforting and unsettling. I count one, two, three cruisers just in front of our window, their lights still flashing. The vans, emblazoned with logos from channels I don't even know, crowd around like vultures, their satellite dishes pointed skyward like accusing fingers.

As the next pancake cooks, I watch this invading army plan their attack. They mill about with notepads and cameras, hungry for any morsel of gossip or dirt they can twist into a headline. They'll be knocking on our door soon.

In the center of it all, our home—Thad's and mine—stands like a fortress under siege. I wonder, for the hundredth time today, what the hell happened.

I continue to flip, trying to inject some normalcy into

Grace and Elias's morning routine, but the atmosphere has got them extra antsy.

"Who's ready for pancakes?"

They exchange wary glances.

"Me." Grace usually bounces in her seat and repeats the word until her food arrives. That single word, with no enthusiasm to back it up, troubles me.

"Sure." Elias is equally uninterested.

I pile three pancakes onto each of their plates, cover them with blueberries, and add syrup. Not even a smile from the kids. Crossing to the freezer, I pull out some ice cream and place a generous scoop on the hot pancakes.

Grace's eyes light up, but Elias just nods. He's growing up. I wish he wasn't. Or at least, not this way, not this quickly.

A horn sounds as a vehicle rushes past, lights flashing.

I gulp coffee, wishing the fog would lift.

Thad blusters into the kitchen all shiny and clean, but his voice is raw and bitter. "Still think I was sleeping with Maggie Donovan?" he hisses as he passes.

I shoot him a warning glance and nod subtly toward the children. "Not now."

He shrugs and grabs a coffee. The rattle of cups and cutlery drives the hangover knife poking through my right eye even deeper.

When Grace finishes, she pushes her plate away, and her eyes plead for release. Elias pushes his away too. "May we leave the table?"

"Go ahead."

As they grab their tablets, I usher them to the family room. The colorful screen lights flicker across their faces as they settle into the cushions. Guilt rears its ugly head at how much screen time they've already gotten this morning, but I brush it aside, needing them to stay engrossed. I rush back to the kitchen, head pounding. The remnants of last night's wine weigh heavily, still blurring my thoughts. I disagree with Thad that I have a problem in general, but last night I did drink too much.

Yeah, you don't say.

Thad's nursing his second cup of coffee, his hands pressing against his temples. Poor little man. What a shame. *Now who's the drunk?*

We need to talk sensibly. "So another one of your playthings ended up dead." Sydney would be so proud.

"The Donovan woman was not my 'plaything,'" Thad snaps back. "And for all I know, you're the one making my 'problems' disappear." He takes a drink, so annoyingly calm. "For the family, of course."

"Bastard." Was that out loud?

From the way his eyebrows rise, I guess it was.

"I can't believe you said that."

A flash of snow in the darkness settles before my eyes. "Why? You just accused me. What did you do last night?"

His tone is cold. "You banished me to the couch. You were drunk and out of your mind with your crazy, pill-induced accusations. Who's to say you didn't grab a butcher knife and head out into the snow because you were jealous of this…of Maggie?"

The accusation hits like a punch to the gut. "You…how could you?" I recoil. Did he believe I was capable of such a thing? Or was this just another deflection, a way to shift the blame from himself? "Don't be ridiculous."

He shrugs. "Don't throw it if you can't take it."

I bite down a twenty-dollar swear-jar contribution.

He's rattling my cage, lashing out like a wounded bear. But his words make me think. No matter how hard I try, I can't remember much from last night. The time after the party is shrouded in a fog of confusion and fragmented memories.

I'd tossed and turned for hours, needing to escape. Who wouldn't, faced with a cheating jerk like him? I remember sneaking out to the garage for a secret smoke. But all I did was have that one illicit cigarette.

I remember the cold biting at my cheeks, the anger, the smoke swirling in the frigid air as I took hurried drags.

After that, the night becomes a blur.

Think, Cooper.

Flashes of snow. But nothing else. I must've come straight back and gone to bed. I woke up in our damn bed. But the actual act of leaving the garage, climbing the stairs, slipping under the covers...I can't grasp those details.

There's no way I could've sleepwalked my way to murder.

Grabbing another coffee, I nurse the cup. Thad's watching me. Cold, calculating, or maybe a little hungover. Right now, I hate his smug face. I can see echoes of Miss Pointy Face in his jawline. She would love this.

"Dammit, Thad, I'm not the one who cheated. I'm not the one who has history."

"I'm not the one who's an addict. You could've done this as easily as me. Neither of us has an alibi."

"Alibi? What the...we don't need alibis."

All I get is a raised eyebrow as he calmly sips his coffee. How can he accuse me? Only, it's the same motivation I have for accusing him. What was he doing all night? He could've slipped out, done something terrible, and returned without me knowing. If I don't know what I did, there's no way I can know what he did.

Our morning feels like a minefield. Each step, each word, could trigger an explosion. My trust in Thad, once unshakable, hangs by a thread, frayed and fragile.

Is Thad a murderer? Am I?

I yearn for a pill.

CHAPTER
FOURTEEN

"Evening, Sheriff."

Sheriff Joni White's steely gray eyes meet my puffy, bloodshot ones. I've been crying on and off all day.

Shit.

I knew this was coming. But opening the door to the sheriff makes this real. I want Thad to pay for the crap he's put me through. Though the thought that he might've killed her niggles at me, it's just jealousy. I don't really believe Thad's a killer, but here's the sheriff to arrest him.

Dammit, slow down.

She's gonna talk to everyone, and as Maggie was at our party, she was bound to come here. I'm only surprised it took her most of the day.

My throat's dry. My focus pulls straight to her badge, and another slice of pain goes through my skull. The hangover from last night's overindulgence still hasn't lifted, not entirely.

"Good evening, Mrs. LaRue."

She's known to be tough and direct. Practical, like her short gray hair and unmade-up brown face.

"Please, Sheriff White. Call me Cooper." I'm grinning like a loon and trying to relax my jaw. A deputy stands behind her.

"I'm sorry to disturb you, but there's been an incident. We're talking to everyone in the neighborhood."

"Of course." I step back. "Please come in."

Thad's presence vibrates behind me as Sheriff White wipes her feet. Her gaze flickers between us, her expression unreadable.

"Evening, Dr. LaRue. I'm sure you've both noticed the activity outside." She gestures vaguely toward the street where the cruisers and news vans sprawl like vagrants. "This is Deputy Byer. We're interviewing people in the area."

They step inside.

The deputy nods politely. He's pale and taller than all of us but looks young and timid. In his early twenties, I assume. His gaze scours the room, landing on Thad and hovering a moment before shifting away. He seems uncomfortable, as if he doesn't want to be here. Maybe this is his first day on the job.

Sheriff White pulls off her gloves. "I'm sure you've heard about Maggie Donovan. We have some routine questions for you both, as she attended your party. This appears to be the last place she was seen alive. All day, we've been collecting and reviewing security footage from the neighborhood. We'd like to review yours. It might help us understand her movements after she left here."

Thad nods, his face unreadable. "We don't have security cameras, Sheriff White. The island's safe. At least, it's always felt that way."

He's as infuriatingly unflappable as ever. Part of me admires his composure. Another part is chilled by it.

Safe. Will anything ever feel safe again?

A flood of last night's disjointed memories makes me dizzy. Maggie walking into the party, all boobs and swagger.

Her laugh carrying over the music, drawing attention like that deep-V dress. I remember the look that passed between her and Thad.

Rage boils up my throat as my mind shifts between Maggie and Laurel Hackert. Two women connected to Thad, whose lives ended in tragedy.

Unlike Thad, who looks like he's wandering through the country club after parring the course, my thoughts are a whirlwind of confusion.

I reckon it shows on my face. Someone like the sheriff will see it as easily as a hound spots a duck.

"Let's do this in Thad's office." I point the way. "Would you like a drink? Coffee, I mean, not a drink-drink." I sound like an alcoholic.

Sheriff White gives me a *what the hell are you even talking about* look but politely declines. Her head tilts slightly, her eyes narrowed and lips parted just enough to show she's both baffled and unimpressed. It's the kind of expression that makes you wish you could rewind the last ten seconds of your life.

As we walk through the den, Grace peeks over the back of the sofa, eyes wide.

"Nothing to worry about, sweetie. Mommy and Daddy are just talking to these nice people."

"This way," Thad says before pulling a monster face at Grace.

She giggles and hides.

"We won't be long." I follow Thad into his office, the room we so recently used for our therapy session. Through the floor-to-ceiling window, I notice a gentle snow is falling. Does it ever stop? I should find it exciting, an excuse for snowmen and hot chocolate. Instead, I imagine bloody slush and frozen bodies. Snow signifies death. Mom, Laurel, Maggie.

Thad walks past his desk and points at the sofa and chairs off to the side. Sheriff White sits down in one of the chairs.

She's not impressed, but Deputy Byer glances around the room like he just stepped into the Oval Office.

Thad spreads himself luxuriously on the sofa like it's a throne. Meanwhile, I sit next to him all tucked into myself, like a criminal.

"Should we call a lawyer?"

"Why?" The condescending expression on Thad's face is infuriating.

I want to say, "Duh," but I clamp my mouth tight.

"If this was serious, the sheriff would take us to the station. Stop worrying so much, honey."

Deputy Byer places a bag on the floor. He scans the room and stops on Thad again. He seems perceptive. So maybe not his first day, but I bet it's his first murder.

Sheriff White opens a notebook. I take a perverse sense of delight that she's always disliked Thad. Though she's never been anything but professional, I've noted the way her mouth puckers like a sour lemon when he speaks at social events. Maybe she doesn't gravitate toward smarminess like everyone else in this town.

She leans forward. Her tan shirt and black pants are impeccable. In sweats and an old t-shirt, I look like I've been dragged backward through a bush, while she could be posing for the cover of *Law Enforcement Monthly*.

Sweat beads on my forehead.

"Now," her gaze flicks back and forth between Thad and me, "I'm sure you've heard about Maggie Donovan, about her murder. Cooper, how well did you know the victim? Can you describe your relationship with her?"

Clearing my throat, I try to ignore the pounding in my head. "Um." This is just what I need. I hardly knew the woman, had barely spoken to her before the party. Why did I invite her? This is all my fault. "I knew Maggie from school. Her daughter is in Elias's class."

The sheriff nods, jotting something down. "Dr. LaRue, how about you?"

"I don't think we'd ever spoken outside my practice. She's a patient of Dr. Hughford's."

"I see. Can you walk me through the timeline of the party? When did the victim arrive, and what was her behavior like? What interactions did you have with Maggie Donovan? You first, Cooper."

"Let me think."

"Take your time." The sheriff taps her pen on her book.

If this is a technique to knock me off-balance, it's masterful. Each tap causes the knife in my eye to go in deeper.

Tap, stab, tap, stab.

I take a deep breath. "Maggie arrived around eight. She was wearing a red dress, deep-V, body contouring." *Envious much? Jeez, she's dead.* "We chatted briefly by the food table, nothing much, just small talk. She seemed to be in good spirits, you know?" The sheriff is still writing, and I feel the urge to keep talking. "She was enjoying being divorced, but I got the feeling she wasn't careful."

"What do you mean by that?" Sheriff White's pen hovers over the page.

"Just that she was," I open my arms and give a shrug, "I don't know, playing fast and loose. Maybe dating the wrong kind of man." Now I'm creating an alibi for Thad. "But we didn't talk much after that. You know how these social gatherings are. So many people."

"Dr. LaRue, how much did you interact with Maggie at the party?"

Thad leans back like he's about to order a scotch on the rocks at the club. "I don't recall speaking with Maggie last night, or much at all. I spent much of the night with my partner, Dr. Simon Hughford. The party was busy. I had a few too many drinks." He cocks a smile at me. "We both did. You know how these evenings can be."

He flashes the kind of charming smile a psychopath would envy.

"Is that so, Dr. LaRue?" Sheriff White eyes him for a moment. There's not a blink, not a blush, nothing. The sheriff's pen moves again. "Did you notice any unusual interactions between the victim and anyone else during the party?"

I hesitate, the memory of the evening blurring. "Um, no, not really. She was mingling, chatting with different groups. Nothing seemed off. But then again, I wasn't paying close attention."

Sheriff White's gaze shifts to Thad. "Dr. LaRue, can you walk me through the party as well? Was there anything unusual about her behavior or mood?"

Thad's expression is as smooth as ever. "Maggie was one of fifty or more guests. I didn't really notice her. She was mingling, just like Cooper said. She didn't seem out of sorts. If anything, she looked like she was having a good time. Everyone did."

The sheriff's eyes narrow slightly. "Were there any arguments or tense moments during the party? Did the victim have any conflicts with other guests?"

I shake my head. "No, no, none that I saw. The party was lively, but nothing out of the ordinary happened."

Thad follows suit. "There weren't any conflicts that I was aware of. It was a pleasant evening overall."

"Cooper, where were you after your talk with Maggie?"

I talk about other conversations, about Beth and me sitting in the corner. But the more we talk, the more memories resurface of a snowy night. It must be last night, but things aren't clear. Snow, Thad, a woman falling, but it's not Maggie. It's Laurel Hackert I see lying in the snow.

"Dr. LaRue, when did you last speak to Maggie?"

"Like I said, I don't recall speaking with Maggie last night, or much at all." His voice is as smooth as silk.

"Did you notice what time she left?"

"I'm afraid not." His smile never wavers. "As I said, it was a busy night. There were far too many guests to focus on just one person."

"I see. So, Dr. LaRue, where were you between two and three this morning?"

"At home with Cooper and the kids. We helped the staff clean up after the party and went to bed." He grins like a cheesy James Bond. "We hit the pillows and were out like lights."

He conveniently leaves out our fight. I jerk my head up and down in agreement, but the sheriff's eyes narrow.

"You didn't leave the house at any point?"

"No, ma'am." Thad's voice is somber. "I was here all night."

She turns to me. "Cooper, can you corroborate your husband's story?"

Trapped by loyalty. "Yes, that's right. Thad was home all night. We both were."

The sheriff's gaze lingers a second longer before she turns back to Thad. "Did you have any contact with Maggie in the days leading up to her death?"

Thad shakes his head. "No, I don't think so. Oh, wait, once at the office in passing."

How can he stay so calm? I'm shaking, seeing flickering images of snow, darkness, Laurel...Maggie in her red dress. So beautiful. I picture Stanley Kubrick's *The Shining*. The Overlook Hotel in the background, a woman running through the snow. Not Wendy Torrance but Maggie.

I'm sweating and finding it hard to sit still while Thad answers every question like he's reading from a script.

The sheriff leans back in her chair. "You seem awfully calm for someone whose party guest was just murdered, Dr. LaRue."

He doesn't blink. "I'm as shocked and saddened by Maggie's death as anyone. But I fail to see how getting emotional would help your investigation. I guess, as a doctor, I'm used to the tragedies of life. I'm used to taking and giving bad news without theatrics."

Sheriff White turns back to me. "What about you, Cooper? Can you tell me exactly when you last saw Ms. Donovan at the party?"

Why can't I pin down the moment? The timeline's blurry. "I...I think it was around eleven, but I can't be sure."

"How was she behaving? Did she look nervous?"

My jaw clenches as I recall the look between Maggie and Thad. "No. She was just...having a good time, like everyone else."

"And after that? Did anyone follow her when she left?"

We both shake our heads. The sheriff appears to understand. It was a big party. She seems satisfied for now. She stands, and Deputy Byer joins her, but a ping has her reaching for her phone. She pulls it out and checks the message.

"I've just received some security camera footage our team has put together from your neighbors. Stay here a moment."

Sitting there is about all I can do. What now? Sheriff White and her deputy walk a little distance away and review the footage. Byer's eyes widen, but the sheriff gives nothing away. I wish I could see what they're watching. Something's happened.

"We have some new information." Sheriff White and the deputy take their seats again. Deputy Byer picks up his bag and pulls out a tablet, swiping and typing as the sheriff looks at Thad.

"I'll ask you once more, Dr. LaRue. When was the last time you saw Maggie Donovan?"

"Sometime at the party." He shrugs. "I don't know what time, and I didn't speak to her."

Sheriff White nods at the deputy, and he turns the tablet to face us. It shows Thad in that midnight-blue suit leaving the house from the front door with snow falling all around him like rain. I dart a look at my husband and watch him turn whiter than bleached linen.

CHAPTER
FIFTEEN

"Would you like to explain this?" Sheriff White taps the screen.

Thad's confidence visibly balloons as if to smother the lie. "I forgot I went out for a breather."

The Persian rug is soft beneath my feet, and its intricate patterns swirl like the questions in my mind. The biggest question tap, tap, taps like Poe's raven—do I think my husband is a killer?

I want a drink of water. No, I want wine and an oxy.

"Do you have anything to add, Dr. LaRue, before we see the rest of the footage?" The sheriff eyes him.

Thad glances briefly at me before facing the sheriff. "No. I stand by my statement. I went out for a breath of air. Nothing more. I forgot to mention it."

"Dr. LaRue, did you speak to Maggie before, during, or after the party?"

"We went over this. No, or at least I don't think so. I may've said something in passing and not remembered. As I said, the drink was flowing freely. That's not a crime, is it?" He raises an eyebrow. I can't believe he's mocking the sheriff.

"Oh, I think you'd remember this." Sheriff White raises her eyebrow in return.

"What?" His Adam's apple bobs as he swallows.

The sheriff nods to Deputy Byer. "This was captured by several of the neighbors' cameras. Our department pieced it together for us. The Masons' camera footage is particularly interesting." Byer sets the tablet on the coffee table, and Sheriff White spins it so we can get a better view. "They live two doors down from you." She presses Play. The footage begins with a grainy image of Maggie leaving the house. A moment later, Thad sneaks out after her. Even in the grainy image, he looks good in that suit.

My ears ring. He couldn't have.

"Here you are, leaving your house just after Maggie Donovan did. Don't tell me. You were just stepping out for some fresh air."

The video changes to another camera, showing Maggie getting into a car a block away. It changes again. Now Thad's approaching the car. There's no hesitation as he climbs in.

No. He wouldn't. We got therapy. He said we were good.

Thad remains motionless, his expression unreadable.

Sheriff White points. "You climbed into Maggie's car as if she was expecting you. But that's not all."

My blood boils.

She pauses the video, her gaze flicking between Thad and me, letting the silence swell before she resumes. On the screen, Thad and Maggie are just visible through the car window. He's kissing her.

I swallow down the bile rising in my throat.

"The video shows you kissing this woman you said you hardly know and didn't speak to."

Thad says nothing as we all watch him get out of the car and walk back toward the house.

"Maggie drove off shortly after, and that was the last time she was seen alive."

Thad's face is a mask of shock and denial.

My vision blurs as the sheriff plays the video again. A tear slides down my cheek, but I'm too embarrassed to move and swipe it away for fear I'll draw more attention to myself.

The damning footage plays again. Thad and Maggie kissing. The cheat and the homewrecker caught in the act.

"It's bullshit." Thad's voice is low and vehement. He runs his hands through his hair.

"The footage doesn't lie, Dr. LaRue. You're now a person of interest in Maggie Donovan's murder. You're the last person to see her alive, and you lied about it."

Thad's face drains of color. He looks like he might be sick right here on the Persian rug.

"And it's not just the footage." Her full focus never leaves Thad. "Maggie's phone records show constant calls and texts between you two in the past few weeks. That also raises questions." She arches an eyebrow. "Would you like to change your statement about where you were when Maggie was killed?"

Thad slumps in his chair, a mix of anger and fear etching deep lines across his face. "If the cameras caught that," he stabs his finger at the device, "wouldn't they have caught me leaving the house to go kill her?"

"They would have if you'd left by the front door, Dr. LaRue. Our investigation shows blind spots in your backyard and the surrounding woods, areas with no camera coverage. In fact, you can get from the back of your house to where Maggie was found without passing a single security camera."

"But...but you know I wouldn't do this." He reaches for my hand like a drowning man reaches for a lifesaver.

I yank my hand away.

Right now, buddy, I'd let you drown.

We're good, my ass. I was right. He cheated. Again. So much for therapy.

Thad scoffs, rubbing his temples as he leans back. "So I kiss some sleazy woman when I'm drunk, and that makes me a murderer? That's pretty messed up."

The sheriff says nothing.

"I didn't do it." His voice rises several octaves. "Have you checked out her son, Manny? The kid's a psycho."

"Is that your professional diagnosis?"

"No. He's not my patient. It's what I've heard. What Maggie told me."

Shut up, shut up.

"We're exploring all possibilities. Everyone connected to Ms. Donovan is being considered. But you were the last person to see her alive, and you lied about it."

The silence that follows is suffocating. Thad, the man I married, the man I thought I knew, won't even look at me. Two years of therapy down the tubes, and for what? A cheap fling?

"I didn't kill her. I didn't kill her."

He cheated. He lied. *Again.* What a fool I've been.

Sheriff White stands and picks up the tablet. "We'll have more questions. If you want to change any part of your statement, now is a good time."

Thad merely stares at her.

"This video footage is damning. We'll find the evidence, so the sooner you come clean, the better." She walks to the door.

We follow her past the kids, through the kitchen.

"Like I said, check out her psycho son," Thad throws out as she exits the front door.

Deputy Byer, who's been silent throughout the visit, gives me a brief nod as he follows Sheriff White.

The door closes behind them. I don't know how to feel, what to process first, the affair or the murder. It should be easy, but nothing's easy when a husband cheats for the second time. The trust I'd rebuilt, brick by brick, just came tumbling down.

"Guess we're not having dinner with your parents tonight, huh?" My words are acidic.

"So much for standing by your man."

Really? "I *did*."

I'm riffling through snippets of the past—every late night, every unexplained absence, every moment of distance I brushed off or explained away. Now, with the image of him getting out of her car frozen in my mind, those memories morph into accusations, each one a finger pointed straight at the man I thought I loved. How can I possibly stand by him now?

"This never would've happened if you'd kept it in your pants." I stalk away.

Are we over? Do I throw his shit out on the street or grab the kids and go? Is it time for a lawyer, not criminal but divorce? I honestly don't know. I need time to think.

CHAPTER
SIXTEEN

I go through the motions of getting the kids ready for bed, supervising Grace while Elias goes through his bedtime routine. They brush their teeth, put on pajamas, and claim their forehead kisses while I try to think.

The roller coaster is climbing. Once it gets to the top, there will be no stopping it.

What would Sydney suggest?

I almost laugh. Is there an appropriate response to believing your husband's a killer? When the sheriff left, all I could think about was him and Maggie. The betrayal. The lies.

Visions flash before my eyes. I see him lying to me, straight-faced and unflinching. I see him sneaking out of our party—out of our home. I see his lips on Maggie Donovan's. I see him on the snowy cliff top with Laurel. Her on the ground. Lying in the snow.

Closing my eyes, I try to remember last night. If only I wasn't so wasted. I can't think. I see the garage when I snuck out for a cigarette. The snow falling. It's cold, but that's it. I can feel the snow on my face. Did I check on Thad before or after the cigarette? I can't remember, and I can't remember going back to bed.

I check my watch. It's just past ten. This has been the longest day ever.

I make my way to the kitchen. Time for a drink.

He's like a professional liar. How many times has he done this over the years? As I twist the top off the bottle, heavy footsteps come up behind me. I tense and pour a glass, drinking before I turn. I'm a fool for believing he could change.

"How could you?" My words are full of contempt. That grainy video feed is almost as real as the moment the sheriff showed it to us. Without it, he would've buried the truth along with Maggie.

Thad's reply rips back at me. "How could *I*? You're not so perfect. You think I don't see the pills you pop? The bottle of wine you drink every night?" He tips his head at the glass in my hand. "Living with you is like walking through a minefield. I never know when you'll explode." He shakes his head in that dismissive, *you're a naughty child* way. "I've covered for you, kept your secrets so the whole damn island doesn't know what an addict you are."

He's right. I'm the laughingstock of the island. Not because of my addictions—well, not *just* because of my addictions—but because he's out there sleeping with anything that moves. It hurts. But I'm alive, unlike Maggie. Unlike Laurel.

"At least I haven't left a trail of bodies in my wake."

He doesn't even flinch.

"What really happened last night? Did Maggie threaten to expose you? Did you feel the need to 'take care of' another problem?"

He just stares at me like I crawled out from under some bush. "I don't know what you're talking about."

I want to scream at him. *Why did you throw it all away? Where did the love go?*

He takes a step closer. "But maybe you do. I'm not the psycho stalking people."

A few seconds pass as I take in his words. "What?"

He saw me.

"Oh, yeah. Maggie told me you were following her. How creepy it was. Apart from that, I saw you sitting in the car. I saw you in the foyer at my surgery. You just stood there, staring. Maggie was right. It was creepy as fuck."

"Creepy? You asshole. I was trying to be sweet. Did you see the coffees? The excited faces of your children? You can't stalk your own fucking husband!"

He lets out a cold laugh. "You'd think. But, hey, you've proven you can. Who knows what else you're capable of? What your deranged, drugged-up mind could justify and just conveniently forget."

His low blow hits home. I can't remember what I did last night after that cigarette. But there's no way I did this. I didn't know for sure about Maggie. Why would I go after her?

Unless I caught her sneaking around the house. What if I saw her and Thad?

No. I didn't.

"Screw you." I grip the glass to stop myself from flinging the contents into his face.

"Screw me?" He crosses to the cabinet and grabs a goblet, holding it out for me to fill. To wait on him like a bloody maid. I don't move, half wanting to hit him with the bottle for all the lies, the cheating.

Control yourself. Think what Sydney would say.

Screw that. If therapy had worked, he wouldn't have cheated.

"Do you remember what you did last night?"

He's trying to turn this on me. I know he's clever,

persuasive, and capable. He's smart enough to murder Maggie and get me sent down for it. Why is he doing this?

Frustration streaks across Thad's face, along with something else. Fear? Guilt?

"What I did? Did you see that video?" I'm trying to stay calm, but the betrayal hurts like a mother.

"I did. I saw me come back to the house. I know what happened next. I remember what I did last night. I curled up on the sofa with a throw, and I slept. But you...can you remember? Take a look in the mirror, honey. In your drug-and-drink-addled state, you could've killed Maggie. You might not even know it happened. And that's my medical opinion."

My vision blurs at the edges as I squeeze my eyes tight. "I could've killed her? Are you kidding me?" I snarl. "I didn't even know for certain that you were having an affair with her until they showed me that! How dare you, you piece of shit!" I want to hit him. I almost do it. "After all the bullshit I've tolerated from you, the damn lies, the late nights, the lame excuses, you have the audacity to throw this at me?"

"If the glove fits."

"If either of us is capable of something so vile, it's not me, you cheat. It's the man who can't keep his dick in his pants." My lips are covered in spittle and my cheeks with tears. "You take that look in a mirror, Thaddeus James, 'cause the monster in this marriage isn't me."

"You think you know everything, Cooper. But you're clueless about so much."

"I know more than you think. And I'm not just some paranoid wife you can gaslight into submission."

Thad grabs the wine bottle, dismissing me with a shrug. Our home sweet home feels so wrong, broken by lies. I want to run. To grab the kids and get out of there. I wish I never had to see him again, and I'm so close to letting it all out.

Thad barges through the kitchen door with a force that

sounds like it damages the hinges. "Great. Glad we've established we're both capable of murder. 'Tis the fucking season."

He doesn't look back. He just strides away, rigid with anger. I hold the empty wine goblet as tears stream down my face.

CHAPTER
SEVENTEEN

I make my way up the stairs, each step seeming twice as high as usual. All the anger and fight has gone out of me. I'm suddenly exhausted.

First, I check Elias's room, opening the door as quietly as I can. His night-light is on, casting spaceships, stars, and planets onto the ceiling. Grace is on his bed, too, watching something on his tablet.

"Sorry. We were..." Elias starts.

"It's fine." This is not like them. They must sense the tension in the house. "Everything's all right." I cross to the bed and lie down. Grace crawls over me, and soon, I'm sandwiched by them. I fight to hold back tears.

This is what matters. This is what I need to protect. I lie with them for a few minutes, holding on to the most important thing in my life.

Kissing them both on the head, I sit up. "Right. Time for bed."

"Is Daddy mad at us?" Elias's fingers twist together.

"No, sweetie. He's just tired. We'll talk in the morning."

They're soon tucked into bed. I despise myself for not

shielding them from the turmoil. I know there's more to come. This close to Christmas, life should be joy, fairy lights, and too much food, yet here I am, thinking about starting over. I have to fix this.

It's not fair. Dammit, why should I be the one to save it? When's he gonna make sacrifices?

I'm tempted to slide down the wall, sit on the floor, and let the tears fall, but this is my family. I have to fight. I need something to help, so I walk down the stairs and robotically head to the wine rack again. Bypassing the pretentious labels, I reach for a bottle of Columbia Crest H3 Merlot. This wine, a reminder of simpler times with my father, evokes memories of hearty laughter and casual dinners.

Uncorking the bottle, I release a rich aroma of dark cherries with a hint of spice. The liquid sloshes into my glass like blood against my pale, shaking fingers. A flash of blood on the snow.

I step into the living room to retrieve my laptop. Thad sits on the couch, the empty wine bottle at his side, a glass of cognac in his hand. His gaze latches onto me as I pass. This is how the roadrunner feels under the gaze of the coyote. And this roadrunner is about to turn the tables. Watch out for that dynamite, you schmuck.

In the sanctuary of the den, I sit down with my laptop, the bottle and a generous glass at my side. My fingers hover over the keyboard. Should I leave it? I go over the options in my mind.

Leave it or dig? Dig or leave it? Yup, it's time to dig deeper, to look beyond Maggie Donovan and uncover the full extent of Thad's deceptions.

"Laurel Hackert," I whisper to myself. It's where it all began. Or at least, where I first became aware of Thad's infidelity.

Taking a big swallow of wine, I will the liquid to fill me

with warmth and open Facebook. Laurel was young. Did she have an account?

I've largely avoided thinking about Laurel since her death. Now it's time to tear off the bandage and face the problem.

Typing in Laurel's name, I'm sickened, saddened, and oddly relieved to discover her Instagram account was never deactivated. Until now, I'd steadfastly avoided seeking out Laurel's online presence. Viewing pictures of Thad's lover—so vibrant, lovely, and painfully young—is akin to sticking needles in my eye. Yet here I am, willingly subjecting myself to these emotional wounds, driven by a need for answers.

It looks like Laurel's profile is publicly accessible. I scroll for a moment. That young lady was an active social media user, with each post accompanied by a string of comments.

Emptying the glass, I begin my investigation with the first year we lived on the island. Scrolling back takes some time. I meticulously comb through Laurel's account for any hint that she might've encountered Thad earlier than he admitted. According to Thad's version of events, he met her toward the end of our second year on the island, sometime after Thanksgiving. He claimed the affair lasted for one year.

Refilling my glass and washing down an oxy, I scrutinize each photo, searching for any familiar faces or locations in the background, any clue that might contradict his story. I scroll and scroll. There's nothing.

Fatigue nibbles at my brain, and my eyes feel like I really did stick needles in them. It's all telling me to stop, that I'm wrong, but I'm just getting to the third year of our island residency, the pivotal period. To my mounting frustration, I haven't found a single indication that Laurel was involved in any relationship, let alone with a married man.

The young woman's posts are filled with innocuous updates about her job, hobbies, and outings with friends. Every now and then, there's a post about her depression. It's always a sudden change. Everything goes from happy, young, and excited to morbid and increasingly despairing, a steep descent into darkness. Then she's back to the young, carefree woman. It's dizzying and corroborates her suicide.

As I scroll, approaching the time when I discovered the affair—that fateful day on the cliff—I can't help but notice Laurel grows more beautiful with each passing image. So young, with perfect skin and a body that hadn't borne two children.

Even now, there's no mention of Thad or even a hint of a mysterious older man. As far as I know, Thad doesn't use his Facebook account, though I realize he could've lied about that too.

Despite my thorough search, I've come up empty-handed. I feel foolish. The police considered Laurel's death an open-and-shut case of suicide. She had a well-documented history of depression throughout her teenage years, and there was no reason to suspect foul play.

But the police didn't know the whole story. They didn't know Laurel had an affair with a much older married man or that his wife found out. Thad and I kept that information under wraps. Now I wonder if that deception was a grave mistake.

He broke it off with her, but maybe she didn't take it kindly. She could have pushed him too far, threatened trouble, backed him into a corner. I always assumed their breakup was the final straw that pushed her over the edge, literally, but what if I had it wrong? What if Thad pushed her because she wouldn't accept the breakup?

Just as I'm ready to abandon my search, my eyes bleary from staring at the screen, a comment on Laurel's last profile picture catches my eye. It's dated December tenth, two years prior—a week after I uncovered the affair and just seven days before Laurel's fatal leap from the cliffs.

Thad had sworn he'd severed all ties with Laurel by then. He pledged on his life—on our children's lives. Yet I cannot look away from the comment. My heart pounds against my ribs as if it's trying to escape.

You'll always be my lucky day, posted by drlove2021.

There's no need for an internet search to know that such a common name will yield countless results. "Dr. Love's" profile picture is the Maine state flag, a dark-blue field with a pine tree, offering no clues to the user's identity.

I put down my glass. I'm halfway through the bottle, but suddenly I want to stay sober.

With shaking fingers, I click on Dr. Love's profile picture only to find the account is empty. Pictures, posts, comments, friends—there's nothing, not even in the bio section. It's as if the profile was created for the sole purpose of leaving that single cryptic comment.

Thad swore he cut ties two weeks before Laurel took her own life. But this "lucky day" comment tells a different story. If Thad went to such lengths as creating secret profiles, what else might he have done? Was he still seeing her, leading her on? Had he met with Laurel on the day she died?

Sitting there, tears dripping on my laptop, I stare at that message. What am I going to do about this?

I can't deal with it. Not now. Not tonight. I sign out and close my laptop. I can't face the wine and leave the half-empty bottle. There's one other thing I can't do, and that's share my bed with him. Not tonight. My feet drag me back to the lounge.

"Thad." My voice is low and controlled.

"What now, Cooper?" His words are slightly slurred. "Come to accuse me of something else?"

"I'm going to bed, but I don't want you anywhere near me or our bedroom tonight. Do you understand?"

Thad lets out a bitter laugh. "Oh, I understand perfectly.

You think I'm some kind of monster. Your husband, the killer."

"I don't know what to think. But I'll find the truth."

He stands. "The truth? You wouldn't know the truth if it slapped you in the face. You're so caught up in your own little world of suspicion and paranoia—"

"Enough." I lift my chin, refusing to cower. "Just stay away from me. I mean it."

As I turn to leave, Thad calls out, his voice suddenly vulnerable. "Cooper, please. Can't we just talk about this?"

I pause in the doorway. "There's nothing left to talk about. Not until I know everything."

I walk away, leaving him alone with his cognac and his secrets.

CHAPTER
EIGHTEEN

The sheets tangle around my legs as I turn over and over. I kick them free and try to relax.

Sleep, dammit.

The room is dark. The clock reads 3:37, the yellow numbers taunting me. I've tossed and turned the night away. Each time I close my eyes, I see the Maine flag. He lied. He cheated. What if he killed her?

You'll always be my lucky day. Six words I wish I never heard.

Finally, I can't take it anymore. I blow out a breath, throw back the duvet, and march downstairs, my bare feet slapping the wooden floors.

When I enter the living room, snores rattle the walls. The cheating sleazeball, who's currently suspect number one in a murder case, can sleep like a baby while I lie awake, seething about the lie that is our life together.

He doesn't stir when I flick on the lights. In other times I'd be charmed by the way his face relaxes, the way his jaw drops open in his sleep. Not tonight. He's gonna tell me the truth for once.

Standing above him, my instinct is to bring something down on his head—like a pillow or a sledgehammer—to keep my children safe. That thought terrifies me. Maybe he's right. I could be a killer.

I push this new possibility away. I'm just a mother bear wanting to protect her children. A woman scorned.

I shake him awake. My intention is to blast him about that comment on Laurel's Facebook post. It proves he was in contact with her right up to the end. But at the last minute, I change my mind. I'll keep that in my pocket for now.

"What the hell?" Thad's voice is thick with sleep. He blinks rapidly, trying to focus on my face. He looks disoriented, hair a mess, and there's a crease on his cheek from lying on the couch.

"You're unbelievable." I barely manage to keep my voice steady.

Thad rubs his face. "What?" His irritation kicks in, and his eyes widen. He's waking up. "What are you even talking about?" He glances at his Rolex. "It's the middle of the night. Can we not do this right now?"

"Oh, we're doing this. Laurel, Maggie, all of it. How could you lie to me, betray me like this? Have there been others?"

"Cooper, honey, you're not making any sense. You're tired and upset." He scoots up the sofa, leaning back and folding his arms. "Are you drunk again?"

"Don't you dare," I hiss. "Don't turn this on me. You slept with her. Did you go out again? Sneak out the back to meet Maggie? Is that why she's dead? Was she out there to meet you?"

"No, honey. I went to the car, but that was it." He sits straighter, his eyes narrowing to slits. "What about you? I heard the door open. Did you go out?"

"No." *Of course I did, but what then? Did he hear me come back in? How long was I gone?*

"This is crazy. Shouting at me in the middle of the night. Honey, maybe you need help."

"Stop gaslighting me."

Thad tosses off the throw, swings his legs off the sofa, and stands. He towers over me. "Dammit, I can smell the wine on your breath. How much have you had? How many pills? Is that what this is about? You know how oxy messes with your head."

I want to retort, hurt him with a zinger, but I have nothing.

He puts a hand to his head and closes his eyes for a second. When they open again, they're filled with such compassion that I rock back a little. Only it's all a crock of shit. He's playing me. "I worry about you so much, honey. We can get through this together."

My entire body is like a block of cement. He knows I'm not buying this.

His lip curls. "More than that, I worry about the kids when you're messed up like this. What you might allow to happen to them."

He's pushing my buttons. Using a threat where his charm failed. Even so, the accusation stings. I'm beginning to realize—*beginning*? Listen to me!—I have a problem. I need to admit it and deal with it. But I'm not drunk. Not tonight.

"I didn't finish my wine. I was too busy catching up on your betrayal and lies." My words break my paralysis, and I poke him in the chest. "How many affairs have there been?"

I sound like a spoiled kid, but I hit the mark. Something flickers in his eyes before he masks it with an indignant smirk.

So I'm right. There've been more. I'm clenching my fists and know I'm close to losing it. I want to beat his smug face, to hurt him the way he's hurt me.

"I want you out." I'm suddenly calm. "Stay with your

parents. Go to a hotel. I don't care. You're not staying here while you're a suspect in a murder case."

Fury and fear are at war in his expression. "I—"

"If you want any chance of saving this marriage, of keeping this family, you'll do this without a fight." I raise my chin. For a moment, I think he'll refuse, but his shoulders slump, and he nods once before turning and heading upstairs.

My feet pound across the cool floor before sinking into the rug as I follow him. I can do this, beat the pills and the drink. I'm not an alcoholic. I've just been pushed. Been through too much. Anyone would snap under the circumstances.

We can work through this. Sydney will know what to do. We can save our marriage.

For the briefest of moments, I wonder if I want to.

In the walk-in, he grabs a bag and throws clothes, shirts, and pants into it. The sound of zippers and slamming drawers echoes around the space. He moves like a caged animal.

"This is bullshit. You know I didn't do this." He turns to me with that hurt look that used to melt my heart. Only, I know it's all an act. He's not hurt. He's pissed. "Let's just go back to bed and sleep this off. We'll talk about it in the morning, honey." A flicker in his eyes betrays his attempt at composure.

It's too late. The man I loved has been deceiving me, probably for our entire marriage.

"Get out. I won't have you near our children. Not until we know the truth about what really happened to Maggie."

And to Laurel.

He blinks as if caught in the headlights. "You can't believe...don't do this to our family. Don't destroy everything because you're mad at me. We still love each other. I love you."

I want to give in, to fall into his arms. "Just go. For once in your life, put someone else first."

Thad's face twists into something dark, a fury I've never seen before. His whole body tenses like a coiled spring, ready to explode. Without warning, he grabs the vase off the dresser and hurls it across the room. It shatters against the purple wall, gouging out a chunk of plaster. The crash is deafening as shards fly in every direction.

"Thad." I grab his arm.

He turns eyes as cold as ice toward me. For a second, I think he might hit me. "After all this, you think you can toss me out like *garbage*?" His voice is a roar.

"Keep it down! The kids—"

"Who the hell do you think you are?"

My mouth flaps, but he's already reaching for something else—this time, a jewelry box Grace gave me. It hits the wall, spilling earrings and brooches that glint like Christmas lights.

A door opens, followed by the sound of footsteps in the hallway. Elias peeks into the room, his eyes wide. He's frozen in place as he takes in the scene. I didn't hear another door, but Grace is behind him, clutching her bear.

"Thad, you need to...the kids."

He doesn't stop but swipes his hand across the dresser, sending a cascade of brushes, combs, bottles, and jars to the floor. "You think you can get rid of me? You think I'll let you ruin everything, Cooper? You and your paranoid bullshit."

"Thad, stop." Placing myself between him and the door, I stare in his eyes and watch as the anger fades, replaced by shame. "You need to leave. You're scaring all of us. Go now."

Elias's voice breaks the tension, shaky and quiet. "Mom?"

"I'm sorry." Thad glances at the kids before refocusing on me. "I'm sorry." He grabs the bag and storms out of the bedroom.

I pull the kids to me, and we watch as he walks down the hallway like a man on death row. "Go back to your room, sweeties. Mom and Dad just had a fight. It's nothing to worry about."

By way of a hug, I push them toward their rooms before starting for the stairs.

Thad is already across the foyer. He gives one last look before going out the front door.

It slams behind him with a resounding thud. He's gone.

My feet sink into the runner as I rush down the stairs, stopping on the cold wooden floor of the foyer. Hands trembling, I check the door is locked and double-check the dead bolt. The cheery glow from the Christmas lights mocks everything. Thad's gone, but the wreckage left behind is more than just broken vases and shattered jewelry boxes—it's the pieces of our life, scattered right in front of the kids.

The silence after his departure is deafening.

My entire body trembles as the realization of what just happened sinks in. A low, fearful whimper echoes from above—Elias and Grace.

I hate that they saw this, saw their dad angry, aggressive. Taking the steps two at a time, I race up the stairs and along the hallway.

Elias is standing in the doorway of his room, his face pale, gripping the doorframe. Grace is next to him, her little face red and streaked with tears.

"Mom?" Elias's voice is barely more than a whisper.

The sight of them breaks what's left of my composure. Kneeling, I pull them both into my arms. "It's okay." My voice shakes with uncertainty. "Daddy's just...he's gone for now. Mommy and Daddy were just having a fight, just like you two do sometimes. It's nothing, and he won't hurt us."

Grace clings to me, burying her face in my shoulder. Elias looks on with wide eyes, searching for reassurance. He grips my hand, trusting but unsure. It takes everything in me to push back the fear and keep my voice steady. "Let's get you to bed, okay?"

"Can we sleep together?" Grace holds Beary Potter close to her chest, glancing at her brother.

Elias nods, looking relieved to have company for the night. "Sure."

"Of course." Tucking Grace under Elias's covers, I smooth down her hair, kissing her good night. Elias looks up at me as I kiss his forehead, his wide eyes never leaving mine. "Mom?" His little voice is low. "Is Daddy angry at us? Will he come home?"

For a second, I can't answer. Not with everything that just happened fresh in my mind. Not with the threat hanging in the air like a storm waiting to break.

"He's not angry at you, sweetie. We just had a silly fight. He might be away for a while. He has to work, but he'll be back soon." The lie comes easily, and Elias seems to accept it.

"Were you fighting about him always working?"

"Yes." I leap at the excuse. "Now, you don't need to worry about that. Just get some rest."

They close their eyes.

Once they're settled, the exhaustion hits me. My whole body feels heavy as I press my back against their door, sliding down to sit on the floor.

Tears well up, but there's no time to give in to them. What am I supposed to tell them in the morning? That everything they know is crumbling? I don't want to lie, but how can I explain the real danger?

As tears spring to my eyes again, the enormity of the situation hits me. A cold sweat leaves me weak and nauseous. Thoughts racing, I replay every interaction, every conversation with Thad since I first suspected him of cheating—again.

I'm searching for clues I might've missed. My stupid mind

is finding nice things. The coffee he brought me in bed a week ago. The way he helped Elias with his homework. Little smiles that passed between us. But there are just as many dismissals. Him grabbing his phone and leaving the room, anticipation all over his face. The late nights. The...

"Shit." Thad could easily come back and type in the security code. Am I safe from him? Are the children? The thought that he might kill me to make this go away would've once seemed as crazy as he thinks I am. Now, who knows? But there's something worse. What if he comes back and takes the children?

I swipe the tears away. This is crazy, even to me. There's no way I can explain the danger to them. I'll have to lie. Does that put them in more danger?

I change the code, but the action does little to calm my fears.

It's drastic, but I'll call a locksmith first thing tomorrow. I'll have all the locks changed. Until it's done, I resign myself to a sleepless vigil.

As I make a pot of coffee, my attention keeps flicking to the junk drawer. It'd be so easy to take another oxy. To let the sweet relief come. To let my problems drift away. But I have to stay strong to keep my kids safe.

It'll be morning soon. Hugging the coffee, I climb the stairs and grab a robe. Positioning myself in the hallway between the kids' bedroom doors and the stairs, I set my back against the wall. My muscles are tense and ready to spring into action. My phone rests in my lap, its screen unlocked, the numbers 911 pre-dialed and waiting for the slightest touch to summon help.

There, I spend the rest of the night—or rather, the early morning hours—wide awake and on high alert, my nerves frayed.

It takes two to tango, and part of me feels like this is all my fault. If only I'd been a better wife, he wouldn't have strayed. Shell shocked and motionless, I wait out the night, straining my ears for any sound of intrusion.

I'm fervently praying, something I haven't done in years. Praying that morning will come quickly and bring some semblance of safety, however fleeting it might be.

CHAPTER NINETEEN

Light streams in through the windows, searing my eyelids. I'm slumped against the wall, my head throbbing with a dull ache. A groan escapes as I stretch my neck. I hear nothing. No chatter, no TV blaring. I'm awake before the kids.

Phew.

The last thing I need is to have to explain why I'm sleeping here in the hallway. *"Drunk again, Mom?"* It's Elias's voice I imagine, even though he's never hinted that he knows.

My mind's groggy. The events of last night swim in and out of focus. The fight. Thad's tense jaw, the anger in his eyes. The kids seeing him in that rage. How do I explain that? Then the door closing behind him. He's gone, and we're alone.

What now?

Though I'm certain I must be out of tears, more form in my eyes, and a lump gathers in my throat. There's no time for self-pity. The kids will be up soon. I have to pull myself together and decide what to tell them.

I imagine Grace, the big *O* of surprise that would appear on her face if she were to catch me slumped in the hallway. Thoughts tap, tap, tap at my mind, relentless and accusatory.

The looks from the neighbors. Their whispered judgments. Shame burns hot in my chest.

My addiction, once a secret indulgence—is it already out? Have I been fooling myself? I've let it spill over into the lives of the kids. I've become the thing I swore I'd never be.

Dragging myself to the kitchen, I look for signs Thad tried to come back. Nothing.

He wouldn't. You know that.

No, I know nothing about him.

First is a fresh pot of strong coffee. I head to the kitchen and go through the motions mechanically. This I can do right, at least. I can make myself coffee without screwing up.

As I sip the scalding liquid, I grab my tablet and search for locksmiths. My body aches for a shower, but this needs to be started first. All the while, I chew on what I should tell the kids. Maybe just leave it at "Dad's working for a few days." We had a fight. There's nothing to worry about. Will they believe it? Only time will tell.

I spend the next hour calling every locksmith listed, but to no avail. No one's picking up. The whole time, my focus keeps returning to the junk drawer where the oxy bottle sits waiting. The desire to stay clear-headed clashes with the pull of that pill. One wouldn't hurt. Just one.

The bottle feels real, familiar, like home. One pill is in my mouth. I chew slowly, savoring the bitter taste before washing it down with a swig of coffee.

The kids are still in bed, hopefully. Panic claws in my throat. What if he took them? Stepped right over me in the hall and carried them out, one by one? No. They went to bed late. There's no need to worry. The longer they sleep, the longer I have to get my head on straight and the locks changed.

Only, it's Sunday morning, and to make matters worse, it's just days before Christmas. Most small business owners are already enjoying their holidays. With each unanswered call, my frustration and desperation grow.

Another call. At last, someone answers, but they can't do the work until well into the new year. What now? Should I forget this and trust Thad won't try anything? It seems the logical answer. He loves us. But the look in his eye as he threw that vase haunts me.

He cheated. He was so angry. And he could be a killer.

Taking a deep breath, I steel myself and dial Sheriff Joni White's number. The phone rings twice before she answers.

"Sheriff White."

"Sheriff, it's Cooper LaRue." My words come out in a shaky breath. "Sorry to bother you, but I'm feeling uneasy about my situation."

Uneasy doesn't begin to cover it. Thad's capable of anything. He may be a killer. He could take the kids. My neck aches dully from sleeping slumped against the wall for hours, and the stale coffee scent curdles my stomach.

"What's going on, Cooper? Something you need to tell me?"

"Thad...we had a fight. Seeing him kiss Maggie..." The words catch in my throat. What am I doing?

"Did he get violent?"

"Not exactly. He broke a few things and got angry. It's just got me worried."

"I get it. Go on."

"I asked him to leave, and now, with everything that's happened...Maggie being killed so close to our house. She was at our party. I'm worried about the kids. Maybe I'm overreacting, but I can't shake the feeling..."

"That's understandable, and you're not overreacting at all. Your concerns are valid. What can we do to help you feel safe?"

"Well, I was thinking about changing my locks, you know, just as a precaution. Not that Thad would...I mean, I'm sure he wouldn't...the problem is, everyone's closed for the holidays."

"Say no more. Changing your locks is a smart move, regardless of the circumstances. I'll send a locksmith over right away."

"Oh, you can do that? That's very kind of you." Relief mixes with the feeling that I'm overreacting. He cheated. Nothing more. "You don't have to go to all that trouble."

"Nonsense. In fact, I'll come over and oversee the job myself. It's no trouble at all."

"Thank you. I really appreciate it. And hope you don't think I'm implying anything about Thad. It's just..."

"You don't need to explain. Your safety and the children's safety come first. We'll be there soon."

Hanging up, I'm grateful for the sheriff's quick response, but I worry I've cast more suspicion on Thad. It's a delicate balance, trying to protect my family without jumping to conclusions...and not letting my fear spiral out of control. Let's hope I've hit the right note.

I sit at the kitchen table, nursing my coffee. The warmth of the mug does little to ease the knot in my stomach. I tap my fingers rhythmically on the table, the clicking of my nails like a mantra. I'm surrounded by a life that was supposed to be good, solid, unshakable. The weight of the mess sinks in.

The feeling of being lied to churns like grease in my stomach, a hollow ache that won't go away. It's not just about poor dead Maggie, though that's enough to make me sick. It's the betrayal, the audacity of it, and the fact that he made a fool of me. Images of them laughing together flash before me. How many times has he looked me in the eye, pretending everything was fine?

That burns.

Did he ever feel guilty? That seems impossible. His

confidence and belief in himself seem unshakable. He believed I'd stick around no matter what. No way. I'm done.

We should go to my dad's for Christmas, yet I sit unmoving at the table, stuck in a moment that feels impossible to escape. A million things call for my attention—packing for the trip, organizing the kids' things, making sure everything's ready for Christmas, calling a divorce lawyer—but I'm paralyzed by the lies, the way he twisted everything until it seems like I'm the crazy one.

Should I wake the kids?

Before I can muster the energy, soft footsteps on the stairs interrupt my thoughts. Grace appears first, her curly hair a mess of tangles, her eyes still half closed. She looks at me with that sleepy innocence that makes my heart ache. "Morning, Mommy."

Elias follows her in, still rubbing sleep from his eyes.

I give them both the best smile I can muster, though my mind is miles away, tangled up in everything I've learned and everything I still don't know.

"Morning, sweethearts."

Elias looks exhausted as he scans the kitchen. "Where's Dad? Is he back?"

"What happened, Mommy?" Grace steps back, hands on her hips. "He shouldn't be so mad."

"Well, sometimes adults get angry, like you do when Elias takes your tablet."

Her eyebrows wrinkle, and her mouth screws up. "Okay. But where'd he go?"

What can I say? "Dad had to go away for work for a few days, sweetie."

Both kids groan in unison, and Grace's shoulders slump.

Elias throws his arms up in grown-up exasperation. "He's always working."

"I know." I smooth Grace's hair. "He's very busy helping

people," that sticks in my throat a little, "but he'll be back soon."

Elias frowns. "But he said he'd play *Minecraft* with me this morning."

"I'm sorry, sweetie." A pang of guilt causes my smile to wobble. "Maybe I can play with you instead?"

Elias shrugs. It's not the same.

The thought of the locksmith and Sheriff White arriving any minute springs to mind. Time for a quick decision. I reach for my phone and dial Allison's number.

"Hey, Allison. I hate to ask on such short notice, but can you take the kids for the morning? Something's come up."

"Of course, Mrs. LaRue." Allison is as cheerful as ever. "There's a Christmas decoration event at the community center in about an hour. There'll be cookies, and it should be fun. Lots of other kids too."

"Perfect. Thank you so much."

After hanging up, I turn to the kids. "How would you two like to go with Allison to make Christmas decorations?"

Grace's eyes light up. "Really? Can we make our own?"

"Sure you can." I turn to my son. "What do you think?"

Elias nods, a small smile forming. "That sounds cool. I'm gonna make a monster ornament."

"That's the spirit."

"'Tis the fucking season," as their dad said.

Grace dances in a circle. "I love Christmas!"

I pat her bottom, urging her toward the stairs. "Now, why don't you both get dressed? Allison will be here soon, and I'll give her money to take you to the Pancake Shack."

With more enthusiasm, they head upstairs to get dressed, leaving me alone with my thoughts. There's so much to juggle, so much to do, and I want it all to go away. I want our life to be back to normal, happy.

Unfortunately, that ain't gonna happen.

Almost as soon as Allison and the kids have gone, Sheriff White arrives at my doorstep, accompanied by the same young deputy and another man.

"Morning, Cooper. You remember Deputy Brent Byer, and this is Pete Barlow, the locksmith."

Deputy Byer nods politely, towering over us with that wiry, tough-looking frame. He's definitely more comfortable now, more confident. Maybe last time, he was just thrown by the whole Maggie situation. Can't blame him for that.

"Come in. Can I get you a coffee?"

Pete, a stout man with a ruddy complexion and hands roughened by years of labor, offers a polite nod. "I'd love coffee. Milk and two sugars. I'll get to work." He plops down a weathered canvas bag, his thinning sandy-brown hair flopping over his eyes as he pulls out an assortment of tools with the practiced ease of a seasoned pro.

I make the beverages and invite Sheriff White and Deputy Byer into the living room. The sheriff watches me closely, like I'm a puzzle she's trying to figure out.

We sit down, and I hesitate before bringing up the subject of additional security. "I hate to ask, but is there any way we could have a police detail assigned to the house?" As soon as the words leave my mouth, I feel foolish.

Dammit, Cooper. He's still your husband.

But I can't shake the fear. I don't want Thad lurking around like some horror movie villain. "I'm worried Thad might return. If he does, I'd feel better if he knew there was a police presence."

The sheriff raises an eyebrow. Great! I just announced I'm scared of my own husband, though honestly, she probably figured that out when I asked to change my locks.

"I understand." She's thinking. I can practically see the

gears turning as she weighs resources, staff allocation, and the practicalities of my request, especially with the holidays so close. "There's a lot to take into consideration. And you would need a restraining order to keep him away."

Fuckity fuck, fuck, fuck.

"Sheriff, that's true, but there's nothing stopping a police presence," Deputy Byer adds in a reassuring tone. "A presence might prevent aggravation. I'm happy to volunteer to keep an eye on things. I can park out front occasionally. If anything does happen, I'll be here to ensure Mrs. LaRue and her children are safe."

The sheriff's other eyebrow joins the first.

"With what happened so close, and with a woman alone, it wouldn't hurt." Deputy Byer shrugs.

The sheriff nods. "Okay, Deputy Byer. That's an excellent idea." She turns to me. "I'll have him keep an eye on things and assign another deputy to watch Thad. We'll protect you and your family."

I nod, trying to let that sink in, but as I glance at Deputy Byer, he seems so young and green. Sure, he's taller than Thad, and he's eager to help, but I can't shake the feeling that Thad'd eat him for breakfast. The kid can't be more than a year or two out of the academy.

As if reading my mind, Sheriff White quickly adds, "Don't let his age fool you. Deputy Byer graduated top of his class both in college and the police academy. He's sharp as a tack. We're very lucky he joined us on the island. With his record, he could have gone anywhere."

Deputy Byer's face flushes red, and he shifts uncomfortably in his seat.

Seeing his discomfort, I change the subject. "Thank you, Sheriff. I trust your judgment. The kids and I will stay with my father on the mainland for Christmas, so I'll be fine during that time. When I come back, I'll leave the kids there until the investigation is over and Thad's cleared. My dad'll love having them."

"I think that's a smart move." She searches my face, as if looking for something written there. She stares so long that I start to fidget.

"Do I have something in my teeth?" My attempt at a laugh is weak.

Her eyes narrow. "No...I'm just weighing how much to share with you, considering this is an ongoing investigation."

My mouth pops open. "Oh. I understand, but if there's anything I can do to help, I want to."

After what seems like a full minute, she nods. "Please keep what I'm about to tell you under wraps, but I want to ensure your safety."

My stomach tightens. It's not like I have enough to worry about. "Oh?"

"We're taking a harder look at Maggie's son. Dr. LaRue was right about him being a nasty piece of work. But until we know more, keep your distance from both men, just to be safe."

A chill ripples down my spine, spreading unease to every corner of my body. The sheriff's words are measured, careful, but they don't settle my nerves. Safe? What does that even mean when the danger feels this close, this real? My chest tightens, and I have to remind myself to breathe. Safe isn't just about me—it's about Grace and Elias. Every decision I make has to be for them.

Breathe. Think about something else. I focus on escape, and it comes to me. Our impromptu trip to the mainland will work for getting away from Manny in addition to Thad.

As much as believing in Thad's innocence would be nice, protecting my children is my top priority. The investigation will bring the truth to light, whatever that truth may be.

I'll never trust Thad again, whether he killed Maggie or

not. And now an ugly thought has wormed into my mind—that maybe he had more to do with Laurel's death than I believed. But these thoughts, these fears, have to be locked away, a secret burden.

Plus, there are the gaps in my memory—the blank spaces after the Christmas party that I can't seem to fill. Did I see him do something so heinous I've blocked it out?

The resurfacing memories of Laurel and Thad on the cliff nag at me, a persistent itch that refuses to leave. These, too, I keep to myself, aware they might haunt me forever.

We make our way to the kitchen. Pete the locksmith is tidying up his tools. "All done, Mrs. LaRue. Here are the keys." He gives me a quick rundown on the new locks before they all leave.

As I stand in the doorway, watching their retreating figures, my doubts and fears linger. But for now, I have a role to play. The strong, protective mother. Ready to face whatever comes next, one careful step at a time.

CHAPTER
TWENTY

Picture-perfect Cape Fleur Island, with its twinkling lights, fades into the darkness as the horn on the ferry blasts, and the vessel chugs and vibrates out into the water. The cold December wind bites at my cheeks and neck, and my jaw aches from keeping a smile on my face for the kids.

Is that what happened to my love? Has it faded? Have we been separating since before Laurel, taking minuscule steps away from each other this whole time? Have our children, his practice, and my career blinded me to this fact?

Has two years of therapy?

No. Thad pulled away. He was looking forward from the deck of the ferry with his signature cool grin, while I was stuck on the shore.

How many times has this happened? Have there been more than two women? I know I'm torturing myself, that it's pointless. And tomorrow is Christmas, so I'd better shift focus.

My emotions are all over the place. Fear that Thad's a killer. Shame that I'm a paranoid addict. Concern that I should stand by my man, you know, in case he isn't a killer. I don't know how long I can keep this from the kids, and I feel like one shitty mom.

Grace and Elias huddle close to me, their small hands on the railing.

"Mommy, why are we going to Grandpa's?" Grace's voice is barely audible over the rumble of the engine and the wind.

"Just for a little holiday visit, sweetheart. Won't it be fun?"

Elias gazes up at me, his eyes narrowing. He's always been perceptive, my little man. "Is it because of Dad and all the police? He was so angry. Did he do something wrong?"

"No, sweetie. He has to work, and this will be a nice surprise Christmas trip."

The lie tastes bitter on my tongue.

As we approach the mainland, I spot my father's familiar figure on the dock. His silver hair gleams beneath the terminal lights, and even from a distance, the worry etched deep into his face is clear.

"Grandpa!" the kids shout in unison as we disembark. They rush to him, momentarily forgetting their confusion about our sudden trip.

My father gathers them in a bear hug, his eyes meeting mine over their heads. The question in his gaze is clear, but I shake my head.

Not now.

"It's so good to see you all. We're going to have such fun this Christmas. Who's ready for some hot chocolate?"

"Me, me, me, me!" Grace seems to be feeling more like herself. My dad scoops her up into his arms and grabs a suitcase from me. Carrying the other suitcase, I hold Elias's hand as we make our way to Dad's car.

The ride to my childhood home is filled with the kids' exclamations, punctuated by Dad's occasional questions about school and friends. I stare out the window, watching the familiar landscape blur, my mind racing with everything left unsaid.

Dad chatters to the children throughout the short journey, pointing out Christmas lights.

The house looks exactly as it always does—a Cape Cod-style home with weathered shingles and white trim. As we step inside, the scent of cinnamon and pine embraces us. Dad's gone all out with the decorations, draping garlands over every surface and installing twinkling lights in every window.

"Wow, Grandpa." Elias's eyes are wide. "It's like Christmas threw up in here."

We all laugh, and for a moment, I can almost pretend this is just a normal holiday visit.

The evening unfolds in a cozy haze. The warmth of family pushes aside the shadows. After dinner, Dad pulls out a worn Monopoly box, a staple of good memories since my childhood. The kids' eyes light up as we gather around the kitchen table.

"The car's mine." Elias snatches up the silver piece before anyone else can claim it.

Grace deliberates for a second before choosing the Scottish terrier, carefully placing it on the Go square. "Maybe we can get a dog."

"Not a chance." I tickle her before the sulk comes.

Dad picks up the top hat and places it jauntily on his head. The tiny piece is hardly visible. "I'll be the dapper gentleman tonight, so it's just you to pick, Coop."

As the kids giggle, I settle for the boot, the last choice since the rest went missing long ago.

Grace grabs the dice and rolls first. The kitchen fills with the sounds of dice rolling, paper money shuffling, and players gasping and groaning. Stress drops from my shoulders as the night passes much easier than expected. Maybe we can get through this.

"Boardwalk again! You're bleeding me dry." Dad's exaggerated look sends the kids into fits of laughter. This might even be a Christmas to remember. *No kidding.* But maybe for the right reasons.

I'm crossing my finger, toes, legs, you name it that this blows over. Maybe they'll never have to hear that their dad was a suspect in a murder investigation. We can just get back to normal.

Who am I kidding? With all the shit that's gone between us, there's no going back—even if he isn't a killer.

The night's over in a flash, and soon, I've tucked the kids in bed.

Downstairs, my dad's in his study with a glass of whiskey. He looks up as I enter, gesturing at a chair.

Even though I'm on my third glass of wine, the thought of facing this is unbearable. Grabbing an oxy and sleeping it off is a much better option, but it's too late.

"Okay, Coopie, spill it. What's going on?"

I take a sip of wine. What do I tell him? "You haven't used that name in a long time."

"Yeah, you have that same look in your eye. Lost, frightened. It just took me right back." His eyes narrow with concern. "Something's wrong. Talk to me."

"It's just...there's been a lot. Can we leave it?"

"Not a chance. I know when you're dodging. It's Thad, isn't it?"

That's one can of worms I'm not ready to open. "You heard about the murder. I'm just shaken. It was near our house. We're safer here." I take another sip of wine, put the glass down, and curl my legs up into the old comfy chair. It's a warm brown cord with a sagging bottom. The sort of thing Thad would never have in the house. It envelops me like a hug. I cross my arms. Conversation over.

"That's not gonna hack it. Not with me. Where's Thad?"

"He's busy."

Dad sips his whiskey. Those old brown eyes never miss a thing. "Dammit. You're scared. I can feel it. This is more than a random murder." He shakes his head. He's never been anything but supportive of Thad, but now... "If my wife was in danger, scared, I'd be with her. Any true man would."

"Look, there's been a lot. With the murder and everything."

"Just like your mom. Stubborn." He points his finger at me. "Don't give me that 'everything' bullshit. It's Thad, isn't it? You tell me and tell me now."

The old nickname and the stern, demanding tone clash with each other, but it somehow works. I down the wine in one gulp. His eyes widen.

Looking at him, I try to keep my expression neutral, but he's not buying it. "Okay, yes. But it's complicated."

"Complicated how?" He leans forward, his glass of whiskey forgotten on the desk. "Tell me. What's Thad got to do with this murder?"

There's a lump in my throat. Voicing my suspicions about my own husband, the man I've shared my life with, feels wrong.

"He had an affair with her. I don't know if it's more than that." The words are finally out, and it's like draining an infection. "But something's not right. I can feel it."

His eyebrows shoot up. "You're just telling me this now?"

I shrug and stare at my feet.

"You're staying here. It's over." The anger in his voice makes me look up. "What are you hiding?"

How does he see right through me?

"If there's more, tell me."

"Thad...he was the last person to see her alive."

"What are you...what are you saying?"

"I don't know." My voice cracks. "I don't know what to

believe. But I think...the cops think Thad might have been involved."

As the words leave my mouth, there's a subtle shift. Dad's steady eyes flicker with a deep, sinking worry that settles into the lines of his face. He glances away briefly, processing what I've said, his thumb nervously tracing the edge of his whiskey glass. It's not fear for himself but for me and the kids—the kind of fear that comes from realizing the danger is closer than he ever thought possible.

He runs a hand through his silver hair. "Are you saying he killed her?"

"No, no...it's just...he was there. I'd suspected he was cheating. I called him out on it, and she turned up dead. But no. He's a lying, cheating jerk...not a killer." The words rush out of me like I've been holding them in too long. "But I can't shake this feeling. There's something off. He's been acting strange, and...and I just don't know anymore."

"Your instincts were always good." My dad takes a long, hard look at me. "You can't go back to that house...to him. Not until this is figured out."

"I have to go back. I have to know for sure."

"No. I don't want you there. Not if there's a risk. I can't lose you."

"It won't come to that." Facing the nightmare and figuring out what the hell happened is my only way to peace. "I need to look into things."

"What things?"

The problem is I don't know. I only know that I have to go back. "Things in our marriage. But don't worry. Thad's out of the house, I've changed the locks, and a cruiser will be right outside when I return. I'll only see him where it's safe. I promise. You just take care of the kids for me."

He takes a sip of whiskey before slamming the glass down on his desk. "Dammit, I can't lose you too."

CHAPTER
TWENTY-ONE

Watching the kids unwrap presents, I try to relax. How did Christmas morning ever get this crazy?

"Cooper, let me show you something." Dad leads me down the hallway into his bedroom. The threadbare carpet, the old quilt, and the furniture that hasn't changed since mom died is hardly noticeable. This is his room, and it's home.

Without a word, he heads straight to the closet and pulls out an old, weathered gun case. My heart skips a beat as he spins the lock and pops it open, revealing his old Smith & Wesson Model 10 revolver.

"You can't be serious." I'm eyeing the gun like it's about to grow fangs.

He turns to me, all gruff determination. "Be sensible. There's a killer close to you."

"But I...I don't know that. Maggie was wild since her divorce. The killer could've been anyone, and they could be anywhere by now."

He holds up a hand to stop me. "That may be. We went target shooting and hunting when you were a kid. You know how to handle a gun. You'll be safer with it than without."

Crossing my arms, I shake my head, backing up a step. "No way. I'm not taking it." Accepting the weapon would mean admitting I'm involved. That Thad…no, that can't be right. He didn't. He couldn't. "This had nothing to do with me, with us."

His eyes lock onto mine, filled with a mix of worry and that stubborn, fatherly love. "Please, Cooper Anne. Just for my peace of mind. Humor an old man, will you?"

"No." I rush back down the hallway to the living room, pushing what dad just offered me out of my mind. Is he crazy?

Grace and Elias are still tearing into their presents like it's the Olympics of unwrapping. Their laughter fills the room.

My phone buzzes. It's a text from Beth. I desperately want to tell her what's going on. Of course, she probably already knows.

Merry Christmas, babe. Hope you're having a blast. Things are wild here, as usual. Aunt May brought a "friend" to dinner. You can imagine the gossip. It's juicy! Call me when you can. Miss ya.

Beth. Of course she's having a fabulous time. Gossip and drama fuel her more than Christmas ham ever could. Not that I'm bitter—good for her, really. She deserves the distraction. Unlike me, who's apparently dodging guns now, thanks to dear ole Dad.

My thumbs fly over the screen. *Merry Christmas, Beth. Sounds like Aunt May's up to her usual tricks, haha. We're good here—just the usual madness with the kids. Hope you're having a great time. Miss you too. Talk soon.*

The urge to pour my heart out to Beth is strong. But she would drop everything and show up at my doorstep, no questions asked. That's the last thing I want. She needs her holiday fun, not to worry about me and this absolute mess. Best to keep it light…for now.

"Mom. Look what Santa brought me." Elias beams,

holding up a model airplane kit. His ice-blue eyes sparkle with excitement. He's so like his dad, and for a moment, I'm transported back to happier times, when Thad would look at me with that same childlike wonder.

Was his love ever real?

Smile.

"That's awesome. Maybe Grandpa can help you build it later."

Watching him, my hope grows that he's inherited more than just the striking ice-blue LaRues. I send up a silent prayer that Elias has received a kinder heart than his father or grandfather.

Grace unwraps a doll, balls up the wrapping paper, and throws it at Elias.

It catches him on the ear, and he chuckles. "You want to fight?

Grace giggles. "Wasn't me." She looks over at my dad.

"Don't bring me into this."

The shrill ring of my phone cuts through the festive atmosphere. Thad. The urge to ignore it is strong, but my feet take me to the kitchen, and I answer the call.

"Merry Christmas. I miss you." His tone is like a crackling fire, drawing me closer. "Look. That should never have happened. I was out of line. I'm sorry, to you and the kids."

"What do you want?" I'm not in the mood for him, even as the wish lingers that he was here, that none of this ever happened.

"Just want to speak to them. I'm sorry. Don't keep them away from me."

"But—"

"What did you tell them?" Worry creeps into his voice.

What does this asshole think I said? *"Hey, kids, I think your dad may've killed Maggie Donovan, you know, the divorcée that's all knockers and swag? So we're going away for Christmas?"* "That you were working."

A sigh of relief comes through the line. "Good. Thanks. Please, honey, let me speak to them."

"The phone will be on speaker."

"Of course."

The paper fight is over, and the kids are unwrapping more presents.

"Do you want to talk to Dad?"

"Yes, yes, yes!" Grace is reaching for the phone.

"Sure." Elias is next to her.

"Go ahead."

"Merry Christmas, my little elves." Thad's voice booms through the speaker, full of forced cheer. "Are you having fun with Grandpa?"

"Yes, Daddy." Grace, as usual, goes first. "Santa brought me a Barbie. She's got a pink dress. And the movie *Barbie and the Diamond Castle*. Will you watch it with me?"

"Of course. Can't wait. That's wonderful, princess. And what about you, buddy? What did Santa bring you?"

Elias launches into a detailed description of his airplane kit. His animated gestures mirror Thad's so perfectly. It makes my chest ache.

After the kids have finished recounting their gifts, I take the phone off speaker and step into the kitchen for privacy.

"Cooper." Thad's voice is softer now, vulnerable. "Isn't *Barbie* too old for her?"

"The new one is. This is an old movie. She'll love it."

"Oh, okay."

There's nothing. Just the empty line. Has he gone?

"Coop…Cooper, honey, I…I'm so sorry. I don't know what's wrong with me. I love you, all of you. All I want is for us to stay together and be a family. You have to believe me."

Leaning against the cool countertop, I close my eyes

against the sudden sting of tears. "I want to believe you. You have no idea how much I want that. But..."

"But what?"

"But I can't ignore what's happened. I've never seen you like that. Never mind the fact that you cheated...twice. That I know of. And both women are now dead. How do I process this? Especially during the holidays?"

Thad's breathing is ragged. "I never meant for this to happen."

Is he...crying?

It doesn't matter.

"Listen, I—"

"Please. Give me a chance to make things right."

"Time. We both need time." Ending the call, I toss the phone on the counter, creating physical distance. Thad's persuasive charm and regret won't pull me back in. Not yet. Maybe not ever.

For the rest of the day, I bite back my tears. We eat a wonderful meal. Dad and I buzz in the kitchen as we bring out the turkey and trimmings. As evening approaches, my bags are packed, my preparations made to return to Cape Fleur Island.

Dad helps me load my few things into a taxi.

"Do you really have to go?"

"I have to face this. For the kids. For myself."

"Then here. You take this." He hands me the gun case. It's heavy, cold, comforting.

We lock gazes. His eyes are filled with fear.

I nod. "Okay."

He kisses my cheek. "Let's hope you never have to use it."

"Yeah. But if I do, I'll make it count."

"Mommy, don't go." Grace runs out, clinging to my leg as I shove the case into the trunk. Elias stands behind her.

I kneel, and they fall into my hug. "Hey, sweetie, it's fine.

You have fun with Grandpa. He's looking forward to that movie. I'll be back before you know it."

"Be careful, Cooper. And call me anytime, day or night." The look in my dad's eyes makes me hesitate, but I have to do this.

"Take me home, Mom." Elias looks up at my dad and grimaces. "Sorry, Grandpa. I just miss Dad."

"No problem, kiddo. You'll be home soon, but your mom has things to do." Dad nods at me as I climb in.

I gaze out at the dark, choppy waters as the mainland shrinks behind me. The cold wind whips my face, and I'm lost in memories.

I remember my hand in Thad's the first time we made this journey together. It was spring, and the air was full of promise. Thad had just been offered a position on Cape Fleur Island, and we were giddy with excitement about our new adventure.

"Can you believe it, Coop?" His arm was around my waist as we watched the island grow larger on the horizon. *"Our own little slice of paradise."*

Leaning into him, I'd felt safe and loved. *"It's perfect."*
Perfect.

Looking back, it's laughable—how that word slipped out so easily, with all the confidence of someone who thought life could be wrapped up in a flawless bow. But back then, that was how it felt. I'd come from humble beginnings—a dad who worked in a factory, day in and day out, covered in the grime and sweat of honest labor.

My dad was a good man, a hard worker who didn't believe in shortcuts or excuses. And while he wasn't rich, he gave me the best he could.

I was a girl from a state university—Central Maine State—

who slung beer at a college bar to help pay for tuition. It was always a hustle. Up at six for early classes, cramming in the library between shifts, pulling taps and tossing out rowdy frat boys at night. Nothing was handed to me.

If I hadn't gone to that alumni gala my senior year—if I hadn't borrowed my roommate's too-tight dress and splurged on the cheapest heels at Payless—I never would've met Thad.

And what did I fall in love with? The opposite of the man I'm tangled up with now—not a cheat, liar, or killer. No. Back then, Thad was a dream come to life.

He was smooth and polished, with a charm that made every woman in the room feel like she was the only one he saw. Confident, thoughtful, ambitious. But no one thought of him as a player.

I can still see it—me standing there, all doe-eyed in that dress that pinched my ribs, thinking, *I've made it*. Thad was the handsome, successful doctor who seemed completely captivated by a girl with callouses from bartending. He wasn't just a step up—he was at the top of the whole damn staircase.

He asked what I was doing there. I answered with something nervous and awkward. He laughed—not at me but in that warm way that made me feel clever, like I belonged in his world. And that night? The way he pulled me into his orbit, I felt like the universe had rearranged itself just for us.

Now, standing on this ferry that once felt like a dream come true, it's funny to look back on that young girl with her wide eyes and hopeful heart. What would she think if she could see what Thad really turned out to be? Would she even recognize him? Would she recognize me?

I'm coming home to…what? A cheat, yes. A liar, definitely. But a killer? I don't know, and I intend to find out.

CHAPTER

TWENTY-TWO

As I pull into the driveway, the sight of Deputy Brent Byer parked in front of the house in a marked SUV offers a small comfort. Gathering my bags from the trunk, I feel a twinge of guilt that he came out here on a holiday, even though I said I'd be out of town.

I tap lightly on his window.

He rolls it down, his expression friendly. "Everything okay, Mrs. LaRue?"

"Yes. I'm so sorry you're out here on Christmas." The words are inadequate.

He waves off my apology with a smile. "Don't worry about it. I'm an orphan. Nowhere else to be, and that's just fine. I love my job."

His easy demeanor loosens the knot in my chest. "Still, I appreciate it. Let me at least bring you some coffee."

Inside, the house yawns around me, all echo and excess, like it's mocking how small one person feels in so much space. The children's absence is wrong, their laughter and bickering replaced by the ghostly hum of the fridge. A fresh pot of coffee bubbles in the background, but we're out of creamer. A job for tomorrow.

With a steaming mug in hand, I head back outside. "Sorry. No milk."

Deputy Byer accepts the coffee gratefully, his hands wrapping around the warm ceramic. "No worries."

He holds onto the cup like he's settling in for the long haul.

"Any updates on the Donovan case?" I try to keep my voice casual, though my curiosity is anything but.

He finishes a sip before looking up. "Not yet, I'm afraid. But it's a small island. There are only so many people who could've done this. More evidence will present itself soon enough." There's something solid in his gaze, something that feels like a lifeline. "Sheriff White won't give up until the murderer's behind bars, and neither will I. That's a promise."

"Thank you. I really appreciate everything you're doing."

He gives me a slight nod. There's a determination there, an edge that tells me he's not just being polite. "It's my job, Mrs. LaRue, but it's more than that. I want to make sure you and your kids are safe. I'm not going anywhere until this monster's stopped."

"Do you want some food, or..." Should I ask him if he needs to pee? "Is there anything else you need?"

"I'm good, thanks. I prepared." He waves a bag at me, and I get a faint whiff of fried chicken.

"Sorry you're missing Christmas."

"Don't be. It's part of the job."

That calm certainty makes me feel a little safer, but there's something else—an intensity in his words I can't quite put my finger on. Right now, I'm too tired to figure it out. All I know is that with him here, I feel like maybe, just maybe, I can breathe a little easier.

Back inside, I carefully type in my new keypad lock code,

the beeps echoing in the quiet house, and I double-check the brand-new dead bolts on both the front and back doors. The extra security measures should make me feel safer, but instead, they constantly remind me how much has changed.

I stow Dad's gun case somewhere easy to grab but out of sight, behind a huge vase of silk flowers. Because nothing says welcome like a bouquet hiding a revolver.

With a cup of coffee, I lean against the counter, surveying the room. The Christmas decorations seem out of place, mocking me with their cheerfulness. I should take them down, but I can't bring myself to do it. The kids will be back soon, and they deserve some semblance of normalcy.

My phone buzzes, startling me. It's a text from Dad.

Hope you're doing okay, Coopie. The kids are having a blast. We just finished decorating gingerbread houses. Call if you need anything.

The thought of Elias and Grace covered in frosting and candy is nice. At least they're having a good Christmas, even if it's not the one we'd planned.

What has Thad told Howard and Miss Pointy Face? Probably some well-rehearsed tale, dripping with charm and just enough truth to keep his dad nodding along like a bobblehead.

"It's all a misunderstanding." Thad will use his best doctor voice. *"You know how people love to talk in small towns."*

And Howard, bless his oblivious heart, will nod and mutter, *"Of course, son. Just envious folks trying to drag down the LaRue name."*

But Miss Pointy Face? Oh, she'll be cutting right through the BS with that razor-sharp tone of hers. *"Thaddeus, dear, it's understandable, especially being married to* that woman. *But if you have your little indiscretions, they must be more discreet. We can't have stains on the LaRue name."*

Thad will hide his smirk under a perfect mask of contrition. *"Of course not, Mother."*

Meanwhile, I'm here thinking maybe I should take up something relaxing—like dodging the knives Miss Pointy Face is mentally throwing my way.

Scrolling through my phone, I find a missed call from Thad.

My thumb hovers over his name, but I decide against calling back. Whatever he has to say can wait. Right now, I need to focus on keeping it together. With that in mind, my hand is already in my purse and grabbing a pill.

I wander into the living room, my gaze landing on the framed photos lining the mantel. Happy faces smile back at me.

I linger on a photo of Thad and me from last summer, taken at the annual Cape Fleur Island Festival. We're laughing, oblivious to the camera. His arm is around my waist. I remember that day—the warm sun, the smell of fried dough, the sound of live music drifting through the air. The post-Laurel Hackert, pre-Maggie Donovan days. The window wherein I thought things would be okay.

Picking up the frame, I study Thad's face. "Did you kill them?" Posing my question to the silent room gives me as much of an answer as I got from the man himself.

Setting the photo face down, I move to the window. It's dark, and the security lights cast long shadows across the lawn. Despite Deputy Byer, I can't shake the feeling of being watched. I draw the curtains to shut out any prying eyes.

Needing something to fill the silence, I click on the big screen and grab a twist-off bottle of red and a glass before slumping down on the sofa to sip the wine. The TV is more for background noise than anything else, but the local news is on. I catch the tail end of a report about Maggie's murder.

They're now calling it the "Christmas Killing," as if it needed a catchy name.

I flip to an old Christmas movie, the kind I love to watch with the kids. The familiar story and cheerful music provide a much-needed distraction.

After another glass of wine, I wonder about Thad. Where's he spending Christmas? With his parents? In some hotel room? I experience a touch of sympathy for him, alone on what should be a day for family. But I remember why he's not here, and that sentiment evaporates.

The movie plays on, but I'm barely watching. Instead, thoughts of the kids, my husband, and my husband's two dead ex-girlfriends won't leave me be.

As the credits roll, I realize hours have passed. The house is dark, save for the glow of the TV. The bottle is empty. I should go to bed and try to get some sleep. But the idea of lying alone in that big bed, surrounded by memories of happier times, is too much.

Instead, I curl up on the couch, pulling a throw over me. The Christmas tree lights twinkle in the corner. I dream of the cliff top, of crashing waves below. Thad is there, kissing a woman. Laurel. He turns to look at me.

In the space of a heartbeat, his hands are around her throat. A snarl crosses his face as he strangles her to death.

He smiles as Laurel drops, lifeless, to the ground. He's laughing by the time he swings a leg back and boots her over the edge.

I wake up screaming.

CHAPTER
TWENTY-THREE

The day after Christmas, ingredients litter the counter. Chicken, broccoli, mushroom soup, mayo. Making this casserole and taking it to Maggie's family feels both right and terribly wrong. It's hearty comfort food and an easy dish to make. A winter favorite in this house, if a little too pedestrian for Dot. My hands move on autopilot, mixing and layering, as my mind wanders.

Sliding the casserole into the oven, I wonder if this is just inviting more trouble into my already complicated life.

Maggie's children come to mind, their grief crushing and raw. No matter what kind of mother she was—and how would I know?—losing her so violently, so suddenly...my chest hurts at the thought of it.

Memories of my mother's death resurface, of the hollowness, the grief, the way the world tilted on its axis. Those kids must be going through hell. Even her oldest, the sixteen-year-old.

Manny.

Thad's warning comes back to me. *"Manny's a psycho."* What does he know? The fact that Sheriff White's looking into Manny only fuels my curiosity. Could this visit provide some answers? Could it even, in some roundabout way, exonerate Thad?

The thought of Thad brings a fresh wave of confusion and pain. As the scent of creamed chicken fills the air, part of me wants to believe in his innocence, wants to find some explanation that doesn't involve him being a murderer. But another part, the part that's been betrayed too many times, whispers, *Naive*. The cheating bastard deserves everything he gets. He could be a killer.

The timer dings.

This is it. Either I'm eating chicken Divan for the next week, or I'm doing this.

As I pull the steaming casserole from the oven, the aroma reminds me of countless dinners. Of family. The sense of loss hits me hard and bitterly.

The drive to the Donovans' is short, but each turn brings a new wave of doubt and second-guessing. Before I know it, I'm pulling up to their house, the casserole a warm weight on the seat beside me.

A curtain next to the door twitches as someone peers out at me. It's too late to turn back. I may as well see this through. Stepping out of the car while balancing the casserole is more awkward than expected. I'm here for the kids, for Elias's friend Samantha, and for answers.

With one final moment of hesitation, I approach the front door. The house is a little run-down, small and neglected. My finger hovers over the doorbell for a second before pressing it. The cheerful chime is at odds with the somber visit.

The dish is heavy in my hands as the moments pass. Rational thoughts urge a retreat—go home, and stay out of this mess—but I stay, bolstered by images of Maggie's children, their world shattered by their mother's death. Losing a parent at a young age...I know that pain all too well.

Because of that, I spent the morning cooking a dish I hope will bring comfort. What a fool.

Food can't replace a parent.

But I can't deny that I'm here out of curiosity too. Maybe Manny really is a psycho, like Thad insists. It will feel pretty stupid if he is the killer. If I ruined my marriage for nothing.

Only, it wasn't for nothing. Thad's a cheat. That won't go away, and I doubt it will ever change. Once is forgivable, but twice, or however many times it's been, is a pattern. And while I might not be a saint, I'm nobody's doormat. Not anymore.

The door opens, and Samantha Donovan peers up at me, her small face a mask of sorrow that makes my heart ache. Her eyes, red-rimmed and wary, remind me of my own reflection in the days following my mom's death. Her hair is unkempt, and there's an odor. I can't tell if it's coming from her or the house. Maybe I should stay awhile, clean for them.

"Hi, Samantha." I keep my voice gentle. "I'm Elias's mom. You've seen me at school. This is some food for your family. I'm so sorry about your mom."

Samantha's lower lip trembles, but before she can respond, heavy footsteps thunder down some stairs. Someone angry is coming fast, and it makes me want to hightail it out of there like a scared little rabbit.

A tall, lanky teenager appears behind Samantha, his face twisted into a scowl.

Manny Donovan towers over his sister with his gangly frame. He's at that age where he hasn't grown into his limbs. Grungy red hair hangs in greasy strands around his neck, disheveled and wild, a huge contrast to his mom's gorgeous, shimmery tresses. He's glaring at me through cold eyes with an intensity that's both intimidating and desperate.

"Beat it, Sam," he barks, and she scurries away, just like that rabbit. "Whaddaya want?"

I swallow hard, suddenly aware that I'm alone with

Manfred Donovan and holding a heavy, hot casserole in aching arms. "Manny." My voice shakes a little. "I'm so sorry for your loss. I can't imagine—"

A harsh laugh cuts me off. "What loss?" Manny sneers. His eyes narrow as he studies me, sizing me up like prey.

"Your Mom. I'm so sorry." It's time to get out of here. Thad was right. He really is a psycho.

His lip curls, and a light shines in his eyes. He puts his index finger on his chin in a gesture of thought. "Wait a minute. Aren't you the wife of that doctor my mom was screwing around with? Her latest sex toy?"

The crude words hit me like a slap. Truth hurts. I take an involuntary step back, and the casserole slips in my arms. "I...I don't..."

Manny steps onto the porch. His breath, hot and sour, brushes my face as he leans in closer. "Well, aren't you?"

Swallowing, I hold out the casserole. A pathetic gesture, but it's all I have. "I'm sorry."

"Sorry? No need to be sorry."

"I'm...here to..." I'm still holding the casserole. He's not reaching for it. Maybe I should put it down and go. "I'm sorry. I should go. Here."

He cocks his head to the side, looking at me like I'm an ant trapped under a magnifying glass. "Sorry! Don't be." He lets out a bitter laugh and leans in closer, voice low and menacing. "My money's on you. I bet you fucking killed my mom. Jealous bitch. You couldn't help yourself, could you?"

My mouth goes dry, my heart pounding so loud, he must be able to hear it.

Before I can respond, Manny's hand shoots out, and he grabs the casserole. But instead of taking it from me, he gives it a sudden, violent shove. I stumble back, and the heavy dish flies out of my hands, crashing onto the concrete walkway behind me. The glass lid shatters, and the food splashes across the ground and over the legs of my black Eileen Fisher pants.

So much for smart casual.

"Thank you." His tone is eerily sincere. "Someone really needed to end that whore."

I want to deny his accusation, to express my shock at his words about his own mother, but nothing comes out. My mouth is just flapping open and closed like some dying fish.

"Get off our property." He flings out his arm, and for a second, I think he'll strike me. Instead, he points toward the road. "Before I return the favor and carve up that tired old face of yours." His eyes are staring, manic. "I've got knives, too, you know."

CHAPTER
TWENTY-FOUR

Manny walks back inside and slams the door.

What just happened? I stumble back, nearly falling down the porch steps. The casserole dish lies shattered on the snow, and the contents are soaking through my pants.

Not bothering to clean it up, I rush to my car, fumbling to find my key fob. Once inside, the doors locked, I sit, hands shaking.

What. Just. Happened?

"My money's on you. I bet you fucking killed my mom."

He tossed the accusation out there so casually. Is this what people are thinking? That I killed Maggie out of jealousy? It's a good motive, an age-old motive, but I didn't do it.

Images of the snowy yard flash before my eyes. I can't remember going to bed that night—or even going back to bed after my smoke.

Thinking of Manny's cynical, chilling "*thank you*" makes my skin crawl. The way he spoke about his mother...I guess Thad was right on this one.

Manny is clearly a natural-born psycho. And his accusations and behavior certainly don't discount him as a suspect, though he basically said he didn't kill her. His mind could be playing tricks on him, creating a false reality to hide an act so terrible, he can't face it. The human mind is capable of remarkable feats of self-deception.

I should know.

But Manny doesn't seem the kind to feel that sort of anguish. Maybe his accusation is simply a lie to switch suspicion onto me.

Backing out of the Donovans' driveway, I bounce my focus between the backup camera, my rearview mirror, and the Donovans' front door. Manny's accusation echoes in my head, a relentless drumbeat of doubt and fear.

"My money's on you. I bet you fucking killed my mom."

No matter how blurry that night is, there would've been blood on me. On something. Or a wound from the struggle. Or at least I'd be sore from the effort it took to stab another human being to death. Yes, I would've been covered in blood. And there'd be a murder weapon. No one's found one. The logical part of my brain knows this, but the seed of doubt has been planted.

Driving back, I promise to double-check the garage, the laundry, my closet, and even my body for any signs of, well, anything. The very thought makes me sick to my stomach. Even contemplating this is crazy. I'm not the one in question here.

I shake my head, but these horrible thoughts won't go. Even if I can't remember shit, I'd have to be capable of murder to commit murder. Me. Someone who walks spiders outside in springtime rather than flushing them. I'm no violent criminal.

My phone buzzes. It's a text from my mother-in-law.

Keeping both hands on the wheel, I instruct my car on what to do. "Hey, Lexus, read my message."

"Text from Dorothy LaRue. We need to meet. It's of the

utmost importance. I assume you'd prefer to sit down and have a civil, solution-based conversation rather than have rumors running rampant around town."

Well, Miss Pointy Face, what solution is there to repeated infidelity and two dead mistresses?

I want to go home, to forget Dot, but I find myself driving to their place.

It doesn't take long, and there it is. The sheer size of Howard and Dot's second home never fails to make me roll my eyes. It looms ahead, all grandiose columns. The manicured lawns are covered in snow. Maybe next year they'll install under-lawn heating. They'd probably add a moat if they could figure out how to do it without ruining the grass.

The driveway is about as long as a football field, winding through sculpted, snow-topped topiaries that are just a bit too perfect, like everything else in their lives. The house itself is a monument to over-the-top opulence—massive windows and a front door that's practically cathedral-worthy.

Every time I pull up, I half expect a butler in tails to greet me, like I've stepped into some modern-day *Downton Abbey*.

But really, it's always been too much. Ostentatious to the point of absurdity, as if they're trying to prove a point. The whole place is just as fake as Dot's smiles and as stiff as Howard's upper lip.

A deep breath steadies my nerves enough to deal with their brand of "concern." It'll all be about their name and reputation, not about family or loyalty. It sure as shit won't be about finding the killer.

Just before I can knock, the door swings open, and there's Howard, looking every bit the part of the concerned patriarch, his face a mask of polite worry, though his concern doesn't quite reach his eyes. Those ice-blue LaRues have seen too much, or maybe they've seen just enough to know when to keep quiet.

Time to step into their little kingdom of pretense.

"Cooper, dear." He ushers me in like I'm about to attend an audience with the queen. How's my curtsey? The entryway alone is enough to make anyone feel underdressed, with its marble floors gleaming like a museum exhibit and a chandelier that could light up a small village.

"Thank you for coming so promptly." Dot glides in from the living room, perfectly coiffed as always. The walls behind her are adorned with heavy, gold-framed mirrors and portraits of ancestors who look like they've never cracked a smile. The furniture is all dark wood and rich fabrics, the kind that screams, "Look but don't touch." The whole place reeks of money, and they want everyone to smell it.

Unlike me. I reek of chicken Divan.

Dot's face is even more pinched than usual, her perfect hair an almost comical contrast to the heavy bags under her eyes. She's tried to spackle over the exhaustion with layers of makeup, but no amount of powder can hide the tension in her sharp features. Still, her back is as straight as ever, as if slouching would be the ultimate failure. "Coffee?"

Her nose wrinkles. Of course she can smell the chicken. Her eyes widen as she takes in the stains on my pants. She probably thinks I've taken a job at KFC.

"Sure." I'll need the caffeine to survive this conversation. The coffee is probably some imported blend that costs more than my dad's weekly grocery bill, but I'll take it. It'll give me strength and time to think.

Once we're settled in the living room—complete with a fireplace that the kids could use as a den—an uncomfortable silence descends. The kind of silence that bounces off the solid wood floor and echoes in the cavernous space.

I bide my time. They'll crack first. They always do.

"Cooper." Dot's voice is syrupy sweet. "We're aware of the

ridiculous rumors circulating about Thaddeus and that Donovan woman."

Here we go.

I take a quick sip of the coffee, which is predictably perfect—too perfect, like everything else in this mausoleum masquerading as a home. Even now, they can't believe he could do anything wrong.

Howard leans forward, his hands clasped. "You shouldn't believe such ludicrous lies. We believe it's in everyone's best interest if you were to...reconsider your current living situation."

"Reconsider. You want me to take him back?"

Dot's smile tightens. "Think of the children, dear. They need their father."

"They need a father who doesn't cheat on their mother." *Or commit murder.*

Howard waves a dismissive hand. "These accusations are baseless. Thaddeus would never—"

"Never what?" I hold up a hand. "Never cheat? Never lie?"

Never kill? I hate myself for thinking it. *Stick to what you know, Coop.*

"Because I have evidence that proves otherwise."

Dot's eyes narrow. "Evidence can be misinterpreted. If you just spoke with Thaddeus—"

"I've spoken with him." My voice is steady despite my anger. "He lied to my face. Repeatedly. He even lied to the police."

"Marriage isn't always easy, Cooper." Dot's tone is patronizing. "Sometimes we must overlook certain indiscretions for the greater good."

I set my coffee cup down with more force than necessary. "And what about murder? Should I overlook that too?"

A flicker of something—fear, or maybe concern—passes

over Howard's face. "Now, Cooper, let's not get carried away. There's no proof that Thaddeus had anything to do with that woman's death."

"But there's no proof he didn't."

That shuts them up for a moment.

"What if we could make certain things go away?" Dot leans forward, her voice dropping to a conspiratorial whisper. "Ensure that any misunderstandings are cleared up?"

My eyes bug right out. Mirroring her actions, including the whispered tones, I look back and forth between my in-laws. "So you guys think he did it too?"

Dot's head almost pops off, and I have to bite down hard before my face twists into my first smile in days.

Howard clears his throat. "What? No. Of course we don't."

Dot heads to the liquor cabinet. I've broken her. *Welcome to the club.*

"We just happen to have considerable resources," Howard continues. "We could make things very comfortable for you and the children. All we ask is that you stand by Thaddeus during this...difficult time."

"Oh, you want me to be his alibi."

"We want you to be loyal." Dot sits back down, a glass of aged scotch in her shaky hand. "To remember your vows. For better or for worse. Isn't that right, Howard?" She bears a brittle smile.

Unable to sit still any longer, I stand. "I don't think 'for worse' was meant to cover murder."

Howard pushes to his feet too. "Now, Cooper—"

"No. I won't do it. Thad and I will discuss the future of our relationship after the police investigation is completed. Not before."

Dot's face hardens. "Standing by your man only after he's proven innocent just shows what type of wife you truly are."

The words sting. I round on her. "You're always harping on about Elias and Grace getting a proper upbringing. It's time to face the fact that your precious son has done more to jeopardize their future and happiness than anyone. He didn't have to cheat. He walked right into this mess, all on his own, for his own selfish desires." I sling my purse over a shoulder. "And I've been loyal, Dot, in every way that counts."

Don't make me go into details.

It looks like Miss Pointy Face wants to dive into her Glencairn crystal and disappear. She received that unspoken message loud and clear.

I cross to the door, and my hand is on the knob when Howard's voice stops me.

"Think carefully about what you're doing, Cooper."

I turn.

Howard sits beside his wife, placing an awkward hand on her arm. It's the first time I've seen them touch in...ever. "You wouldn't want to find yourself unsupported in these trying times."

"Is that a threat?"

Howard adjusts his cuff links. "Of course not. We're merely concerned for your well-being. And the children's, of course."

"Of course," I echo, my voice oozing with sarcasm. "Thank you so much for your concern. I'll be sure to file it under Things Not to Lose Sleep Over."

As I walk to my car, their gazes burn into my spine. Sure enough, when I look back, there they are—standing at the window, watching me like vultures. I give them a small wave and a tight smile, but inside, a flicker of unease presses down on me.

They're not done with this—not by a long shot—and I'm not sure just how far they're willing to go.

CHAPTER
TWENTY-FIVE

As my hand touches my car, there's a crunch of tires on snow. My stomach drops as Thad's Mercedes pulls into view. Of course his parents would summon him. Should I make a dash for it? But he's already out and striding toward me.

"Cooper, wait." He approaches me as if I were a lion about to rip his head off. "Please. We need to talk."

Keeping my distance, I cross my arms tightly. "We've said all we need to say for now."

He runs a hand through his hair, a gesture I once found endearing. Now it only irritates me. "You don't understand what this is doing to me." There's a whine in his voice that's unfamiliar. "There's a cop parked outside my hotel room 24-7. Everyone knows I'm a person of interest in Maggie's murder. Half a dozen patients have already left the practice."

"Aw, poor baby. Guess your patient count and your reputation are the most important things here."

As Thad takes a step closer, his scent hits me, that mix of sandalwood, musk, and fresh linen. I'm tempted to close my eyes and forget everything. To lean against his chest and feel his arms around me.

Instead, I back away.

Hurt flashes across his face. "If you'd just let me come home, it would show I'm not some monster. That we're working things out. That you believe in me."

A laugh escapes before I can stop it. "Working things out? Thad, you cheated. Again. And now you're mixed up in a murder. There's nothing to work out until this is over and done."

He changes tactics, his voice softening, trying to reel me back in. "Remember our first date? The way you looked under the stars on the beach? We can have that again. I love you. I've only ever wanted to be with you. Why don't we have a bottle of wine tonight, sit by the fire, and make this another great Christmas?"

My mind wanders back to that time—the way my shoes filled with sand. I kicked them off, my toes warm, feeling giddy and carefree. When we ate the picnic he brought, I spilled shrimp on my white dress. He bit it off me, calling me his "messy princess." For a moment this is what I want. To give in.

I think of the video, of Maggie, and my stomach turns. "Don't. Just don't."

Frustration clouds his features. "What do you want from me?" The warmth evaporates, leaving his words sharp and brittle.

"Honesty, fidelity, the darn truth. Did you kill her?"

"Now you're just being stupid. Paranoid."

I turn to my car, but his harsh laughter makes me whip back around.

"When she's done with me, Sheriff White's likely to knock on your door. You had motive and opportunity, and you were out of your mind on oxy and wine. A jealous wife has motive. It doesn't look good."

Rage mingles with fear. "You wouldn't."

"I wouldn't lie, honey."

The implication is he wouldn't have to.

"Do us both a favor and stay away until this is over."

"This isn't what you want. Divorce isn't the answer. You're not thinking clearly." He pauses, his next words carefully measured. "If we're being fair, you haven't been thinking clearly in years. Not since your hiking accident. Not since the pills. Not since the wine."

"You absolute asshole!"

"I'm not a killer." His face is placid, calm. "And despite my actions doing little to prove it, I love you. If you end it now, you'll regret doing this to our family."

"If I stay with a man who has cheated on me twice and get betrayed yet again, that's what I'll regret."

"I swear, Cooper, I will never cheat again." Thad holds his hands up. "And I didn't even sleep with Maggie."

Can he even hear himself? "You've got to be kidding me. We've been here before. Why should I believe you now?"

"You might want to think carefully about this." Something dark flashes in his eyes, and his voice turns low and dangerous. "I can't imagine any judge would allow two young children to stay with their alcoholic, pill-popping, paranoid mother."

The threat catches me off guard, and I struggle to find my voice.

If he'd never cheated with Laurel, I would've never followed him to the cliffs, never tripped and injured my back. And there'd be no oxy hiding out in a kitchen drawer taunting me daily. Still, his words terrify me, because he's not wrong. I'm responsible for controlling my own actions, what goes into my body. I'm a mother first, even before I'm a wife.

"I've only been drinking at night. Just at night." The words finally come out, but my voice cracks. "You know that. It's under control."

His features rearrange themselves into an expression of

horror. "Honey, I'm sorry. I never meant that. You know I'd never do that. My anger is just getting the better of me. Just take me back."

"I have a legal prescription from a doctor." My words are a harsher snap than I intended. "And I'm done talking about this. Done talking to you." My eyelashes are wet with tears.

Fumbling with my key fob, I practically dive into the car before the tears fall. As I drive away, in the rearview mirror, I see Thad standing in the snow, watching me leave.

Disgust bubbles inside me.

The wine, the pills...I've justified them as necessary to deal with the pain, both physical and emotional. But how would it look through the lens of a custody battle?

No. That can't happen. It won't come to that. It can't.

CHAPTER
TWENTY-SIX

After leaving the LaRues', the car seems to steer itself. I can't stay still and can't face the house. Around and around, I go. Past landmarks that blur together in the snow, and still I drive. The sun goes down, but nothing soothes the static in my brain. My headlights show a muted white, but my thoughts are deafening.

The low fuel light flicks on. Just like me, the car's running on empty. Clarity hits me. I know what I need to do, so I turn for home, and in a few blocks, I pull into my drive. My hero is parked in the nighttime shadows. I toss Deputy Byer a wave, but once inside, the house is hollow and mocks my courage.

My stomach growls, reminding me I should eat something. But the thought of food makes me queasy. The reek of that darn casserole lingers. Besides, there are more pressing matters at hand.

The walk-in is my first target. In a panic, I run my hands over every piece of my clothing, shaking out jackets, pants, bathrobes, purses. Upturning boots. Searching for...what, exactly? A bloodstain? A hidden weapon? The absurdity of the situation isn't lost on me.

Switching to Thad's side of the walk-in, I rifle through his things. As the familiar scent of his cologne hits me, memories surface unbidden, and a few shirts fall off the hangers to the floor. Tears form, but I can't now.

Be strong.

The laundry room is next. Upending the baskets, scattering clothes across the floor, I catch a flash of red. My heart leaps into my throat. But it's just Grace's sweatshirt, innocently mixed in with the whites. A shaky laugh escapes me. Man, I'm on edge.

Everything in the laundry room is normal. Disturbingly normal. I'm not sure whether to be relieved or disappointed.

The garage is my final stop. Retracing the steps I would've taken that night after the party, I head for the back corner where I hide my secret stash. The coffee can sits undisturbed, just where I left it. Popping off the lid, I find my cigarettes, my lighter, and the smaller jar for the butts all in place, but no knife, no evidence of murder.

Everything is normal. Nothing points to murder, but I can't shake this feeling.

Standing there, staring at the evidence of my guilty pleasure, I'm oddly detached. Is this what my life has come to? Sneaking cigarettes and searching my own home for evidence of a crime my husband and I have accused each other of committing? With no clues in Thad's things, the question remains—did he do it?

Shit, if he committed murder, he'd be clever enough to hide the evidence. We have a wood burner. His clothes could've been destroyed that night. What was he wearing? I close my eyes to help me remember. The Tom Ford midnight-blue suit with the Turnbull & Asser white dress shirt. I laughed when he bought it. It's from the James Bond collection.

The walking definition of *GQ*, Thad believes he's

Gentleman of the Year. But the clothes get me nothing. The suit is ready for dry-cleaning, the shirt in the laundry. There's nothing on them.

Sure, he could've changed, but he would've needed to come into the bedroom to do it, and Thad's not the stealthy type.

What's wrong with me? He didn't kill her. He did not kill her.

My gaze drifts to the window. Moving to it without thinking, I peer at the street beyond. The view stretches for a block before disappearing into the grove of snow-covered pine trees.

For a split second, I watch a figure walking down the sidewalk. A woman, her red hair trailing behind her like a banner. My heart stops. Maggie?

The ghost of Maggie?

I blink so hard it hurts and rub my eyes. Looking again, all I find is an empty street. The apparition, if it was ever there, has vanished.

Is Thad right? Am I losing my mind? The stress, the lack of sleep, the constant fear...it's all taking its toll. As I step back from the window, my hands are shaking.

A drink. I need a drink. The thought comes unbidden, and I hate myself for it.

"One empty wine bottle in the recycling bin every morning isn't 'under control.'"

But it's calling me. The familiar burn of alcohol, the way it softens the edges of reality. It would be so easy to give in, to lose myself in the bottom of a bottle.

I can't let Thad get under my skin. I have to keep a calm head to work my way out of this. But I need to make a decision about what comes next. What do I want?

I wish none of this had ever happened. That his affairs were still hidden, both of them. What kind of wish is that?

Wandering from room to room in the house, I scan for possible hiding places for bloody knives.

In the living room, family photos mock me from their frames. Happy faces, frozen in time. Was any of it real?

There in front of me is the wine rack. How did I get here? My hand reaches out, almost of its own accord, fingers brushing the cool glass of a bottle.

"No." My voice is loud in the quiet house. I yank my hand back, turning away from temptation.

Instead, I head for the bathroom. A hot shower might clear the fog from my head.

As the water cascades over me, I try to piece together the events of that damn night once more. The party. The look between Maggie and my husband. Her leaving cocky and confident. The fight with Thad. Going to bed. Tossing and turning half the night away in a drunken, angry stupor. Going to the garage. The cigarette.

That's it. That is all I can pull together. It's like trying to grab a fistful of smoke—the more I reach for the memories, the quicker they slip through my fingers.

After the shower, wrapped in my robe, I sit on the edge of the bed. The house creaks and settles around me, ordinary sounds that suddenly seem sinister.

My gaze falls on my bedside table, where my prescription bottle sits. There's no need to hide it when no one's here. The pills would help. They always do. But Thad's voice is there again.

"I can't imagine any judge would allow two young children to stay with their alcoholic, pill-popping, paranoid mother."

With a frustrated groan, I flop back onto the bed, staring at the ceiling. How did my life become this? A maybe-murderer husband, a drinking problem I can't seem to shake, and now the very real possibility of losing my children.

CHAPTER
TWENTY-SEVEN

To keep my children, to stay ahead of Thad, I need to know what happened. But the more I try to remember, the worse it becomes. What's happening? I can't have seen Maggie. She's dead, gone, brutally killed. Whether by Thad or crazy Manny or someone else is anyone's guess.

Without thinking, I beeline straight to the wine rack and grab a bottle. Thad's voice follows me, sarcastic and cruel. *"Who's to say you didn't grab a butcher knife and head out into the snow because you were jealous of this...of Maggie?"*

Pretending he didn't know her. What an ass. I hate it, hate that he looked so good in his suit, the way it clung to his broad shoulders. Hate how composed and sharp he was, like he hadn't just shattered my world.

I still have no memory of what happened after the party. We fought—nasty words, raised voices, his face smug, as if I were the one losing it. I went to bed. But the sheets were like sandpaper, and my thoughts were spiraling, so I dragged myself to the garage for a cigarette. The nicotine barely hit the mark. Then nothing.

Snow, cold. The trees swaying in the darkness, their shadows long and twisted across the pavement. The image blurs like an old, flickering film. I close my eyes. Why won't it come back to me?

I force myself to imagine Maggie, what she was wearing, her smile, the way her hair moved, her scent. The vision is clear. Across the dining room she floats.

Remove the party. Feel the snow.

My eyes are closed, and the temperature dips as I immerse myself. Is she walking toward me, her breath misting, raising her hands to stop me, fear in her eyes? Do I see her bloody and dying in the snow? I conjure it. Red spreading around her. The contrast between white and red too jarring, too vivid. Her eyes staring blankly at the sky.

Do I see this, or have Thad and those stupid pills pushed the image into my mind?

Stop. It's all lies.

Why am I torturing myself? The thought of me killing her is so ludicrous, not even the police are considering it. Thad's throwing shit my way in hopes that none will stick on him. He knew her. He kissed her. He screwed her. I'm sure of it.

A vision of them sneaking along a hotel corridor takes over.

Her glorious hair cascades down her back. He nuzzles into it. Her red heels barely make a sound on the carpet. Thad grabs her tush and leans into her neck. Now they're kissing like they're the only two people in existence.

They stumble into the room, their bodies almost joined, her fingers running through his hair. Their lips lock like she's trying to suck out his tonsils. He pulls back and strips off his jacket, laughing as he throws it onto the huge bed. The look in his eyes is how he used to look at me, only hungrier, more desperate.

He grabs her, his hands roaming her body like he can't get enough. Like the very touch of her sets him on fire. His shirt drops away, and she's caressing his chest as he fumbles with her dress. They fall onto the bed. He's gonna fuck her.

I push it away and grab a corkscrew.

My fingers are like sausages as I fumble with the cork. More of Thad's scornful words swirl, triggering a taunting waltz of self-hatred and guilt. *"If we're being fair, you haven't been thinking clearly in years. Not since your hiking accident. Not since the pills. Not since the wine."*

His accusations are true. I let this happen. But two of *my* inconvenient lovers aren't dead.

"I can't imagine any judge would allow two young children to stay with their alcoholic, pill-popping, paranoid mother."

Pushing harder, I grit my teeth as the corkscrew rotates into the bottle. How dare he judge me?

Despite my anger, those words are a reminder of my darkest moments—time cloaked in a medicated haze. The countless mornings spent hungover. Precious moments of Elias and Grace's childhood slipping through my fingers like sand.

Do my children realize their mom's a drunk? It hurts. "I will change, sweet peas, I promise. I'm gonna beat this and be there for you. I swear it."

I just need to get through these very trying times first.

A moan escapes me as the cork pops. The rich aroma of merlot usually grounds me, but I want to throw the bottle. To smash it against our alabaster walls. Only it would run down like blood. Maggie's blood.

I didn't kill her. I couldn't have.

I pour the wine and take my first sip. I'm steadier now. This isn't about escapism—not tonight. It's about staying in the present. I need clarity.

And I know I've done wrong. Drunk too much. Mixed alcohol with oxy, and maybe just as bad, I've pushed away my suspicions about Thad. Letting things ride instead of stomping down on him when I first suspected he was cheating again was a big mistake.

The pain, the hurt, the self-doubt were hidden in my haze. It didn't help.

That clarity I craved hits me hard. I've been a terrible mom, with my indulgences and my dependencies. Still, I've improved. During the day, I'm more often sober than not, and my back healed long ago. The painkillers are no longer medically necessary. But I got them legally, and they help me cope. No judge could damn me for that. Could they?

However, a judge might not like that I mix them with a bottle of wine every night. What have I become? Why do I keep doing this?

The answer is clear. It dulls the sharper edges of reality, at least long enough for sleep to take hold.

I've wallowed in this hell, all the while pretending it was perfect. Making believe I was happy, we were good. Stupidly acting out a fantasy of a happy family. It's time to grow up. To find the truth.

In the dim light of the kitchen, I lean against the counter, wine glass in hand, contemplating the tangle of my life. Thoughts of Laurel Hackert—and now, unavoidably, Maggie Donovan—dance through my mind like specters I can't exorcise.

The questions circle relentlessly. Why Thad? What allure does a married father in his thirties hold for a nineteen-year-old girl? Did Laurel believe she loved him, or was it just a fleeting infatuation?

And Thad? Did he love her despite his vehement denials? He always insisted that he didn't. Of course he insisted. He's a liar, a cheat, a bastard.

My trust in Thad was shattered when I discovered his affair with Laurel. It wasn't some sudden revelation. It crept up on me like a bad hangover. I wasn't stupid. I had suspicions long before the truth hit me square in the face. The late nights were the first red flag. "*It's been crazy at the clinic,*" he'd say, like I didn't know what crazy looked like.

Then came the perfume—floral, musky, fruity, and not mine. It lingered on his shirt, in his car, like a slap in the face wrapped in a pink vanilla kiss.

And don't get me started on the phone. He'd guard it away like a lifeline, never letting it out of his sight. The man couldn't let the damn thing charge in peace without checking it every five seconds.

One time, he locked the screen so fast, I half expected him to yell, "Classified information!" Instead, he caught himself and said, "*Just patient stuff,*" delivered with that slick smile, like I was too naive to know what was really going on.

There were other things, too—his mood shifts, the little things he used to do for me that suddenly stopped. He was pulling away, like a thread unraveling, little by little.

When I finally caught him, he eventually admitted to the affair. But even that wasn't easy. He tried to pretend it was innocent, even after what I saw. I had to force him into therapy when he finally came clean. He even handed over his passwords, as if that would fix everything.

But trust doesn't come back just because you can now scroll through someone's emails. It wasn't his inbox I was worried about—it was the watering down of our love, every excuse, every late night that came before it.

Searching his emails and social media was torture. Fruitless torture, for I found no evidence of further infidelities. There was nothing incriminating in the careful curation of his digital life. But the absence of evidence isn't evidence of absence.

Kicking off my shoes, I grab the bottle and glass and pad through the house, flicking on lights. They sparkle off Christmas decorations, a sad reminder that it's still the season to be jolly. A sudden urge to wrench them down hits me, but I don't have the energy.

I take a drink, but tonight isn't just about numbing the pain or clouding my thoughts. It's about seeking answers, about piecing together the fragments.

It's about digging deeper, sifting through the digital traces of Thad's past liaisons. If there are secrets left to uncover, I will find them, starting with Laurel and stretching into the murky waters of his recent behaviors. I need to know how much he lied, how much is true, and if he can ever be trusted again.

The truth is out there, and the search for it begins tonight.

Crossing to his home office, I open the door and flick on the lights. It's neat. The sofa and chairs where we had our recent therapy session look so empty. The big mahogany desk is clear and ultra tidy, with just a planner and a screen. Being here, violating his space, feels wrong, like I'm a naughty schoolgirl sneaking into the principal's office.

I push the thought away. He deserves this. Sliding into the huge leather chair, I open the bottom drawer and move files. Panic flutters in my gut until I find what I need. The password book he made for me has been forgotten and untouched for months.

His passwords are a predictable assembly of personal milestones and cherished names. They now seem like clues to his hidden life. Each is formatted with an exclamation point, a meaningful name, and a significant date, followed by another exclamation point—a code he seems to follow instinctively.

I'm about to go back to my laptop, but there's no need. He's not here. When I click the mouse to his desktop computer, the screen fires up. The screensaver is a picture of our family. Smiles, always smiles, that make my blood boil. I gulp wine. "No emotion, Cooper. This is about facts."

Next, I pull up his Facebook account and click on the profile shot. It opens an almost empty account, one we set up years ago that he doesn't use. I switch to Instagram, searching for the drlove2021 account that had commented on Laurel's post. I use different password combinations, but I can't get in. Flipping the pages in his book and trying different variations gets me nowhere. Everything I think of fails.

"*Arrrrghh.*" If it's a date that's special to them, I have no chance. Frustrated, I leave the office, throw a lasagna in the microwave, and pop an oxy before I give myself time to overthink it. The wine bottle is three-quarters empty. I think about getting another, but no. I need to be sharp.

Relatively speaking.

The microwave pings. The plate burns my fingers on the way to the table. I drop it quickly onto a mat.

It hits me. I've been working on his computer and completely forgot the operating system offers a free password keeper. The only reason I remember is because my computer keeps prompting me to set mine up. I never bothered, but I bet Thad did.

Food forgotten, I race back to the office.

A flashlight sweeps past the window, and I freeze in my tracks. Tiptoeing to the blinds, I peek out. It's Deputy Byer, walking the grounds, bathed in the glow of the security lights. I whisper a prayer of thanks.

Throwing myself into Thad's chair, I root around for his password manager. Once found, it asks for a password, but that one's easy. It's in his book under *PM*—I'd wondered what it meant. *!Elias06032018!*

A long list of apps appears. The usernames are visible, but the passwords display as strings of asterisks. I scroll down until I find Instagram. There are two accounts. One is for Thad LaRue, the other for drlove2021.

Next to the row of asterisks is the eye symbol. I click it.

The screen prompts me for his browser password again. I enter it, and the string of asterisks becomes *!Laurel0806!*.

My stomach turns over. He used her name the same way he used our children's.

I switch back to Facebook and enter the details. The screen refreshes, and I'm in. Vomit rises in my throat. Until now, a tiny part of me believed the "lucky day" comment was a coincidence. Now I know it was him. *My lucky day* is always him.

Admit it, Cooper.

I click through the account, but it's empty. No posts, no pictures, nothing. Was all this for naught? Was it just that one comment?

When I notice the icon for messages, I slap my head. This was for secret texting, a way for them to communicate.

My finger hovers over the mouse. "Do I wanna do this?"

I click on Messages. There they are, a long thread of communication between them. The evidence of Thad's duplicity. The messages, hundreds of them, go back a long time.

You really think you can just walk away? After everything we had? I'm not some fling you can toss aside. You don't get out. Not that easy. You still think about me. I know it, and I'm not done with you yet...and I don't think you're done with me either. Let's meet.

They were breaking up, but that does nothing to ease the pain radiating through every part of me. I take a deep breath before reading Thad's reply.

You need to stop. We agreed it was over. But you know damn well I can't forget what we had. I still dream about you, about us. The way you make me feel...no one else does that. But we have to lay low until Cooper starts to believe in me again.

The words blur. Each word and sentence unravels the remaining threads of trust I'd clung to. The truth is as clear as it is devastating—my husband, the father of my children, lived a double life. He lied again and again. He betrayed me for so long. I want to throw the screen at the wall. It's too painful to grasp in this wine-blurred hour.

Determination replaces my tears. I'm no longer a woman kept in the dark. I will read every painful, lying, cheating message and find out just how far this went.

CHAPTER
TWENTY-EIGHT

The urge to speak to Beth, to run this whole mess past her, overwhelms me. I grab my phone.

"Dammit." It's after midnight, too late to call.

I'm back to scrolling through the endless stream of messages. They whiz past too fast to read. I keep scrolling back, back, back to the start, where this all began. To find out why.

Turn away. Go to bed. Forget this.

Back and back they go. Past a year, and still, there are more and more of them. I've stumbled upon a digital Pandora's box, and now that it's open, I can't look away. Thad's been living a double life for years.

"Two years." The words taste bitter on my tongue. "Two fucking years."

He hadn't cheated on me for one year, as he'd claimed when I caught him. No, he'd been sneaking around with Laurel, with that beautiful, vibrant young woman, for two years before I busted him...before her death.

One year hurt enough, but two? He was sleeping with that

young girl the first year we were on the island. So much for a loving marriage. What is wrong with him?

What's wrong with you? a spiteful voice whispers. I tune it out.

I tell myself to breathe, to read, to let my fury burn. It will keep me strong.

His messages are sweet, loving. It hurts.

Finally, I reach the start.

Hi, Lorelei, my love. I told you I had a surprise. Now we can message in private. Sending you my prescription of love.

Lorelei. He calls her Lorelei, the siren who lured sailors to their doom with her beauty. All I get is *honey*, and it's often accompanied by a sneer.

I luv it like I luv my Dr. Love. Kisses.

I want to barf.

Just thinking about you. Meeting you was amazing. You're my lucky day.

Emotion and hate sear my sinuses. "His fucking lucky day. If I hear those words again!"

Miss u, Dr. Love. Luvd the flowers and chocolates.

He sent her presents. Asshat.

He sends back a stethoscope emoji.

Miss u more than I thought possible...especially the way u can't wait to get ur hands on me. Bet u're missing me 2...
There's a photo of her in her underwear. A sexy two-piece. *Send me my prescription, Dr. Love.*

If he includes an eggplant emoji, I just might punch the screen.

You know exactly what I'm missing, Lorelei. How about tonight...I administer that injection you're craving?

Oh, god. I swallow down the bile creeping up my throat. This. Can't. Be. Happening. My thirty-six-year-old doctor husband just responded with a dick pic...to his teenage lover.

Oh, Dr. Love, that's 1 big prescription.

He's behaving like a besotted teenager. I can't read anymore. But I do...

Scrolling on, I find more of the same. My nerves thrum. I gulp my wine, locking my total attention to the screen like I'm watching the world's greatest car crash. I want to look away, but I'm glued.

Just saw this guy at the coffee shop trying to flirt with the barista by dropping a line about "good bedside manners." It made me laugh and immediately think of my Dr. Love. U're the only one who gets my twisted sense of humor. Excited about tonight. Lots to tell u...and show u.

There's a photo of a package, a piece of red lace just showing.

They carry on much the same, but a sickening realization hits me as I delve deeper into their conversations. Laurel was only nineteen when she died. Which means...

"Seventeen." I gasp as bile rises in my throat. "She was only seventeen when it started." She was a child, overawed by this rich and handsome doctor. Groomed. She was groomed. The outrage burns, but there's sadness too—sadness for her, which surprises me. Thad took advantage of this beautiful, sweet girl.

It's disgusting. Every part of me wants to turn away, to switch off. I feel like a sneak looking at a young girl's diary.

One message stops me. It looks like even Thad was worried about her age.

After what we talked about last night, I know u're worried, but I rechecked the law. Look at this link. We're not doing anything wrong.

The tackiness of it all—pulling up a government law website to justify their disgusting relationship.

Sixteen! The age of consent is sixteen.

But he's a doctor, a person in a position of trust. A bitter laugh escapes me. "Well, isn't that just peachy? It wasn't *technically* statutory rape."

So, legally, my husband might not be a sexual predator. But the line feels too gray and gross to ignore.

Thad knew it too.

I read on for a while. It's one sickly message after another, like horny teenagers. Well, technically, she *was* a horny teenager. I guess I can't blame her for writing like one.

After about eight months, the first tiny cracks begin to show.

Thad, we need to talk about our future. I can't keep living like this.

We did talk. I'm busy tonight, but I can see you tomorrow.

Sure. Let's meet at that little restaurant at 8.

We have to be careful. There's a big age gap and other things to consider, my little Lorelei.

Such as? If u love me, leave Cooper. Then we can meet anywhere.

It's not just about love. You know I love you, but there are other factors at play.

Like what? Ur reputation? Ur career? What about us?

Even though I want to, I can't stop reading. I begin mimicking their voices, giving her a mouse like squeak while he talks on something closer to Goofy. Somehow, that makes it easier.

"'My sweet, you know it's not that simple. There's professional ethics to consider. If this came to light, I could lose my medical license.'"

"'So your career is more important than our love? You said you were ready.'"

"'I am ready, in my heart. But we need to be smart about this. We can't just rush into things. How would I support you if I couldn't work? Be smart.'" I add a very Goofy *ah-hyuck* to stop myself from going crazy.

"'I am smart.'" She sounds more like a drunk Minnie Mouse now. My apologies to Walt. "You know that. But I'm tired of waiting. You need to make a real commitment. You have to choose…choose me.'"

"'I do. We'll talk tomorrow. Let's make it special. I have to go. Patients. Love you.'"

She wanted more commitment and for him to leave me, to separate. How could he have these conversations behind my back? And Thad doesn't even mention his family. Their arguments are about how society would view their relationship, regardless of state laws, not how his leaving me would affect his children.

Laurel seems appeased for a while, but after another couple of months, she asks again to meet in public.

I love you, my little Lorelei, but I can't help but worry about us. You might be legal in Maine, but there's still a big age gap. We have to keep this secret. It looks bad. Very bad.

I growl low in my throat. "No shit, Sherlock. What gave it away? The fact that you're banging a teenager?"

Her sweet reply only shows the difference between the predator and the prey.

We're not doing anything wrong. Luv transcends everything. Emojis of a legal document and hearts add to the juvenile feel of the message.

It carries on, and the nub of things soon emerges. Thad fears losing his medical license for being involved with a patient.

She's not just a child in a relationship with a doctor. She's a child in a relationship with *her* doctor.

I snort. "Of course. He was banging a child in his care. And the great Dr. LaRue was worried about losing his precious title."

The hearts and kisses on each of her messages highlight her youth and naivete. I know what she was thinking. Young, with hormones surging, she's so in love, she wants to shout it from the rooftops. That's why Thad was so careful, trying to get her to understand she had to stay quiet. How hard it must have been.

I understand, my love. I don't want to lose you. I couldn't bear it, but if this gets out, I won't be able to see you again.

Bile churns in my stomach as he gaslights her. Just like he's gaslit me.

Don't let their opinions scare u. I've never been more sure of anything. I'm in this because I love u, not because of some rule.

I know. I love you so much that it hurts. But trust me on this.

Ok, 4 now. Guess what...some new lingerie for tonight. Get ready 4 take-off.

The full horror of the affair is laid bare before me. Tears run down my face. I'm blubbering, but I still keep reading. What hurts the most is that this doesn't look just physical—they were in love. Truly, madly, deeply in love. The words they shared make me want to vomit.

My dearest Lorelei, your smile lights up my world. I can't imagine a day without you in it.

"Thad, did you plagiarize a Hallmark card?"

Eventually, Laurel wonders if Thad would ever break things off due to the complications of their relationship.

His response is a punch to the gut. *Of course not. I need you in my life. I love you so much that I couldn't live without you.*

It's too much. The final straw. Lunging for the wastebasket and barely making it in time, I violently empty the contents of my stomach. As I retch, I think how fitting it is. Thad's lies have made me sick for years—now they're doing it literally.

CHAPTER
TWENTY-NINE

Reading through their chat history, it's like I've entered the Twilight Zone. The messages go on and on in predictable patterns. The sweet banter from Thad. The occasional bout of self-pity from Laurel. The intermittent attempt to get him to leave me.

This has to be an alternate reality. One where I don't even exist. I didn't to Thad. That's for sure.

The content is much the same, over and over again. Them telling each other how much they are in love. Sharing ridiculous things that make my jaw clench. And the sexy pictures. Despite her occasional mentions and his deflections of a future, a year on, they're still sharing sexy pictures. They seem to have a sense of humor that's in sync. So either Laurel is, or was, old beyond her years, or Thad really is a horny teenage boy with no control over his body or actions.

Likely the latter. How did I miss it?

Every time I close my eyes, I see your smile. It's what keeps me going through the day.

Did my stuffy, uptight husband really write that?

Then there's one from Laurel. *Found the cutest café today,*

The Nook. It made me wish u were there to share a coffee w me. It's our kind of place. I even went in, ordered a latte, and pretended u were w me.

That stings. I asked him once to stop there, and he said it wasn't our type of place. I assumed it wasn't quite up to the stuffy LaRue standards. Now I wonder if he didn't want to spoil the fantasy of being there with her.

It's almost one in the morning. My fingers hover over the mouse as I scroll through message after message, each a fresh blow.

"Dammit, Thad. What the hell were you thinking?"

It's like some tragic romance novel chronicling a love story that spiraled into bedlam. I can't stop reading, though I'd like to.

The tone of the messages gradually shifts. The honeymoon phase gives way to something darker and more volatile. Laurel becomes increasingly desperate and demanding.

Why are u still w her if u luv me like u say?

You know why. We have to be patient. My medical license. We need a safe buffer of time, since you were my patient so recently. And there's my kids.

"Way to go on priorities." My voice makes me jump.

Easy, Cooper.

Keeping going is unhinged. But if I let go and start screaming, I may never stop.

The desperation gets more and more severe on Laurel's part. Thad played it cool for a while, but I imagine he was shaking like a leaf in a hurricane.

I can't do this anymore. You have to leave her. You know how I feel about you.

I scoff. It's a faint noise, the bitterness boiling within me. How naive was she to think he would abandon his life for an affair?

Our time will come, my Lorelei.

Did she fall for that? It seems so, as her pestering stops for a few months. I scroll down, racing past the flurry of exchanges, but something catches my eye, drawing me in like a moth to a flame.

"'Leave her,'" I read, my voice barely above a whisper. "'Leave Cooper. Don't live another day in a loveless marriage with a woman so perfect she even poops on a schedule.'"

A feeling of violation starts in my chest. How much of our life did he share? He mocked my perfectionism. Well, girl, I could share a few things of my own. Deep, dark, dirty things. Things only a wife knows. But I can't, because she's dead.

Despite the hurt, a twinge of sympathy for this girl I never knew creeps in. She was so young, so trusting. She really believed Thad would leave his family for her. It's sad.

His answers are constantly placating. *Soon, but we have to do this right.* Or another. *You know I will when Grace is a little older.*

I clench my fists so tight, my nails dig into my palm. He brings Grace into this sordid affair. It's another level of sick.

But the messages change again. Laurel's tone becomes pleading, frantic, desperate, and depressive.

Plz don't leave me, Thad. I'm sorry. I'll do anything. Please, I don't know what I'd do if u left me.

His reply to that one is still committed.

Hey, I'm not going to leave my Lorelei. Enjoy what we have.

The poor kid. Enjoy being a bit on the side. Enjoy being used, hidden, and ignored.

It wld be better for me to just disappear. It wld be better for every1. It would stop the pain, don't u think?

Don't even think about that, Lorelei. You have so much to live for.

He was worried about her.

But I can't sleep...can't eat. Everything feels pointless. Maybe it'd be better if I wasn't here at all.

Please, Laurel, you're scaring me. Your life is precious. I'll be there tomorrow. We can talk about this. Promise me you won't do anything rash.

I won't.

Then it's as if she changed back to the happy-go-lucky teenager.

Bought a new lipstick today. U're gonna luv it. That and a can of Reddi-Wip!

A few months of sweet nothings, then another change.

U promised me, Thad. Leave her, or I'll tell every1.

No, Thad replies, the weight of authority leaking through the screen. *You have to understand it's complicated. You don't want to do this. Think of your mom. She'd be so disappointed.*

She'd understand. We can make her.

But if it comes out, your friends will call you a homewrecker. We don't want that, do we? Some might even call you a slut. Let me end my marriage at the right time, and after a decent interval, we can come out in public.

When? she fires back.

The tension practically crackles. This is like a novel I hate but can't put down, the destruction of a life. It's clear Thad was manipulating Laurel all along, keeping her on the hook while playing the devoted husband to me.

She's easily fooled, but their spats are increasing, and we're getting closer to me finding out. It's late October on the thread. I caught them in December.

I can't face this pain much longer.

Her desperation is back. It looks like he feels it too.

I'm on my way to see you.

Just two days later, she's back at him. His little affair is becoming less fun, more aggressive by the day.

Remember our promise? U said u'd leave ur wife 4 me! Don't u want this? What's stopping u?

Thad's response stings like a brand. *You know I can't risk my medical license. Not now.*

His license. This is all about his reputation, not about love. Not about the family I built, while Laurel was whispering sweet nothings and getting the best parts of him. But the cruel twist is that it wasn't even about her.

Later, she becomes so melancholy.

I understand. Please don't end things. I need u. I luv u.

He doesn't reply.

Her next message sends a shiver down my back.

Sorry, Thad. I can't do this anymore. It hurts 2 much. I just want the pain 2 stop.

Laurel, listen to me. Whatever you're thinking of doing, don't. I love you. You know that. I'm coming over right now. We'll get through this.

I scroll further, my stomach twisting.

And around the time I caught them, it's like a switch has been flipped, and Laurel's messages turn threatening.

I'll tell everyone.

His reply is sugary sweet. *Don't, my love. This was just a misunderstanding. We have to keep it quiet a little longer if we're to be together forever. You know that. You're smart. You're my girl.*

There's no way she could have believed that, could she?

Maybe. The messages return to sweet nothings and arranging meetings for a while, but he starts to not answer as quickly, to put off dates. The next message raises the hair on the back of my neck.

I'll go to the paper. How does this headline grab u? Beloved doctor sleeps w 17y/o patient.

I lean back in my chair, and a long, ragged breath comes

out, followed by a whistle of admiration. "Damn, girl. You went for the jugular."

My mind flicks to Thad's words from other messages, his fears about how society would view their relationship regardless of its legality. His certainty that he'd lose his medical license.

"Guess you didn't think that far ahead when you started this little affair, did you, darling?"

He arranges to meet her after that one. Until Laurel's final message.

I gave up everything for u. I'm done. Imagine the headlines. U've taken advantage of me 4 2 yrs now. Don't act like u're the victim here. I will tell everyone unless u leave her. I will destroy u. I promise.

And just like that, the messages stop. Of course they do. Laurel's dead. She jumped from the highest cliff, the spot where I found her with Thad.

CHAPTER
THIRTY

Two years earlier...

My life was a circus—minus the cute animals and fun snacks—on the best of days. The past couple weeks, though? Far from the best.

Grace, my three-year-old tiny terror, was permanently glued to my hip while Elias, now five, had developed a passion for screaming, "Mommy, look at this," every five seconds like it was his life's mission to drive me crazy.

Meanwhile, I attempted to run a graphic design business from home—or my shiny new office—in an effort to keep myself sane. At home, it meant trying to be creative while finger painting with one hand and answering client emails with the other. At the office, it was trying to balance work around the sitter's schedule.

And there was Thad. My husband. My charming, lying, cheating husband. The man I caught kissing another woman on the cliffs fifteen days ago.

I still couldn't believe it. Not just his actions, but mine.

For years, I thought I knew myself. I always imagined I was the kind of woman who, if caught in that kind of circumstance, would storm over, rip them apart, slap the slut across the face, and kick the bastard in the balls for good measure. The kind of woman who'd grab the kids, file for divorce, and leave him wondering what truck just flattened his life.

But that wasn't what I'd done. Not even close.

No, I'd stood in the pouring snow like an idiot. Staring. Snapping pictures with my phone like a wannabe private investigator who'd never taken a class. I didn't say a word. Didn't stomp over. Didn't even glare. I just...slunk off with my tail between my legs. Like some extra in a bad soap opera.

And then I fell. Of course I fell.

The snow had hidden a tree root, and down I went, flat on my back. The pain was instantaneous, a sharp explosion that left me gasping for air. I might have lain there forever if the thought of being found by the happy couple hadn't acted as a prod to my frozen ass.

Somehow, I'd dragged myself to the car. Not exactly a triumphant escape. More like a pitiful limp through the snow with tears and snot freezing on my face.

Now, over two weeks later, my back still hurt like the devil plunged his pitchfork into my spinal column. Dr. Hughford diagnosed a herniated disc and prescribed oxycodone. It helped with the pain but made everything...distant. Blurry. Like I was living someone else's life.

And Thad? He swore he loved me and that the affair was a mistake. Promised it would never happen again. Therapy, he swore—hand on the figurative bible—would fix us. Therapy, I hoped, might fix him.

But here I was, fifteen whole days after the cliffs, still married, still checking his phone obsessively, still finding excuses to follow him around town like a paranoid lunatic.

Every other night, there was another excuse. A patient emergency, a late meeting, traffic.

Sure, honey. Traffic at nine? On this little island? Not buying that one.

Because the truth was simple. I no longer trusted him. Not after Laurel. Not after the excuses. And especially not after the whiff of perfume on his shirt last night—a floral scent I didn't wear.

Tonight, he'd claimed difficult patients and lots of paperwork would keep him at the office late again. Did I believe him? The fact that I'd called the sitter to watch the kids and was currently parked near the cliffs again should've been answer enough.

This time, though, I had enough wine and oxy on board to keep me warm.

I stared at Laurel's car, the same one as before. Thad's Mercedes was nowhere to be seen. There was another vehicle, though, parked just before the lot.

An old truck. Blue, I think.

Did that mean he was at his office like he'd said? Or had he caught a ride with her?

I was going to find out.

With visions of them kissing dancing in my head, I made my way to the cliff top on the treacherous path, just to see if they'd gone back to the same spot. It was cold out, but I was more prepared this time.

Ready for anything.

The wind whipped around me as I struggled up the steep path. My movements were clumsy, stiffened by the cocktail of pills and wine that numbed the pain of my injured back.

Am I really here, or is this all in my mind?

My rage cut through the drug-addled blur. Each step was a battle against gravity, my uncooperative body, and my need to see.

"Come on, Cooper." Teeth grinding together, I pushed forward. "One foot in front of the other. You can do this."

The path is endless. I keep losing focus. Why am I here? What will I achieve climbing this godforsaken cliff?

I should've been home wrapping presents instead of checking to see if my husband was with another woman... again.

The urge to turn and run home was strong, but sitting in that house for one more minute would suffocate me under the weight of my husband's lies.

Nearly at the top, I paused as a wave of dizziness washed over me. I stumbled, catching myself against a rough tree trunk. That spiked the pain in my back but sharpened my mind some. The bark bit into my palm, and I welcomed the sting. It was real, tangible, unlike the nebulous ache in my chest.

That was when I heard it. Voices carried on the wind. Shouts.

I froze before diving into the trees. Though the voice was muffled, I could tell it was a man's. *Thad?* And another, higher, feminine voice that could only belong to one person—Laurel Hackert.

"Shit, shit, shit, shit." They were here. Together. Again. I'd known it, yet I'd prayed it wasn't so.

Creeping forward, I was careful to stay hidden behind the thick pine trees. Through the boughs, I caught glimpses of them. Thad's back was to me, his posture rigid. Laurel faced him, and even from this distance, the fury etched on her features was clear.

"You can't do this to me." Laurel sounded shrill with desperation. *I barely hear the words, my mind filling in the blanks where the wind snatches her voice away.* "You don't get to make decisions for me. I'm not some damsel you need to rescue."

His reply was clipped, too low for me to make out, but whatever he said only seemed to enrage her more.

"Don't you dare!" She raised a hand to strike him. He caught it, holding it inches from his face. "Don't you dare. You're not some knight in shining armor. I'm not some child. Stop treating me like I'm fragile."

My insides boiled. How dare they come to this beautiful place, once a place special to Thad and me, and taint it with their breakup? Sure, I'd wanted Thad to end things with Laurel, but he should've let her down over a text, if even that much contact. Not...whatever this was. Not here.

"You don't understand." He was shouting now, the voice strange, distorted in the wind. "If you stay—"

"Stay?" She let out a bitter laugh. "You think I want to stay? After everything?"

He wasn't breaking up with her—he was asking her to stay. To stay. How could he? I wanted to step out, to confront them both, to unleash all the hurt and rage I'd bottled up.

But before I can move, the scene before me shifts. It's as if I'm not here, not seeing this. My mind is grasping, but the image slips away.

The yelling stopped abruptly as Thad pulled Laurel close. From my vantage point, I saw her face over his shoulder. The look of revulsion on her face rocked me backward, and I almost fell into the snow.

"I can't do this anymore." His voice drifted to me, soft but clear in the sudden silence. "You can't do this Laurel. I won't let you."

The young woman's face crumpled. "No." Her agony was hard to witness. She tried to pull away from him.

This was what I'd wanted—for it to end—but there was no triumph. All I felt was a deep, aching sadness. For the crumbling of my marriage and for Laurel, so young and clearly in over her head. I even felt some sadness for Thad, trapped between his obligations and desires.

There was pity, yes, for myself, the unwitting victim in this mess. And rage. A rage that drew a red mist over my eyes and made me want to push them both off the cliff.

The wind has risen. I can't hear a word they're saying, but he's hugging her now. He's changed her mind.

He pulled her deeper into his arms, and they hugged on our spot. Our special place.

My rage turned into blinding fury until it was all I knew.

CHAPTER
THIRTY-ONE

Present day...

Waking up sprawled on the bed with my neck twisted at an angle draws out a groan. I have no memory of climbing into bed, no recollection of falling asleep. I must've passed out without even changing into pajamas or bothering with the lights.

That's ridiculous. My head throbs. My neck aches, and my throat is as dry as a week-old biscuit. Forcing my eyes to focus, I think about the last of the messages again. Laurel threatened to destroy Thad's life. And then nothing.

The abrupt end. Instead of destroying Thad, she killed herself. Is that true? Was Laurel truly suicidal? It's possible. Every now and then in her messages to him, she slipped into a melancholy mood.

Some of her messages made me feel sad for her. It wasn't the emotion I was looking for, but...

Sometimes I feel like I'm drowning. Like the world is too heavy, and I can't breathe. Do u ever feel that way?

"Thad, c'mon, you should've seen it. You're a doctor, for pity's sake. Why didn't you help her?" But no, he came back with some platitude about her strength and him always being there.

Did she take her life? Or did she become too big a problem for Thad? And if he killed Laurel, he could've killed Maggie. Thinking my husband could've killed two people should horrify me. Instead, I'm simply empty, drained, and angry. And filled with too many questions to face.

It has to be a coincidence. Laurel took her own life. And Maggie Donovan was killed behind our house. Not directly, but close enough. Thad wouldn't be that stupid. If he was going to kill Maggie, he wouldn't do it in such an obvious place, so close to our home, directly after she left our party. What moron would do that? Unless she became too big a problem for my wayward husband. Maybe he was too drunk to think properly...

I reach for my phone to call Beth. Maybe she can talk some sense into me. I need someone to make this all come together. To talk me out of this nonsense. But Beth's away. A short break for the holidays. If I speak to her, she'll rush back. Spoil things for her and the kids. I can't do that to her.

A glimpse at the time. It's just after eleven. Shit. I promised Marco I'd stop in at noon to look over the ideas he's implemented so far.

It's the last thing I need. Should I cancel? No, it will do me good to get out of the house. I fire off a message that I'm running late.

After a quick shower, I rush through my morning routine. Gulping down a coffee, I spot Deputy Byer walking around the house. He gives me a wave. I'm sure it was him I saw last night. How long are his shifts? I pour another quick coffee and head out to see him.

"Morning, Deputy Byer." I hold out the steaming mug to him. "You look like you could use this. Long night?"

His hands wrap around the cup like it's the first warm thing he's touched in hours. "Thanks, Mrs. LaRue. You didn't have to."

I wave it off, trying to act casual. "So when's the next shift coming in? Gotta keep up the LaRue watch, right?"

He looks down at his boots and shuffles on the spot. It's almost cute, in a completely awkward way. I get the feeling he hasn't had much experience talking to women. Or maybe it's embarrassment because they're pulling my protection.

"Well, uh...you see...the sheriff only authorized me to do the night shift. Technically, I'm off the clock now."

I blink. "But...you're still here."

He rubs the back of his neck and sips the coffee. "Yeah, I, uh...well, with what happened..." His gaze flicks toward the back of the property. To the area where Maggie was found. "Figured I'd keep an eye on things. You know, to make sure. I mean, I'm used to living in my vehicle, more or less." He glances at me, a half smile playing on his lips. "Until this is over, you can be sure I'll be here. Gonna keep you safe."

Deputy Byer is young, but there's a sincerity to him that catches me off guard. He actually cares. This is more than a job.

"Well, aren't you my knight in shining SUV?" I tease, raising an eyebrow. "But seriously, thanks. You don't have to do that, and I can't tell you how much I appreciate it." I tap my chin with mock thoughtfulness. "Though I feel bad about you living out of your vehicle like some vagabond."

He chuckles softly, shrugging. "It's not so bad. Besides, a bit of discomfort is better than if something happens and no one's around."

I nod, trying not to let on how much his words mean to

me. "Well, I'm glad someone's got my back, even if it's not official." I take a step away. "Let me know if you need more coffee. Or, I don't know, a blanket or something."

Byer's grin widens, a little sheepish.

"I'll hold you to that. Coffee is always welcome, Mrs. LaRue. If you're going out, you take care, all right?"

"You got it. And call me Cooper. I think we're past Mrs. LaRue at this point, don't you think?"

He nods and raises the mug.

Leaving him to return to his patrol, I set off for my meeting and arrive at Marco's a few minutes late, slightly out of breath.

Marco doesn't seem to notice. "Cooper. It's so good to see you. Come quick. This is *benisimo*." With a huge grin and eyes that are bright and way more awake than I feel, he leads me to the back. "You will love what we've done."

For the next half hour, I listen as Marco walks me through the changes he's already implemented. The room is coming together. The walls look rustic Italian, but there's graffiti that makes them pop. He's started building booths for gaming and an area for talking and, more importantly, eating. It looks great, just as we designed it.

Offering a mixture of congratulations and suggestions, I try to focus on the task at hand rather than the turmoil in my personal life. My head still pounds. My mind keeps flashing to Thad, Laurel, and Maggie. To deciphering what happened. Laurel's state of mind was not good. How callous could Thad be? The man who wrote those sweet words—surely he couldn't have killed her.

"It's great." I have no idea what Marco just asked, but his grin tells me I hit the right note. "These changes will really boost your business."

"Good, good. One more…" The ding of the pizzeria's

front door interrupts us. Marco rushes off to greet his customer.

"I'll grab that for you, Mrs. Hackert. Give me just a minute," he says before the door to the kitchen swings shut.

Mrs. Hackert. The name has me whipping around, my pulse racing.

Sure enough, Vicki Hackert, Laurel's mother, stands at the counter. It seems like fate. Vicki looks diminished since I last saw her. A sad shell of a woman, her shoulders hunched under an invisible weight. Her hair is limp, and her face is drawn. She's wearing black trousers under a coat that looks three sizes too big and like it could do with a trip to the dry-cleaner. Grief weighs her down.

My heart aches for her, even as my mind races with possibilities. Here, right in front of me, is someone who has insight into Laurel's life throughout the affair and her mindset leading up to the day she supposedly jumped from the cliffs.

Don't do it.

What sort of a bitch am I? Bothering a woman who lost her only child about said child seems distasteful. But finding out what Vicki knows could be crucial. It could catch a killer.

My better judgment loses out. My feet are already propelling me to the counter. I have to talk to her. This worry can't continue. Maybe she holds some insight into Laurel's state of mind in those final days. Did she know her daughter was spiraling? Did she suspect anything about an affair? If so, did she know it was with Thad?

As I push my morals down, my stomach twists. I need to tread carefully. She's been through enough without me dredging up painful memories. I want to stop, but I can't.

It seems I'm quite a bitch.

The feeling that I'm on the verge of uncovering something important is strong. Something that could change everything I thought I knew about Laurel's death.

And somewhere buried deep in my subconscious, there's a nagging feeling that I'm missing something crucial. Something about Laurel.

Every time I try to grasp it, it slips away. I should probably go reread all those Instagram messages.

Vicki's eyes meet mine, and there's a flicker of recognition.

"Vicki, Mrs. Hackert, I'm..."

"I know who you are." Her voice is flat.

She knows. It's clear as day. She knows about the whole sordid debacle. Why didn't it come out? Why didn't she tell anyone?

"You're the doctor's wife."

Resentment bubbles up at being known only in relation to the cheating scumbag. It hardens my resolve. "Mrs. Hackert, could I ask you a question about Laurel, if that's all right?"

Vicki stiffens, her shoulders tensing visibly. Her color fades even more. After a moment's hesitation, she gives a curt nod. "Go ahead."

I keep my voice as gentle as possible, even though I'm excited to have this chance. "This might be difficult, but did you believe Laurel was suicidal at the time of her death? Did you suspect the fall was due to something else?"

Vicki's face hardens, her eyes flashing with a mix of pain and anger. "My daughter was in a very dark place. She killed herself." Her voice is firm and unwavering. "There's no question about that."

"You seem very certain," I press, wanting to shut up but unable to help myself. "Why are you so sure?"

Her eyes widen with pain. "Because I know where my daughter was at." Her voice cracks. "She'd been mistreated." She raises an eyebrow, letting me know it was Thad's fault and that she knows I know he was to blame. It's hard to look her in the eyes, to witness her pain. There's guilt there too.

Shit, to lose a kid? I can't imagine. "Laurel made mistakes. She was in a dark place. She killed herself. Now just let it go."

Searching her face, I look for any hint of doubt, any flicker of uncertainty. There's just a deep, hollow sadness—the kind of grief that only a mother who's lost everything can carry.

I'm about to ask more.

Her eyes narrow as she regards me with newfound suspicion. "I'm not entirely sure why the doctor's wife is asking these things. And I'd prefer not to say any more about my daughter."

"I—"

"But I will say one thing." She lowers her voice even more. "I know that Laurel was seeing your husband for well over a year. Mothers don't miss these things." Her gaze sharpens. "And wives don't either, do they? That's probably why you're so interested in a random dead island girl, right?"

My throat aches. I try to speak, but nothing comes out.

"But," Vicki adds, her words short, clipped, as if she's having to fight for control, "it's for the best that we never speak of this again. For everyone involved."

Still reeling, I can only nod mutely.

"Let my daughter rest in peace. The doctor and the doctor's wife can at least give Laurel that much, considering I've kept the entire despicable nightmare to myself."

Why? Why didn't she tell anyone? Was it to protect Laurel's reputation? I would scream it from the rooftops if this had been Grace.

A blast of warmth covers me as Marco returns with Vicki's pizzas. The smell of melted cheese and tomato sauce seems out of place against the heavy atmosphere between the two of us.

"Here you go, Mrs. Hackert." Marco's oblivious to the tension. "Two large pepperonis, just as you ordered."

Vicki turns away from me, her face smoothing into a

polite mask as she pulls out her wallet, the leather worn and creased. She counts out the bills carefully.

Taking the boxes from Marco, she balances them in her arms, turns, and walks out without another backward glance. Her dismissal is clear and cutting.

I'm frozen. She knew, and she said nothing.

CHAPTER
THIRTY-TWO

My head whirls as I navigate the snowy roads of Cape Fleur Island, heading to my office to check on the mail and review a few designs. The events at Marco's pizzeria have left a sick feeling in my stomach.

Vicki Hackert's words spin in my mind like a broken record. She kept calling me "the doctor's wife," and the disdain in her tone was unmistakable. She must hate me, hate both of us. I understand. If Laurel had been my daughter, I would want to rip Thad's balls off. If I thought his wife knew, would I hate her too, or would I pity her?

I can't make my mind go there. Losing a child like that is almost unfathomable. What if this had been Grace, sometime in the future, groomed by an older man? Manipulated by him. Abused by him.

Am I taking this too far? Was it abuse?

Laurel would've argued that she knew what she was doing, that she went into the affair with eyes open, but did she? He charmed her, and she believed him. Believed he would leave his family.

It's a story as old as time.

She was pushed to suicide while he still swans around the island like the world is his oyster. And she was a child. Technically a legal adult when she died, but the age and power disparity is unconscionable.

If this happened to my daughter, I'd be bitter. Unlike Vicki, I'd want him to pay. I'd want the whole island to know what he did. Why doesn't she?

Yet this is the answer I wanted. Vicki believes Laurel killed herself. If that's true, all my worry has been for nothing. I dreamed up Thad as a killer who pushed Laurel from the cliff to stop her from talking. If he killed Laurel, my logic insists he could've killed Maggie to solve another problem.

And if he killed them both, it's my fault. The only reason he had to silence them was because I found out.

Only now, I can see how crazy I've been acting. A fake suicide was one thing. Stabbing a woman to death behind our house is quite another. And Thad didn't kill Laurel. She killed herself. Why would he kill Maggie?

My mind won't let it go. Laurel died because Thad couldn't keep it in his pants. It will be a cold day in hell before I can forgive that.

But this changes my thinking. I've been working toward believing Thad killed two people. None of it is true. The two deaths must be a coincidence.

And who knows what other kinds of men Maggie hooked up with?

One of her biker lovers could've been following her. If they saw Thad leave the party and climb in her car, saw them kissing, that could have enraged them.

And the woods out back were the perfect place for a scorned lover to kill her, especially if they wanted to frame Thad. Maybe even Manny would've been driven over the edge if he saw his mom like a teenager in her car with a married man.

But the police would've seen them, unless the murderer cased the area and knew where the cameras were. That is the heart of the matter—the reason I keep coming back to Thad. Who else would know how to avoid the cameras?

My head throbs with theories and endless questions.

I flick on my turn signal to change lanes and glance in my rearview mirror. Behind me, some asshole is following too close for comfort. An old black Mustang is right on my tail, its headlights glaring off my windshield.

"Back off, asshole," I growl through gritted teeth, resisting the urge to brake check and teach him a lesson.

My shoulders ache as I tense up while spending more time looking back than forward. Doesn't he realize how treacherous these mountain roads are, especially with the icy conditions? One wrong move, and we could both end up wrapped around a tree or plummeting down a ravine.

The headlights are so close, they're blinding me.

"Just back off, dammit."

As the parking lot of Cooper LaRue Design comes into view, I breathe a sigh of relief. The tailgater zooms past. Some people have no regard for safety.

Inside my office, I stare at the stack of projects on my desk, overwhelmed and distracted. The room, usually my little oasis of creativity, feels like it's closing in on me. My perfectly curated space—sleek modern furniture, bold splashes of color—mocks me with the clutter that's built up.

My prized drafting table, a beautiful piece of reclaimed wood and steel, sits unused in the corner. Rolls of blueprints and design sketches are scattered across its surface, projects I should be excited about but can't bring myself to focus on. The soft hum of my high-end computer, usually a soothing background noise, makes my nerves thrum like a badly tuned violin.

My mind is like a monkey on speed, constantly jumping

back to Thad, Laurel, and the sordid affair that Vicki apparently knew about all along. Why didn't I see what was happening right under my nose? Unlike the young woman's mother, I didn't know. I had my suspicions and worries, but I kept dismissing them as nothing.

Not until close to the end did I start playing detective. Only when I trailed Thad like some paranoid psycho did the truth hit me—hard, fast, messy—like a house of cards collapsing in a hurricane.

The irony isn't lost on me. Here I am, a successful designer known for my keen eye and attention to detail, but I missed the glaring deceit in my own home. It makes me want to laugh and cry at the same time.

Deep down, I knew something was off, but I shoved those doubts aside, burying them beneath layers of denial and false hope. He wouldn't cheat, I told myself over and over. We had a good marriage, didn't we? He loved me—at least, that was what I convinced myself. What a damn fool I was, clinging to that comforting little lie like it was a designer throw pillow that made everything appear perfect.

Looking back now, all the warning signs were there, but I chose to ignore them. The late nights at the clinic, the way he'd become distant and distracted. I'd chalked it all up to the stress of a busy doctor, convincing myself things would get better. But they never did. Instead, the cracks in our relationship only widened, finally shattering when I followed Thad and caught him in her arms.

Closing my eyes, I fight back tears as I remember all the times I defended him to friends and family who expressed concern.

"He's just busy."
"We're going through a rough patch, but we'll work it out."

How pathetic I must've sounded. Desperate to maintain the perfect marriage until my suspicions goaded me into following him. The shame of not seeing it burns. The shame that Vicki saw it humiliates me.

After an hour of accomplishing absolutely nothing, I give up. Maybe some caffeine will clear my head. Grabbing my coat, I head for the Bean Dock.

The warm aroma of freshly brewed coffee envelops me as the doors slide open. Forgoing my usual half-caf latte, I order a double shot of espresso because, damn, I need it today. Waiting for my drink, I move to the window, my attention drawn to a car parked outside.

"What the…" It's the same old black Mustang that was riding my ass. The driver is staring right at me, his gaze intense and unsettling. I squint, trying to make out his features. Scraggly red hair, angry eyes.

It's Manny Donovan. Maggie's son.

Our gazes lock. I want to run, to hide. Why is he following me?

Manny raises his hand and flips me off. With another sneer, he backs out of his spot and drives away, leaving me standing at the window with my mouth agape.

"Ma'am? Your coffee." The barista's voice snaps me back to reality.

I grab my drink, fingers unsteady, mind racing. Was Manny following me? Stalking me? No doubt he's still pissed about my drop-in at his house. The memory of his accusation rings in my ears.

"I bet you fucking killed my mom."

Is he out for revenge? I remember how he thanked me for it. He's a psycho, everyone said so, and he's a person of interest in Maggie's murder. If he killed his own mother, what's to stop him from coming after me?

CHAPTER
THIRTY-THREE

As I hurry back to my car, I examine the lot, half expecting Manny to jump out, flailing a bloody knife, but there's no old black Mustang, just families enjoying the night.

Manny's gone.

I slide into the driver's seat. Even so, I can't shake the feeling of being watched.

The drive home is tense. Every car in my rearview feels like a potential threat. Maybe it's just a coincidence. Maybe Manny just happened to be at the coffee shop at the same time as me. He saw me, and like a kid, he had to show his rage.

A black car changes lanes behind me. My nerves thrum. I crane my neck and swerve a little. "Hold it together." It's not close. It's too new. It's not him.

I ask the car to call the sheriff and tap my fingers on the wheel as it dials. It takes forever. *Ring, ring, ring.*

"Cape Fleur Sheriff's Office. How may I help you?"

"My name is Cooper LaRue. Can I speak to Sheriff White? It's urgent."

I imagine Manny sneaking into my house, shouting,

"Someone really needed to end that whore," as he plunges the knife into me again and again.

I see him stabbing me ferociously, blood flying over his face and clothes. His psychotic sneer, dripping in my blood beneath that scraggly red hair...

A horn screams, and I realize I've drifted from my lane. Hauling the wheel back, I skid on the ice before I'm back on the road. "Dammit. Keep it together."

"I'm sorry. Sheriff White's not available. If you need urgent help, you should speak to Deputy Byer. Shall I connect you to him?"

My throat is dry. Did she hear my outburst? "No, thank you. I'll contact him myself." Why didn't I think of Byer? No way is Manny getting past him. I'm safe.

Just chill.

Close to home, the street looks desolate. With the cold weather and the holidays, many of our neighbors are away. Only a few houses have lights on. It's like some apocalypse movie.

Though many houses sport Christmas lights, they don't thrill me like in other years. Driving down with the kids, them oohing and aahing at each new display, was always a holiday highlight. Now it all seems staged. There's more darkness than light. Manny could sneak down here without being seen. He wouldn't even need to sneak too hard.

By the time I pull into my driveway, my palms are clammy, whether from my almost crash or the fear of Manny, I'm not sure. The sight of Deputy Byer's marked SUV steadies my nerves. He's here, reliable, ever watchful. There's nothing to worry about. He waves as I drive past and park in front of the garage.

The house looms above me, big and hostile, with endless places to hide. The garage door opens, and I pull in. There are countless windows, so many nooks and crannies where a deranged psycho could gain entrance.

"Stop it!"

My mood is all over the place. One minute, I feel safe—the next, I'm terrified. Deputy Byer's been my constant shadow since Maggie's murder. I need to trust him.

Approaching his vehicle, I tap on the window. He rolls it down, his boyish face looking up at me expectantly.

"Deputy Byer, would you mind coming inside? There's something I need to discuss."

He nods, following me into the house. In the kitchen, I turn to face him, taking a deep breath.

"What is it, Mrs. La...Cooper?"

Now that he's here, I feel paranoid, like I'm making too much of this, but he's staring at me like an eager puppy. "Manny Donovan's been following me. He tailgated me when I left my office. Then he was outside the coffee shop watching like a creep. And, real classy move, he flipped me off before driving away." I cringe at how pathetic that sounds.

His face tightens. "Did he approach you or make any threats?"

"No, but I went over to the Donovans' house yesterday to drop off a casserole. Figured I'd do the neighborly thing. I know what it's like to lose a parent." I rub my temples. Why do we do that? As if a casserole is like some consolation prize. *I know you lost your mom, but here, have this baked dish instead.* Deputy Byer is staring at me, and I realize my mind has drifted. "Only, Manny lost it. Accused me of...of killing his mother."

His brow furrows. "He accused you of murder?"

"Yeah, he went full-on psycho mode. He looked like he wanted to strangle me right there. Told me I was to blame, shoved me, the whole nine yards. Trust me, that guy is...well, he's not right. He was talking about having a knife. I half expected him to pull one from behind his back and come at me." I cross my arms. The memory still makes me uneasy, but I force a shrug to prove I've gotten over it.

"You're worried he might show up here?"

"Yes," I admit, hating how vulnerable that sounds. "I know it's ridiculous, but—"

"It's not ridiculous at all, Mrs. LaRue." His voice is so calm. "But please, don't worry. Like I said before, I've got nowhere else to be. I'm patient and diligent. Manfred Donovan isn't getting anywhere near this house, not while I'm around. You have my word."

Relief washes over me. Sheriff White was right about this kid. He might look like he's barely out of school, but there's a quiet competence about him that makes me feel safe. What's more, he's committed to this case. More than committed. Does he ever pee, eat, or sleep?

"Thank you, Deputy Byer." I manage a small smile. "I appreciate that more than you know." An idea strikes me. "Have you eaten? I'm about to make dinner. The least I can do is offer you some food for your protection."

He hesitates before nodding. "That'd be nice, Cooper. Thank you."

"Great. Sit. I'll get coffee and have something ready in no time."

I'm in full-on multitask mode, tossing pasta in the pot and dicing garlic like I'm on *Chopped* and trying to beat the clock. "So the whole casserole thing...I thought I was doing the right thing. After Maggie died. I figured Samantha Donovan, she's just seven, you know? I figured it could offer comfort. Food's supposed to be like that." I click my tongue, realizing I'm overexplaining. "Maybe I'm projecting my own shit. Losing my mom...I don't know. It was just instinct."

Deputy Byer responds with a thoughtful hum.

I glance over at him, stirring the sauce. "What about your family? You got people, Deputy Byer?"

My phone rings on the counter.

"Brent. Please call me Brent." He's got that look, the one that tells me not to go there, but I've already pried the door open, so why not push?

It's Beth. I press Decline. I'll call her later.

"Brent, great. Do you have any family?" I raise my eyebrows.

"Only child." His gaze is on the floor.

Throwing in a pinch of salt, I keep stirring. "Only child, huh? Me too. It can be lonely sometimes." My phone buzzes again. A text from Beth.

Hey, girl! Just heard about crazy Manny Donovan and your chicken Divan shower. Tell me you weren't wearing your black gabardine? I'll kill the kid myself if he wrecked it. Seriously...don't hesitate to call if you need anything. ANYTHING. I mean it! Xoxo.

A small smile tugs at the corners of my mouth. She has to know about Thad. I want to text back, but the deputy's speaking, and he deserves my attention.

"Yeah, well, my parents passed when I was young." For a second, something flickers across his face. Grief, or maybe just exhaustion.

My hand stills on the spoon. "I get it. I lost my mom when I was ten. I can't imagine losing both of them."

"It was rough, but my grandparents raised me." There's a hint of sadness in his voice. "They were amazing, but they're gone now too. My grandma passed a couple of years ago. I miss her a lot."

Setting down the spoon, I turn to him. His young face is etched with a grief that seems too old for his years, and something else too. Anger. It makes sense. He's had it rough. "I'm so sorry. I can't imagine how hard that must be for you."

He shrugs, offering a small smile that doesn't reach his eyes. "No need to be sorry. My past just made me stronger. It's why I became a cop. To help others, to make a difference. To make sure the ones who hurt people get what they deserve."

"I get that." I toss the pasta into a bowl. "I appreciate you doing all this. But is there anyone special in your life? Someone keeping you grounded?"

His face turns beet red, and I nearly laugh out loud. "There was, but it didn't work out."

"Figures. All the good ones are taken or too busy chasing bad guys." I bite my lip. Was that me? Has Thad turned out to be one of those bad guys?

He laughs, seeming a little embarrassed but maybe a little relieved too. I want to ask more, but the meal is ready, and I get the feeling it's too soon for him to talk. Maybe when this is all over, I can introduce him to someone. Who might I know?

As we dig into the pasta, Brent opens up a little more, his earlier stiff formality melting away. "I'm not going to let some little idiot like Manny bother you." There's such confidence that it makes me feel guilty for worrying. His voice softens. "But I get it, his anger. His grief. Teens lash out. They're all emotions and no common sense. I can handle him. No worries."

Nodding, I twirl my fork into the spaghetti. "I believe you." And I do. For someone who looks like he'd get age checked to rent a car, Brent's got this weirdly calm intensity about him. He doesn't swear, and he's always polite, but there's a fire when he talks about justice. Like it's not just a job but a calling.

And I bet he never sent anyone a pic of his dick.

Sheesh, where did that come from?

"So what do you do for fun? When you're not saving damsels in distress?"

His ears turn pink, and he looks down at his plate.

"Honestly? I guess I'm all in for my career right now. I have a plan. I've been working on it for some time. Since I lost my grandma."

"A plan, huh?" I'm genuinely interested. "Sounds mysterious."

He shrugs like it's no big deal. "It's just something I've been working toward for a while. To advance my career, so I can make my grandma proud. You know, college, police academy, get a job on the force. I have a few more steps, hopefully leading to detective. Once I get through them, maybe I'll relax a bit."

Intrigued, I tilt my head. It's nice to see someone so committed to their career. "What happens when you reach the end? You take up golf? Start a stamp collection? Become sheriff?"

He lifts his arms. "Maybe. I guess it sounds foolish."

"No, and I know your grandma would be proud of you. Just don't forget to live along the way. Trust me. Work can't be your whole life."

A nerve twitches in his right eye, and he glances away. "Yeah, I guess. But I've got a few more steps to go before I'm ready to ease up. I'll get there when I get there. You know?"

"Hey, I hear you. Just don't wait too long. Life doesn't wait around for you to finish your steps."

Beth's familiar rap on the door rings through the house.

"I should check that." Brent is already on his feet.

"It's okay. It's my friend. I recognize her knock." We both arrive at the door, and he opens it first, a hand on his weapon that moves as soon as Beth breezes past him.

"Give me a hug." Beth pulls me into her arms. Pulling back, she nods at the deputy, her eyes widening a little. "The man of the hour, looking sharp in that uniform, but I bet you'd look even better out of it."

Brent's face turns red again, and his ears glow. He shakes

his head as he backs out the door. "Gotta get back to work, ladies."

"Thanks, Brent."

Beth pulls me into the living room and plops onto the couch, patting the spot next to her. "Damn, he's good looking. A little young but yummy." She wiggles her eyebrows, and I elbow her.

"Seriously, Beth." I try to look stern as I take a seat. "It's great to see you."

"What? Don't pretend you didn't notice Mr. Hotty." She grabs my hand.

"He's too young for me."

"So tell me what happened. Tell me about Thad."

I raise my hands. "Not going there tonight."

"Okay. I understand, but I'm here." She moves a little closer, bumping shoulders before leaning back, still holding my hand. "But how are you really?"

A heavy sigh escapes, but that's it.

"You need anything, to shout and scream, someone to punch him, to slash his shirts and throw them out the window...I'm here, okay?"

"I don't know. One second, it's like I've got it all under control, and the next, everything is unraveling."

"You should've called. You know that, right?"

I squeeze her hand. "Didn't want to spoil Christmas. How are the kids?"

"Stuffed and spoiled. I needed a break. I practically sprinted out the door to get here. So let's grab a bottle." She gives me a conspiratorial smile. "We can just gossip and bitch. Whatever you need."

We talk for an hour. I don't go into details about Laurel, but it feels so good to have someone on my side. Someone who understands. When she gets up to leave, I almost beg her to stay, but pride stops me.

The door clicks shut, and the house is too quiet. It's that weird feeling—like I'm forgetting something, but I can't figure it out. Like I've left the stove on, or maybe it's the memories I can't quite put my finger on.

My gaze keeps drifting toward the junk drawer. The familiar pull of the oxy tugs at the edges of my resolve. It would be so easy. But I stop myself. I'll delay for now. I have to start cutting down. Maybe I can do that now. After all, with Brent outside, I can sleep safely, assuming I can sleep at all.

But first, I need to talk to my kids.

CHAPTER
THIRTY-FOUR

I pick up the phone, my fingers hovering before dialing. It rings twice before the unmistakable pandemonium comes through the line.

"Mom." Elias's voice is a mix of joy and that *I miss you, but I'm trying to be cool* vibe.

"Hi, sweetie." I force cheerfulness that's almost more than I can muster. "How are you and Grace doing?"

"Mom, Mom, Mom." Grace's screeches are accompanied by a grunt from Elias. Yep, she elbowed him, so he put the phone on speaker.

"Love you both." I cling to the phone, knowing that whatever comes next will be pure bedlam.

And there it is—both of them talking over each other. I catch snippets about missing home, wanting to see Daddy, and how Grandpa's cooking is one step above school cafeteria food. It hurts. I want them home, but that's not happening until it's safe.

"I know it's hard, babies," I soothe. "But you need to stay with Grandpa a little longer. Mommy and Daddy are working on some grown-up stuff."

"Mom, really, we can be really quiet." Elias's voice hits that pitch where he's going into negotiation mode.

"As mices," Grace adds.

Elias scoffs. "Mice."

"Listen, sweeties. It's just for a little while."

"I miss my room, my nightlight, you reading to us, and your hugs." Grace is clearly aiming for a full emotional hit.

"I miss home too."

Great, now they're tag teaming me.

"I miss you more than I can say. But this is the holidays. You're with Grandpa. You're having fun, aren't you?"

"Yes," they answer in unison, but with the enthusiasm of kids agreeing to eat vegetables.

I'm the world's worst mom. I want to bring them home, but I can't. Not with all that's going on with Thad and now with Manny lurking like a horror-movie villain. And there's a killer out there somewhere. If the killer isn't Thad or Manny.

Nope, too dangerous.

"There you go. Treat it as a little vacation and have fun."

Their disappointment is palpable. There's a lump in my throat as I hear my dad's voice take over.

"Okay, kids. Go play while I talk to your mom."

Groans are followed by the door closing.

"Cooper? What's going on out there?"

Oh, you know, the usual. My husband's a cheat. I'm being stalked by a deranged teenager. I've somehow managed to screw my life up so bad that leaving sounds like the only option.

But I can't dump that on him.

It would be so nice to talk to someone. But I didn't even lay all this on Beth, and she's my best friend. I can't lay it all on Dad either. I have to tell him something, but not too much.

"Dad, Manny Donovan, the son of Maggie, the woman who was killed...he's been following me. He...he's angry about his mom's death."

So much for not worrying him.

"What in the actual hell? Cooper. Pack up and come back to the mainland. You'll be safe here, and the kids will love it."

"I can't. I have to deal with this mess. Take my life back."

There's frustration in the heavy breath he draws. I don't mention that nagging voice taunting me with the fact that someone else knows the ugly truth about who I'm shackled to. The sheer embarrassment of it.

His sigh feels like a full-body eye roll. "At least you've got that deputy outside, right? And the...you know. The item I loaned you." He doesn't want to say *gun* with the kids nearby.

Out the window, snowflakes drift lazily to the ground. Brent's SUV is covered, but the windshield remains clear. Does he ever take any time off? He seems to be in that vehicle 24-7.

"Yeah. The snow reminds me of Mom. Of that night." The words are like lumps in my throat. I didn't want them to come out, yet here they are.

Steady. Next, you'll be blurting out that you think Thad killed two women.

The line goes quiet. I imagine him tiptoeing around the next words. "Cooper..." His voice is as soft as air.

"I was so upset when the play ended." The memories flood back, angry and raw. "Mom didn't come. And you walked out in the middle of 'Winter Wonderland.' I didn't know what to do. I was so embarrassed, so hurt, so selfish."

"Honey, you were just a child."

My younger self was confused and on the verge of tears. "When it was over, I ran outside, ready to chew you out for ruining my concert...but you were crying. Miss Carter, too, and there was a police officer. You scooped me into your arms and held me."

"I remember."

My voice catches. "I asked what was wrong and where

Mom was. And then you said…you said, 'Mommy's been in an accident, Coop. Mommy's passed away.'"

"That's when you started screaming. I'll never forget it." His voice cracks.

I nod, even though he can't see me. "Yeah, I remember that scream. It felt like it was tearing me apart. But the silent scream after…when I learned Mom was rushing from work for my stupid play…that's the part that's been harder to block out all these years." Tears are flowing freely now. "I'm sorry, Dad. We lost Mom because of me."

"Cooper, no." His voice is back to full strength, almost hard. "It wasn't your fault. It was never your fault."

"But—"

"Coopie. I need to tell you something important." His voice is strong now, no sign of hesitation. "I never realized you were blaming yourself just like I was. You never showed it."

My throat aches as I listen, squeezing the phone tighter.

"All those years, I was drowning in guilt, thinking I pushed her too hard, wishing I'd gotten her a better car, wishing I was there with her." Each word is heavy with regret.

"I thought it was my fault," I whisper. "That I should've done something to stop her."

He sighs, and it spans the years of grief. "No, sweetheart. It was an accident. None of it was your fault, or mine. It took me years to see that, but I'm at peace with it now. I hope you can be too."

It's all too much. I need to shut it down. Grab a drink or something. "I am. I should go. I love you. Kiss the kids for me."

He tells me how much he loves me, how much Mom loved me, and ends the call.

As I hang up, something inside my psyche adjusts. Not some grand epiphany, but a little crack in the darkness. Like someone opened a window to let in a tiny stream of fresh air, making room for cautious relief.

But even though I believe his words, even though it was all those years ago, the guilt doesn't simply pack up and leave. It's still here—fresh, raw, and lingering.

All this time I've been lugging this guilt around, believing my mother's death was somehow my fault, Dad was carrying his own burden. We could've been sharing the damn thing.

Closing my eyes, I remember the countless times I found him lost in thought, his face tight with pain. I always assumed he was just missing Mom and never realized he was battling his own demons.

We should've spoken about it. We would've helped each other.

Staring out at the falling snow, something shifts inside me. The weight of the guilt lifts a little. It doesn't fully let go, but it's not crushing me anymore. For the first time in twenty-four years, I feel lighter.

"It wasn't my fault." The words feel foreign, but there's comfort in them just the same.

Mom. I've spent so long wallowing in the tragedy that I've almost forgotten the good parts.

The way her eyes would crinkle when she laughed. The way her perfume smelled when she hugged me. The way she sang me to sleep.

A memory surfaces. Mom helping me practice for the Christmas play. Her patience as I stumbled over the words, her encouragement when I got them right. The pride in her eyes as she watched me sing.

"*She loved you*," Dad said before we hung up. *"She would've moved heaven and earth to see you perform. That's not something to feel guilty about. That's something to cherish."*

Taking a deep breath, I let it out slowly. The guilt isn't gone completely—I don't think it ever will be—but it's more of a scar now than a gaping wound. A reminder of what I've survived, not a weight crushing my chest.

My gaze falls on her photo on the wall. It was taken just a few months before she died. She's laughing, her head thrown back, full of life. I've always loved this photo, even though it brought a twinge of pain.

Now, looking at it, I feel something different. A warmth spreads through my chest, a mixture of love, longing, and, surprisingly, gratitude. Gratitude for the time I had with her, the love she gave me, and the memories I still carry.

"I miss you, Mom. I'm sorry I've spent so long feeling guilty. I think...I think maybe it's time to let that go."

For the first time in days, I can take a deep breath. Sure, Thad's infidelity, Maggie's murder, and Manny lurking like a shadow are still issues I must face. But unburdened by decades of misplaced guilt, I'm more equipped to face them.

"Good night, Mom. I love you."

Tomorrow's gonna be a whole new circus. I should try to get some sleep, but before that, I have one more call to make. I doubt it will go as well as the last one. But, hey, a girl can dream.

CHAPTER
THIRTY-FIVE

The phone feels heavy as I call my husband. It rings once, twice. I imagine him in bed with some young blond.

"Cooper?" His voice is cautious, wary, with a hint of resignation.

"Thad." My tone is neutral, though I have to clench my jaw to maintain it. "Meet me for coffee tomorrow morning. We need to talk."

All the messages on that Facebook account are seared into my mind. Should I let him know my disgust? That I saw the dick pic? The stupid, pathetic messages he sent to a teenager? Clamping my jaw, I decide against it.

He lets out a heavy sigh. I can almost see him narrow his eyes as he thinks of the best response. The one that will bring me back in line. Not this time, babe.

I know your tricks, and I see through them faster than you can say jailbait.

"That's good. We need to have a rational talk. We can get through this."

I say nothing.

"Cooper?" Thad's voice grows urgent. "I missed you so much. Getting our marriage back is all I'm thinking of."

"We're not at that point yet, but I want to talk." I don't add that I'm considering divorce, settlement, and getting my kids away from him rather than reconciliation. I'm thinking about what he did to get us in this mess.

But hearing his voice, I want to believe. I wish we could go back to a time when none of this had happened. But we can't.

The moment stretches. I'm not giving the answers he wants, and he's probably gritting his teeth, expecting me to play my part and agree with him.

Sorry, hon. This isn't one of your fantasies.

"Listen to me. Don't make any rash decisions. Splitting us up is making a bad situation worse. It was nothing to me, just a game I was playing, a persona." Thad's voice is so calm. The doctor telling the silly patient she's imagining the illness. But I detect agitation. Good.

"A game? A persona?" I want to ask what I was. Another game? Another woman for him to play with until he was bored? I bite back the accusation.

"You know what I mean. Maggie was never important. Not like our family."

Silence.

He clears his throat. "Look, you accepted the affair with Laurel wasn't worth throwing our family away for. Maggie was even less than that. I'd only seen her a couple of times."

Can he hear himself? What do men think when they spew this drivel?

"This changes nothing...and these insane rumors that I killed Maggie Donovan? Ridiculous. You know that. You know me. The most important thing is keeping our family together. Focus on the future." His voice rises a bit. "Dammit, Cooper, the woman isn't even alive anymore. Neither of them is. Don't let them destroy us."

The casual dismissal of two women's lives, women he was intimately involved with, should tell me everything. He's a monster. A charming monster.

"You disgust me. But you know what? I disgust myself more for staying with you. For trusting you."

"Cooper, please—"

"No. I don't want to hear it. Not now. Tomorrow morning, eight, at The Nook." I wonder if he remembers the exchange he had with Laurel about that café or how he told me that it wasn't our kind of place. "Be there, or we're done for good."

"What's this about, Cooper? What are you planning?"

A deep breath steadies everything. The calmness in his voice remains, but there's an edge creeping in. He knows something's shifted, that I'm not gonna roll over and play dead. My plan is to push just enough to get answers. The key will be looking into his eyes when the moment comes.

"This isn't a conversation for over the phone. Meet me or don't, but it's your last chance."

"Honey, let's be grown up about this. Using 'last chance' is just silly. You know I love you. We can do therapy. We can work this out."

So he can sit in front of Sydney and tell her how great everything is? Not anymore. "Therapy! Yeah, that went great. It wasn't supposed to be a gateway to your next affair."

I'm cold inside. Calm, even. Brent walks past the window again. No doubt his head's on a swivel. That's loyal. That's what protection looks like. The comparison to my lying cheat of a husband is stark.

All Thad wants is to keep his reputation. He's just a snake slithering around to protect his image. He doesn't love me. How could he, after what he's done? What would he tell our kids if I ended up dead?

"Don't let it spoil the holidays, kids! She's not even alive."

Unbelievable.

I have to get away from him, but the truth still needs to come out. It's clear that if we ever got back together, he'd jump into another affair as soon as the urge took. Being nice won't stop a coon hound from scenting other bitches, especially those in heat, as Maggie surely was.

I despise the thought, even as it lingers. She's dead. That kind of thinking isn't fair to her memory.

The line is silent. Maybe Thad hung up. Before I can check, his voice comes through, low and strained. "Fine. I'll be there. But let's be adult about this. Have a conversation and work on our problems. Let's look for solutions."

Adult? I can barely keep myself from laughing. I end the call without another word and throw my phone onto the sofa beside me. My revulsion for Thad is overwhelming, but it's nothing compared to the self-loathing that's creeping in. How could I be so blind? How could I stay with a man capable of such callousness?

"The woman isn't even alive anymore. Neither of them is."

Two women, both involved with Thad, are dead. He brushes it off like a piece of lint on his suit. No remorse, no guilt. He sounds as psycho as Manny.

Grabbing a bottle of wine, I stare at the junk drawer. The oxy's calling, but I have a lot to do. I'm unsteady as I uncork the bottle and pour the wine. A pill would help, but not yet. I wander back to his office, his computer, wondering if Thad will confess. Will he lie through his teeth? Or twist the truth just enough to make me doubt myself again, as he's done so many times before?

One thing's for sure—nothing will ever be the same after tomorrow. I intend to look my husband in the eyes when I ask him if he's a murderer.

CHAPTER
THIRTY-SIX

The screen dims, the soft glow a cruel reminder of what I'm about to dive back into. I crack the knuckles of my right hand, the sound echoes in the stillness. This feels like the start of some grim ritual.

Am I feeling trepidation? Sure. But also a shot of pure determination.

Don't cry. Blink back the tears.

There's no time for a breakdown. It's time for the truth, and I'll rip it out, even if it cuts deeper than the jagged rocks on the cliffs where our marriage really ended.

It's my fault for letting it come to this. I should've been stronger. I should've walked away while Laurel was still alive. But hindsight is always a smug little bitch.

Once more, I'm staring at the messages between Thad and Laurel. Scrolling through this disgusting saga of deceit. The plan is simple—save them as evidence. Copy them to a thumb drive and hand them to the sheriff.

The only problem? Thad, the charming snake, doesn't say anything incriminating. There are threats, but none are violent. However, they paint a pretty nasty picture. Enough to rip that golden medical license from his hand. That'll sting, and he deserves it. His patients deserve better than a predator in a white coat.

It's a mammoth task, like shoveling through a sewer. I start at the end with the most damning messages, the ones they exchanged after he'd supposedly broken up with her but just before she died. The ones in which she threatened him, in which she didn't seem suicidal. In which he was sweating over his reputation, his perfect life. That's motive.

But I want to get those first messages too. The ones in which the young, innocent, and naive girl—his patient—tells him it's fine for him to screw a teenager.

Each scroll and click makes me despise him more. Soon, my wrist aches. The wine hasn't dulled my senses enough. My pain is raw and visceral, and I know if I saw Laurel now, I would fly at her like an animal.

Am I any better than him? As I scroll and click, scroll and click, I wonder. Could I have been pushed to solve our most recent problem? Could anything push me to take a life to save my marriage?

No, I would never.

But Thad could. Not to save the marriage but to save the LaRue reputation. That perfection and standard they live by. He would never let the affair come out and take his precious career.

He'd kill for that. I'm sure.

These messages won't prove he murdered Laurel. Far from it. But each screenshot tells a story. His lover, the one who was threatening him, is dead under shady circumstances. That shines a light on Maggie's murder. Once a cheater, always a cheater. One dead problem lover is a coincidence, but two is a pattern. And patterns get noticed.

Armed with only his computer and a bottle of merlot, I keep going. The wine flows faster than my sanity. Tears hit the mouse, making my fingers slip and my vision blur. Great, now I'm drunk and tech challenged. Perfect.

Many of the messages are tame enough. *Missed you today. Can we meet later?*

Love you, my little Lorelei.
Can't wait to see my Dr. Love.

I shudder at the memory of the dick pic, the wine suddenly bitter.

"Oh, yeah, Coop, you're really hanging onto that 'strong woman' title right now." Instead of strength, I feel like I'm unraveling, one screenshot at a time. "You need this. You need it to take him down."

The freight train of revulsion hits. Their banter—so disgustingly intimate, dripping with secrets shared and boundaries crossed.

"What the hell were you thinking, Thad?" My once-loving husband is neck deep in this sordid mess.

I scroll and copy, message after message.

After what feels like hours, I've captured every single wretched detail. This won't just shine a light on Thad. It will condemn him. There's no way around it. I don't care. He did this, not me.

Sure, he'll lose the practice, but so what? He never needed the money. As callous as it sounds, I'll be okay. I earn enough to live here. Or, hell, I could pack up and go back to the mainland. That would mean starting over, but with Dad's help, I could do it.

I scan the screen, the chair creaking beneath me, and a twisted sense of accomplishment flickers inside. I just might have the ammunition to blow his perfect little world to smithereens.

But here's the kicker. If Thad tries to flip the script, tries to gaslight his way out of this, I'll be ready. Maybe I'll record our meeting. The thought makes me flinch. What if he admits something? What if he confesses to making Laurel "disappear?" To Maggie's murder? A chill slithers down my spine. Thad might not say anything specific, but any slip of the tongue could point to his involvement.

"It's just you and me, Thad." Sarcasm drips as I mock the vows we took all those years ago. The more I think about it, the more I realize my life, our kids' lives are hanging by a damn thread, and he's the one with the scissors.

With a sudden adrenaline rush, I grab my phone and open the voice-note app. My fingers hesitate over the button. Could I do this in my pocket? I think so.

I hit record. This will be my proof, my insurance policy, my ace in the hole. "I'll give you one chance, dearest husband. One chance to tell me the truth."

I play back the recording. It's faint but clear enough. This'll work.

Once this is over, I'm done with Cape Fleur Island, done with the lies, done with living with a man who can't choose loyalty over temptation. The kids deserve better than this. They'll go to school on the mainland, close to my dad. We'll make new friends, new routines. It'll be a fresh slate as they navigate their new lives, free of their father's indiscretions.

I might not know how to heal from this disaster or whether healing is even possible, but I do know one thing. I'm not letting him screw up the kids the way he screwed up everything else.

After this, I'll be sober, and I'll dedicate my life to seeing them thrive.

My body aches. The bottle is empty, and the sharp pangs of anxiety are strong. Thad thinks I'm a drug-addled mess. My quaking limbs tell me he's right. I need to stop. To give up the pills and stop the bottle-a-night habit.

But quitting cold turkey? No, thanks. I'm not about to add hospitalization to my list of problems.

Instead, I'll target just one pain pill at a time. I split it into quarters, like a prisoner cutting their meager rations. Three of those quarters go down with water, my hand twitching for that second bottle of wine. I hope this compromise will be enough to maintain my buzz just a little longer—while at the same time starting on the journey to sobriety.

In our walk-in, I lay out my clothes for tomorrow. A white blouse, a blue cashmere sweater, a blazer, and black trousers.

Will he threaten me or kill me? I won't be afraid. I'm not that woman. Not anymore. I won't let him control me. This marionette is done dancing to his twisted whims.

Reaching into the case I brought back from my dad's, I pull out his revolver and tuck it into my jacket pocket. Its cold weight promises I won't become another solved problem of Thaddeus LaRue.

CHAPTER
THIRTY-SEVEN

The Nook is warm, filled with the rich aroma of brewing coffee. It's eight o'clock sharp, and while the world outside might as well be in a snow globe—all fluffy, white post-Christmas cheer—I'm stuck in a parallel universe.

One wherein sobriety is a cruel joke, and the idea of hope feels like grasping at vapors.

I woke with the flu, only I know it's not. The headache is sharp, threading its way from the base of my skull to my temples. The usual morning fog feels thicker today, like my thoughts are wading through syrup. Cutting down the pill was supposed to help me feel clearer, more in control, but right now, all it's done is strip away the buffer, leaving me raw and exposed.

As I shuffle to a booth by the window, my stomach twists as I think about Laurel sitting there, playing out an imaginary date with her married lover. And I hate to admit it, but this is exactly the kind of place I used to frequent before I became Mrs. LaRue.

My pulse thumps in my ears like a bad drum solo. The gun is heavy in my pocket, and I instantly regret bringing it. What am I? Some secret agent? A headline flashes through my brain. *Jealous Wife Gunned Down by Police for Bringing Firearm into Local Café.*

Is it even legal to conceal carry in the state of Maine? I probably should've googled that.

The sunlight is too bright. Squinting, I drop onto the vinyl seat. My head's post-wine-and-oxy throb is worse than usual, and there's a fine sheen of sweat on my skin. That and the tremors in my fingers remind me that cutting back on the pills is going to be a rough ride.

Glancing at the menu, I consider breakfast, but it's a performance, just like this whole damn morning. I order the standard—eggs, toast, and, of course, coffee. My stomach cramps, unable to face the food. "Just one more thing to waste." The server raises an eyebrow, but I'm too caught up in my own misery to worry if she thinks I'm rude.

I touch the phone in my pocket. Check that I can go to record without looking. It's easy. I pull it out.

Yep, recording. Leave the mother running. He'll be here soon.

The coffee arrives hot and steaming. I take the first sip, willing it to somehow make my headache go away. But nope, it's just as bitter as my mood. *Great choice, Cooper.* Thad's about five minutes late now, and I'm already shredding my dreams of what was supposed to be a "grown-up" conversation.

Time stretches, bending painfully as I sip my coffee, push my eggs around the plate, and run my fingers along the cool surface of the table. Where is he? My mind drifts back to last night, to the messages I painstakingly documented. Laurel Hackert knew far too much, and her parting threats hung like a noose around Thad's neck.

Not that he sees it that way. He never takes responsibility for anything except the good bits—the public persona, the compliments about his medical successes, all the shiny coins that keep his little world spinning.

After another glance at the clock, I tap my heel to ease some of the tension building in me. Where is he? Ten minutes becomes thirty, and it feels like a damn lifetime. "This isn't happening."

I yank out my phone and call Thad. Each ring is like a personal insult—another reminder that he's somewhere else, anywhere but here. I try his office phone, his hotel room. Nothing.

"Piece of shit."

A few heads swivel my way.

The heat in my chest boils over as rage blooms like a violent flower. If people weren't staring at me, I'd kick this table across the room.

Another thirty minutes pass. I'm tweaking like a junkie, unable to sit still.

Finally, I stand to leave, my foot tapping angrily on the tiled floor, when my phone buzzes in my pocket. I fumble to answer, and the caller ID stops me dead—Sheriff White. Great. Just what I need.

"Cooper? This is Sheriff White." Her voice is steady but heavy, like she's about to drop a bomb.

"What?" I've no patience left for pleasantries. I'm beyond niceties at this point.

"Thad's been attacked. He was beaten badly last night, knocked unconscious by a masked assailant. He was found in the hotel parking garage."

For a second, the world spins. I see his face and want to run to him. "Is he...?"

"He'll be okay."

Of course he is. Thad's a cockroach—nothing really takes him down. But I can't help the flicker of fear, the tightening of my chest at the thought of him in a hospital bed. The thought of telling the children he's gone.

"Where is he?" My voice carries an edge of concern I can't quite stop. The urge to run to him—to tell him I'm sorry, to forgive—is strong.

"Island Medical Hospital. They're treating him for a concussion, among other injuries. He wants to see you. Given the circumstances, I won't blame you if you don't come."

"No, no, I'm on my way."

I hang up. I was fired up to confront him, to blow his world apart with the messages, the threats from Laurel, everything. But now he's lying in a hospital bed, and despite all that's happened, my stupid heart still gives a damn. I hate that it does.

Throwing some cash on the table, I bolt out of the café.

Pulling into the parking lot of Island Medical Hospital, I'm a mix of nerves and adrenaline. I toss the gun in the glove box. Why did I even bring it? I'm pretending I'm some action hero. *Real smart, Coop.*

Each step across the lot feels heavy. My head swims from last night's lack of indulgence. Could just a quarter pill less make me feel so out of it?

Focus.

Thad's inside, likely lying in a hospital bed and milking the "poor me" routine. But he *is* hurt, bad enough to be in hospital. If they hadn't found him, he could have died, lying there all night.

The smell of antiseptic greets me as the doors sweep aside, and my heels click sharply against the tiled floor. The hustle of nurses and doctors blends with the muted tones of worried relatives. Everything about the scene screams to stay alert.

I'm marching toward some twisted version of judgment day as I make my way to the reception desk.

"Cooper," Sheriff White calls out. Turning, I find her striding toward me. "I need to speak with you."

Great, just what I need—a lecture. Will she see the state I'm in? Realize I'm an addict? "I'm not here to make small talk." That was sharper than I intend. Her eyes widen.

Steady, Cooper. You could skewer Thad with that kind of attitude.

"This is serious." She drops her voice. "Thad's injuries were surprisingly mild. It's raised some red flags. I have a deputy outside his room, but something about it doesn't feel right."

My patience is thinning. "What do you mean? He got beat up, maybe by an angry husband, bad enough to be admitted. It seems straightforward to me."

She shakes her head. "He did get beaten up...it's just a feeling. It looks like a simple beating, a bad one, but it could have been so much worse. He could be playing the victim to gain sympathy, from you especially. You have to consider that."

The words land heavily. "So you think this is all a charade?" This doesn't make sense coming from her. From me, sure, but not from the sheriff.

Following her along the hallway to Thad's room, I keep my mind on today's purpose. I'm not here to make him feel good but to get answers. The fluorescent lights blur. I need a drink. Way to go in front of the sheriff.

"There's nothing that points to that. It's just a hunch." She glances back at me. "Be careful."

We stop in front of a door. A deputy stands to one side, but I can't go in. Not yet. I imagine Thad trying to reel me in with the wounded-puppy act. Hoping to draw me back with a flutter of his pretty lashes and an earnest tone. Staged or not staged, he'll use this for sympathy. But I won't fall for it again. Not this time.

Taking a deep breath, I bend forward and press my hands against my knees. A wave of nausea rolls through me, cold sweat beading my forehead as my body protests last night's decision to cut back. I'm done playing the fool in this sick game he thinks is just for the two of us.

"You okay?" The sheriff rubs my back as if I'm a child about to be sick.

I swallow to moisten my dry mouth and nod. "I need a moment." I have to be smart. I can't unleash my fury on him, and I won't let his charm cloud my vision.

"Prepare yourself. He looks bad, with black eyes, a cut on his cheek, and bruises, but we can't rule anything out. Thad is a person of interest in Maggie Donovan's murder. You need to be cautious."

In spite of myself, I snort. "If he staged this attack, he wouldn't risk his face." My nails dig into my kneecaps. Could it be Manny? He came at me. He hates us. He's just a kid.

Forgetting Manny, I wish I'd been the one to mess up Thad's face instead of whoever this mystery assailant is. But I keep that juicy thought to myself. I straighten up to standing and move to the door.

CHAPTER
THIRTY-EIGHT

Pushing open the door to Thad's hospital room, I steel myself for the confrontation ahead.

I've got this. I'll be strong, call him out, and get the answers I deserve. No more playing games. I walk in, expecting to find the usual smug smirk, but what greets me makes my breath catch.

Thad's a mess, black and blue all over. His right eye is swollen shut. He looks like he's been beaten within an inch of his life. I want to rush to him, offer him water, make him soup. It takes all my self-control to not rush to his side and kiss him better.

"Hey, Coop, honey." His voice is slurred, but there it is—the same damn grin I've seen a thousand times. It's like he's trying to charm away his misdeeds. A smile stretches across his battered face. Will the cut on his lip bleed again if he keeps it up?

His charm offensive is already working. I blink back tears and clench my hands at my sides. He's behaving like he just got home from a tough day at the office. Like nothing has happened.

"Looks like...I'm ringing...in the new year in an unforgettable way. Quite a costume, huh?" It's hard for him to speak. With his condition, it's probably hard for him to even think. His eyes are swimmy and unfocused.

Seriously? Take a moment and a breath. Don't run to him, hug him, and tell him it'll be all right.

He's all hurt puppy now, but this won't last. Once he's well, he'll slither off to the next affair quicker than I can pack away my nurse's outfit.

"It's lucky you're able to celebrate at all." My voice comes out sharper than I meant. Seeing him like this, I expected to experience a flicker of satisfaction against the backdrop of my simmering betrayal. Thad finally got some kickback from someone who didn't fall for his smooth smugness. But all I feel is worry for him, fear, and sadness.

Taking a couple of steps closer, I cross my arms defiantly. I will not feel sorry for him. "What happened?"

Thad winces. He thought I'd be an easy mark, but he tries to remain cool. "Just a little mishap." He brushes it off, as if getting his face rearranged is not a big deal.

"Sure." I motion toward his eye. "Looks like someone really worked out their frustration on you. Tell me, was this a passage into the world of husband dodging?"

"It was a robbery, Coop." His tone becomes serious as he shifts in the bed.

My arms twitch to help, but I lock them against me.

"When I came to, my cash and cards were gone from my wallet. They caught me off guard." He stops and sips from a cup with a bendy straw. I want to hold it, to wipe any dribbles, but instead, I tighten my jaw. "Luckily, someone found me."

My eyebrow arches. "Did you recognize the attacker?"

"No. The first blow was from behind." His words are slow, and talking looks painful. "They took me by surprise, and when I did get a look, they were wearing a mask. I couldn't see a thing." He tries to waggle his eyebrows, his sign for *you know what I mean*, a mannerism I've always loved. His bruised face won't comply.

But I don't know what he means. He looks as if we're sharing a joke, the smug bastard. "You were knocked unconscious and then some. Your attacker didn't just steal. He kicked you around for fun, Thad. They beat the shit out of you. This was personal." I look to the door. The deputy is facing away.

Keep cool.

He blinks slowly, pain flickering in his good eye. "Maybe... I don't know. It all happened so fast." He shifts again, and I sense something bubbling beneath his bravado. "Regardless, you wanted to talk about more than just this, right?"

"Damn straight." Here it is—the moment I tell him everything. That I know the real story behind his pathetic charm. I recheck the door, move closer, and lower my voice. "I broke into your secret Instagram account. In your office, on your computer." His eyes widen. He doesn't like that. Tough shit. "I read the messages. All of them." I'm still whispering, but he hears every word.

His smile has slipped, and his battered, bruised face is set between petulance and rage. Now he knows how it feels.

"What messages?"

"Don't play coy. You know exactly what messages I'm talking about. Drlove2021. Laurel Hackert, your young mistress. Your little Lorelei." I've angled myself with my back to the door. I'm close to Thad, my voice low. This is between us and us alone. "The details of your oh-so-charming affair with your teenage patient."

"There are no messages. That's the drugs, honey."

I ball my hand into a fist and barely stop myself from punching his gaslighting face. "I guess the screenshots I captured are all in my mind?"

His Adam's apple bounces. He didn't expect that.

"I'll let the sheriff see them and ask what she thinks." Vicki Hackert's name is on my lips. She knows about the affair. I have corroboration, but I'm gonna keep that tinder dry for a little while longer.

"Let's talk this through." Thad pats the bed and forces a smile. He doesn't like me being one step ahead of him. The color has drained from his face. Except for the bruises and the cuts on his cheek and lip, he's as pale as the sheets he's lying on. And lying is certainly his game.

Stepping closer, I lower my voice even more. No one can hear but him. "I'm still not sure what's more shocking. The fact that you cheated on me or the corny messages you shared about whether your patient was of legal age. I have the full script of your filthy little escapade. It makes for great reading."

"Look, Cooper, I'm so sorry about everything that happened with Laurel. I really didn't know she was that young. She lied about her age." The words are coming fast now, despite the slurring. He comes off a little deranged. Is this how I look when I'm on oxy and wine?

"Really? You couldn't just check her medical chart?"

He keeps going as if I didn't say a word. "I thought she was older. It was a mistake. I swear. I never cared for her. I was just saying those things. It was what she wanted to hear. It was a game." He leans forward, his voice growing earnest as he continues his long list of excuses. "I'm sorry for being weak. She came on to me. She pursued me, but I never loved her. It was always you."

"Games, lies, excuses, Thad." I refuse to let his words take root. "Even if you're telling the truth, do you think that changes anything? You used that poor girl, whether you admit it or not. You betrayed me, the kids, for a teenager."

"There were so many things going on. I was stupid, and I

didn't have the strength to say no. Especially with what was happening with you."

For a moment, I almost feel sorry for him.

Push those emotions down. Don't make it that easy, not this time.

"What was happening with me?" My voice rises. I glance over my shoulder. The deputy doesn't appear to be listening.

"You were day drinking, reckoning you could handle it, but flipping out every time I asked you to cut down. You lost it in front of the kids, mixed wine with oxy like it was nothing. You didn't care about anything...just the next drink." He tries for a concerned expression through his bruises, but it's hard to tell what's real with him.

As I look at him—really look at him—something shifts again. Dammit. I don't know if it's the years of history between us or that he looks so hurt, but my mom mode kicks in. I hate myself but can't help it. I want to soothe him, and for a brief second, I almost forget everything I read last night. But only for a second.

I cross my arms, forcing myself to stay rooted. "That's not what drove you to cheat. The pills started when I hurt my back after I caught you with Laurel. Two years after you started the affair. Two years!"

"You have to accept responsibility if you want to change."

"Do you think I wanted to end up like this?" I'm still trying to keep my voice low, but it's creeping up there. "My fall. I was running away from you, Thad, from your affair. You're a cheating, lying jackass. And you blame me?"

"Look, it was a mistake. I wasn't even sure if you loved me anymore. I told myself I should give you room."

"Give me room by banging a teenager?" I look around. The deputy outside hasn't moved.

"I should've come clean, but I was trying to save our family. Trying to spare you. You would've left me, Cooper, and I hated the idea of our kids growing up in a broken home. I still do. We can fix this. If not for us, for the children."

Every word is an excuse. According to him, none of this is his fault.

Strangely calm, I lean over the edge of the bed and drop my voice to a whisper. "Just two weeks after I confront you, she's dead. She jumped from the cliff top. Or did you kill her?"

A mean look grows in his eyes, and he stares straight at me. "My memories of the last two years are crystal clear. I certainly never killed anyone. Not Laurel. Not Maggie."

"What are you insinuating?"

He just shrugs.

But I know he found me asleep in the car in our driveway the morning after Laurel died. Instead of driving home, I'd taken off. No plan. Just my foot on the gas and my mind stuck on repeat, replaying the scene over and over until I couldn't breathe. At some point, I'd pulled over. I didn't even remember where. I'd just cried until I passed out in the driver's seat.

If Thad hadn't found me, I might've frozen to death. The irony. The man who'd betrayed me saving my life.

Why was I in the car? Was I thinking of leaving him that night but too stoned to drive? And damn, I wish I could remember the night of Maggie's death.

"You're still taking the oxy. I can see it in your face."

I answer him with a shrug of my own. There's my alibi. I was too stoned to kill anyone.

CHAPTER
THIRTY-NINE

Thad is staring at me, baiting me. I want to stay calm, but I'm all over the place. His words make me itch to punch the wall.

"My memories of the last two years are crystal clear."

The implication being that mine aren't. And he's right. I can barely remember this morning. The night Maggie was killed and the night Laurel died are just misty, murky glimpses. I don't even know if they're real or my stupid imagination.

That smug look on his face. I know it's a defense, but it stings. It pushes me. He's trying to turn this around on me? Seriously? I can hardly believe my ears.

"You've got to be kidding me." My voice is climbing like a kettle about to scream. "After everything, this is your move? Shifting the blame to me? Gaslighting 101. No, Thad, no. What's next, you accuse me of witchcraft too? Maybe I put a love spell on you. Maybe the affairs were all my fault. Maybe I beat you up? How dare you accuse me of...what? Of murder?"

He tries to lift that smug eyebrow, but it pulls a stitch. The sight of blood dripping down his cheek almost makes me laugh. "Don't dish what you can't take. You're constantly stoned, and you accused me first, remember. How dare *you*?"

I laugh out loud, but it's the kind of hysterical laugh you let out when someone's testing your sanity. "That's rich from the guy who's been living a double life," I shoot back. "Sure, I've got issues. I'm working on them. But I'd never stoop to killing...to murder. What is this, an episode of *Dateline*?"

He scoffs, waving his hand dismissively, like I'm some fly that keeps landing on his nose. "Don't act like you've got the moral high ground here after the way you've behaved these last two years."

"Me? Let's not forget, you're the one who's dead to rights." My chest tightens. "Do you remember me catching you kissing another woman? Not the other way around, pal. And, yes, I still have those pictures on my phone, just in case you've forgotten about that little rendezvous."

"Yeah, you got a few crappy photos of me with Laurel." His voice drips disdain.

"The pictures were just the start." Despite my steady tone, I'm raging beneath the surface. "You think I'm here to play this game? I read everything. What you admitted to. Her depression, your lies, your manipulations. Her links about the age of consent. That was barf-worthy. The dick pic. Imagine that coming out. How old was she when you sent that?"

His eyes narrow, but I'm not done.

"Then there's your threats. Don't even try to play the innocent card with me."

He exhales and tries to look bored. I'm not buying it. The cracks are forming in his tough-guy act. "Sure, all of that's true...but do you know what you've done?"

A nerve flares. "What *I've* done? Seriously, are you listening to yourself?" My nails are close to breaking the skin of my palms, but I welcome the pain. "I won't stand for this bullshit. You think you're gonna flip this script and make it look like I'm the one who's blown our marriage to pieces?"

He leans back against the raised mattress, the bed creaking

under his weight. "You've got your own demons. Half the time, you can't remember what you did. Maybe in a fit of jealousy, you hired someone to kick my ass. Maybe you did something worse."

For a split second, his words dig under my skin. What if...? No. That's ridiculous. *Isn't it?* Could he be swapping my pills for something stronger, something that makes the fog worse? The idea sends a chill skittering down my spine, but I squash it just as quickly. He's goading me. Trying to mess with my head.

Paranoia successfully ignored, I roll my eyes so hard, I nearly give myself whiplash. "Yeah, sure. In between my pill popping and wine chugging, I hired some thug to do what? Teach you a lesson? Please."

"Maybe."

I back away from the hospital bed. "I felt sorry for you when I came in, but I know one thing for sure. You're gonna milk it for every ounce of sympathy you can get. But guess what, buster. I'm not buying it anymore."

"Cooper."

He tries the puppy dog eyes, but I'm not listening. I storm out of the room and past the deputy, who clears his throat as he steps aside. Guess I wasn't that discreet.

A new dread settles in as I race through the hospital corridors. Is he right? Am I to blame for our problems?

Things can't have been perfect, or he wouldn't have cheated. Does every wife think that when her man goes astray? Do we all blame ourselves? When my suspicions were aroused, I got a little paranoid and started drinking. But his affair came first. He cheated when things were good. Weren't they?

Stepping into the biting air, I pull my coat tighter and glance around. The world seems distant and surreal, as if I'm watching from the sidelines as my life careens off the road.

Confusion clouds my mind, Thad's accusations ricocheting around in my stupid, drug-addled skull as I drive.

I realize I'm home and don't remember getting here. Wondering if I remembered to record our confrontation, I check my phone. A blank audio file mocks my good intentions. Ugh. If I'd just hit the button, I could've gone back over Thad's words and sorted out some of my confusion.

"Dammit. Can't he see how twisted this situation is? How twisted he is?"

Thad is manipulative. That's for sure. I know he's just throwing shit, hoping something will stick, hoping it will make me come around. He wants to make me need him, make me think I can't manage without him. Well, he's wrong.

Thad's voice hounds me, coated with concern but laced with an unsettling edge. Is he genuinely worried about me or just trying to drive me insane, to deflect blame? I tap my fingers rhythmically on a wine goblet. I don't remember opening the bottle or pouring the wine. I ache, and sweat runs down my back. I want more oxy—probably need it, but I have to start cutting back somehow.

"Why are you doing this to me?"

But the truth is a slippery beast lurking just outside my grasp.

CHAPTER
FORTY

The wooden floorboards creak under my feet as I pace the living room, my mind a whirlwind of fragmented memories and unanswered questions. I've spent into the early evening hours trying to piece together the events of the fateful night Laurel died, but the details remain frustratingly elusive. It's like trying to nail Jell-O to the wall—every time I think I've gotten ahold of it, it slips right off the nail.

Closing my eyes, I will myself to remember. Flashes of the cliff top dance behind my eyelids. Thad and Laurel, their voices raised, then suddenly embracing. The memory feels both vivid and dreamlike, and I can't be sure if it's real or a product of my imagination.

It was cold. There was snow. My feet were wet, and my mind was foggy. Nothing could break through the drugs.

My phone buzzes again. Thad's twentieth attempt to reach me today. I send it to voicemail, focusing instead on the gaps in my memory. Did I go out that night? If so, how did I get home? I can envision flashes of the trail as I raced away from the cheating piece of crap. I can almost taste my fury. I can't recall getting in the car, the drive, or arriving home. I certainly don't remember the rest of the night. Is any of this real?

Thad said he found me asleep in my car the next morning.

The more I try to remember, the hazier it becomes. Images of him cheating with both Laurel and Maggie seem real, yet I know they're part of my imagination. A way I torture myself. Why? My perfectionist personality believes this is my fault. If I'd been a better wife, he'd never have cheated, and Laurel and Maggie would both be alive. From that, my logical mind is feeding me guilt.

Let it go.

Grabbing a glass of water, I fight the urge to reach for another bottle. Cutting back on the oxy and alcohol has not been easy. The cravings nag at me, especially now, when I'm desperate for clarity.

As I sip the water, another memory surfaces—Thad and Maggie, their eyes meeting outside the bathroom at the party. It ignites a fresh wave of rage. During my fight with Thad after that, my accusations flew like daggers against his weak denials. He slept on the couch that night.

I went to the garage for a cigarette, needing to escape the suffocating tension. The details filter back—the cold metal of the coffee tin against my fingers as I fished out a cigarette, the satisfying hit of tobacco as I took a deep drag, the crisp snow crunching under my feet as I stepped outside.

But what happened after? Did I go straight to bed? I must have. The alternative is unthinkable.

The phone rings again. Why won't he leave me alone? Only this, time it's not Thad but Sheriff White. I swipe to answer, my pulse pounding.

"Cooper, it's Sheriff White. We've got some news about Thad's assault."

"What is it?"

"We think we know who attacked Thad. There's only one

way in and out of the hotel parking garage where Thad was staying." She's clipped and professional. "We've checked every vehicle going in and out that night. They all check out as hotel guests or employees...all except for one."

Holding my breath, I wait for the other shoe to drop. Was it me? It couldn't be. I didn't black out last night. I went to bed. I'm not violent. I'm not a killer. That I'm even thinking this shows that Thad has done a number on me.

"It was a late-nineties black Mustang."

Manny!

"It belongs to Manfred Donovan. The timeline matches when Dr. LaRue was attacked. We have every reason to believe Manny did this."

Maggie's son. I'm not surprised, but my mind reels with the implications. "Why would he—"

"You know why. He blames your husband for his mother's death. Manny thinks your husband killed her or that she died because she was with him at the party. Or maybe Manny just thinks she neglected him because of Thad. The problem is, we can't locate Manny."

The hair on the back of my neck rises. That teenage psychopath is out there somewhere.

"We've tried to pick him up for questioning." The exhaustion in her voice is evident. "We have a warrant for his home, and we're searching for any sign of your husband's blood as we speak. We've put out an APB across the island and at the mainland port in case he tries to leave by ferry."

I'm about to ask why she's telling me this, but it clicks. "You think he's coming here?"

"It's a possibility we can't ignore." Someone shouts in the background. "Manny likely blames Thad for Maggie's death, but he may blame you too."

"Jealous bitch. You couldn't help yourself, could you?"

"Given his current state of mind, we can't trust he won't come after you."

I turn to the windows and step to the side. "What should I do?"

"Stay inside your home." The sheriff's voice is firm. "Deputy Byer is there to keep you safe while we continue the search."

When she disconnects the call, the silence in the house takes on a menacing quality. I've barely processed the revelation about Thad screwing a teenager for two years, and now this? It's like I'm trapped in a labyrinth where each turn reveals a big, scary monster.

My feet tap, tap, tap across the room as I pace, my mind racing. Not only do I have to worry about my husband, but now Manny could be coming for me. Maybe another oxy would help take the edge off my panic.

No. I have to stop—to get my life back.

As night falls, the house grows increasingly oppressive. Every creak of the floorboards and every rustle outside makes me jump. Somewhere out there, Manny Donovan is on the loose, possibly seeking revenge. And here I am, caught in the crossfire of secrets and lies I never asked to be part of.

I recheck my phone to find more missed calls from Thad. Part of me wants to answer. But another part, the part that's struggling to piece everything together, hesitates. If I talk to him, he'll twist things to try to make me believe whatever suits him. He might even convince me to stay with him. Until my head is clear, until the drink and drugs are under control, I need to stay away as much as possible.

Standing by the window, peering into the darkness, I spot Deputy Byer's SUV. I'm safe. But I can't shake the feeling that everything is about to change. Whatever happened on those nights, I can't remember. Whatever is happening now with Manny, I'm trapped in the middle of it all.

And I have no idea how to find my way out.

CHAPTER
FORTY-ONE

"You're safe, Cooper. I promise." Deputy Byer is the definition of serious and confident.

On one of his patrols past the window, I invited him in for a coffee. The need to talk to someone, to hear a voice, to feel safe, is overwhelming, but his confidence strikes me as patronizing. He's not the one who got a Manny Donovan Special. Chicken Divan with a side order of violent threats.

"Thanks, Deputy," is all I can manage as the worry of being stalked by a psychotic teenager scratches at my mind like a cat locked out of a tuna factory.

Behind him, the kitchen clock blinks quarter after eleven, inching toward midnight. I should be tired, but the wine on the counter is calling my name like a long-lost lover. I want to down it, guzzle it straight from the bottle. Thad would lap up that scandal faster than a starving dog on a slab of unattended steak.

Nope, can't give him the ammunition.

"Cooper?" Deputy Byer's expression is intense.

"I'm okay." I wonder if he's tired, if he'll fall asleep and let Manny get past him. He doesn't look it, though. His uniform is pristine. I don't remember when he wasn't stationed out front. Always alert. On this, at least, I'm lucky.

His expression softens. "Thanks for the coffee. You sleep easy. I'll be right outside if you need anything." He heads for the door.

I force a smile, though it's more like a grimace. This is stupid. Being afraid when he's there for me, when the whole Cape Fleur Sheriff's Office is hunting Manny.

When the door clicks shut, I'm alone in the soulless house, its silence pressing in like a heavy fog. My mind whirls like a damn top around Thad, Manny, the kids, and round again. Is it withdrawal? Manny, already up to his eyeballs in his mama's murder, was creeping on me yesterday. The psycho beat Thad to a bloody pulp.

Now what? I wait? Manny's after me, I feel it, no matter what soothing turns of phrase Deputy Byer spins.

My attention pulls to the half-finished bottle on the counter before I glance at the clock again. It's only twenty past eleven, but that's close enough to bedtime. Grabbing the glass and the bottle, I head upstairs to the bedroom, snagging my pills on the way.

Sinking onto the edge of the bed, I recall how this room was once a sanctuary. The theme, opera mauve, once whispered elegance, but now it mocks me as too refined for the sham this room has become. The Egyptian cotton sheets, the Maria Theresa chandelier, each crystal a shard pointing my way in judgment. Yes, the message is clear. A fool lives here, and it's me.

The velvet armchair near the window is another posh shade I can't remember—purple to a girl like me. Thad used to drink his coffee there, making me feel loved and secure. Now it sits empty like a throne of lies. Was he humoring me while planning his next tryst?

Biting down the bitterness, I look around the room,

searching for something to hold on to. With the antique furniture, all rich wood and intricate carvings—the place is a mausoleum for a love that was all in my mind.

The bottle of pills rattles in my hand, a reminder of my constant internal debate. Take more? Cut back? Take more? Should I try to cut back more tonight? Go down to half a pill instead of three-quarters? Has it been two nights?

Who knows?

But as I pour the wine, my hand trembles enough to give away the truth. Cutting back won't happen. Not tonight. Not with Manny lurking somewhere out there.

Three-quarters of a pill goes down, followed by a hearty gulp of wine. The familiar warmth spreads, dulling the edges of my fear. The glass empties too quickly, followed by another.

By the time my pajamas are on and my teeth are brushed, the wine is almost gone, and the world has softened around the edges. Locking the bedroom door feels good—but it's a flimsy, almost laughable barrier. Slipping into bed gives me the pretense of safety, at least.

Sleep won't come. I try thinking about the kids, about anything pleasant, about nothing at all. But my mind keeps circling back to Manny, with his greasy red hair and angry eyes. His attitude toward his mother has turned him into a crazed psychopath, if he wasn't one to begin with.

He's full of spite and bitterness and fueled by the most dangerous emotion. Love. Add to that all those teenage hormones and that undeveloped prefrontal cortex. He hates her. He loves her. He wants her dead. Did he kill her?

What if he comes here? What if Deputy Byer can't stop him?

The bottle is empty. It's time to try to sleep. I reach to turn off the lights, but I stop, unable to face total darkness. The house creaks, and I expect to toss and turn the night away.

Let it go. You're being paranoid. You're safe.

But light holds all the crap that's gone down. Darkness will let me rest. I turn off the main light, leaving the bedside lamp to give off a soft glow. I drift off to sleep...

Until a crash jolts me awake.

What the...?

Disoriented, I try to blink my grogginess away, my head swimming in a fog of sleep. Something woke me. A bang. It must be a dream.

But no. There it is.

The bedroom door shakes, vibrating with another crash. It's bending under force. Manny Donovan, redheaded and furious, bursts through the splintered door like a demonic Kool-Aid Man.

Instinct kicks in, my body moving faster than any conscious thought. I scramble back in a desperate attempt to escape. Light sears my eyes. As he moves, I try not to look into the flashlight on his phone. The bright light disorients me, making me wince. He's closing fast. He's already coming around the bed, and soon, he'll be close enough to grab me. He must want to kill me.

There's nowhere to go. My phone is somewhere, but I can't find it. Where's Deputy Byer? Reaching for anything I can use as a weapon, I find the lamp. I hurl it at the teen's head with all my strength.

It connects with a sickening thud. He drops the phone and stumbles backward. Darkness overtakes the room, broken only by a thin stream of light that dances across the far wall.

The lamp barely slows him down. He's coming closer. Blood trickles down his face, his eyes wild with a rage that chills me to the bone as he rushes at me. His body lurches in and out of the light.

"One of you did it. One of you killed her." Drool sprays from his lips as he advances on me. "You're the reason she's gone."

I glance around wildly for something that might stop him. There's nothing. I'm pressed against the headboard, the carvings digging into my back. Why couldn't we have a soft, comfy headboard like normal people?

Dammit, think.

"But you hated your mother," I blurt, immediately regretting my words.

His face contorts with fury. "Mind your own business, bitch!" He takes a step closer. "She was my mom."

"I know. I understand."

"No, you don't. But you'll pay."

There's nowhere to go. I pull the quilt around me, but that won't stop him.

"I'm gonna beat you to a pulp and stab you to death for what you did."

What I did?

"Your stupid husband, that cheating piece of shit, should be dead. I would have stabbed until he was dead and gone and then some if I'd had more time."

Stab Thad. Stab me.

Maggie was stabbed to death. Did he kill her and forget, block it out?

Time stands still. I catch glimpses of the conflict in his eyes —hatred warring with love, grief tangled up with rage. He's a walking contradiction, a teenager drowning in emotions he can't begin to process.

I scoot over to the other side of the bed, but he's faster. He jumps up and is on me. My arms come up to block him, but I'm too slow. His fist hits my cheek like a freight train, and I'm knocked back into that darn headboard, tasting blood. The world spins. *Move*, my brain screams, but I can't seem to make my body work.

My arms fly up instinctually for protection, but he knocks them out of the way. His fist hits my cheek again, and pain flares. Kicking out, I slam my foot into his leg, sending him stumbling back. A sharp grunt escapes him, his face contorting with pain. "What the hell?" He pauses, glancing at the door. For a split second, I think it's over. I stopped him. But Manny's far from done. He's up and on me again, a sneer on his lips, his fists raised as he screams, "Go to hell." His knuckles crash through my arms and into my eye.

Stars burst across my vision. My consciousness fades, but I can't give in. I'm dead if I don't fight. In the distance, I think I hear a voice, but all I can focus on is trying to save myself.

"Please. I didn't kill her. I couldn't kill anyone." I hold my arms in a defensive position, my legs ready to kick. My head aches, and I'm spinning from the blows raining down on me. Or is it my nightly cocktail?

Manny stops. I peek from beneath my arms. He's beyond reason, a look of manic hate animating his eyes. He pulls a knife from a sheath at his waistband. It glints in the light. He raises it above me.

This is it. This is how I die.

A gunshot rings out, the sound deafening. Manny's body jerks before crumpling to the floor beside my bed. The knife clatters away.

Deputy Byer rushes to my side, his face a mask of concern and shock. "Shit." His eyes dart between me and Manny's still form. "I saw a light moving across one of the windows. It looked strange, so I was already on my way to investigate when I heard the crash. Are you okay? Did he stab you?"

Shaking my head, I taste copper. "I'm okay," I croak, though "okay" feels like a stretch.

Deputy Byer's jaw hangs open, and his gun shakes slightly. He holsters it. It appears he's in shock too. He can't believe what just happened. I get it. He's just killed someone in my opera mauve bedroom, all over our cream, king-size comforter. But Manny didn't leave him much choice.

"I...I thought he was going to kill you. I had to shoot."

"You did. He was. Thank you. He gave you no choice." My words are choppy as I try to form coherent thoughts. My head is throbbing, and my eyes want to close. "Manny wasn't going to stop. He said he was going to stab me to death. He said he would've stabbed Thad if he'd had more time. You saved my life."

Deputy Byer nods, still looking dazed.

"How did he get in here?" I wonder how he got past the ever-vigilant deputy.

"Sorry. I didn't see him approach the house. Not from the front. I didn't hear a thing. I just saw this light across one of the windows. It seemed strange that you'd use a flashlight."

The world's starting to tilt and blur around the edges.

"You're bleeding."

"What?"

"Let me get you something for your face, and I have to call this in." Deputy Byer pivots this way and that, looking for a bathroom, I would imagine.

As consciousness starts to slip away, I can't shake the feeling that this is far from over. In fact, it might just be the beginning. But for now, I let the darkness take me. I'm grateful to be alive and hoping like hell this will all have been a bad dream when I wake up.

CHAPTER
FORTY-TWO

Beeping is the first thing I register as I claw my way back to consciousness. Where am I? I recall Manny and the knife plunging toward me. I attempt to blink. My eyelids are made of lead. Still, I force them open, immediately regretting it as harsh light sends daggers through my skull.

The room is all white. I catch a whiff of antiseptic. The beeping is a heart monitor. I'm in the hospital. I'm safe.

"Hey, Cooper. Welcome back to the land of the living," Sheriff White's voice comes from somewhere to my left. "How are you feeling?"

I turn my head, wincing at the movement. "Like I've been hit by a truck and backed over for good measure." I sound like a frog with laryngitis. "What's the damage?"

Sheriff White's lips twitch in what might be a smile. "You took quite a beating, a couple of good blows to the face and more on your arms. After that you passed out, and you've been here all night. The doctors say you have a concussion, so you need to take it easy. You've also got some nasty bruises, especially on the right side of your face and the back of your skull."

"Stupid antique headboard."

"What?" The sheriff raises an eyebrow.

"Nothing." I search for the bed controls. I want to sit up.

"Here." She understands. She grabs the remote and raises the head. "How's that?"

The movement makes me dizzy, but this angle is comfier. Less vulnerable. "Good, thanks. What...how...I remember Manny...Deputy Byer..."

"He saved you."

It all comes back, Manny's manic eyes and the blade. "Yes. If he hadn't taken the shot..." I swallow, thinking about it. "That deranged kid was gonna stab me. Said he would've killed Thad if he hadn't been interrupted."

The sheriff pulls out her notebook and sits in the chair next to the bed. "This might be difficult right now, but I need to take your statement."

I nod, immediately regretting the tiny movement. "It's not like I have anywhere else to be."

"I just need you to go through it step by step. Give me as much detail as you can remember."

"Okay."

Sheriff White listens intently, jotting down notes as I recount the events.

"Manny burst through my door. He attacked me. It was confusing. I tried to fight. I kicked him, but he kept coming. He pulled out this knife. I thought I was dead. He lunged at me, and then it was over. Deputy Byer saved my life. If he'd waited even a second, I'd be dead."

"Thank God Deputy Byer got there when he did. Manfred Donovan would've killed you. There's no doubt about that."

"No kidding." I touch my bruised face. "I owe him a lifetime supply of donuts or whatever cops prefer. The guy's been like my shadow. I don't know how he does it."

"He's been so dedicated. Maggie's murder must've shaken him." She purses her lips. "It looks like Manny is responsible for more than just the assaults on you and your husband. We think he killed his mother."

I blink. That is not what I expected at all.

"No, you're wrong." My befuddled brain is searching for the words Manny used. "Manny told me he was there because he knew 'one of you,' as in me or Thad, did it. He believed we were the reason his mother was gone."

Sheriff White shakes her head. "Manny was a deranged and probably psychotic kid. He could've said anything in the state he was in, but it won't change the evidence. He shared video rants with friends, talking about his desire to kill his mother. To make her pay. He even described how he'd do it."

I shudder, trying to imagine Elias wanting to murder me. It's unthinkable.

"That young man harbored a lot of hate, a lot of resentment. His "friends" were too scared of him to even talk to us at first. One of the particularly brutal videos showed how he would stab her over and over until she was dead. Trust me, the look in his eyes as he mimed the actions said it all."

"But..."

"Rest easy. The killer's dead. The case is solved." The sheriff closes her notebook as if that's the end of the matter.

My mind reels, trying to align this information with what I saw. "That seems convenient." Skepticism leaks into my voice. "Like finding a signed confession next to the murder weapon."

"There's nothing convenient about a mentally ill boy from a broken family killing his own mother and attempting to kill the couple he blames for causing the final rift between his parents." Sheriff White's tone is even and controlled. "In Manny's eyes, his mother would've been home if it wasn't for Thad. Maybe he would've been more important to her if you, the LaRues, had never moved to the island. It makes sense."

Though I'm not exactly sold, I'm too tired to argue. She's the professional here. I was scared out of my mind and knocked senseless, plus sleepy and washed out on oxy and wine. Who knows what I really saw or heard?

"What about Deputy Byer?" I switch gears. "How's he holding up?"

"He's down at the station. He's pretty torn up about having to take such a young life. Any life, really. Deputy Byer has never had to use his gun before." Sheriff White purses her lips. "We'll conduct an investigation into the shooting, and he'll be on administrative duties until that's over, but it's routine and nothing to worry about."

My heart goes out to him. "Tell him I wouldn't be here if he hadn't come running. Sheriff White...he did nothing wrong. I owe him my life."

"I know that, but guilt after a shooting, even one as cut-and-dried as this, takes time to get over. He'll be evaluated before he can be on duty again." She gives me a gentle smile. "Don't worry. This is all standard procedure. It'll take a couple of weeks, but it doesn't reflect on his performance."

"Good. If he hadn't been so brave, I'd be dead." Goose bumps rise on my arms. "Tell him not to beat himself up. Manny didn't leave him much choice."

"I'll pass that along."

As Sheriff White turns to leave, a thought strikes me. "Sheriff." She pauses at the door. "I'm beyond thankful I've kept Elias and Grace on the mainland at my dad's house for the duration of this nightmare. What if Manny had gone after the kids?"

The sheriff's face softens slightly. "Don't waste time thinking about what-ifs. Focus on getting better."

I sigh and rest my head back. "You bet."

"Try not to worry too much. The doctors want to keep you under observation for twenty-four hours, but then you should be free to go home. Thad will likely be released today, but where you go from here is up to you."

"I feel guilty about..." Thad didn't kill Maggie, but he's still a lying, cheating asshat.

"Thad may not be a murderer, but you deserve a faithful husband, at the very least."

I laugh and wince at the pain it causes. "Thanks for the relationship advice, Sheriff."

She's right. I need to take a long look at my marriage.

CHAPTER
FORTY-THREE

The hospital room feels smaller by the minute, the white walls closing in on me like a shrinking box. I need to hear a familiar voice, one that doesn't belong to a cop or a doctor. Grabbing my phone off the bedside table, I call my dad.

"Cooper?" His voice is bright and cheery. "It's good to hear from you. When you coming over?"

He doesn't know what happened. I wish I could keep it from him, but I can't. These bruises will last a good long while.

Taking a deep breath, I wince at the pain in my ribs. "Hey, Dad. I'm okay. But there have been some developments." That's an understatement. I have to tell him what happened. Or at least some of it. I just don't want to. This will hurt him.

"Something wrong?"

"Oh, yeah. I have a few things to tell you. First of all, I'm fine. You don't need to worry."

He lets out a sharp bark of a laugh. "Never tell a father not to worry."

As I fill him in on the events of the past twenty-four hours,

I can practically see his face paling through the phone. When I finish, there's a long pause.

"What the hell?" His voice cracks. "You could've...I could've lost you."

The horror in his voice makes my chest tighten. "I know. I'm sorry."

"Sorry? You have nothing to be sorry for. Just, please, come back to the mainland. Please. Right now, or I'll come over there and fetch you. That damn island has been nothing but trouble."

As I close my eyes, the weight of everything crushes me into the bed. "I plan to, but..."

What can I tell him? It looks like Manny was responsible for Maggie's murder, which clears Thad from being a killer. But that doesn't clear him of the lies, the cheating, and the fact that I will never trust his shifty ass again.

"But what?"

I might as well spit it all out. "Thad cheated on me. Lied to me. There's no trust between us anymore. That's no way to spend my life." Maybe some men can change, but this is one leopard whose spots are seared into his bones.

There's another pause. I can almost see my dad nodding, processing this information.

But there's Laurel. Manny Donovan can't be blamed for her death. There's no connection between them.

Did Thad kill Laurel?

Vicki's words are clear in my mind. Laurel was lost and broken, and Vicki is convinced her daughter died by suicide. Now that Maggie's murder is off the table, the idea of Thad killing someone seems far-fetched.

Maybe I'm the drugged-up paranoid bitch he thinks I am.

Maybe I owe him an apology for throwing that accusation at him.

Or maybe hell will freeze over before I apologize to the

man who started this whole train wreck by sleeping with a patient—a teenager, no less. He owes me more than an apology, and I'll be damned if I say sorry first, or ever.

My dad's voice pulls me from my thoughts. "Cooper, there's something we need to talk about."

We've been silent for some time. There's no need to share Laurel and all that mess with Dad. It'd only add to his anxieties. Now that it's all over, I feel stupid for racing down that rabbit hole. The girl was depressed, and she killed herself.

"Cooper, are you there?"

His tone makes me sit up straighter, ignoring the protest from my battered body. "Yes, sorry. What is it?"

"I'll help you get sober." His voice is gentle but firm. "Life will be better after this. We'll do it together."

The air is sucked from my lungs. Sober! Thad recognizing my issue is understandable. He's a doctor. He sees me all the time. I've been stupid to think I was keeping it a secret. The drugs dilate my pupils. I slur my words and get jittery when I need a dose. But my dad? That's just crazy that he knew.

"Dad, I...I never realized...I mean, I don't—"

"You don't have to say anything. I'm not blind. I know how much you've struggled over the years since your fall. I know you, and I understand, but it's time for you to move forward and get healthy."

My throat tightens. All this time, he knew. How many times has he sat alone, worried and scared? He probably prayed and cried and had nightmares about losing me while I was oblivious, drowning myself in pills and alcohol.

He lost Mom, and here I've been, making him go through the possibility of losing me too. I hate myself for putting him through that.

"I'm sorry," I whisper, tears stinging my eyes. "I'm so sorry, Dad."

"Don't be sorry. I understand. Just be ready to fight. Are you ready, Coopie?"

Taking a deep breath, I ignore the pain. "I am." I'm surprised to find I mean it. "I've already started cutting down. It'll be slow going, but having your support makes me think it might actually be okay. That I can do this."

"You can. We can. It will be okay." How many times has he said that to me over the years? "We'll make it okay, and we have as long as you need. Just come home."

"I can't thank you enough."

"Come home soon, or I'm coming to get you."

"I will. I don't know what I'd do without you."

"We're a team. Don't ever forget it."

"I love you, Dad. Give the kids my love."

As I hang up, a mix of emotions swirls inside me. Guilt, fear, hope, determination. The road ahead won't be easy, but for the first time in a long time, I feel like I might actually have a shot at making it.

CHAPTER
FORTY-FOUR

"How are you doing?"

Thad's words jerk me away from the conversation with my dad. He enters with caution, clutching a tote from the hospital shop. His face is a mess. The right eye's no longer swollen shut, but it's a lovely shade of eggplant that could rival any avant-garde makeup. We almost have matching bruises.

There's a cut above his eye that's stitched and puckered, and his split lip is puffed up like he's auditioning for a Botox ad. He looks like he went ten rounds with a cement mixer and lost, but he's strutting in here like he just walked off a runway.

The familiarity of his voice is a double-edged sword. I stare at him, leaning against the pillows. Why he thinks I should greet him like my beloved husband mystifies me. I'm more inclined to treat him like a stubborn stain that won't wash out.

"They released me, so I brought you a few things." He holds up the bag before depositing it on the bed. "I've got three broken ribs, a few bruises and cuts, and a concussion, but I'll be okay." He waves his hand at his face. "If you call this okay."

He's expecting me to feel sorry for him. Crossing my arms, I keep my face stony.

His eyes narrow and seem to focus on my bruises. Just as bad as his. "Look, I'm really sorry you had to go through that alone." He seems earnest. Desperation lurks behind it. Guilt drips from his words like a leaky faucet.

"Oh, please." I shift in the stiff bedding. I'd be happier to see the pigeons that roost in our sycamore tree and shit on my car than I am to see him. But there's a bottle of wine or something in the bag. Would he dare bring that? My leg drifts across and touches the bag. Not a bottle. What then?

"I should've been there." He brushes aside my sarcasm like it's nothing. "From now on, I promise, I'll never let you down."

"You won't let me down again?" I can't keep the bitterness from seeping into my words. "It's too late for promises." Does he really think a promise will stick this broken mess back together?

Thad shifts uncomfortably, the change in his body language a telltale sign that he feels like he's losing. "Honey, I've made mistakes. I'm sorry. Manny was responsible for Maggie's murder. With the videos he posted and the assaults... it's all there."

His words rattle around my brain like stones in a jar. I keep silent, and his bluster slips a little. A muscle jumps in his cheek.

"I've been trying to tell the sheriff what a nutjob Manny was." Frustration draws lines across his forehead. "I told her the kid was unstable. Maggie was afraid of him, and so was her daughter. Now the entire island will know it was him."

A jagged laugh escapes, though it feels wrong, bitter. "Oh, great. Let's gather around like it's a damn island festival and watch the gossip mill grind out what we learned too late. Maybe that'll bring back Samantha's mom and brother." I narrow my eyes at him. "That'll make everything better, right?"

"Enough!" The force of his vehemence is surprising. He steps closer, and the walls crowd us with unspoken words. "We're done playing the blame game. We need to think about our future"

"Future?" I scoff, unable to believe we're having this conversation.

"We won't have one if you give the sheriff those messages. Have you?"

I haven't, and they're eating away at my soul. I'm sure Manny didn't kill his mom. The problem is one minute, I think Thad could've, the next, I know he couldn't. What do I do?

"You're thinking about our very public demise?"

"Yes. The messages?" He rubs a hand through his hair.

"I've still got them, for now."

"Good. Let's rebuild. It's time we move back to the mainland. We need a new start. Everything here's tainted. "

Mostly, it's his reputation that's tainted. I'm still not convinced Manny killed Maggie, but looking at Thad, I'm pretty confident he didn't either. Cutting back on the oxy has been a mixed blessing. Sweats, aches, and anxiety come and go. In between, it's done wonders—my brain feels less like scrambled eggs. It makes me realize I've been a fool.

Thad's a cheat, sure, but a killer? Come on, I know him. He's too busy preening to plot a murder. It's downright scary to think how out of my head I was to ever entertain the idea.

"It's for the best." He sounds so sure, but I wonder whose best he's really talking about—his, mine, our children's? Somehow, it's easier to pretend leaving will fix something that's utterly broken.

"Right, because running away will sweep anything under the rug. What's next? New names and a fresh start?"

"If we don't leave now, we'll drown in implications and accusations. The island isn't safe for us anymore." His voice lowers, turning almost pleading, like he's losing me and would do anything to hang on.

"Safe? What does that even mean?" The words rip from me before I can stop them. "Just last night, I was fighting for my life, literally."

"That's why we need to go. Join the kids. Leave this behind..." His voice trails off, and I can almost see what he's imagining. Cozy days, our children's laughter, me back to being the blind, trusting wife, a fresh beginning. A new setting for the same old tragedy.

And how long before his next affair?

"Okay, let's leave the island behind." I stare at my hands. Thad doesn't understand. I can't just erase Laurel, Maggie, and the cheating. I'd much rather start over without this man I've come to detest. But I'm not willing to let the Laurel situation be forgotten. "Do you mean leave Laurel behind too?"

There's a flicker of something—guilt, fear, anger, or maybe just the sting of truth. He puts a hand on my shoulder, that fake doctor's pity in his eyes. "Look, if you're willing to forget what I did, a foolish affair when I wasn't myself, then I'm willing to forget how you behaved when you were out of your mind on pills."

I freeze, blinking. "How I...?" The words feel foreign on my tongue, and I can see him squirm. I expect him to shrug it off, but no, he watches me carefully, his eyes narrowing just a fraction.

Before I can say anything else, he doubles down. "You were all over the place back then, honey. Drinking, popping pills like candy. You don't remember things right." He looks at me with that quizzical eyebrow puckering its stitches. He's expecting me to acquiesce, to give in because of something.

What?

"There was the time you threw the china my mother gave us for our wedding. The fire at Marco's Pizzeria because you weren't paying attention to your paperwork. You'd drive weird places and pass out, like that one time I found you in the car in the driveway. I don't even know why you were there when your back was so messed up anyway. And you don't either."

He rubs at his bandages.

I hope they itch like a bitch. "I have always been in control of myself."

Thad continues his litany of my alleged crimes. "You forgot parent teacher conferences. You slept at all hours of the day or night. You fell asleep while we were making love, Cooper."

I suck in a shocked breath. Part of me wants to refute what he's telling me, but I know I was in a fog for a while. Pieces of what he's saying flicker through my hazed memory. Out of all the accusations, the only one I really remember is sleeping in the car. His girlfriend had launched off a cliff in that same twenty-four-hour period—those kinds of things are hard to forget. And I do vaguely recall shattering a bunch of dishes after Dot said something…

His eyes change, grow more predatory. "You were not a good mom, not a good wife." He goes in for the kill, dropping the truth like a bomb I don't see coming. "But I forgive you."

Stunned, I shake off his hand and push back into my pillows. How dare he try to blame our marriage problems on me. All of it started because he cheated. My mouth opens and flaps for a second before I can get the words out. "How can you possibly say that?"

Thad sighs. "It's not important. Let's just move on. For the kids. They deserve a mom and a stable home."

I shiver at the way he says *stable*, the word full of insinuation.

But can I move on? Does he really think I can overlook everything? The betrayal, the lies, the way he used Laurel? He may as well have pushed her off the edge. His deeds forced her to that point. And now that his style of manipulation is aimed at me, my thoughts whirl around each other like the merry-go-round from hell.

Why do I feel like the situation is my fault, though? Because I caught them? If I'd never caught them, he'd never have broken her heart, and she'd still be alive.

The silence stretches uncomfortably. He touches my shoulder again. I flinch. "Cooper." His voice feels constraining, like a weight that's never been light enough to carry. "Let the past go." He touches my cheek. "If you keep holding on to that…it'll destroy not just us but you."

I blow out a long breath.

"Forget the past." His voice is mellow, like he's trying to convince a cornered animal to relax. "You and I have to move forward for our kids."

He kisses my cheek. The gesture makes me want to recoil, but I'm too stunned.

"There's a couple of my oxy and a thermos of the gift shop's finest merlot." He points to the bag at my feet.

I finally meet his gaze. "You accuse me of being a pill-popping drunk and you think offering pills and booze will help?"

"I know you're in pain. It's better than nothing…" He tries to sound flippant, but his words sit like a heavy stone. There's a warmth in his eyes, which makes it worse. The affection I can't reciprocate stings to the point of agony.

"Whatever." I dismiss him with a wave of my hand. "Just don't think I can forget the hell you put me through."

He leaves the room quietly, leaving me with my thoughts and the insistent noise of hospital machinery. It fills the room, reminding me this won't last forever. Whether it's healing or a new world entirely, I need to figure out how to piece my life back together, even if that means tearing apart the familiar.

I grab the bag. It's good he brought his oxy. He's right. I'm hurting. The hydrocodone they gave me isn't cutting it. Taking that would be like going cold turkey. Meaning, no way I'd be leaving the hospital in the morning, and I need to get out of here and off this damn island.

It's time to confront what's lurking in the darkness—inside myself, my memories, all of it. When I leave this hospital, I want to emerge as someone who won't run away, who won't be controlled by guilt and fear.

CHAPTER
FORTY-FIVE

With midmorning light poking golden rays through the hospital windows, I'm dressed and ready to get out of the hospital. It's only been a night, but it feels like I've lived a lifetime inside these sterile, suffocating walls, searching my soul under the dull fluorescents. Not ideal, but it's helped. It's time for a change. Time to face the mess that awaits me, to leave Thad behind and let my dad help me become the mom my kids deserve.

My phone rings, and Beth's name flashes across the screen. My stomach does a little flip, part relief, part dread. She's the one person who would drop everything and show up on my door with ice cream and cheap wine if I needed her—hell, even if I didn't. The urge to let it all spill out, to fall into her arms and unload every ounce of this chaos, is strong. But will that weaken my resolve?

"Coop! I heard what happened." Beth is the usual whirlwind of energy. "Are you okay?"

"I'm fine. I didn't want to worry you."

"Don't ever do that again. I'm here for you."

"I know." Her voice is like hot chocolate, comforting and

warming, and it makes everything feel easier. "How did you hear?"

"Oh, from the usual gossipy moms. Is it true that Manny did this to you? That lunatic. I'm coming over right now." Kids scream in the background. "Ethan, stop it now."

My eardrums almost burst.

"Sorry! Kids!" She yells something else before refocusing on me. "So where are you? I can be there in...oh, wait, my gas tank's low. I'll stop for gas, then I'm all yours."

I almost laugh, but it would hurt too much. That's Beth, ready to play my knight in shining armor but missing details like gas. I wouldn't put it past her to forget and run out. It wouldn't be the first time.

"I'm fine, really. I haven't even left the hospital yet. You don't need to rush over." There's a crash in the background, followed by the squeal of a kid. "It sounds like you have enough on your plate."

"They're still on a sugar high since Christmas, but are you kidding? You were attacked. That psychopath could've—"

"I know, I know, but trust me, the last thing I need is you barreling around these slippery roads, risking your life to swoop in and save me. Leave it a day or two. I have to...I need time alone with Thad first."

Beth huffs, clearly not happy with the brush-off. "Thad? You need to focus on you, not that sleazy..." She sighs so hard, her breath crackles the line. "Okay, okay, I'll back off. But I'm keeping an eye on you, you hear me? I'm here whenever. Whatever time, if you need an ear, call me. And I mean it. Three in the morning, I'm there. Might be in my jammies, but I'm there."

"What would I do without you? But I think the last thing we need is you pulling a *Fast and the Furious* in that old jalopy of yours. Pretty sure it's got fewer lives left than a one-eyed cat."

She laughs, a warm sound that feels like a hug over the phone. "Fair enough. She's a clunker, but she bounces well. Just don't push me away for too long. I'm worried about you."

"Hey, girl, I'm much better after this call."

After a bit more back-and-forth, we hang up. For the first time in forever, I feel a little lighter. Sure, I still have a mountain of issues to deal with, but knowing Beth's on my side, ready to swoop in with all that chaotic energy, makes it easier.

Everything's packed and ready to go. A wave of nausea washes over me, the remnants of the night, the fear, the attack, and the hazy memories that refuse to solidify. "Shit."

I bend to check the cabinet is empty. I didn't put anything in there, but it's a reflex. Always check the cupboard and drawers before you leave a place.

It's a form of procrastination, a way to delay stepping back into life. Because I've racked my brain over and over, trying to work out what Thad's getting at. Why he keeps poking me about my problem. It's almost as if he's blaming me for Laurel. Whatever happened the night Laurel jumped from the cliffs has nothing to do with me.

Yet I carry guilt about her death. If I hadn't caught them together at that very same place, maybe...maybe she'd never have jumped.

Around and around my thoughts go. Is this all about control? Making me feel like I'm a bad person? Not a fit mom?

He finally realizes that I might walk away, fears losing me and the kids and his perfect family. The snake has sunk so low and is trying to manipulate me into staying with him to keep my kids. That has to be it, and it eats at my soul that the man I loved could do such a despicable thing.

With that conclusion, my skin buzzes with anger and hurt like a fly over a picnic. I've hardly slept a wink. I force my brain to remember any incidents when I neglected the kids, anything he could use against me, but all I get are images of snow, Thad, and Laurel. This time of year, the snow always haunts me. Flashes of snow, of blood. These things have haunted my dreams. Is any of it real, or is the oxy just messing with my mind?

"Ready to go?" A nurse enters with a wheelchair.

Behind her, Thad hovers in the doorway, looking sheepish, like a bewildered puppy caught with his nose in the chow. But an air of victory clings to him, a smugness that makes me want to claw at his arrogant grin. He thinks we'll carry on as if nothing happened.

Oh, Thad. You poor, clueless sap. Don't you realize this is just a temporary truce?

I bite down my exhaustion-induced fury. He's the one who's been having secret affairs with anything that catches his eye. He's the one with the reputation that means more to him than the air I breathe. I'm a good mom, and I will play his game until I'm safe at my dad's.

"Yep." I manage to maintain a neutral expression, a near-impossible task when all I want is for this awful marriage to be over.

Thad grins at the nurse. His smile is a little too wide, a little too fake. The bruises add an air of horror. "Come on, then. Let's get you settled back at home." He grabs the tote with my few possessions.

People ogle us as the nurse wheels me through the hospital, their gazes bouncing between Thad and me. We must look like we've been through a car wreck or are modeling for photos in a domestic abuse campaign.

"You seem enthusiastic about a fresh start," I mutter to him. It seems every onlooker is playing detective.

"It's what we need." His voice, too chipper, grates on my nerves. "We could get away, take some time to figure things out."

A snort escapes me, loud enough to draw more stares. "Oh, I'm sure. Maybe a nice beach vacation. Work on our marriage, our tans, and our bruises."

The hospital doors whoosh to the side, and cold reality rushes over me. We're finally going back to that ostentatious house. All I want is to go home to my dad's and hug my kids. But I have to be sharp. To stay calm. I can't give him anything to use against me in a custody battle.

Thad rushes ahead to open the door to his Mercedes, that big gray beast of a sedan. The full brunt of what's to come hits me. It's like we're both playing a game of pretend, wearing costumes that are fraying at the seams.

The nurse helps me out of the wheelchair and into the passenger seat. When I'm strapped in and the door is closed, Thad reaches for me, but thinks better of it and pulls his hand back.

Smart move.

"Cooper, I'm serious."

I twist slightly to face him, squaring my shoulders and daring him to meet my gaze. "Serious? You think we can just hit reset after everything? After Laurel, after Maggie? This isn't some game of Monopoly where you pass Go and collect $200."

He stumbles over some excuse, something about "rebuilding trust," but I turn away and stare out the window. I'm too busy imagining the look on his face when I kick him out the door.

Don't get too cozy, dear husband.

The mistrust between us is a festering sore, but I'm over it and out of here as soon as possible. For once, I'll be the manipulator. I'll be nice until we get to the mainland. Then I can dump his cheating ass and start again.

"Come on, honey." He's like a teacher to an unruly pupil.

"I've been looking forward to having you back. I'm so sorry I wasn't there the other night. I would've saved you."

My jaw tightens as "honey" sets my nerves on edge. I used to love it when he called me that. But I'm not his little Lorelei, just *honey*. And that word can be used as an insult. He's like those people who send a sarcastic and cutting text but add a smiley, thinking they can get away with murder as long as they cover it with a generic yellow happy face.

"You didn't save yourself."

His jaw clenches, and he pushes the ignition button a little too hard. I bite back more sarcasm. Maybe if I ignore him, I'll somehow be able to imagine this is just a bad dream, a temporary nightmare waiting to fade.

The car engine purrs as Thad pulls out of the lot. As we drive past the familiar sights of Cape Fleur, still dressed in her Christmas finery, I catch myself wondering when I'll leave this island for good. Once, that would've terrified me, but now, I can't wait to see the back of her.

"I've already started packing. We'll leave today."

Even though I want this, his words sting. This is a preemptive move, making me wonder how much of my life he's willing to uproot for his benefit. Once we're off this island, the stage will be set.

"We have to talk to the kids first. And what about your practice? Shouldn't you stay while Dr. Hughford looks for a new partner?"

He's fidgeting in the driver's seat. The tension in his shoulders, the set of his Miss Pointy Face jaw. I think he knows that if I get out from under his influence while he stays until the practice finds his replacement, he'll never get me back. His perfect family will be gone, and he'll be a failure.

Losing control over me terrifies him.

"I've spoken to Simon. It's all set."

Of course it is. "Okay."

My hands clench around my purse, a physical reminder of how tightly I'm trying to hold on to a semblance of composure.

The silence stretches as I shrink in my seat. This car feels like our marriage, an empty box designed to show off his wealth and domination. The engine's hum and the road noise are the only things between us.

"I'm sorry," he finally whispers.

Sorry he cheated? Sorry he's wrecked our lives on this island? Sorry his deeds have gotten both our asses kicked, almost killed? Sorry for his contribution to my drug problem? Sorry for Laurel's death? Maggie's?

Thad likes to hold things over me.

The fear, the trauma of the attack, the agonizing stress of Maggie's murder, and the knowledge of his repeated betrayals have left my mind feeling like a scrambled mess, compounded by a bottle of red and a pill or two for good measure.

I know I'm a drunk, a drug-addled fool, as Thad would have me believe. How can I expect to piece together the events of the past when my memories are scattered like confetti in the wind? When they're mashed up like eggs in an omelet and tangled like old charging cables tucked deep in a drawer?

Thad studies my face as if searching for acceptance, his attention moving back and forth between me and the road. He's probably hoping I'll look meek or maybe even loving, that I'll toe his line and do as he wants. But I've learned a thing or two since our wedding vows. All I feel is a quiet, creeping rage.

Snow begins to flurry as we drive toward home. It's a beautiful day for a fresh start, but I know the reality will be much more complicated than just walking away. Even so, when we get back to the mainland, it's over.

This time, it's truly over.

CHAPTER
FORTY-SIX

By late morning, we've barely spoken since returning from the hospital. Thad's holed up in his office like a squirrel with his precious little stash—files, certificates, expensive gadgets. Stuff that's apparently too important to live without.

I wonder if he knows I'm done with him, seriously this time. No, he's too arrogant. He won't imagine the little woman can cope without the grand LaRue empire behind her. Boy, is he in for a shock.

Meanwhile, I've devoted a solid hour to sifting through our vast collection of photographs, my heart aching with each memory. I've carefully selected the ones featuring the children, their bright eyes frozen in time, either by themselves or with me in the picture. It's bittersweet, choosing which fragments of our life to preserve.

I doubt he'll even notice that none of the pictures that include him are missing from the walls. It's telling, really, how easily I can erase him from our lives.

The worst of it is, I don't feel a thing. Well, maybe a touch of relief. I'll have to tell the kids, but that's a problem for another day. Right now, I just need to get my head straight and escape without letting him know my intentions.

Everything I need is packed. I've got my clothes, toiletries, and makeup. Sneaking in some of my expensive jewelry spikes some guilt, but I might need it for the kids. Another bag contains clothes for the kids, along with the toys they'll want the most. I'm now in the kitchen, surrounded by gleaming appliances and pristine countertops that suddenly feel alien.

The George Nelson ball clock ticks incessantly, a reminder of how everything in this house is over-the-top, even the damn timepiece. Its sleek design and polished metal finish scream luxury. But to me, it's just another symbol of the life I'm leaving behind.

Tick, tick, fucking tick.

All I want to do is rip the expensive monstrosity off the wall, stomp it into silence, and watch its perfect little spheres scatter across the floor like the pieces of my broken marriage.

My gaze keeps pulling to the wine rack, its bottles like sentinels, tempting me to have just a sip. Their promise of escape dries out my throat. I'm constantly swallowing, working up saliva to keep going.

Though my shaking hands yearn for the bottle, I turn for a coffee instead. Clutching the mug and downing a long swig, I let the bitter warmth flood my senses. It's not the same as the numbing embrace of alcohol, but it helps clear my head—if only a little.

I drop things into rustling bags and try to keep looking forward, focusing on practical things. I'll have to close the physical side of my business. The office. How many jobs do I need to finish? Can I do them remotely? Do I just let it all go?

I'll miss my clients and the work. Both are casualties of this upheaval. But as I pack on autopilot, I realize I can deal with most of my clients online. God bless technology.

But Marco, my unofficial cheerleader and biggest fan, will

be devastated. I'll miss his cheer, his ability to brighten even the gloomiest of days with a joke or a kind word. I'll even miss his pizza. His belief in me helped me build the business. But it's for the best. Ties sometimes have to be cut before a person is free enough to start anew.

The doorbell yanks me out of my thoughts. Great. Just what I need right now. Heading to the door, I'm half expecting a well-meaning neighbor wishing us holiday cheer and wanting to come in for drinks and nibbles, or Beth. How long will she stay away? *Not now, please.* I'm in no mood for forced pleasantries or small talk.

Upon peeking through the peephole, relief is like a warm cloak. It's Deputy Byer, welcome amid this turmoil. I swing the door open and instinctively wrap him in a grateful hug, bumping the holster on his hip and almost knocking him over with my exuberance.

"Thank you for saving my life." My voice is thick with emotion. "I can never thank you enough. I don't know what would've happened if you hadn't been there."

He gently extracts himself from my embrace, his cheeks glowing either from the chill of the winter air or embarrassment. I suspect the latter, given his quiet manner. "Just doing my job, Cooper."

He steps inside, and I close the door, shutting out the cold.

"It's good to see you're okay." His voice is steady and calm, a small island of normalcy in the turbulent sea that has become my life.

He's not in uniform today but a black suit, looking like he stepped off the set of a detective show. It makes him look older, stronger, and more confident. Maybe he got a promotion, and I hope that's true. He deserves it.

"Ouch." He winces visibly as his gaze travels over the

bruises scattered across my face, the ugly reminders of that harrowing night.

"The doctors say these will heal in a week or two." I wave away the bruises like they're nothing more than a bad rash.

I try to keep the mood light and push away the memories that threaten to surface. He looks anxious and stiff, his posture more rigid than usual. There's something about him that's different, a tension in his shoulders that wasn't there before, and I wonder why he's really here.

"Yeah, it's a relief." His gaze searches mine, as if trying to peel back the layers of what I'm feeling, to see beyond the brave face I'm putting on. "But I wish you'd never had to go through this. No one should have to endure what you've been through. No man should ever ruin a woman's life."

"Thanks. I appreciate that." I swallow a lump that's formed in my throat. "It would've been much worse if you weren't there. I'll never forget that."

"Just doing my job."

Only he wasn't. He went way beyond his job with the hours he sat outside. He was the only one who thought something might happen. If he hadn't volunteered...I shudder at the thought. "Can I get you a coffee or something? It's the least I can do to thank you, Brent."

"No, thank you, Mrs. LaRue, I won't be here long." He raises his eyebrows and peers into the house, his lips forming a thin line. "This isn't a social call, I'm afraid."

Oh, that's the tension I sensed. Plus, we're back to formalities.

"Well, okay, Deputy Byer. Please, let me know if I can help about the shooting. Anything you need."

He walks farther into the foyer, his expression growing more serious by the second.

I brace for whatever news he's about to deliver. The intensity of his gaze makes me nervous. "You look like you're carrying the weight of the world. Or is this the new detective vibe you're going for?" I raise an eyebrow, hoping for a smile. I don't get one.

"I really did want to check on you, but I'm actually here to see Dr. LaRue."

A knot forms in my stomach, that familiar pit of anxiety that warns me something bad is about to happen. Pity I haven't listened to it more often. "To see Thad?"

"Yes. Is your husband home?"

"Yes."

"Dr. LaRue is no longer a person of interest in Maggie Donovan's case."

So why is he here?

I nod, but the relief that flickers through me is quickly swallowed by a growing sense of dread twisting in my gut.

He licks his lips and faces me fully. "I need to talk to Dr. LaRue about Laurel Hackert."

CHAPTER
FORTY-SEVEN

Thad charges into the room, face flushed with anger and confusion. He must've been eavesdropping. "What the hell are you talking about?" He's shorter than the deputy but broader, and I expect he's counting on his intimidating demeanor and reputation to come off as imposing.

Even though I hate him, years of conditioning—and self-preservation, I guess—cause me to shoot Thad a warning look, trying to convey the need for caution in this crazy situation. He has to tackle whatever this is with sense and rationality, not raw emotion and aggression.

Plus, no one should get to take him down but me. When I'm good and ready.

But Thad doesn't even glance my way. He's too caught up in a swirling storm of agitation to notice his little woman's silent message. His hands clench into tight fists, tension rolling off him. The air crackles with energy.

The kitchen transitions into a boxing ring, and I'm caught between two combatants.

Standing to my left, Deputy Brent Byer remains unfazed.

His expression is calm, almost clinical, as if he's dealt with this kind of outburst a thousand times before.

Standing to my right, Thad looks like he might lose it. He's the underdog, with no plans of losing in the match. His fists are clenched, jaw tight, like he's ready to swing for the final round. Is this the look Laurel saw on that fateful night?

"Laurel Hackert." The name falls from Deputy Byer's lips like a stone dropping into a still pond, sending ripples through the room. "She was an islander who jumped to her death from the cliffs just over two years back. Maybe you remember hearing about that incident?"

Of course we heard about it. It saved our marriage, but now, in hindsight, Laurel's death was the beginning of the end. "Yes." The word somehow escapes the emotion clogging my throat.

"Sure," Thad shrugs, "maybe." But he lacks conviction. He sounds uncertain. And that uncertainty is terrifying.

Deputy Byer's gaze shifts between us, his sharp eyes assessing. He's reading the room, cataloging our reactions, and I know we're not hiding anything from him—not the tension, not the fear.

"New evidence has come up regarding Laurel's case." His tone is steady, almost gentle, as if he's breaking bad news to a patient. "I need to bring you down to the station for some questioning. There's no need for any concern. This is all routine, but it has to be done."

New evidence?

Could it be Vicki Hackert? Has Laurel's mom finally decided to talk about the affair? Vicki's been a silent threat since I spoke to her and found out she knew. I wondered why she never went to the police at the time. What else might she be holding on to?

But what if I'm guessing wrong? Maybe it's not Vicki.

What if the police have found something else, something they overlooked?

What evidence or witness could've come forward?

Thad reacts just as I feared he would. "I'm not going anywhere." He crosses his arms like Elias when he's having a tantrum. "What the hell could that possibly have to do with me?"

His words are a challenge that Deputy Byer doesn't rise to. "I'll make it as quick as possible. But you do need to come with me, Dr. LaRue. It will be discreet. Forcing me to get a warrant could draw public attention. We both know you don't need that."

Though wrapped in a thin veneer of politeness, the threat is clear. Thad's jaw tightens, his eyes narrowing as he processes the deputy's words. He's cornered. He's been outplayed, and he knows it. The realization flickers across his face, but there's something else there too—something darker, something like fear.

Thad turns to me, his eyes meeting mine, and for a moment, I see something raw and desperate. It's the look of a man who knows he's in deep trouble but doesn't know how to admit it, address it, or escape it. And for a second, I feel sympathy for him, despite everything.

"Keep packing. I'll be back." He leans in, pressing a rough kiss on my cheek. It's not affectionate—it's a gesture of reassurance, more for him than me. "This is bullshit," he adds as he follows Deputy Byer to the door.

Thad moves like a man holding on to the last shred of control. I watch, my mind spinning with questions I don't want to ask, with possibilities I don't want to consider. I blame Thad for Laurel's death. I blame myself too. If I hadn't found out and forced him to dump her, she would be alive today. I know it's ridiculous to blame myself, but the guilt sits heavy in the pit of my stomach.

Deputy Byer turns to me. "I apologize for the inconvenience, Mrs. LaRue." However, he doesn't seem sorry.

Before I find the strength to open my mouth, they're gone, Deputy Byer leading Thad out the door and down the path to the waiting unmarked navy blue Subaru Impreza. It's solid and dependable, much like the man himself.

I watch from the window. *New evidence.* The phrase plays over and over in my head, growing more ominous with each repetition. What could they have found? What could Vicki Hackert have told them?

For two years, I've lived with the weight of what happened to Laurel Hackert. Two years of uncertainty, of not knowing what really happened that night. Two weeks before Laurel died, I caught them together—Thad and Laurel, on the cliff top. The affair that had been a nagging worry was suddenly a reality, undeniable and raw. It shattered everything I knew about my life and marriage and injured my back to boot.

From the start, I've known Maggie's death was a murder. The woman didn't stab herself to death. But I never had reason to doubt Laurel died by suicide until Maggie was killed. Thad was a major contributor to Laurel's demise, but it was suicide all the same.

Yet ever since Maggie's murder, doubt has gripped me like an invisible hand trying to choke me. And Deputy Byer's words are tightening its grip.

What if Thad killed her? The rumors about her death were light on details. She'd been in the water for some time before she was found. There could've been a physical altercation. She could've been pushed. The damage to her body would've been covered by the fall and the water.

My fingers twitch as I look at the junk drawer—anxiety, sweats, aches are all telling me to give in to the call of my mind-numbing pills. Just this once. Just to cope with today. Sweat traces down my back, and my throat is sore. It wouldn't hurt, just this time.

No.

My focus flicks to the wine rack, but it won't help. I have to be strong. I can't afford to fall apart. Not now. Not when everything is hanging by a thread.

Deputy Byer isn't just fishing for answers. He's on a hunting expedition. He won't stop until he gets what he wants. And whatever that is, I'm not sure I'm ready to face it.

They stand next to the SUV, Thad's head lifted as the snow floats gently down. What are they talking about, and why is it taking so long? No doubt Thad's giving snark as he tries to worm his way out of this.

Despite his insistence that he's innocent, that this is all some big misunderstanding, I can't shake the feeling there's more than he's letting on. He's been hiding something. I'm sure of it. I run some of our recent conversations through my brain, how he's tried to figure out what I know, what I remember. And he's trying to manipulate my memories. Use them to keep me pliant.

Now the police are questioning Thad. My husband. He's a liar, for sure. But is he a killer, too, after all?

CHAPTER
FORTY-EIGHT

In the kitchen, chaos is scattered across the counters. New evidence—against Thad. Should I celebrate? No. This is serious. Everything I've pushed aside slams into me at once. I should've told the cops about the affair.

Laurel Hackert has haunted our lives, lingering like a storm. Always threatening to tear us apart. Two years of silence. Maybe it's time I stop ignoring her.

I pace, each step an attempt to stay grounded. Recollection and regret swirl in my mind, a cocktail I've sipped on since I caught Thad and Laurel together. I think about everything I've kept from Sheriff White, the truths I uncovered then buried. The affair, Thad breaking things off just before her death.

Why didn't I give the sheriff those Instagram messages? I knew they painted a picture of Thad manipulating her, pushing her over the edge without ever laying a hand on her.

She was a kid, broken, and he discarded her like she was nothing. Dr. Thaddeus LaRue, healer and destroyer. He knew about her depression. He didn't care. No matter what, he's one cold bastard.

Laurel. That beautiful, broken girl gone too soon. She jumped from the cliffs, they said. A final act of desperation, a scream into the void that nobody heard until it was too late. But I heard it—in the way a woman scorned understands. That bitter, twisted way that made me forget about justice for Laurel and only want it for myself.

I always knew it was Thad's fault. Even if he didn't push her, he may as well have. He knew about her depression. He's a doctor, for heaven's sake, but he used that young girl for his own selfish needs.

The Cape Fleur Sheriff's Office finally found something. They must realize Thad was involved. But I know my husband. He'll deny everything, twisting the truth until it snaps. Just like he denied the affair with Maggie until the police slammed the video footage in his face.

I picture him in an interrogation room, wearing his smug grin, thinking he's untouchable. "*That's not what happened,*" he'll say, all smooth and slick. Or "*You're reading it wrong,*" like he's the one holding all the cards and in control.

I glance out the window as the Subaru pulls out of the drive.

The LaRue name and reputation have always saved him.

Not this time. I'm done. I won't sit back and watch him twist everything. I grab my coat. Swiping my keys from the counter, I grab the carry-on I packed days ago when things started to unravel. At the bottom, hidden in a pair of socks, is the thumb drive where I copied all the Instagram messages.

It's time to act. I need to be there, to witness Thad squirm under the weight of his own lies. If he thinks he can talk his way out of this, he's in for a shock. This time, I'm taking control. This time, Thad will face the truth.

I step outside, the cold air biting at my skin. I'm going to the station to watch it all go down. Thad might think he's untouchable, but he's about to find out how wrong he is.

Pulling onto the road, I spot Deputy Byer's unmarked vehicle in the distance, its taillights just visible through the light flurry of snow. There's hardly any traffic, just an old, dented SUV that's seen better days and a light-colored sedan between us. Not that it matters. I know exactly where they're going.

I'm giving evidence of Thad's affair with a dead girl to the cops.

Deputy Byer is navigating the familiar twists and turns of the island's roads with the ease of someone who's driven them a thousand times. I know these roads too, every bump and curve ingrained in my mind from years of living here.

But the Impreza makes an unexpected left at the intersection where I know they should be turning right. The station is in the other direction.

Does he know some secret route? A back way to the station I don't?

My shoulders knot. *Relax*, I tell myself. Whatever happens, this secret needs to come out. This boil of lies that's been festering for years should've been lanced long ago. The way it's poisoned our lives, corroding everything it touches, must end.

Taking the turn a little fast, I skid on the slippery roads. "Steady." Back under control, I follow as they veer onto another road, one leading them farther away from the police station. My stomach twists. "Where the hell are you going?"

We head out of town, the landscape around us growing wilder, more untamed. The road narrows, and the trees on either side loom closer, their bare branches covered in a coating of snow. I've eased back now, letting a bit more distance grow between us. Byer can't know I'm following. I don't want him to catch a glimpse of my headlights in his rearview. I can't shake the feeling that something is terribly wrong.

The road he's taking goes to two places—the ferry or the trail. The one I've come to think of as Laurel's Trail. It used to be that special place for Thad and me, but now it's someplace I never want to visit.

The Impreza passes the turnoff to the ferry. That leaves the trailhead. Which leads up to where I caught Thad with Laurel. Where everything fell apart. Where she jumped to her death.

Byer rounds a bend in the road. He's gone from sight. I stop momentarily. The world around me is barren, with just the swish of the wipers to clear away the soft flakes. I hate the snow. It heralds death.

"Stop it," I shout, as if I can banish the unease with sheer force of will.

There must be a logical explanation for all this. Maybe Sheriff White is waiting for them at the trailhead. Perhaps she wants to see Thad's expression when he's confronted with the new evidence there.

Back on the winding road, I take my time. This drive is treacherous this time of year, and the road hasn't been plowed. I inch along, afraid of sliding into a ditch or getting stuck.

At last, I pull into the parking lot of the cliff trails. Images flash across my mind. Snow, Laurel, and Thad with his back to me. The memories threaten to pull me under. I squeeze my eyes shut.

Thad and Laurel, their bodies entwined on the cliff top. The day I caught them, the day my world shattered. My fall, the pain that followed, the pills that numbed it all. My descent into addiction.

It all started here.

I park beside the Subaru, the only other vehicle in the lot. The emptiness of the place makes my skin crawl. The sheriff isn't here.

I'm back here at Laurel's Cliff, and something is very wrong.

CHAPTER
FORTY-NINE

Thad and Byer are nowhere in sight. Why on earth would they come here? They must be planning to judge Thad's reaction at the scene of Laurel's death. I wonder about calling the sheriff, but the thought leaves my mind as quickly as it comes. She's here, waiting somewhere. She must be. *Just follow.* Every instinct tells me to follow.

I glance down at the carry-on nestled in the passenger footwell. It's more than just my go bag with the incriminating Facebook messages between Thad and Laurel.

"Go bag." Who do I think I am, a spy? A doomsday prepper? What's next? A bunker full of canned beans?

Hidden at the bottom is my dad's trusty Smith & Wesson Model 10 revolver. The thought of its presence is comforting but also unsettling as I ponder my next move.

You didn't think that through very well, Coop.

I imagine unzipping this suitcase at the station in front of a room full of cops, rooting around for the thumb drive, and pulling that gun out. *"Here. Hold this a sec while I search for the thumb drive."* I can picture their startled faces, hands instinctively reaching for their weapons. All those Glocks pointing at me as I stammer like a drunk.

Each time I think I'm coping and have it all under control, moments like this tell me I'm off my game. Only a drugged-up fool would drag their dad's gun along to the cop shop to hand deliver evidence against their own husband.

But I'm not down at the station.

I grab the go bag and set it on the passenger seat, fumbling with the zipper. My fingers refuse to cooperate and slip again and again. Calm. I have to stay calm. I finally get it, flip up the top, and dig through until I touch the cloth wrapped around the gun case.

I glance around to ensure I'm alone before unwrapping and opening it. The familiar scent of gun oil hits my nostrils, and the cool metal sends a shiver up my spine. What am I doing? Am I really thinking of following a police deputy and my loser husband up a trail with a loaded gun?

And if so, why?

It's been years since I last went target shooting with Dad. Still, muscle memory takes over as I flip open the revolver's cylinder. Six .38 Specials are loaded and ready, a silent promise of protection. Or peril.

I tuck it into my coat pocket—yes, I'm taking it—and get out of the car. As I hustle toward the trail entrance, my breath comes in short, visible puffs. The frigid wind stings, but it's nothing compared to the chill of the memories this place holds. It's like that day all over again. Déjà vu.

I want to go home. I want to curl up on the couch with a bottle of red and forget this place ever existed.

Twin sets of footprints lead the way, a breadcrumb trail in the snow, guiding me forward. This can't be. I start to run, and the gun bashes against my hip with each stride.

What is happening? What if I get to the top, and the Cape

Fleur Sheriff's Office has Thad surrounded? No, no one's here. Just two sets of footprints stand out in the snow. I push on, my breath heavy.

A long way ahead, I catch a glimpse of Byer's back. He and Thad appear briefly between the snow-covered pines before disappearing as the trail winds. They have quite a lead on me, but I don't want one of them to look back and spot me, so I get off the trail and weave through the trees.

My adrenaline surges as I dodge between trees as fast as my detoxing body will allow. I'm racing toward that cliff edge. Memories of Thad and Laurel flash before me, disorienting me and reaffirming my hatred for this place.

Each footfall, each bash of the gun against my hip, fills me with dread.

Was it Thad's idea? If he did push Laurel, will he try the same stunt with Byer? I wouldn't put it past him to think he could overpower an officer of the law.

This trail is unused this time of year—desolate, cold, and treacherous. My heart pounds like a jackhammer, a mix of exertion and the reduction in my oxy messing up my system. I'm trying to outpace the chaos spiraling through my mind.

Go back. Call for help. Thad needs you. Or maybe Brent does. Either way, Laurel deserves justice.

All these thoughts whip at me like the naked tree branches I'm weaving between.

Glimpses of brighter times flash through my mind—lazy afternoons spent hiking, laughter shared under the sun. Now those memories are tainted, marred by betrayal and a girl's death. The weight of it presses on my chest, threatening to suffocate me under layers of guilt and regret.

Unable to breathe, I stop, bending and gasping in air. Images flash before my closed eyes. Snow, Thad, Laurel. Laurel falling. I push the thoughts away, focusing only on placing my feet safely, each step a conscious effort to stay grounded in the present.

Nearing the edge of the clearing, as the trees begin to thin, I expect to find Thad standing before Byer, likely embroiled in a heated conversation. But as the summit comes into view, my stomach sinks.

Thad didn't agree to come here. He didn't have a choice.

Thad stands close to the cliff's edge, his hands lifted high above his head. Byer's back is to me.

I want to stop to see if I can work out what's going on, but I keep walking. The scene compels me closer. It's windy here, enough that I've come on them unnoticed. My mind screams at me to pull my gun and shoot, but that makes no sense. *What's happening? Is this some sting?* Only, I know it isn't.

Deep inside, I know Deputy Byer—the man who saved me —has gone rogue.

Stepping to the side, I slowly circle around so I can see the man's profile. A shiny piece of metal glints in the gray light. The Glock 19 service weapon is just six feet from Thad's chest. Too close to be anything but a kill shot.

"Deputy Byer." I keep my voice steady despite the terror building in my chest. "What's going on?" The words are inadequate, barely scratching the surface of this madness.

As if he's not even surprised to see me, he turns his head, his movement slow and deliberate. "You shouldn't be here." His tone is matter-of-fact, as if discussing the weather rather than a life-or-death scenario. His cold focus snaps back to Thad, leaving me invisible and helpless.

"Deputy Byer...Brent. What are you doing? Why are you here?"

"Mrs. LaRue." Byer sighs, the part of his expression I can see contorting into one of utter disgust, his features twisting as if he's just tasted something rancid. "You should've stayed home."

He doesn't even bother to look at me, his focus, laser-like, bloodless, and unyielding, stays on my husband. The contempt in his voice makes me question everything I knew about the man I recently considered an ally.

Holding my breath, I pull my father's revolver from my coat pocket, my fingers trembling as they wrap around the grip. The cold weight of the gun is foreign in my hand, and it catches briefly. I pull harder, and it comes clear.

I'm drawing down on a cop! Have I truly lost my mind?

"What's going on?" My voice cracks.

A gust of wind pushes at my back. I stumble.

Steady. You need to be steady here.

Thad's breathing is labored, each gasp ragged. He's terrified. I step a little closer, the gun still at my side. Beads of sweat glisten on Thad's brow despite the falling snow. He's close to the edge.

His gaze darts between Byer and me, silently pleading for help or understanding. The world narrows to this singular, terrifying moment—the jagged cliff edge, the roaring sea below, and the two men caught in a deadly standoff.

"Put the gun down." I sound amazingly calm as I raise the revolver. On the outside, I might look confident, but inside, it's a damn hurricane. "Seriously, what's your grand plan here, Brent?" I use his first name again, hoping to make this more personal.

Byer looks over and notices my gun for the first time. He even smiles a little.

"It's over, Byer," Thad shouts, ducking as the Glock waves at him once more.

Byer takes a step in my direction. "Shut up, killer."

Keeping his weapon centered on Thad, Byer turns to me. His face changes, relaxing from the insane animal to the man I've come to know. "Put the gun down, Mrs. LaRue. I'm a cop. This is police business. I won't hurt you."

For a split second, his tactic works. I waver in my conviction, my grip on the weapon faltering just enough for him to seize the moment. He lunges for me, crossing the frigid ground in two giant strides. His wiry strength catches me off guard as he rips the revolver from my hand, nearly breaking my wrist in the process.

Even as I'm attempting to understand what just happened, he flips open the chamber to find it loaded. His face darkens with fury.

"Loaded?" He snaps the gun shut and glares at me like I'm some reckless child playing with fire. Without missing a beat, he holsters his own gun and grabs me.

Great. Just fantastic. I'm gonna get shot with my dad's gun. Poetic.

He shoves me, and the force sends me stumbling toward Thad. I scramble on the slippery ground. For one horrifying second, I picture myself falling to my death, to land, broken, on that rocky beach just like my husband's mistress did two years ago.

My arms wheel frantically, and Thad grabs me. Our gazes lock for a brief, harrowing moment as he pulls us away from the edge.

"That's perfect. The killer becomes the protector, but not for long."

"What are you doing, Brent?" I use his name once more. Hoping he remembers the time in our kitchen. Hoping he remembers we talked, laughed, and shared personal details. "I thought you cared about me."

"Stay by your husband."

He comes closer, the barrel of the revolver so large, it fills my vision. The cold metal gleams menacingly. Wind whips around us, and every fiber of my being screams for a way out of this nightmare.

"You should've stayed home, Mrs. La Rue." He seems genuinely sad. "Why didn't you just stay home?"

It's a good question. I should have stayed home today, just like I should have stayed home before.

CHAPTER
FIFTY

Two years earlier...

The cliff loomed around me, stark and silent, its beauty turned into something cruel. Snow swirled through the air, stinging my cheeks as my breath fogged in short, sharp bursts, as if attempting to shield me.

My back spasmed, nearly doubling me over, and I popped another pill. Two weeks ago, this trail had broken me—physically and emotionally.

And yet here I was again. Same cliff. Same woman. Same betrayal.

But as I take a step closer to get a better view of the couple near the edge, I realize it's not the same man.

The figure standing with Laurel was taller than Thad, his build leaner, his movements sharp where Thad's would be confident and relaxed. Even through the swirling snow, the differences were glaring. His hair was darker, his shoulders narrower. And there was something else—something dangerous in the way he held himself, like a predator stalking its prey.

I stepped forward, the snow crunching beneath my boots. A cold, mocking echo of two weeks ago. Back then, I'd taken pictures like some cowardly voyeur. Back then, I'd fled, tail between my legs.

Not tonight.

I'd rehearsed what I'd say a thousand times…sharp, biting lines designed to slice through Thad's lies. But this wasn't Thad. This wasn't infidelity. This was…

Something worse.

As I drew closer, the scene shifted. Laurel wasn't clinging to the man like she had before. She wasn't kissing him either.

She was fighting him.

My breath caught as his hands closed around her throat, her desperate struggles growing weaker by the second. This wasn't a lover's embrace.

For a moment, I couldn't move. My mind screamed at my body to run, to shout, to do something…anything. But my legs were rooted in place, my heart hammering against my ribs.

His arms began to tremble as the life squeezed from Laurel's young body. She continued to struggle, clawing at his hands, but she was getting weaker, her face an alarming shade of purple. They moved like dancers, do-si-do-ing to give me a better view.

I wanted to rush forward but froze in terror, my witty remarks dying on my lips. This wasn't a lover's tryst gone wrong. This was betrayal.

Laurel continued to struggle, but her hands hardly scratched at his. He was completely focused on her, oblivious to my presence. I had to do something, but what? I was no action hero. I was just a stupid woman who came to confront her cheating husband and stumbled into a nightmare.

Scrambling for cover, I hid behind a nearby boulder, my heart pounding so loudly, I was sure her attacker might hear it. I'd barely made it to my hiding spot when the man's head snapped in my direction. I crouched, trying to shrink into nothing.

Finally, I peer around the edge of the boulder, my chest heaving. The man tightened his grip, his face obscured by shadows. Laurel's gasps grew faint, her movements sluggish. My stomach churned, bile rising in my throat, and I covered my mouth to stop a groan.

This wasn't just betrayal. This was murder.

And I know exactly who the murderer is.

CHAPTER
FIFTY-ONE

Present day...

"You." The word escapes my lips, barely a whisper, as I come back to the present. All those memories I've tried to piece together are suddenly so clear. I tilt my head, studying Byer like I'm seeing him for the first time. The clean-cut deputy persona crumbles away, revealing the monster beneath. "You strangled Laurel. I came looking for Thad, but I found you with her. You killed her. I saw you."

Now everything's so clear and vivid, and the way he purses his lips tells me it's true. This is not oxy or wine playing tricks. He's a killer. Deputy Brent Byer is a killer.

Byer's sigh is heavy, laden with a weariness that seems out of place given the circumstances. "That's unfortunate, Mrs. LaRue." His voice is eerily calm. "I wish you'd just stayed home."

His fingers tighten around the gun, the motion controlled and deliberate. As if the weapon were merely an extension of his hand. Every movement is calculated, a quiet menace that's more than terrifying.

Beside me, Thad's face is a mask of shock and confusion. He's paler than I've ever seen him. "What the hell is going on?"

Byer flushes as a roar rips from his throat. "This isn't some game. This is justice!"

"What?" I move forward, but he waves the gun and shakes his head. It hits me then. There'll be no negotiating with this man. He has the patience and fortitude to sit outside my house without a break for days. He's been planning this for a long time. Two years, in fact.

"I loved her."

Though I didn't expect that admission, I should have. It would take something like love to make a man so obsessed, so filled with hatred, as to kill.

"I loved Laurel Hackert more than anything in this world." His focus darts between Thad and me, his eyes manic and gleaming. "And this bastard," he gestures wildly with the gun toward Thad, "abandoned her like she was trash, like the sack of shit he was, *is*, and always will be."

I want to argue, to defend my husband, but I can't. He's not wrong.

Byer's face twists with rage, the revolver jerking erratically as he glares at Thad. He's losing it, unraveling before our eyes. "You destroyed her." His voice cracks under the weight of his fury. The revolver barrel jabs the air between them, a vicious punctuation to every word. "She was so tender, so delicate, and you destroyed her." His chest heaves as spittle flies like miniature bullets.

"I...I..." Thad stops before I can elbow him into silence. The slightest wrong word, and Byer will fire.

"You know what's worse?" He's looking through us now

as if he's peering into the past. "Laurel was pregnant." There's a strange mix of pride and anguish in his words.

Pregnant. Laurel was pregnant. Thad shudders so hard, it draws my attention to him. It's clear from his face that he knew.

The scumbag. I think of Laurel's last message to Thad. *"I gave up everything for you."*

"She knew this piece of crap would never stand with her, but I told her I would. I promised her I'd raise that baby. I'd support her, support both of them, and love the baby as my own. It could be our child." He sneers at Thad, coming a step closer, and we both inch back, so close to the edge. One gust of wind, and we'll be over—like Laurel.

The muzzle rises, centering on Thad's forehead. "You just walked away like it was nothing. Like she was nothing."

Thad flinches, and I can do nothing but stare at them both.

"She was my destiny. I could feel it in my bones. It was meant to be. I'd loved her for so long and knew she would return to me when he let her down." He's ranting, not looking at us.

Thad takes my hand and starts to inch us forward, away from the edge. Step by tiny step.

"But her mother convinced her to have an abortion." Byer slaps his own forehead with the hand holding the revolver.

We take another couple of small steps. The gap between the cliff's edge and us widens. Byer seems to be following us around, unaware that we're moving. If he realizes, he'll shoot. It'll be over.

"Can you believe that? Her own mother!"

So many things make sense now. The way poor Vicki Hackert couldn't hold my gaze. How angry she was, destroyed. It was her own guilt. She convinced her daughter to have an abortion and believed it had driven her to suicide. I can't imagine the torment she went through. I want to give her the truth. But what is it?

"Laurel was devastated." Byer shrieks. "She couldn't handle the guilt, the loss. She never wanted the abortion. I could've been there for her, but he," the revolver waves at Thad, "destroyed everything. He took her from me, and now he has to pay."

I have a brief mental image of what Thad and Laurel's baby would be like. Beautiful, no doubt, with Thad's striking ice-blue eyes. Another little ice-blue LaRue that will never be. The thought brings unexpected tears, which I blink away furiously.

Byer's voice cuts through the haze. "She told me about the abortion. I couldn't believe it. I hated her for killing our baby. She admitted she came here to jump, but in the end, she chose life. She chose to move forward. Without me."

The gun in his hand trembles. I can't tear my eyes from it. Any second now, Dad's gun will fire. I'll never see my children again.

I look Byer in the eye, trying to make him see me. He glances around, frantic, searching for something—an escape, maybe, or a way to make this all disappear. The calm, composed deputy has been replaced by a man crushed with the loss of a child and his love. They may not have truly been his, but his mind made them so. He's teetering on the edge of sanity. How do I get through to him?

My mind scrambles, searching for a way out of this nightmare, a way to talk him down, but every scenario ends with blood on the snow.

Beside me, Thad clears his throat, the sound rough and strained. His voice is hoarse when he speaks, each word laced with grim realization. "So that's it. You killed her. You killed Laurel because she didn't love you."

"She did love me! She was confused." Byer's face contorts

with rage as he gestures wildly with the gun. "You messed her up so bad, she didn't know what real love looked like anymore."

I watch, frozen, as the deranged, lovesick deputy locks gazes with Thad. The hatred in his stare is a living, breathing thing that pulses between them. Just as quickly as it appeared, the rage subsides. An unsettling grin spreads across the deputy's face.

"I've killed two people now," he admits, his tone eerily casual. "The other was Manfred Donovan."

"You're not a killer." I need to turn this around. "You killed Manny to save me. I'm so grateful for you doing that. You gave me the chance to see my kids grow up. My Grace and Elias. You saved their mom."

The cold glint in Byer's eyes tells a different story. "I would've shot the kid regardless."

"Why?" The word escapes me before I can stop it.

"I couldn't let Manny kill the great Thaddeus LaRue. Which the little psycho would've done sooner or later." A chuckle escapes him, dark and humorless. "I'd worked too long and too hard to be denied the privilege of killing this piece of shit myself."

"So you killed Laurel because she rejected you." Thad's voice is less than confident, and I want to tell him to shut up.

"I didn't kill Laurel." Byer's eyes seem to clear. "I might've hurt her. I might've been furious with her. I might've crossed a line. But I left her here alive. It was you." He sticks the revolver against Thad's forehead.

I close my eyes. I don't want to see this.

When the blast doesn't come, I open them again. Byer has stepped back, and Thad has a red indentation on his forehead.

"She jumped because of you. Because you used her like you use everyone."

Byer starts to pace back and forth, the gun waving

dangerously in his hand. His gaze darts between Thad and me, never settling, as if he's watching ghosts we can't see.

When he stops, he grimaces as if he's hurt. He's pointing the gun at Thad again.

"Two people." The words come out without me thinking. He said he'd killed two people.

His eyes narrow, his lips sneer. "I had to find justice for the woman I was meant to be with. For the baby I was supposed to raise." A chilling fervor creeps into his tone. "I needed to prove he was a murderer. So I framed Dr. Thaddeus LaRue, the big shot, the user of women, for killing Maggie Donovan. Once that was confirmed, it would be easy, so easy, to convince everyone that long before that, he murdered Laurel Hackert."

Thad shakes his head. "But I—"

"I didn't just want you to die, you loser. I wanted you to go down in flames. Boom!"

I flinch.

The revolver seems to have a mind of its own, swaying and jerking. It's like watching a cobra, coiled and ready to strike, the tension in the air so thick, it's suffocating.

Thad's voice cuts through the madness, defiant despite the gun aimed at him. "This is all bullshit," he snaps, glaring at Byer. "Brent, you're crazy as hell. I didn't kill Laurel. I've never killed anyone."

For a brief moment, I catch a glimpse of the man I married —unyielding, even with death staring him in the face.

"You might not have her blood on your hands..." Byer smiles. "But her blood is on your head."

Like a thunderclap, the gun fires.

CHAPTER
FIFTY-TWO

"No!"

Splashes of wet warmth hit my face as Thad's head jerks. His lifeless body falls backward and hits the snowy ground. His eyes are open, but...

Dead. He's dead.

Tears blur everything, creating a watery haze. I can't look away from him or process the reality of what's just happened. My husband, the father of my children, is dead. The man I've loved, hated, and everything in between lies motionless on the cold, unforgiving ground of the cliff we once treasured.

"The lives Thad stole that night didn't end with Laurel's death."

Byer's voice cuts through my shock. He's justifying his actions. An urge rises within me to scream, to wail, to throttle him, but my survival depends on understanding his twisted logic. I have to make it back to my children.

"I hurt Laurel, too, and seeing her lying here," he points at the ground before me, "knowing our future was dead, was too much. I drove to the Last Call and drank the night away. Whiskey after whiskey until I couldn't even stand. I was drowning in my grief and my hate for the man who stole my future."

Thad's dead. Shot. Lying in the snow.

My mouth's open in a silent scream, my body rigid, but my mind clings to Byer's words. I know the place. It's on the outskirts of town in a rough area. I can almost smell the stale beer and whiskey on his breath as he speaks, even though it's been two years since that fateful night. But why is he telling me this?

"Drunk, I slept in my truck that night. Didn't get home. That's Thad fault too. If he hadn't destroyed Laurel, I never would've gotten so wasted."

Why? Why does this matter?

A glint of tears brighten his eyes. Is he remorseful about what he's done?

"You see, I lived with my grandma. She looked after me for years. When the dementia started to steal her memories, it was my turn to look after her." He looks at Thad as if he might kill him again. "But that night, I was out drinking, so I couldn't remind her to take her heart medication. All alone and confused, she died of a heart attack. Probably wondering where I was, why I'd left her all alone." His lip curls. "Chalk up another death to our beloved doctor."

I'm numb as Byer weaves a narrative of cause and effect. If Laurel had chosen him, he wouldn't have been drunk. She'd still be pregnant and with him. In his mind, it all comes back to my husband—Dr. Thaddeus LaRue, leaving a trail of destruction in his wake.

Though the habit of defending Thad kicks in, the words lodge somewhere between my mind and my throat. Even if I could, the crazed man in front of me waving a gun would never hear it.

"She was the only family I had left."

I almost feel sorry for him. But our children are waiting

with my dad, blissfully unaware that their world has just been shattered. When I glance at Thad's body on the snow, any sympathy I have for Byer evaporates like morning dew in the summer sun.

Thad's dead. The instinct to run to him, to wail out my grief, almost overwhelms me, but that revolver still weaves back and forth. If I move, it'll fire again. I'm sure of it.

Byer drones on. "I never hurt Laurel on purpose," he insists, as if that somehow absolves him. "But I wasn't myself that night. Only a broken version of the man I could've been." It's a pitiful attempt at justification that does nothing to ease the weight of his actions.

His description of Laurel is like a twist of the knife. I think of all the times I cursed her name, all the anger I harbored. Now it seems so pointless, so petty in the face of this tragedy. She was a victim. She didn't deserve to die. In my mind's eye, she's young and vibrant, full of life and potential. A life cut short by jealousy and obsession.

"Mrs. LaRue, you're beautiful too. Just not quite as youthful."

Seriously?

"What does it feel like to sacrifice your best years to give the man you love a family, only to have him reject you because you're no longer young?"

A scream builds in my throat, a desperate desire to tell him he knows nothing about my life, my marriage. The years of love, laughter, arguments, and reconciliations. The sleepless nights with colicky babies, the proud moments at school plays and sporting events. The quiet evenings spent together, comfortable in each other's silence. But fear keeps me quiet.

All I can think of is getting home to them. I see their faces in my mind—hopeful, innocent, trusting. They're expecting both parents to come home. How will I explain this to them?

How can I possibly make them understand when I don't understand it myself?

"I need to get back to my children." My voice is steadier than I feel. "I'll leave immediately. I won't tell the sheriff. That gives you time to flee. Do whatever you want. Just let me live. They need me. Like your grandma needed you. Please, Brent, let me go."

I'm bargaining for my life and hate myself for it. But I'll do anything, say anything, if it means I can see Grace and Elias again.

His response crushes that fragile hope. "I want to." He sounds regretful. "None of this was your fault, and we've gotten along so well, but..." The "but" hangs between us, heavy with dread. "But if you're alive, you'll tell everyone I killed Thad. And the world needs to believe you killed him in a jealous rage."

As the words sink in, he closes the distance between us. He's still holding my revolver—the one he used to kill Thad. The same revolver my dad gave me for protection is now being turned against me. He presses it against my head. The metal is warm. I smell the gunpowder, an acrid reminder of Thad's fate.

"Murder-suicide is such an epic way for the perfect couple to go out." His voice is almost dreamy. In his mind, this is just the final act in his twisted play. It's nothing. Just tying up loose ends.

How did we get here? How did a simple confrontation about infidelity turn into this nightmare? I think back to this morning, when my biggest concern was walking out of my marriage and starting again. It seems like a lifetime ago.

"If you'd only stayed home, Thad's death would have been just another accidental cliff fall, and life could've gone on for me and you and the rest of the island...peacefully. Mrs. LaRue, you and I could've been friends. Maybe more."

The implications of his words knock the air from my lungs. Thad's lying lifeless at my feet, and Byer wants to talk about the lost potential of our friendship? My stomach clenches, and bile fills my throat.

How could I have missed it? His friendly but shy smiles. How safe he made me feel. How he was always there, protecting me, when all along he was lurking. Watching and waiting for this twisted moment. Was he always this unhinged, or did Laurel's death push him over the edge?

Nausea churns so violently, it threatens to drop me. Thad's blood creeps ever closer to my boots, and Byer's twisted notion that we could be something wrenches my stomach further.

"But now I have to do what I have to do." The gun presses harder against my temple.

This is it. This is how my story ends.

I close my eyes, warm tears slipping down my cheeks. I pray my children will grow up strong and happy. I pray my dad will survive this, that he won't blame himself. I can almost hear their voices over the wind roaring across the cliffs.

Is this really how it ends? After everything I've been through, everything I've survived, is this where my story stops? On Laurel's Cliff, next to my dead husband, at the hands of a man I trusted?

I hold my breath, but the roar of gunfire washes all my thoughts away.

CHAPTER
FIFTY-THREE

The gunfire still rings in my ears. Was I shot? Am I dead? At that range, I have to be dead.

"Mrs. LaRue. Cooper. Are you all right?"

My eyes snap open. Sheriff White is running toward me, her gun drawn. It's only then I realize I'm alive. My legs are numb, and my chest aches, but I'm still here, standing on this windswept precipice I hope to never see again.

My gaze falls to Byer, sprawled on the ground just a few feet in front of me. His body is still, unmoving, a dark mass next to another vibrant red pool of blood spreading into the snow.

There's Thad, his blood already coagulating.

"Are you hurt?" Sheriff White is a calm anchor. She kicks away my dad's revolver, checks Byer's pulse, and reaches down to throw the gun away from his holster.

"What happened?"

She holds up a finger. She's radioing for EMS and backup, her calm voice describing the scene. "Light it up. Code three."

I drop to the ground next to Thad. He never killed anyone. He was innocent after all.

"I'm sorry I didn't get here sooner." Sheriff White is at my side, gazing down at her struck-down deputy. She shakes her head. "I tried not to let it come to this. I tried to stop him."

"How?" It's all I can manage when I look up at her.

"I was yelling for him to stand down. But he ignored me. You're safe now." She places her coat over me, leaving only her jacket underneath. "Brent was supposed to be on leave while we investigated the Manfred Donovan shooting. That's standard procedure." She leads me away from the bodies to a rock, dusts it off, and helps me to sit.

"Oh." I still don't understand. When I thought I heard the kids' voices, was that actually Sheriff White?

"He hadn't turned in his service weapon as instructed. He told me he was off the island and would do it when he returned, but Beth Hopner spotted him getting gas in plain clothes but wearing his gun. She asked him about it, and he said he was on his way to the station to turn it in."

I pull the coat a little tighter. "Oh." That seems to be the only word left in my vocabulary.

"I'd been trying to contact him for a while, with no response. He'd gone AWOL."

The phrase "AWOL" hangs in the air, heavy with implications.

In the distance, sirens begin their mournful wail. The sound grows steadily, piercing the fog in my mind. They're coming for us, coming to help, but they're too late for Thad.

"Beth went to see you after she filled her tank and saw Byer leave with Thad, with you on their tail. She followed."

"Sounds like Beth." I almost smile.

"She dropped her phone trying to text you as you turned onto the cliff road and ran into a snow drift."

"That really sounds like Beth."

"She called me after that."

"Her crappy driving saved my life."

"We were already looking for Byer. This morning, Vicki Hackert called the station. She was desperate to speak to me." Sheriff White pauses, her gaze settling on Thad's unmoving body. "I should've spotted this. Should've known."

Thad lies just a few feet away. It breaks my heart that I'll have to tell our kids their father is dead. And despite all our battles, it breaks my heart that I'll never hold him again. The reality of it smothers me.

I try to collect myself, to focus on the present. I cling to Sheriff White's coat, the warm brown fabric heavy on my shoulders.

"Cooper, are you listening?"

"I...what?" I try to refocus on her words.

"Vicki Hackert walked into the station this morning. She had that air of a woman who's been holding on to something for far too long. She said she'd talked to you recently and couldn't keep quiet any longer."

I can imagine Vicki speaking with Sheriff White, her voice trembling underneath her air of authority. Vicki would've taken a deep breath and confessed whatever she needed to in a logical, unemotional fashion. She seems like the kind of woman who only breaks down behind the scenes.

"Cooper." The sheriff's voice brings me back again. "Vicki told me about the affair between Dr. LaRue and Laurel. She was concerned about the age difference." Her voice is calm, but her eyes betray the weight of what she's about to share. "She told me how Laurel thought it wasn't just some fling but something deeper, something stronger. How Laurel would fall into depression whenever things slowed down."

My stomach twisting, I nod. I saw the affair with my own eyes, caught them together in that moment of betrayal. But hearing it again, hearing what Vicki went through, makes it fresh, like the scab's just been torn off an old wound.

"She was pregnant." My words come out in a mumble. I

wonder distantly if I'm in shock. About everything I've just learned. About everything that just happened. "Vicki pressured her into an abortion."

Sheriff White shakes her head as if she still can't believe it. "Vicki confirmed that too."

A shiver runs down my spine, the kind that starts at the base of your neck and works its way down to your toes. It's not the revelation of her pregnancy. Byer already dropped that bomb. But hearing it without a gun to my head makes it real in a way I wasn't ready for.

Laurel wasn't just a girl broken by the grooming of an older man. She was a girl broken when she got an abortion she didn't want at the urging of her own mother. Another wrong choice in a long series of wrong choices. No wonder she'd found herself here on this clifftop, ready to end it all.

But she was ready to survive. She came through so much. It makes Laurel's death even more tragic.

Voices echo across the clifftop as an EMT crew arrives with stretchers. I watch as they break off in pairs to kneel in the snow, checking vitals on Thad, then on Byer. I'd think the buckets of blood in the snow would tell them all they needed to know.

My hand goes to my forehead. Despite my memory returning, events still seem so blurry. "How does Byer figure in? I never even saw this coming. He was so..."

The sheriff places a reassuring hand on my shoulder. Her voice drops to a whisper. "Actually, Vicki told me about Deputy Byer and Laurel."

My head snaps up at that, and I see the seriousness in Sheriff White's eyes and the way her jaw sets as she delivers the next blow.

"Brent and Laurel went to college together on the mainland. He was in love with her, deeply in love, but it wasn't mutual. She was caught up in the affair with Thad when he admitted his feelings. Byer didn't take the rejection well."

Brent Byer, the steady, reliable deputy who seemed so level-headed, harbored feelings for Laurel all along. It's almost too much, the idea that, this whole time, Byer's motivations were rooted in something so twisted and basic as anger and jealousy.

"Vicki wasn't surprised when Brent ended up here, on the island. His grandma was his only family. However, he hung around Laurel so much. Called her all the time. To Vicki, it felt off. She believed he was pursuing a woman who'd rejected him. It was like he couldn't let go. Laurel laughed it off, but it made Vicki uncomfortable."

The pieces are falling into place, each one heavier than the last. Byer came here not to escape his past, but to be closer to it, to keep it alive. And when he saw Thad, the man he blamed for taking Laurel away from him, cheating with yet another woman as if Laurel never mattered to him at all, his plan fell into place.

"Sheriff White, Byer told me..." I have to swallow. "He said he killed Maggie Donovan with the intent of framing Thad. He wanted to establish Thad as a murderer so he could blame Laurel's death on him."

Sheriff White nods as if this confirmation is precisely what she expected.

How could this happen?

Sheriff White gives me a look that's both sympathetic and resolute. "Hang in there, Cooper. You'll be okay."

Nothing feels okay. Thad's dead. The secrets are out. The lies are exposed, and the nightmare I've been living in is far from over.

"Cooper." She touches my arm and squeezes it. "Trust me. You'll get through this."

And for a moment, I believe her.

CHAPTER
FIFTY-FOUR

One year later...

Snow blankets the ground as we make our way up to the top of the cliff. When Thad died, I expected to pack my ass up and leave the island, to race away and never return, but here I am, and life is good.

Arms full of bouquets, we trail the kids as they dart ahead, laughter filling the air. Dot walks beside me—no longer the bitter, stiff woman I used to dread being around. Grief chipped away at her hard edges, softened her.

Now she pours her heart into her grandkids in a way I admire. Bringing up the rear is Howard. Dependable as ever, trailing Dot with the loyalty of a well-trained retriever.

Elias bends and makes a snowball, a glint of mischief in his ice-blue LaRues. He's full of energy, like a whirlwind with no off switch. I can't help but smile as he lobs a snowball straight at Grace. She takes it square in the chest and stomps her foot, her lip curling into a pout.

For a moment, she's on the verge of tears. She's emotional

today. She looks at me, and I shrug. She scrunches her nose. It makes her look like me. Instead of breaking into tears, she bends and makes her own snowball, and the fight is on. They race ahead, lobbing snowballs back and forth.

"Full of life, just like their dad." Dot's voice is tight with grief or pride or maybe both.

Dot's grief is honest, but the rest? Maybe that's her perfect lie. We all have them, don't we? The stories we tell to make the past bearable.

The weight of Thad's demise hangs in the air, but I don't let it take root. Not anymore. I'm in control of this, of myself. Dot accepts me now. She's learned not to push too much. She knows I won't take her nonsense any longer. She lives for time with her grandkids.

"They are." We've stopped to watch, but there's a chill in the air. "Let's get to the top before the kids turn into snow people."

We continue walking, the cold nipping at my cheeks. Howard puffs as he tries to keep up.

For me, each step feels purposeful and steady. I'm not the woman I used to be—the one who wavered at every mention of Thad's name, the one who once stumbled through life from oxy to wine like she was always one breath away from breaking.

No, I'm different now. I'm almost twelve months sober, thanks to Dad, and I can handle this, can handle her. Dot doesn't scare me anymore. Nothing does.

The climb is no longer so hard. My body is healthy, and I'm enjoying the walk through the trees and the trek to the top. There are so many memories on this trail, good and bad, but I'm fighting to keep my mind here, anchored in the present.

We reach the top, and the view is as breathtaking as it is tragic. Snow covers the ground. The sky is gray, heavy with clouds, and the ocean sparkles below us with the mainland in the distance like a postcard. It's a long way down to that stony beach, but you can smell the salt air and feel a tint of sea breeze.

The kids are racing around the place where Thad died. "Keep away from the edge." My voice is sharp, and they immediately turn and come back.

"Is this where it happened?" Grace's eyes are so very sad.

"It is." I hand her the bouquet of daisies she picked out this morning. It's off-season, so even the normally happy flowers also appear somber.

Howard has already walked over to the spot. Not quite the right place. It's close enough, and this is not the day for being picky.

Visiting the place where Thad died is wrenching, but it doesn't pull me under like it used to. Instead, I'm calm. I've finally made peace with the ghosts of my past.

We each place our flowers down—Dot with her crisp white lilies, Howard with forget-me-nots, Grace with her daisies, and Elias with the purple irises he loves so much. I'm the last to go.

I step forward, my breath catching as I kneel to lay my bouquet on the snow. *I wish it hadn't ended this way, Thad.* I set the roses down. They flare, bold and jarring, the petals spreading like spilled wine on a pristine tablecloth. Or blood on snow.

I don't know why I bought them. Maybe part of me wanted to remember the messiness, the rawness of it all. Or maybe they just seemed fitting. Red like love. Red like pain. Red like the kind of wounds that take years to heal. Acting on instinct, I pluck one from the bouquet.

As I stand, Grace takes my hand and Elias hers. "Rest in peace, Thad," I whisper. Snow starts to fall in thick, chunky flakes that swirl in the wind. It's like we're in a snow globe.

Elias moves away from us, trying to catch them on his tongue. He's done his grieving and moved on. It's a good philosophy. A reminder that life continues, even in the shadow of loss. Grace copies him.

"Can we build a snowman when we get home?" Grace is full of excitement and innocence.

I hug her to my side. "That sounds like a great idea."

How far I've come through infidelity, addiction, and the loss of Thad and nearly myself. But this snow is always there, hovering in the back of my mind like a shadow. As Grace races after her brother, well away from that horrific drop, I stand and watch the flakes fall. It takes me back. I don't know if it'll ever stop being a trigger. A harbinger of death, of the past, of secrets.

Still clutching that single red rose, I step to the edge of the cliff and look down.

I toss the rose and watch it sail to the snow-covered rocky beach below. It takes but a few seconds before the wild sea crashes against the shoreline and steals it away.

CHAPTER
FIFTY-FIVE

Three years earlier...

I crouched behind the boulder, barely daring to breathe. The rough surface bit into my palms where I tried to steady myself, but my body betrayed me. My hands trembled. My knees ached. My chest burned as I stifled the desperate need to gasp for air.

He was still out there. Brent Byer. Killing Laurel.

Daring to peek around the side, I watched in terror as Brent's entire body began to tremble with effort as he squeezed the life from her.

With a howl of rage and grief, he opened his hands and let go.

Laurel crumpled to the snow at his feet, her body folding awkwardly, her head lolling to one side. For a moment, everything was still. My breath caught in my throat, my heart pounding so loudly, I thought it might give me away.

Brent stared down at her, his shoulders rising and falling

with ragged breaths. His hands twitched at his sides, as if even he couldn't believe what he'd just done.

With another cry, he dropped to his knees beside her.

"No." His fingers hovered over her face before he grabbed her shoulders and shook her violently. "Don't do this. Don't leave me!"

His voice was raw, broken. He let out a guttural cry, throwing his head back as the wind whipped around him. For a second, I thought he might collapse beside her, but instead, he grabbed her face and kissed her.

It was desperate, almost frantic, his lips pressing against hers as if he could somehow breathe life back into her. But she didn't move. She was as still as the snow beneath her.

Brent pulled back, staring at her pale, lifeless face, and let out another anguished howl. As the sound echoed around us, he staggered to his feet, swiping at his eyes with his sleeve.

I pressed closer to the rock, my breath fogging in shallow bursts I tried to hide behind my hands. The snow stung my face, but the cold didn't matter. Only the sound of his footsteps did. They came closer, so close, I swore I could feel the vibration through the frozen ground.

And then...silence.

I held my breath, listening. A rustle of pine branches. The crunch of snow as he turned and walked away. The sound faded slowly, his boots thudding farther and farther until the world around me went still.

When I finally crept out from behind the rock, my legs trembled so badly, I nearly fell. I crossed to where Laurel lay, each step heavy and tentative, my breath making it hard to see.

Her face was pale, gray, her neck streaked with angry red marks. She was dead. The fog of my brain was fighting to clear. To hold on to reality. Maybe this was just the pills. The oxy was making me see things. Maybe I was asleep at home. This wasn't real. No one was dead.

Just when I'd decided this was all a dream, Laurel's chest rose and fell in a barely perceptible rhythm.

Her eyelids fluttered, and she looked up at me, terrified. She was alive. Barely, but alive.

"Hang in there." Was this real? "You're going to be okay."

A surge of euphoria shook me awake, like rocket fuel in my veins. Laughter bubbled up, wild and unstoppable. I completely lost it. The whole world shook. No, that was just my knees.

Her beautiful hazel eyes latched onto me, and for a brief second, there was a spark—a flicker of hope. It was faint, glowing beneath the pain like a dying ember fighting to stay alive, just as she was. The terror that had clouded her eyes moments ago faded, replaced by relief. She was safe now.

Her lips parted slightly, trying to form words, but only a scratch came out.

"It's okay. Don't talk. You're safe."

She struggled to move, trembling fingers reaching up as snow fell on her face. Her hand, shaky and pale, inched closer. The movement was feeble, barely perceptible, but it was enough to send a surge of emotion coursing through me. She was vulnerable and needed my help.

I'd come here to catch Thad cheating again. I'd driven through the snow, hardly knowing how I'd gotten here. Was this the reason why?

I leaned in closer.

She tried to speak but didn't have the strength.

"It's okay." I knelt next to her, careful with my footing.

She was so close to the edge, to that magnificent drop.

Running my hand through her damp hair, I gave her my best *it'll be all right* face. With my most encouraging smile, I rolled her off the cliff.

Her arms flailed, trying to catch something, anything, but there was only air and snow.

. . .

The End

Acknowledgments

How does one adequately express gratitude to all those who have transformed a shared dream into a stunning reality? Let us attempt to do just that.

First and foremost, our families deserve our deepest thanks. Their unwavering support and encouragement have been our bedrock, allowing us the time and energy to translate our collective imagination into the words that fill these pages. Their belief in our vision has been a constant source of strength and inspiration.

As coauthors, our journey has been uniquely collaborative and rewarding. Now, with Mary also embracing the additional role of publisher, our adventure has taken on an exciting new dimension. This transition from solely writing to also publishing has been both a challenge and a joy, opening doors to share our work more directly with you, our readers.

We are immensely grateful to the entire team at Mary Stone Publishing — a group who believed in our potential from the very beginning. Their commitment extends beyond editing our words; it encompasses the tireless efforts of designers, marketers, and support staff, all dedicated to bringing our stories to life. Their expertise, creativity, and passion have been vital in capturing the essence of our tales and sharing them with the world.

However, our greatest appreciation is reserved for you, our beloved readers. You took a chance on our book, generously sharing your most precious asset—your time. It is our fervent hope that the pages of this book have rewarded that generosity, offering you a journey worth taking and memories that linger.

With all our love and heartfelt appreciation,

Mary & Caroline

ABOUT THE AUTHOR

MARY STONE

Nestled in the tranquil Blue Ridge Mountains of East Tennessee, Mary Stone has transformed her peaceful home, once bustling with her sons, into a creative haven. As her family grew, so did her writing career, evolving from childhood fears to a deep understanding of real-life villains. Her stories, centered around strong, unconventional heroines, weave themes of courage and intrigue.

Mary's journey from a solitary writer to establishing her own publishing house marks a significant evolution, showcasing her commitment to the literary world. Through her writing and publishing endeavors, she continues to captivate and inspire, honoring her lifelong fascination with the mysterious and the courageous.

Connect with Mary online

facebook.com/authormarystone
x.com/MaryStoneAuthor
goodreads.com/AuthorMaryStone
bookbub.com/authors/mary-stone
pinterest.com/MaryStoneAuthor
instagram.com/marystoneauthor

Discover more about Mary Stone on her website.
www.authormarystone.com

CAROLINE CLARK

Caroline Clark is a British author with a penchant for fast-paced crime fiction and the kind of mysteries that keep readers glancing over their shoulders. From an early age, she was drawn to the darker corners of storytelling, quickly realizing that the most terrifying monsters aren't supernatural—they're human.

Inspired by writers like M.J. Aldridge, Freida McFadden, and Daniel Hurst, Caroline developed a sharp eye for twists, always eager to unmask the villain before the final reveal.

These days, she spends her time delving into the minds of criminals, carefully plotting their downfalls (strictly on the page, of course). She lives near the historic town of Lincoln in the United Kingdom, accompanied by two lively boxers and a particularly opinionated Frenchie. When she's not writing, she can be found exploring the ancient streets—quietly deciding where her next fictional crime scene should unfold.

Connect with Caroline online

facebook.com/CarolineClarkAuthor
goodreads.com/Caroline_Clark

Made in the USA
Las Vegas, NV
19 May 2025